The ordinary

Christopher Ritchie

First published 2015
Published by GB Publishing.org

Paperback ISBN: 978-0-9931639-7-5 (paperback)
978-1-912031-07-8 (hardback)
eBook ISBN: 978-0-9931639-8-2
Kindle ISBN: 978-0-9931639-9-9

A catalogue record of the printed book is available from the British Library

Cover Design © Mary Pargeter Design
Cover Illustration by Derek E Pearson

GBP.
GB Publishing.org
www.gbpublishing.co.uk

For
Diana, Madeleine and Henry, my lights in the darkness

Acknowledgements
Grateful bows to Renia Siekierska, Karen Granger and Ian Russ. Warm hugs for DEP. Immense love for G and B, and the humble M. Books do not write themselves, so nods offered to all those who encouraged the writing of this one. Finally a special star for my parents, who gave me the tools, time and temperament to be twisted

Contents

Chapters

One – Cowboys and angels

Piotr swung his legs out of bed, his feet clunking down on the unforgiving wood. He felt drained. His head ached. His teeth felt loose and tender.

Shrugging to iron out the creases in his shoulders, his head hung. His stare fixed on his feet. He rocked forward and stood up with a grimace. He accidentally kicked an empty, crumpled can which the night before had contained a strong shot of thick, heavy hooch, and walked over to the only window in the room.

Pulling the curtain to one side, a blast of bright sunlight smashed into his retinas. He let the curtain go and blinked a few times, shaking his head as if to dissipate the liquid light from his frazzled skull.

The noise that had awakened Piotr came back – a rumble like a motor, thrumming in the walls or somewhere beyond. It was the same noise his own taps made. A motor chugging away, doing its best not to send an irritatingly pathetic flow of hot water in the basin. It was the same noise, he expected, that woke up everyone in the block when their neighbours turned the taps on.

A quick flash of the dream he'd been having prior to this rude interruption struck him still. His eyes closed gently, easing the sting further. He was back at home, another sunny day in the suburbs of Wroclaw. His sister, Halina, skipped over a rope in the front garden. The short lawn, worn grass in patches of yellow and brown with only a few splashes of green, stopped abruptly at the concrete pavement, itself sloping down to the roadside.

It had never been the busiest of roads but in this dream, there was no traffic. Halina called over to Piotr. He walked out of the porch and down to her as she held out her hand and smiled. He took her hand, a comforting warmth spreading into his, as she dropped the skipping rope to the ground. It landed with a reverberating thump, shocking Piotr back to the real world.

He shook his head again, trying to clear the cloud of a hangover, and walked to the basin on the opposite wall. He caught his reflection in the mirror, an unclean and awkwardly hung piece that did no one any favours. He hung his head again, his hands resting on the sink edge.

1

As his head fell his eyes followed, the colour of his vision streaming back into his personal eyelid cinema. Halina led him towards the road. He tried to pull back, his real hand instinctively pulling off the sink and onto his stomach. His dream hand stayed firmly in Halina's.

Her voice was slow, dull and muffled. 'Piotr.'

He tried to speak as they reached the pavement. Nothing came out. A sinking feeling began in his gut as Halina reached the road.

A voice came from behind him, this time not as slow but louder. 'Piotr!'

He turned to see his mother waving and then back to Halina. Her grip on him loosened. Again, from behind, 'Piotr!'

He turned again. His mother came running down the stairs, her arms raised and waving. He tried to swivel around back to Halina but some unseen force stopped him. He pushed against it but could only turn his head a little. It wouldn't let him see her.

His mother ran past him, now screaming. 'Halina! Halina!'

The wall gave way and Piotr turned all the way round.

~~~

'How many?'

'Just two this time.'

'That's not enough, man. That's only three grand.'

'I know. Nothing to do with me.'

'Bollocks. It's *all* to do with you.'

'Fuck off! We're delivering tonight anyway. Two'll have to be enough.'

'Okay, whatever. I'm coming round now.'

'I'll put the kettle on.'

Bleach put the phone down. He looked over at the bedroom door and yawned, clicking his jaw from side to side. The apartment reeked of death. Bleach had become not exactly used to the smell but it had been over a day since he had accidentally over-medicated the girl. It was her fault anyway. She had been far too lively. Far too unpredictable. He'd had a nice time with her at least, before she came to. If she'd not come round, he wouldn't have had to deliver the fatal shot. *Yeah, it was her fault.*

He stood up, turning away from the bedroom and towards the kitchen and second bedroom. He reached the sink and grabbed the kettle from the draining board. He filled the kettle and set it on the worktop, flicking a switch down. The indicator lit up orange.

Bleach felt in his pocket and pulled out a small lighter, then in his other pocket for his cigarettes. The smoke helped to conceal the smell of the dead girl, he thought. He would have smoked it anyway. It burned like a miniature bonfire as he drew sharply. The smoke barrelled down into his lungs and up into his nostrils at the same time, an inhalation technique he felt always gave him the full experience.

He walked casually over to the first bedroom and stopped by the door, pressing his ear up against it to listen. Of course she was dead. He had stamped on her head five times, maybe six, to make sure. He had decided to keep the door shut as he didn't really want to see the mess – a sight he was dreading. It was inevitable though. Jock was almost certainly going to smell her, and it would be impossible to stop him opening the door if he wanted to.

Explaining to Jock why they were fifteen-hundred short would be the real kicker, though. Jock was not going to like that at all. Bleach considered for a few seconds the possibility of disposing of the girl before Jock got there, but he probably only had five or ten minutes. Or he could just kill Jock.

Bleach took another long drag on his cigarette, comically blowing it forcefully out in front of him. He choked a little and let out a chuckle. Over on the table he saw his pipe. There was a wrap of cellophane next to it, slightly exposing the brown chunk inside. He felt hungry all of a sudden and picked the pipe up in one hand, crushing the cigarette into an ashtray with the other.

He fell back into the chair, clicking his lighter to shoot a thin plume of fire into the bulb of the pipe, sucking it down onto the brown powder. It was an entirely different feeling to cigarette smoke, like gaseous glass slipping down the throat; like oysters but with a taste that didn't make him gag.

Although he was as steadily stoned as ever, Bleach felt the extra layer land in his brain. His eyes closed and ears listened as the kettle did its job.

~~~

3

Piotr looked back into the mirror, his eyes red and dark. He closed them again, frantic to get back to the house in Wroclaw, back to his sister. Colour streamed back in easily but he was facing an open road. He ran to the pavement, looking left and right.

She was nowhere to be seen. A voice came from behind him. 'Piotr.' It was her voice. Slow, lifeless again.

'Piotr.'

He turned to see his sister, laid out across the grass, her arms red as if burned. The skin on her face was flayed in patches to reveal the flesh beneath. Her head craned around to face him. She tried to speak again but as her mouth opened, a red river flowed from it, thick as treacle. It seeped down over her chin and into the folds of her neck before pooling under her head.

Halina's mouth opened wider and the red river stopped; cut off. She began to choke. Piotr moved to her and knelt down, cradling her head in his right hand. Her blood dripped from his fingers. His expression was a mixture of confusion and expectation. The croak turned to a gurgle. He leaned in further and saw she had no tongue. A stub poked out of her throat, a fleshy slug emerging from a dark, wet pipe.

The red river had pooled as a lake in her throat, and as he watched its waves gently lapping up against her gums, her teeth like centuries-old rocks creating currents, he felt himself drawn in towards it. His sister's hands grabbed at his shirt and pulled him in, deeper, for the grimmest swim of his life.

~~~

Thump. Thump.

Bleach's eyes opened into a blurry room.

Thump.

His eyes sharpened and he slunk forwards, pushing his hands into the desk to prop himself up.

Thump. Thump.

'All right! I'm coming!'

As he approached the door, he saw out of the corner of his eye that the bedroom door was not shut as he had left it. As he *thought* he'd left it. A

4

rush of anxiety slammed into his stomach and he skipped over to the door, grabbing its handle and pulling it shut with a slam.

Bleach rounded the corner into the alcove housing the front door. He opened it and nodded at Jock, who looked angry and impatient.

'Took your fuckin' time,' Jock said.

'I was napping.'

'Whatever. We don't have much time. Pick-up's in two hours.'

Jock led Bleach towards the kitchen. 'Where's my cuppa then?' He stopped at the first bedroom, nudging the door open.

Bleach made the tea, pouring another for himself and emptying the last few shots of whiskey from a barely one-day-old bottle into it. He hoped that Jock didn't see.

'What's that fuckin' smell, man?' Jock joined Bleach in the kitchen. 'You killed a dog in here or something?'

Bleach angled his head a little towards his 'business partner' and raised a pathetic shrug. 'Nah. It's this gear mate. It's foul.' His thin lips widened, showing off a smile that made Jock shudder a little.

'Your teeth are disgusting, mate. See a dentist after the next drop, eh?'

Years of drug and alcohol abuse and a rather laid-back attitude to oral hygiene had indeed taken their toll on Bleach's mouth – a festering pit of disease, a graveyard in itself.

'Yeah, yeah,' Bleach offered. He wasn't the sort to look in the mirror anyway. His opinion of other people's opinions had become far less important after he first tasted the great crystals and never looked back. As long as he had a regular supply and enough money to keep it regular, life was good. He was living the dream.

'Let's get 'em ready then.' Jock moved back to the bedroom. He opened the door fully this time, met with the familiar vision of chaos. It was, he knew, partly his fault. They always kept the girls in Bleach's flat simply because he didn't want them in his. He enjoyed having *real* girls to stay too. They probably wouldn't take to the idea of sharing the bedroom with a couple of tied-up, half-dead teenagers.

Jock walked to the nearest bed and nudged the first body bag. It shook pathetically. The girl was fourteen. Her clothes and small selection of earthly possessions – what she'd had on her when Bleach entered her life – sat in a holdall at the foot of the bed. The black, shiny cocoon covered her entirely. Two small air holes in front of her head provided enough oxygen. Inside, she was bound and gagged.

5

It was never a pretty sight taking one of these girls out of their bag. This was, Jock acknowledged internally, the worst part of the job. Seducing the girls outside school, or picking them up at a roadside or wherever, and then having some one-sided fun with them – these were the perks. The thrill of the hunt. Playing detectives, tracking down the criminally young and beautiful, handcuffing them and putting them in the holding cells before they could be processed.

Unzipping the bags was horrible. The smell hitting the air like a car hitting a cow – a malodorous slap in the face, the excrement pooled at the bottom of the bag around the girl's feet while some had usually dried and caked around the holes from whence they came. Still, right now they just had to load the bags into the van – by far the easiest part.

Bleach joined Jock in the room, sipping at his hot tea. 'See – nice and tidy this time?'

Jock snorted. 'For once. Yeah, nice surprise. Cheers. Seriously, man, what the fuck is that smell? That ain't gear.'

Bleach felt another surge of anxiety rising from his stomach and settling harshly in his throat. Jock nudged the second sack and once satisfied that the flesh within was breathing, he went back out to get his tea. He picked it up and walked over to the sofa. It was covered with a couple of blankets and a pillow at one end.

'Why're you sleeping out here?'

Bleach joined him. 'Fell asleep watching the box.'

'And the magic bed fairy brought you a blanket and pillow?'

Bleach was about to answer but Jock continued: 'What's in your room then? Let me guess – the other girl.'

Bleach shifted, his hand shaking and spilling hot tea down the side of his mug. 'It's… look, I was gonna tell you.'

'For fuck's sake, mate.' Jock slammed his mug down on the table, tea spraying upwards like a miniature caffeinated volcano. 'This again? I knew I shouldn't let you do this alone.'

The previous day, Jock had cried off at the last minute simply because he'd had a better offer. If Shawna hadn't called him at just the right time, he would have scouted the schools with Bleach. He was mildly impressed that his moronic partner could manage to harvest more than one girl at a time anyway, but this was not the first time he'd gone too far and taken more than he could handle.

'So you've killed her?'

6

'Yeah… I had to mate. Sorry.'

'Sorry?'

'Yeah. Sorry.'

'You'll have to get rid of her, mate. Have you scrubbed her up yet?'

'No… no, I was waiting. Let's get the others out first. I'll sort this out later. Sorry.'

Jock winced. 'Stop saying sorry. I can tell you're sorry. So unabashedly apologetic for murdering another little girl. Sorry, sorry. Whoops, there goes another. Sorry, everyone. It was an accident. She walked right in front of my foot and I accidentally kicked her to death. There was no way around it. Sorry.'

Bleach chuckled.

'Oh, this is funny? You know, I don't think it is. What we do is provide a service. It's supply and demand. What you've done is over-supply and not meet demand. That's a fucking waste of time and resources, and now you've got to dump a dead girl somewhere and hope no one finds her. Well done, mate. Really, well done.'

'Sorry.'

Jock walked over to the second bedroom and opened the door. 'You've got to be joking! What's this?'

Bleach stumbled over to join Jock in the doorway. On the carpet in front of them was a large pool of blood, a selection of broken teeth giving it the look of some kind of sea creature yawning. A few feet further away was a small brown hill of excrement, the source of the smell Jock could now pinpoint.

'Where's the fuckin' girl?'

Two – Obliterations

'We got a name?'

'Don't know. I'll check.'

Mathers flicked his thumb up the screen of his PDA. Text scrolled down. He stopped it and scrolled down a little further.

'No. She's in bad shape. Unrecognisable, so it's going to be dental.'

'Brilliant. More blind alleys. So what's the point of going?'

'Hang a right, just up there.'

Danson did as he was told, turning into a small cobbled patch and stopping short of a set of bollards that blocked access. A small group of people waited, huddled under umbrellas and the canopy of the building behind them.

He stepped out and into a light puddle, a few dirty spurts splashing up onto his trousers. They were only a week old but already looked well worn. He pulled his jacket collar up close around his neck and ducked under the yellow rope.

Mathers was right behind, but he had had the good sense to bring an umbrella. He ducked under the rope, scraping the tip of the umbrella through a shallow puddle, grinding against the wet concrete.

A uniformed officer put his hands up to the gathering. 'I'm sorry. We're working as fast as we can.'

A lady with a newspaper folded over her head responded angrily. 'I'm late for work. My boss is an arsehole and if I get fired for this...'

'Madam. The whole area is closed until we're finished, and possibly longer. I suggest you...'

Before he could finish, the lady turned and disappeared around the building towards the main road.

Mathers sidled up to a familiar face, jokily knocking her shoulder with his. 'Mack. How's it going?'

Mackenzie knocked him back, a little harder. 'It's grim. Hope you haven't just had breakfast. You won't want lunch, anyway.'

Danson acknowledged Mackenzie and walked through, arriving at the scene. 'E118' in chalky paint was daubed large on black wood panels. A small window was mostly opaque with dust on both sides. The door, another black panel, was propped open by a metal rod. He leaned around to see who was inside.

'Ah, Mike. Couldn't sleep?'

'Morning, Dave. I'll sleep when I'm dead.' Danson felt a little inward poke at his insensitivity but the thought was replaced with the knowledge that he could always show his sensitive side later.

'It's not pretty.' Dave Wilson, forensic detective extraordinaire, was somehow always first at the scene, or so it seemed to his colleagues.

Danson stepped in. Wilson and his assistant, Ed Sharpe, had set up a small lighting rig in one corner of the shack, up on a thin tripod and casting light over to the far wall and everything in between. Ordinarily a scene like this would have an assortment of yellow flags on toothpicks, marking out points of interest.

'Nothing at all?'

'Early days, but no. My guess is the body was dumped here.' Wilson pointed over at the corpse, bathed in its own spotlight.

Danson stepped towards it, careful to watch his feet. He reached the body and squatted down, pulling gloves from his pocket and putting them on.

Mathers came in behind him. 'Hi, Dave.'

Wilson smiled and nodded. 'Hi, Pete. We'll move her in a bit. Don't think this was the scene.'

Mathers nodded and stepped carefully over to join his partner. He put his gloves on too and reached into his pocket, taking his PDA out. 'Mind out, Mike.'

Danson stood up. Mathers framed his shot not too studiously and thumbed the screen. A flash hit the room like a sharp bolt of lightning.

'Bollocks.'

'Turn the flash off, twerp.'

Mathers tried again. This time the shot was true – an eerie glow surrounding the dead girl. 'Another one for the scrapbook.' He looked at Danson and shook his head. Danson raised his eyebrows and offered a shrug.

'What've we got then?'

Mathers hunched down a couple of feet from the body. He recalled what Mack had told him outside. 'Body found in-situ by kids. Door was open, they came in, playing pirates or... something. Victim is female, teenage. Face obliterated.'

Danson winced in agreement. Obliterated was a good description.

Mathers continued: 'Punctures on the arms. Hands and feet bound. Lesions around the waist. Your turn.'

He stood and backed away, moving behind the arc of the light. Danson took his place. He lifted the girl's chin slightly, cocked his head down and to the side and nodded. 'Heavy bruising.' Resting the chin back, the light flickered, momentarily dancing over the area where the victim's mouth and nose had been replaced by a red, speckled mess. The eye sockets had become almost one, a large indentation – a crater perhaps – in place of her features.

'The binding's wet, Pete.'

Mathers nodded at Wilson. 'It's raining. Get the snapper in. We'll meet the body at Villiers.'

'Cheers Pete. We'll have to hold off a bit. UV sweep first.'

Danson and Mathers exited the shack, regrouping with Mackenzie.

'Coffee?'

'Very funny, Mike.'

'I'm not joking.' Danson smiled and elbowed his partner.

'Let's get on with it then.'

~~~

Piotr blinked hard. Between short bouts of poor quality sleep he'd been hard at his research and now his eyes were stinging. Reclining on his bed, his head painfully propped against the metal rod across the headboard, his laptop computer was hot on his legs.

His discomfort complemented the uncomfortable task of jumping into the rabbit hole. Page after page of naked men and women, their orifices on show and usually open. As he scrolled down the two-hundred-and-twelfth page on PornTap, one scene caught his eye. He touched his finger to the trackpad, moved it over and clicked the image.

He tapped through until the girl came into view. She was barely clothed – a short camisole hanging loosely off her small breasts and stopping just above her waist line. She was pretty but, on closer inspection, not the girl he was looking for.

This grim daily event hooked Piotr. He remembered when he would do this for fun – for personal sexual satisfaction. Now there was no sex; just brutality. Hundreds of thousands of images of debased flesh had filled his mind. Images of girls showing more than any girl had ever

10

shown him. Men standing proud over them with hungry cocks and shaven balls and tattoos and facial hair. Old women with too much make-up, their legs spread for young bucks and their thin penises to conquer.

The film continued and switched its focus on the girl's fingers to hover over her face. Piotr tapped the pad and stopped it, framing her pretty visage. Her eyes were hollow, almost lifeless, yet something was there – hope, perhaps. He leaned in closer, his neck clicking. Her skin was dry and blotchy. Maybe she had been pretty, once. Now she was a rag doll.

~~~

'Peter!' Mary Mackenzie called from the far end of the corridor that joined the equipment room with the rear section of the front desk of Villiers, the listed historic building that had been home to Malton District Police for over sixty years.

Mathers turned towards her and shrugged, as if to say *what?*

Mack beckoned him to an open doorway. He joined her there, readying himself for whatever lay within. Having seen the body slumped in the shack was one thing, but viewing it in the cool light of the station would be more shocking: each cut, bruise and sign of trauma telling its own chapter in a horror story, laid bare and clinical.

'Where's Mike?'

'He'll be along. Probably shaving his balls or something.'

Mack shot him a look. She counted herself as having a good sense of humour but she frequently struggled to appreciate her colleagues' vulgarity.

Danson appeared behind them. 'Right then, ladies. Let's get this done.'

Mack moved to let Danson through. He approached the corpse, which was covered by a thin blue sheet. He pulled the sheet back carefully and looked back to Mathers. 'Okay, Pete. I did the last one. All yours.'

'No chance!' Mathers smiled. 'You touched her last.'

'For fuck's sake!' Mack was, and looked, frazzled. 'Just toss a coin?'

The men nodded. 'Ah, okay then. I'll do this one. Your turn next time.'

Mathers looked grateful. Danson turned back to the body. He reached up to the large module hanging from the ceiling and switched the UV

11

light on, then pressed a large red button. A camera lens appeared from the underside of the unit and made a faint whirring sound.

'Mike Danson, examining unknown.' He looked up again at a small monitor. 'Victim is female, five-eight. Slim build. A hundred and twenty pounds roughly. Appears mid-teenage.'

Mathers and Mack left the room.

'Puncture wounds indicate recent intravenous drug use − but short term. The face is obliterated.' He tried to separate the jaw. 'Few teeth intact.' Releasing the jaw, the face stayed as it was − like a deflated football taking its time to return to form. The UV light gave the blood an eerie purple hue.

Danson flipped the body to get a good view of its back. 'There's a smudge here.' He reached up to the console and depressed a small blue button. A timer counted down. 'Capture. Mark for Wilson. Mark for Sharpe.' The camera whirred and an audible cue, which most users of the system had come to call a 'tick', told Danson it was done.

'Mike.'

Danson turned around. 'Ah, Dave. Just got up?'

Wilson sneered.

Danson continued: 'Just done some prelims. You should have a pic.'

'Yeah. It just buzzed.' Wilson pulled out his PDA. A thumbnail of the dead girl's back sat in the middle of the screen. He put it back in his pocket. 'Let's have a look then.'

'UV give you anything?'

Wilson approached the corpse. 'Not a lot. I'd say she's been dead for a few days. Looks like she crawled in there. We found some footprints. No blood at the scene either.'

'I'm gonna be a while here. I'll shoot you if anything comes up.'

'Cheers.'

Danson left the room. He looked down the corridor towards the front desk and saw his partner leaning against the wall, flirting with the desk sergeant, Liz. He turned back towards the exam room and walked to the men's toilet door, pushing it open. He entered the middle cubicle and sat down.

Reaching into his jacket pocket, he pulled out a small packet. He pulled the ends apart, revealing a small white tablet. He sat still, staring almost through the pill. As always in this situation, his mind offered conflicting advice.

12

He heard the door swing open.

'Mike? You in here?'

Danson snapped out of his haze. 'Yeah. Hold on mate.' He closed the packet back around the tablet and stuffed it into his pocket before standing, flushing the toilet and exiting the cubicle. He felt dishonest. Wasting water and energy and putting himself through the same turmoil, over and over.

'What's up?'

'We've got something.'

'That was quick, Pete. They'll promote you to chief scrotum soon.'

'Fingers crossed.' The partners grinned. Mathers had no idea that just behind Danson's grin was a bitter twist of desperation.

'Let's grab Dave.'

They exited the washroom and turned straight into the exam room. Wilson was scraping something off the dead girl's foot.

'What's up, Dave?'

Wilson turned around, holding aloft a scalpel covered in a dark brown substance. 'Happily, that smudge is a tattoo, and it is pretty unusual.' He'd spotted something beneath the dirty smudge and peeled back a layer or three of skin to reveal the deeper ink. 'Eastern Europe, possibly Polish.'

'You're *so* subcutaneous, man.' Mathers laughed, looking at his partner for encouragement.

Wilson frowned. 'Okay, okay. I suppose I am. The point is this kind of ink originates in the Eastern Bloc.' He looked back at the body and the tattoo. 'I've found another something down here. Looks like there used to be another tattoo, right... here.' He pointed the scalpel back at the foot, where he'd also been scraping. 'There are some remnants of ink in here too.' He gestured towards a small cavity. 'See, you missed this stuff. Hotshot detectives. Kindergarten level.'

'Yeah, yeah. Whatever, Dave,' Mathers smiled. 'You mean Mike missed it. He's no hotshot. He's a twat.'

Danson and Mathers joined Wilson at the exam table. 'So someone went to the trouble of trying to remove these. That's a bit off. Ruining the artistry.'

'That's right, Pete. A real shame. A tragedy. Still, gives us a potential lead, for which we should be thankful. So what's this other one?'

The three men stared at the tattoo. Although it was difficult to make out any detail, it was circular and about two inches around. Danson grabbed the magnifier arm and placed the lens over the tattoo, angling it. 'Are those letters? What's that... looks like PP,' he said.

Mathers was grateful that the corpse was face-down. He didn't like looking at what was left of her face. The word 'obliterated' seemed to loop around whenever the image leapt into his mind.

'When'll your report be up?' Danson asked.

Wilson didn't appreciate the impatience – but he was used to it. Thirty-two years in the force and most of those burdened with impatience.

'Give me a chance!' He smiled to hide his true feelings. 'Two, maybe three hours. I've got to run bloods, tox and a few others.'

Mathers nodded. 'Okay then. That gives us time to have a think about this PP thing.' He turned to his partner. 'Lunch?'

Danson didn't feel hungry for food. He wanted to reach into his pocket and take the pill. He always wanted to take the pill.

~~~

Mathers and Danson sat on the paved area in front of Megan's, a café not far from the Villiers HQ. They'd just been served by one of Megan's underlings, Katie, who'd brought them a leaf salad and steak sandwich respectively.

'So, Mikeyboy, tell me. Don't you ever feel bad about these poor, defenceless animals, getting maimed in the name of human gluttony?'

'Oh yeah, this again,' Danson said through half a mouthful of chewy meat. 'Here we go. Brilliant. I never tire of your militant fucking vegetarianism.'

'Good. Let's open the debate then.' Mathers took another forkful of assorted greens and reds and yellows. 'I put forward the motion that you're a murderous, scummy bastard with a thirst for blood.' He winked at Danson.

'Yep, that's pretty much it. Well done. Game over.' He took another large bite of his sandwich.

Mathers looked disappointed and then grinned. 'Oh, come on mate.'

'Okay then,' Danson said, chewing his way around to find a comfortable opportunity to speak. 'This house posits that you're a

14

herbivorous freak who isn't man enough to handle real food. And you're destroying the planet.'

'Destroying the planet – how so, my friend?' Mathers was clearly enjoying himself.

'Well, look at it this way. We need animals to fertilise those very vegetables you eat. We need them for all sorts of industrial uses, and we create a beautiful triumvirate of sound ecology by eating them at the end. If you had your way, those animals would just die in their fields and have proper burials, filling the ground with cows and sheep and whatever else and squirrels and bats.'

'That doesn't make any sense.'

'You don't make any sense. Just eat your trees, bitch.'

'Better than a steakwich.'

'Don't call it a steakwich. What's yours? A rocket salad... a rockalad.'

'What about this tattoo then?'

'Oh, you want to talk sensibly now, about work stuff?'

'If we have to.'

'I've no idea. PP could be anything.'

'It looks a bit like a logo. We should ask Mack to cross-check it with the database. Call her.'

'You call her!' Danson spluttered. 'I'm giving my teeth a workout here. It's like chewing a shoe. A *delicious* shoe.'

Mathers took out his phone and clicked Mackenzie's contact. He put it on speaker mode and set the phone down, tucking back into his salad. She answered promptly.

'Pete. What's up?'

'Did you get the photo of the PP thing?'

'Yes. And I've got a match too. Don't get too excited though. We've got two other bodies turned up on the Interpol database from three years ago. Both Eastern Europe.'

'Is the data uploaded?' Mathers asked.

'Are,' said Mack.

'Are what?'

'*Are* the data uploaded. Data is the plural, you imbecile.'

Danson laughed and stuck his middle finger up at Mathers and mouthed: *you imbecile.*

15

'Thanks Mack,' Mathers said, returning the finger to his partner. 'Well, *are* the data uploaded?'

'Right… now. Okay guys, while you two get stuffed some of us have real work to do.' Mack clicked the call off.

'You so fancy her,' Mathers said, grinning at Danson. 'You want her to be your girlfriend.'

'Maybe,' Danson smiled back, but all he could think of was taking the pill. The pill that was burning a hole in his pocket, as if it had actually started cooking itself and was eating its way into his leg. *It's just one pill. Just one. What harm can it do? You've taken thousands of them. Just one. Take it. Let's go and take it now.*

'I'm going to the lav,' he said. 'If I'm not back in an hour, go fuck yourself.'

Three – Young love

'Haven't you finished that yet?' Col leaned forward from the back seat, grabbing the passenger headrest to pull himself up. 'You're shit at this.'

'Shut up, pissface,' retorted Jez, brushing a small pile of marijuana leaves and smaller, dust-like shavings into a cigarette paper resting in his other hand. 'My mouth's dry. I can't lick the paper properly. It's doing my head in.'

Jez had tried twice to construct a joint but both had fallen apart at the sealing stage – his mouth refusing to produce anything even slightly wet.

'You and your crappy tongue,' Col laughed. 'You can't lick for shit. Or so your mum says.'

'Fuck off. Third time's the charm. Pass me the water?'

Col found the bottle and dangled it around the seat. Jez carefully put the unrolled joint down on his lap and took the bottle. He took a swig and sloshed the liquid around his mouth.

'That'll be too wet now, ya prick,' Col laughed again. Although he was growing impatient waiting for his smoke, he could pass the time with a little light banter.

Jez managed to stick the paper down but as he did, the paper creased across the end. 'Bollocks! You do it then.'

'No worries, mate,' Col said, fully aware he had battered his friend into submission. 'If you want a job done properly…'

Jez opened the car door and rolled out, closing it and Col's comment behind him. He walked over to Kerry and Jo, civilised and sitting on their blanket, each smoking a cigarette. 'You've been ages!' Jo said.

'Art takes time,' Jez smiled, although he didn't feel very happy. He was annoyed, frustrated and a little angry. He changed the subject. 'Nice view.'

'Stop looking down my top, cheeky,' Kerry said. Both girls giggled. 'I've only got pancakes anyway.'

'I mean the actual view, duh.' He gestured towards the ocean, the view from their spot taking in lush green and freshly mowed grass, gambolling down out of sight and giving way to the tall townhouses atop the cliff side, the horizon above the Malton skyline lit by a clean, bright sun. The clouds and rain of the morning just a few hours past were almost a distant memory were it not for the moisture in the grass.

'Yeah, whatever. Down my top's better.' Kerry smiled up at Jez. 'So what's happening?'

'My mouth's too fucking dry.'

'I'll help you wet it,' Kerry said. She giggled and poked his leg. 'You gonna sit down or just stand there like a lemon?'

'I don't want a wet arse.'

Col joined the three of them. 'There, easy-peasy.' He sparked up his freshly-rolled joint and took a big drag on it, falling into a sitting position on the blanket and knocking firmly against Jo as he did.

'Oi, careful,' she said. 'And save some of that for us this time.'

'I'm going to head off in a bit,' Jez said. 'If you guys don't mind?'

Col nodded up at him, his second large drag simultaneously emerging from his mouth and nostrils. He grinned and went to take another.

'Oh... that's a shame,' Kerry said. 'Where're you going? Can I come?'

Jo elbowed Kerry gently, flashing her a look of consolation. Kerry frowned.

'I've just got some shit to do. See you tomorrow, probably.' Jez leaned down, snatched the joint away and took a long, deep lug. He held it down for a few seconds and let the smoke out slowly, handing the reefer back to Col. 'Catch ya later, mate.'

Jez walked back to his car. Jo spoke: 'He's been really odd lately. Always running off with *shit* to do.'

Col shrugged. He knew where Jez was going but it wasn't really any of the girls' business. He exhaled again and passed the joint to Kerry. She eyed it suspiciously before taking a drag. 'I guess he just has some shit to do.'

~~~

Jez parked his car along the promenade about two hundred yards from the fairground. He'd always hated this area of Malton. Having been brought up by middle-class parents in the upper town, away from the seedy seafront and its garish tourist attractions, he had followed in his parents' snobbish footsteps to find this part of Malton distasteful.

18

It hadn't stopped him from enjoying days and nights out there. Despite his parents' thinly veiled contempt for the tattooed, orally-challenged populace, living by the sea had its appeal and it wasn't too unusual to be able to avoid those types all together.

He'd also found the ready availability of pills and other thrills convenient, and in recent months he'd found the best reason to hang around the fairground – Maria.

He did like Kerry. She was pretty, slim and funny. But Maria had something else. She had an *accent*. She had an air of mystery he felt drawn to, and she wasn't available on a plate like Kerry. He'd slept with Kerry the summer before but they'd never gone beyond that, despite her best efforts to turn fumbled sex into something meaningful.

With Maria it was already meaningful. Since first approaching her three weeks ago, he'd walked her nearly all the way home twice, they'd been for two coffee dates, and he was most certainly falling for her. She was older than him too. At seventeen, Jez could get served in the pub with his fake ID but he hadn't told her the truth. As far as eighteen-year-old Maria knew, Jez was twenty.

He made it to the fairground and edged past a group of obese adults and children. An elderly woman, presumably the grandmother in this family of fat fucks, had a wilted face but didn't deviate from the tubby trait everywhere else. *I hate fat people*, he thought. *Do I? Do I really hate fat people? Why? They're just... fat. But yeah, I hate them.*

Jez had observed that the girls who worked at the fairground seemed to all be Eastern European. Maria was Polish but her English, Jez thought, was very good. It was better than some of his friends'. Her accent made every word sexy too. He'd never met an English girl who *sounded* sexy. There were posh girls and then there was Maria. She was mysterious but marvellous.

He looked around to spot her. She wasn't working on the carousel or octopus ride and the token booth was manned by a thin, ill-looking blonde girl. Her face reminded him a bit of Prader-Willi syndrome. She seemed to have... *what was it? Shabismus. No...* it was something that reminded him of that old horror writer, Peter Straub. *Yes... Strabismus.* She had crossed eyes. He'd watched a documentary with his parents a week ago and the word had stuck with him. *Almond eyes too*, he thought. *Eyes like almonds. Must be a nightmare seeing through almonds.*

He walked past Strabismus Girl towards the crocodile-themed roller coaster and helter-skelter. Navigating his way through more elderly and obese gatherings, he saw what he wanted – Maria, who was checking the seatbelts of the passengers on the crocodile-themed roller coaster, Croccy's Cradle. He stopped and waited to catch her attention. She walked to the small control booth and flicked a switch to start the ride. She saw Jez and fluttered her fingers at him with a warm smile. He waved back and grinned – the butterflies in his stomach turning fast. Maria put both hands up and flashed them at him twice, then went back to keeping an eye on the ride.

'Twenty minutes,' Jez said to himself. 'Awesome.' He looked around for somewhere to park his backside for the duration and saw, beyond the fairground fence, some police 'do not cross' tape wrapped around some old fishing huts. He could see two uniformed officers standing outside one of the huts, marked 'E118', but it looked like whatever had happened was old news.

'Murder.' Jez jumped a little, startled.

'I- I'm sorry?'

An overweight man in his sixties or seventies, who appeared to be chewing his teeth, had sidled up to Jez. Wearing a holey, stained vest, his arms were flabby with various inked areas melding into each other. *Just my kind of dude*, thought Jez. *A fat old man. Quality.*

'Said it was murder,' the man continued. Jez reeled back a little from the man's breath – a strong, toxic mixture of cigarettes and something unidentifiable but disgusting. 'Police all over it this morning.' Jez noticed spittle coming from the inhuman oral cavity and reeled back further, shifting his weight so he could edge round to stand by the man's other side and pretend to survey the scene.

'Oh, right,' he offered. 'Murder? That's bad, is it?'

The man cocked an eyebrow at Jez, possibly appreciating the deliberately pathetic question. 'I'll say. Young girl. Naked, she was.'

'Naked? You mean she had no clothes on?'

The fat man raised both eyebrows. 'Yes, naked. That's what I said. You thick in t'head, boy?'

'Dunno, am I?' Jez was enjoying this exchange far more than his counterpart. He pushed his tongue firmly into his lower lip, presenting this look of disenchantment to Fat Dirty Vest Man, who took the point and scuttled away. He joined a small group of similarly styled inhuman monstrosities and pointed at Jez, muttering something he couldn't hear.

Jez looked back toward the crime scene. One of the officers caught his eye and nodded at him. He nodded back. He liked policemen. After all, his dad was one.

~~~

Jez loved lots of little things about Maria. As she walked towards him, her dainty handbag slung loosely over her shoulder, he admired her short, quick steps. It reminded him of dominoes falling over in sequence; the way she allowed eye contact only every few steps kept his attention, his stare fixed on her beautiful, soft features. He couldn't help smiling in her company. She seemed to reciprocate. Maria was worth blowing Col, Kerry and Jo out every time.

'Hi,' she smiled. 'How are you?'

Jez felt an instant rush of happiness. 'Hi. I'm great. You look... great.'

'In these?' She looked down at her red T-shirt and black trousers – standard uniform fare for the fairground. 'No, I hate these clothes.'

'Well, I... y'know, I like it.' Jez realised this line of conversation wasn't going anywhere. 'So how long have you got?'

'Fifteen minutes,' Maria said. She looked over to a dilapidated booth next to a token machine. Jez followed her gaze. A heavy-set man in the booth returned a stern look.

'Who's that?'

'My supervisor. Let's go.'

Maria wrapped her hand in Jez's and led him away briskly. They snaked through the obese, unwashed crowds and crossed the road to the Red Snapper café. Maria told Jez that the police had been asking questions around the fairground. She'd heard there had been a murder. Fourteen minutes later, following a hurried downing of still-too-hot coffee, Maria pecked Jez's cheek and said she'd see him at five-thirty.

As Jez walked back out to the main road, a figure stepped in front of him. Looking up from the chest he was confronted with, he saw the face of Maria's supervisor. His name badge read 'Steve.'

'Oh, sorry... excuse me,' Jez said, keeping his voice light.

21

Supervisor Steve bumped up against him, knocking Jez into the side of a vending machine, and carried on. As Jez righted himself and watched Supervisor Steve walk away, he stopped and turned to face him. His expression was one Jez understood to mean 'go away'. So he did.

~~~

Jez got home just after three. Thirsty, he headed for the kitchen.

'Hey, Jeremy. How's it going?'

'Oh, hi, dad. Yeah, good thanks. Just getting a drink. Want anything?'

Jez's father, Robert, was lying in his hammock beyond the kitchen in the conservatory. The sun streamed through the glass onto his torso, giving him a warm glow and making him look not unlike a basking cat.

'What you been up to?'

Jez got on very well with his father but didn't feel the need to explore the minutiae of his life with him. 'This and that,' he said. 'Nothing too exciting.'

'Ah, girls then. I getcha. Chasing the skirt. Good man.'

Jez inwardly approved of his father's well-meaning but distinctly uncool discourse. 'Chasing skirt. Yeah, dad. What am I supposed to do when I catch up with it?'

'We'll tackle that when you do, mate. But bear in mind there's not much skirt actually worth chasing. And always make sure you're chasing the skirt, not the shirt.'

'Yes, dad. Nice line in homophobia.'

Jez opened the fridge and took a bottle of water. He flipped the cap and downed the liquid inside. 'Not working today?'

'No, Jeremy, not today. I've got a case tomorrow over in the New Forest, just come in. I'm cogitating on it now.'

'Cogitating? You might want to see a doctor about that, dad.'

'Funny!' His dad rolled out of the hammock onto one leg, stood upright and stretched. 'Well, I don't have time to lie around cogitating all bloody day, Jeremy. It's fine for you kids, chasing pussy all day.'

'Pussy, dad? Really?' Jez threw his empty bottle into the recycling bin, sighed a mock sigh of exasperation, then grinned at his father. 'Dad, you're a dick.'

They smiled at each other as his father walked out into the living room and then through into his study. He called back: 'Pete's over for dinner tonight, so try not to stink of weed.'

Jez liked his dad's friends too. Pete Mathers was an old friend from his days at Villiers. They'd worked CID together until his father retired. He knew Mathers was paired up with someone called Mike now, but he hadn't met him. He sounded like a good chap from the conversations he overheard anyway.

Jez's father closed his study door and settled into his brown leather swivel chair. He reached his arms up and stretched again before settling his right hand on the computer mouse and his left on the keyboard. He typed his password, '1ps0fact0', and clicked the mouse.

His email list appeared on the monitor. The newest read: 'Case Ref: 45094600072 Painsley CID'. He clicked the email open and read it for the second time.

Attn: Robert Moulder
Consultant

Hi Rob. Here's one for you if you're interested. We've had a murder in our sleepy village. Out in the woods. Nasty stuff. Some photos attached.

A girl, well liked in the community. We're lacking a motive and it looks like we've got transients in the frame. This was a really messy one too. Possibly ritualistic.

If you're up for this one, we're setting up the incident room tomorrow.

Cheers,

Jerry

Robert closed the email and reached over to the printer at the back of his desk. He took the five printed photos and looked through them one by one. The scene was certainly gruesome. A young female had been pretty much butchered. The blood had been splattered about too – someone was making a statement, perhaps, or maybe it was just chaos. Murder scenes generally looked chaotic, Robert thought. He'd seen hundreds of them.

23

He clicked the email open again and responded: 'Jerry. Look forward to seeing you tomorrow. Put the kettle on.' He clicked *Send* and waited for a progress bar to fill, then flicked the monitor off.

~~~

At five-twenty-five, Jez managed to park right in front of the fairground. Maria was now working on the pirates and princesses carousel, just feet from his car. Having exchanged a quick succession of amorous glances, Jez turned his attention to a group of boys standing around a unit with a punchbag sticking out of the top. He watched as each in turn thumped the protrusion, then each other, all the while jumping around like popcorn and whooping noisily.

It reminded him of a nature programme, watching some dumb animals trying to out-do each other to see who would be the chief of the tribe – or in this case, he thought, *chief twat among the most supreme twats in the civilised west*. He made brief eye contact with one of the animals, who first offered a snarl of aggression but then self-awareness set in and, as if his brain had just reset in that brief moment, he went back to whooping and jumping.

Jez looked back at the clock on his dashboard – *5.30* – and then to the carousel. This, he always thought, was the worst way for anyone to spend their time: going round and round in circles, the most irritating, saccharine music soundtracking the mundane, horrible experience, and you have to pay for it too. Yet every time he looked at this 'ride', he saw the faces of contented children; not necessarily happy, often bewildered, but *satisfied*.

At five-thirty-three, Maria disappeared from view briefly then returned with her coat on, her handbag slung absent-mindedly over her shoulder, beaming at Jez. He got out of the car and locked it.

'Maria,' he smiled.

'Where are you taking me then?'

'Where would you like to be taken?' He realised the double entendre immediately but Maria didn't seem to. This was another mark of appeal for Jez: her innocence; ignorance even. For him, Maria was his intellectual match but she simply hadn't developed a grasp of the nuances of the English language. He would teach her. He knew words like *strabismus*.

24

'A drink, a walk, the cinema… you know, I'd not really planned anything. I was just looking forward to seeing you.' Jez shrugged and Maria blushed, shaking her head.

'Okay. Let's walk. But let's go that way.' Maria pointed the opposite direction from the way they usually walked, to where she lived. 'We always end up walking the same way. Let's go up the cable car.'

Jez smiled and nodded, taking her hand in his. They turned up and around the larger of two arcade buildings and once again Jez saw the police tape around the old fishing huts. One of the officers recognised him and nodded.

'I hope it wasn't really a murder,' Maria said, squeezing Jez's hand. 'It's too close.'

Jez nodded. 'Probably wasn't. If it was murder there'd be police all over it. My dad's a copper. He didn't mention anything.'

The couple carried on walking, crossing the road and up past a row of bars and galleries, until they reached the cable car. 'I'll get these,' Jez said. He approached the booth and bought two return tickets, then turned back to Maria.

Beyond her he saw that stark, heavy figure from earlier. On the other side of the road, her supervisor stood staring right at him. Jez felt a little twist in his stomach and focused back on Maria. 'Come on. Let's go up.'

They rounded the booth to the barrier, inserted their tickets and waited for the cable car. From then until the moment the cable car disappeared from his view, Supervisor Steve didn't take his eyes off them.

Four – The numbers game

Bleach stopped the van in the usual spot. Jock looked at him, quizzically. 'You mean to tell me you're actually writing a book?'

'Yeah, I am *actually* writing a book.' Bleach's demeanour had changed considerably since the sobering realisation that the dead girl in his bedroom had somehow got up and walked out of his flat. Even through the haziest of drug fogs, he knew something like that would snap you right out of it.

'So it's about… what – failing to murder people properly?'

'No!' Bleach accepted the jest. 'It's about a group of friends who go to climb a mountain and get attacked. I've written four chapters. I'm really enjoying it. Writing is like… I mean, you get to tell a story and describe stuff, but stuff also comes out that you hadn't planned in a voice you don't recognise. It's amazing.'

'Twat.'

'Huh?'

'Do you recognise *this* voice? It's mine, calling you a twat. Now let's get these girls delivered, get some money, and get wasted.'

Bleach and Jock got out of the van. Jock swung open the side doors. The two body bags and holdalls had rolled down into a heap by the back doors. Jock reached in and grabbed one of the bag ends, dragging it out and then up, over his shoulder. There was a faint moan from inside.

Bleach grabbed the other bag and poked at the head end. The head responded pathetically. 'Let's go,' he said. 'Almost there, love. Let's get you inside and give you a nice cuppa.'

Jock let out a raspy laugh as he slid the doors shut. 'Yeah, cup of tea and some cake. How about a nice hot bath as well?'

They walked around to the front of the van and straight ahead to their destination: the rear entrance to a mid-terrace, four-storey house. A small set of stairs led up to a nondescript door, railings at each side. Down to the left was another stairway leading down and under the back door to a basement door. A sign above that door read 'Deliveries for Stanley.' Out the other side of the house on the main road was the shop front, two large windows showing its wares – the assorted tools and do-it-yourself packages one would expect to find in a hardware store. Given that it was nearing nine o'clock, the shop was shut.

26

The rear of the property was enclosed with a high gated fence running along the access road used by the shopkeepers and those who lived in the dwellings above or below, and of course those making deliveries, such as Jock and Bleach.

Jock knocked on the door. He looked up at the small camera above the frame, waiting to see its red light turn green. Five seconds later it did as the door opened. 'Evening,' Jock said in monotone.

A smart over-middle-aged man, wearing a red dressing gown, beckoned his guests in. They proceeded past the man down a narrow corridor, turning into the second room on the right. The man closed the door behind them and went to join them.

'Only two tonight? That's... disappointing.'

Jock shot a look at Bleach. 'Yeah, it's a shame but it's not always easy.'

'Isn't it? How so?'

'Well, Stanley,' Bleach said, 'there's only the two of us and...'

Stanley interrupted: 'It was only one of you this time, wasn't it?'

Bleach hiccupped. 'It was... well, yeah.' His expression was surprise and bewilderment.

'Yes, Stanley. James went on his own this time. I was otherwise...'

'Were you? I see. Well this is very interesting. I find this all very interesting.' Stanley looked directly at Bleach.

'And where is the other girl?'

Bleach's pulse quickened. He could feel his face reddening. 'I...'

'You... what? Is there something you'd like to tell me, James?'

'She... I mean – no, Stanley. I'm sorry.'

'Oh, you are? Thank you for the show of remorse, James. I'll note that on the wall planner.'

Bleach could feel his legs weakening. He edged back a little nervously.

'Is there something the matter, James?'

'N... no, Stanley.' He felt the walls closing in. The mantelpiece above the fireplace on the opposite wall appeared to shift position. The fact that none of the ornaments on it moved told him it was in his imagination.

'Good. It's quite simple.' He moved his stare to Jock. 'Do you take me for a mug, Neil?'

Jock hated being called Neil. Only his mother and Stanley ever did. 'No. Of course not, Stanley. It's just-'

'Yes, it is. It's always *just* with people like you. Now listen to me, you brainless fucking children. If you draw attention to yourselves, you're going to draw attention to me, aren't you? That's pretty straightforward common sense, wouldn't you agree?'

Stanley didn't wait for an answer.

'Now you, James, have lost your way a bit, wouldn't you agree? Yes, you would. Have you seen yourself in a mirror recently? Have you caught your own reflection in any of the crystals you insist on smoking? And as for you, Neil. You've always been the sensible one. That's why you two work so well together. Thicky and Dicky.'

Stanley looked back at Bleach. 'So what's disappointing here is this: you've got a loose end. You've killed girls before, haven't you, James? Why was this one so much trouble? And what's really, really disappointing, especially today, is that you were going to lie to me. Why do you think today might be special?'

Jock started to speak but Stanley raised his hand as if to say *shut up*.

'Today isn't any more special than any other day, see. Every day of every year, I expect my friends to treat me with respect. I'm assuming you understand. Don't fucking lie to me and don't spoil my merchandise.'

Jock and Bleach replied in chorus: 'Sorry, Stanley.'

'Good. Now, who have you brought for me today? I always enjoy unwrapping my presents.'

Stanley bent down and unzipped the bag closest to him. He looked up at Bleach. 'You two can go and claim your reward. Come and see me when you're finished.'

Jock and Bleach left the room, closing the door behind them.

'Hello there, sweets.' Stanley stroked the back of his hand over the girl's cheek. She twitched. There was, as Stanley had become accustomed to, a look of terror in her eyes. Terror mixed with desperation. The eyes were red, bloodshot. He picked at the silver tape gagging her and began to pull it up.

'Now listen, lovely. If I pull this up, I don't want you to scream. I don't like screaming. Oh, hold on.'

He got up and walked over to a small hexagonal table and opened a drawer. He took out a white mask and put it over his face before returning to the girl.

'My name is Stanley.'

28

His voice was muffled now. *Scarier*, the poor girl thought. Her eyes struggled to adjust to the room; her breathing was short. Looking up as his masked face came into view intensified the horror. Her mind raced with thoughts she couldn't latch onto. Fear ruled her now. The other body bag moaned.

'I'll be with you shortly, dear. Patience, please.' A stronger moan this time.

A sharp click was followed by nine chimes from the grandfather clock in the corner of the room. Stanley barely noticed. His attention was focused on the girl.

'Now then, what should I call you?' Stanley reached back and dragged over the first girl's holdall. He unzipped it slowly, pulling the items out one by one and laying them on the floor beside her.

'Fifteen. We've got a few of you in already. Such a lovely age. I remember being fifteen.' His breath became lighter. 'Olga. What an ugly name for such a pretty girl. That won't do at all. Your parents must be horrible. We'll call you...' Stanley dragged his index finger along the line of Olga's possessions, scanning for inspiration. His finger hovered and swirled over a magazine cover.

'Ah, here we go. Nice to see you take pride in your appearance.' He flipped the magazine open. 'Charlie. Yes, that'll do. Nice to meet you, Charlie.'

Stanley unzipped the body bag further and rolled her over enough to get access to her hands – bound tightly in silver tape. There was a large dried stain, brown and red, covering her back and buttocks. He softly took one of her hands in his and shook it.

'Don't worry, Charlie. We'll get you cleaned up in a little while. Close your eyes and rest for now.'

He zipped the bag back level with *Charlie*'s neck, then got up and stepped over her to the next bag. This time he opened her holdall first. This girl was called Daniela. Stanley told her he didn't like that name at all either. It sounded too much like Daniel. Daniela was fourteen years old. He explained that they hadn't had a fourteen in for a while. This excited him very much. He didn't unzip the bag at all but she heard every word. Daniela's name was changed to Stephanie.

~~~

Jez knew he was falling for Maria. He hadn't experienced love before, or not like this anyway. No girl had ever excited him so much as to make his stomach churn when he thought about seeing her. He leaned in for another kiss. Maria responded, latching onto his lower lip and nibbling it a little.

Withdrawing with a giggle, Jez said: 'Walk you back?' This was just one of many attempts to get closer to Maria; to find out where she lived. Thus far, she'd been cagey, unwilling to let him walk her all the way home. He wondered how soon she'd let him go *all the way*.

He assumed it was just another barrier to break down. He'd never had a real girlfriend like Maria before. She was elegant. She probably had a string of boys after her, following her home. She'd probably had bad experiences.

Maria smiled but hesitated. After a pause, she said: 'Okay. I suppose it's time. You can walk me... nearly all the way.'

Jez chuckled playfully, inwardly feeling hurt. 'Don't you trust me?'

Maria was quick: 'Oh Jez, yes. Of course I trust you. I share this house with some other guys, that's all. And...'

'And?'

'Well, one of them is my ex-boyfriend and he's really jealous. He still thinks we're kinda *a thing*. And we're not. Not at all. But he's Polish too. And he's very... obsessive.' Maria pronounced it *obs-es-if*.

Jez felt relief at understanding Maria's reticence but pushed further. 'If this... goes anywhere, he'll have to deal with it.'

'I think this is definitely going somewhere,' Maria giggled. 'Just a little time. I'll talk to him tomorrow, in my break.'

Jez realised that this ex-boyfriend and Supervisor Steve were likely one and the same.

'It's Steve, from the fairground?'

'Yeah!' Maria prodded Jez in the chest. It hurt. 'How did you know that?'

Jez frowned. 'Just a feeling. Well that, and he gave me the evils earlier.'

'The evils? What is the evils?'

'Y'know...' Jez trailed off. 'Well anyway, sod the walk. I'll just drop you wherever you like.' He started the engine, flicked the indicator up and checked his mirror.

'Hey, baby. Don't worry.' Maria could see Jez's mood had changed and she cared enough to want to make him feel better. She leaned over and kissed him. 'I promise. I'll talk to him tomorrow.'

~~~

Jock got to the top of the stairs first. 'How the fuck did he know about the other one?'

Bleach shook his head. 'I'm trying not to think about it. We need to find her anyway.'

In front of them stood another door, guarded by a stocky man with a full beard. He nodded at Jock, nodding again to the side to suggest they open it and go inside. They did as they were told.

The door closed behind them. Bleach whispered to Jock: 'I don't want to do this now. I don't feel good about this.'

The room was about twenty feet square with armless chairs arranged around the walls in an *N* shape. Jock counted them mentally: sixteen. On each chair sat a figure. Each was dressed in what Jock's mum would have called a 'pretty piece'.

The girls' heads were covered with black, eyeless hoods. They appeared motionless – as if dropped there out of time; static in the room, waiting to be awakened.

Jock walked to the first chair on his right. Mentally he considered this to be Girl Sixteen. Her legs were folded at the ankles, her hands clasped elegantly together in her lap. Her dress was lilac and aquamarine, patterned with sea shells. Jock crouched down and lifted her feet up. He saw the branding on her left heel: *Julianna*. He let her feet drop. They bobbed gently like a buoy in calm water.

Bleach felt the room was all *wrong*. He'd never seen it sober. The haze of drug happiness he normally sauntered through had turned to stark realism. He wondered how Jock saw it. He didn't seem to share the same apprehension. Bleach watched him circle the room, stopping at each girl to check her feet.

'Some of these names are mental,' he said, jarring the grim atmosphere in Bleach's brain with unexpected levity. 'Check it out.'

Bleach didn't want to check it out. 'No, I'm okay for that mate. I'm not up for this.' He felt his voice becoming croaky.

Two gentle knocks on the door behind him got Bleach's attention. He turned and noticed there was no handle on this side. The door swung open and the bearded man beckoned Bleach out. Jock followed. Bleach felt an instant wave of relief replaced with anxiety.

The bearded man spoke: 'Stanley wants to see you.' He pointed towards the stairs going upwards.

They made their way up the stairs and came to a landing bathed in red light. A corridor led off to the left, joining another landing that circled the stairway, several rooms leading off it. Ahead of them they could see Stanley talking to another man. Jock led the way. As they reached Stanley's office, Bleach noticed a door just off the landing. It was open enough to give him a dreadful snapshot – a body hanging from the ceiling by a thick rope. His mind's eye formed the image of his mother hanging from the rafters. He snapped his view back forwards.

'Do come in, chaps. Sit down.' Stanley motioned for Jock and Bleach to take the seats in front of his desk. They were ornate, red leather, suiting the décor of the room's dark wooden and leather furnishings. Paintings of landscapes hung on the walls, lit by downlights. The room seemed stuffy to Bleach, as if full of smoke; some kind of mental fog. His chest felt tight.

Stanley spoke softly to the other man in the room, standing just adjacent to the doorway. He was taller than Stanley but he seemed smaller to Bleach. Everyone seemed somehow *smaller* than Stanley. He patted the man on the shoulder and used his palm to guide him out of the room.

'Now then,' Stanley said, closing the door and walking back and around the desk to take his own seat, a larger and more cushioned version of Jock and Bleach's. 'Thanks to that fine, upstanding pillar of our community, we have an opportunity to tie up your loose end.'

Jock and Bleach sat still and unable to think of anything to say. Stanley took this as the appropriate response.

'Good. We're agreed then. James, your ex-girlfriend has turned up in a hopeless state. She'll not be giving your name and address away but she needs taking care of.'

Bleach felt like he had just woken up. 'That's great, Stanley, sir.'

Stanley nodded in approval. A small crease in his lips resembled the beginnings of an insincere smile.

'I'll make sure she's got no chance of talking this time.'

'And how will you do that?'

Jock knew Stanley was playing with Bleach.

32

'Well, I'll... you know, kill her.'

Stanley laughed. It cut through the room.

'James, you sweet fucking imbecile. The girl is dead. The police have her body at Villiers. Do you know where that is?'

'Oh... yes, Stanley. I know Villiers.'

'Good. Of course you do. You've seen the inside of that place more than most. Our friend in the force has just agreed to give you a free ticket to the dead girl show. You'll see him there at midnight.'

Bleach was alarmed to look at his watch and see the time was ten-thirty. *An hour-and-a-half? We got here before nine. How could... what?* His chest tightened another notch. *I need to get high. Now.*

'That'll have to wait, James,' Stanley said. Jock looked confused. He hadn't heard Bleach say anything. 'You've worked for me for... it's about two years now, isn't it? As I said earlier, James, it's time for you to clean up. You're getting sloppy.'

Bleach nodded. 'Yes, Stanley.' His thoughts: *I wanna get high I wanna get high I wanna get high I wanna get high.*

Stanley laughed again. 'We'll see then, won't we?'

Bleach felt like he'd been invaded but he didn't understand why or how.

Because you opened the door. You invited him in.

'Bring the girl back here. She could still be useful. Or on second thoughts, if you think you can dispose of her properly this time, so be it.'

Jock thought: *Useful? How could she be?* He saw the reasoning behind taking her away from the police, though.

Stanley let it ride. He wasn't too concerned with Neil's behaviour. Neil had always been the one with the keys. James had heart though, as much as that would get him into trouble. Still, Stanley was pretty much invincible. He knew that ultimately he was babysitting these lost souls, and that as long as he kept them in a state of fear and confusion, they were his.

The thought re-settled in Bleach's head: *an hour-and-a-half... ninety minutes... hour-and-a-half... ninety minutes... I wanna get out of here.*

~~~

Dixie shuffled a little in her chair as the man entered the room, closing the door gently behind him. Her mouth twitched a little but no sound

33

came out. The man shot an indifferent glance at her as he rounded the bed. He wasn't there for her.

The man bent forward and grabbed the girl. She screamed. He dragged her over and threw her against the wall and walked back around the bed, pulling the door open just enough to see through. He reached down to his side and pulled a knife out of its sheath.

The silent observer shifted in her seat, turning her face towards the light of the window. The bedroom door sprang open with a thump as the man jumped backwards, grabbing another by the shoulder and thrusting the knife into his neck. He slumped to the floor, a thin spray of blood shooting up the wall. The girl sprang up, pushing herself back into the corner of the room, her eyes full of fear. She screamed again.

The man jumped over her bed, pushing his gloved hand down over the girl's mouth. With his other hand he reached to his belt, unbuckled a pouch and withdrew a small black unit. He pressed it against the girl's leg as she fought back limply. The unit let out a short, sharp *click* and the girl's body stopped pushing. A human *off*-switch.

He cradled the girl and positioned her over his left shoulder. With his other hand he took a revolver from its holster and made his way out of the room.

The silent observer jumped straight from the seat to cower under the bed as shots rang out, loud splashes of orange bouncing off the walls and ceiling outside. She waited a few moments then came out and jumped onto the bed, quickly finding the warmest spot where the girl had been. She curled up, contented, and went back to sleep.

~~~

'What the fuck was all that about?'

Jock turned the key in the ignition, put the gear stick into reverse and began backing out of the gate.

'I don't know. What happened after we left the girls? It's not... it wasn't the same as last time.'

'The money? Why didn't we get the money?'

'We got paid last time, right?'

Jock thought hard. As if someone was cutting off his air supply, he felt mentally suffocated – unable to grasp at the memories. He turned the

34

steering wheel three-quarters, braked, then lurched forward to leave the access road.

'Yeah, we did,' Jock said. 'I'm sure. The house this time was... different. I don't remember being in his study before.'

'That's because we haven't been up there before. Last time we went down, didn't we?'

'How would you know anyway? It's a wonder your meth memory retains any information.'

Bleach felt insulted. 'What is all this shit? Okay, so I *use* a bit, but it's not as if I'm out of control. I can do the job. And I do it well.'

'Which is why we're heading to the police station to steal the corpse of the dead girl you let walk out of your flat, right?'

Bleach remembered something from moments earlier – a fragment of a memory coming forward. He couldn't grab it. He was thinking of the number ninety but couldn't place why. *Ninety-nine, nine-hundred-and-ninety-nine.* He let it go.

Jock too was trying to hold onto a thought. He had an image of a foot with writing on it. He couldn't make out what it said. The image flashed up and away in a second.

'We've got a little time to kill,' Jock said.

'Pop back to mine.'

'So you can get high? No thanks. Let's get this done.'

'You judgemental prick. I operate at my peak after a bulb or two.'

'Yeah, course you do. You can get your fix later. After we clean up *your* mess. You can write about it in your fucking book.'

35

Five – The mighty fall

Jez wasn't the worst channel-hopper in his family but on this particular evening he felt restless and was thumbing the button with greater urgency, as if rushing to find the inevitable conclusion: that there was nothing good on TV.

He was distracted by a buzz from his PDA. Picking it up from the arm of his black leather recliner, he saw in the screen's glow it was a message from Col. '109 – porn debate! ;-) Might get to see some action!'

Jez flicked the envelope icon right and responded. 'If you want to see a big cock, just look in the mirror.' Without really wanting to, with his other hand he thumbed 109 and caught the last in a sequence of commercials, this with a cheery blonde teenager seemingly enjoying washing her hair.

His father crossed the living room from the kitchen and glanced down at Jez. He was pre-occupied after dinner with his old colleague Pete but had time to note that his son looked like some kind of cyborg, augmented with 3D visor and electronic talons.

Jez smiled up from his visor and flicked the screen down over his eyes again as the programme started.

Following a brief intro sequence with a piece of music Jez thought was designed to be urgent but had a greater chance to irritate, the camera zoomed to the familiar face of presenter Donal Henderson.

'Good evening and welcome one and all to tonight's *Blue Horizons*, where we tackle another in our series of moral matters – pornography. On tonight's show we'll be talking to some of the UK's leading thinkers and voices on porn and asking: is porn degrading to women, and what about the men? Is it dangerous in a civilised society?'

Jez had rarely thought beyond the primal urge satisfied by the female anatomy laid bare. He now realised, presumably justifying the objective of the TV show, that he did have an opinion. Yes, he imagined it was degrading for women, but if those women were willing participants...

His thoughts were interrupted. 'Let's meet our panel of experts.' Jez's PDA buzzed again and he decided to check it after the introductions. The camera zoomed to each of the six 'experts' in turn.

'On my left we have George Lazarou, owner of adult entertainment provider SkinFlix; Skip Standings, lead producer at Standings Room Only; and Briony Black, adult entertainment actress.'

Jez recognised Briony Black. He wouldn't class himself as a fan as such, but he'd seen her in action several times. Most boys his age had, he thought.

'And on my right, representing the moral standpoint, we have the Bishop of Heddersley; Stephen Clark, MP for Portwich; and Gloria Davies-Smith, chief executive of women's rights campaign group, StandUp.'

Donal Henderson set the scene as Jez checked his PDA. 'Can't even SEE your dick in a mirror.' He sighed. Col wasn't the funniest guy in the world but normally he'd do better than that. He responded right away: 'I saw your mother in the mirror this morning. Sucking my balls.'

Jez's father crossed the room again. 'What're you watching?' Jez told him.

'Ah, that looked fun. But that guy... Lazarou, isn't it? He's a crook.'

'Everyone's a crook to you, dad,' Jez smiled. His father continued to the kitchen, muttering something cheerily.

Henderson continued: 'Our format tonight is Q and A. Our first question comes from... Mr Yannick Portrou. Yannick?' He looked up and began to scan the audience.

The microphone ran up to the third aisle from the back, then along a few feet to a man wearing a dark red suit jacket. He had a beard that Jez thought was too long, too bushy, and just too *beardy*.

'Good hee-vening,' Yannick said. 'For the goody-goodies.' He paused as a ripple of sighs clashed with a wave of sniggers, a mixture of mockery and anticipation. 'My question is: what is the problem with pornography?' Jez thought Yannick's accent made him sound like a TV terrorist – the sort whose accents alone flagged up their guilt and intentions. 'It is just sex, and sex is all natrool. So why shootn't we enjoy it?'

George Lazarou and Skip Standings exchanged a low-five. Briony Black nodded, seemingly deep in thought. It was a look Jez recognised – glassy-eyed and miles away. The look of a porn actress finding herself out of depth.

'If I may,' Gloria Davies-Smith started, 'this is the simplest answer. Women – and men – can enjoy sex in their own homes, and they can do whatever they like within the boundaries of the law, but as soon as they decide to film that sex and put it on the internet for anyone to see, it becomes something else. It perpetuates an industry which has a core, and on the fringes of that core are the desperately sad stories of girls being abducted, put into porn unwillingly, and depraved sex acts becoming popcorn for fetishists. There's also obvious use of hard drugs, and perpetuation of the idea that women are just holes to be filled.'

Applause and sniggers clashed as Henderson gestured to Lazarou. 'George?'

'Can I swear? Can I?' Lazarou turned out his palms to a shrug, inciting the audience. Jez formed his opinion quickly: lower working class bully. He'd seen snippets of Lazarou before in the papers, but not heard him speak.

'Well, may I first say what a pleasure it is to be here, and next I'd like to put it on record that Lady Smith over there is talking out of her fucking arse.'

Whoops and applause created a cacophony with a sea of disapproving muttering. 'At SkinFlix we have a legitimate recruitment process, all our girls take regular drugs tests, and nothing we put out could be called *depraved*. Seriously, you're way off track, lady. Our business supplies a demand. We've got sixty million turnover last year. People are paying to see our girls, and we look after our girls. If you don't like porn, don't watch it, but don't try to stop millions of satisfied customers enjoying it. Millions!'

Applause grew louder still. There were still some sniggerers. Jez laughed out loud too as Lazarou verbally assaulted his holier-than-thou opposition. The camera zoomed back to Davies-Smith, who had a look of half-grimace, half-apoplexy. Jez's PDA buzzed again. He ignored it.

Henderson set the Bishop up. 'It's a difficult question to answer if you're not talking about God's will,' he said. 'That is how I must approach any such question, and the church's position is that sexual love between two people is a sacred thing to be shared only by them. Anything else is outside of the worship of God.'

'Bollocks!' Lazarou shouted gleefully. Henderson looked like he might try to stop him but Lazarou went full-throttle. 'You show me anywhere in the *Bible* anything about selling videos of beautiful ladies pleasing their men.'

'Well there… there are many scriptures which allude to…'

'Allude? That's the problem with you holy types. It's all implifications and alludements. There's no black and white, hard and fast. In my game, everything is hard, fast and comes in black or white.'

Most of the audience seemed to roar with laughter. The Bishop looked deflated and helpless. Lazarou continued: 'And while I'm bashing the Bishop, that's what sixty-five per cent of my customers want to do while they're watching my movies. Yes, thirty-five per cent of my viewers are women. Women!'

Henderson calmed the rabble as Jez looked at his PDA again. Col had sent him a link and a winking emoticon. He tapped the former absently.

Skip Standings entered the fray. 'I've worked in the industry for over fifteen years. I used to be an actor myself. I can say categorically that I've never worked with a girl, and we're talking hundreds of girls, who has been there against her will. Some girls are good at being doctors or sitting behind reception desks. Our girls are good at having sex.'

Sound buzzed from Jez's PDA. He brought it closer to see what Col had decided to subject him to. A video began with a blonde woman in very high heels and a loose fitting dress knocking on a door. Col often sent him videos like this. Seeing that his father was about to cross the room again, he closed the video and put his PDA back on the arm of the recliner, making a mental note to catch the rest later.

The MP, Stephen Clark, was speaking: '...and we know that a lot of these girls do come from broken homes, there are abductions, and some of these girls just become nameless internet entities. They're lost to the real world. Then there's the content that goes beyond sex. I can't call it anything other than rape. Clearly drugs are involved. The police have got masses of documented cases which show these to be the facts. Now I'm not saying that Mr Lazarou's organisation is responsible for all this, but it definitely contributes to proliferation of a fringe where the acts are approaching or exceeding unspeakable.'

Jez agreed with this, as apparently did the studio audience. However, the Bishop, Jez mused, still looked well and truly bashed.

His father re-entered the room, carrying a large hold-all. 'Okay mate, that's me done. I'm off early in the morning and back in a day or two. Stay in touch, eh?'

'Will do, dad. Take care of yourself.' His father leaned in and patted Jez's shoulder. Jez reciprocated, leaning in and grabbing his elbow warmly. 'Sure I'll see you on the news anyway.'

'Maybe. I'm taking my best blouse.'

Jez went to the kitchen and opened the fridge. Settling on a Chunk chocolate bar, he unwrapped it and went back to his seat. He half-watched two commercials before *The Great Mass Debate* started up again.

Henderson explained why George Lazarou's seat was now empty – he'd been called away on a family emergency. *Live TV, eh?* Jez thought. He wasn't really interested in what anyone else had to say now the star of the show had left. Briony Black he'd *heard* before anyway, and as always with these girls, no one cared what came out of their mouths as much as what went in. He thought it was unlikely to escalate in that direction.

Jez's thoughts turned to earlier in the evening, when he and his father and his father's old friend Pete had shared a nice meal – a Chinese one delivered, anyway – and how much he enjoyed the banter between them. Pete had gone serious for a bit though, talking about the dead girl they'd found that morning, and he'd been at pains to point out to Jez that such talk was strictly confidential.

Jez agreed to keep his mouth shut, but really he had no intention of doing so. It turned out the police thought the girl was Polish. They were investigating a tattoo she had that seemed to say 'PP'. Maria, he thought, might know what that is, being Polish herself. He planned to ask her about it as soon as possible, but it wasn't the sort of thing you might bring up on a phone call or in a PDA message.

Pete had also asked Jez's father about the consultation work he was doing. This turned the conversation to his impending departure for Painsley Forest the next day, where he'd been asked to help with the investigation into a murder of a young girl in the woods. Pete left fairly quickly after they'd finished the food and a bottle of wine, as he'd just received an urgent message to report to the station. He didn't say why.

~~~

'Come with us, Mr Lazarou.'

The pornographer who just moments before had been cheerfully assaulting the 'moralists against masturbation', as he'd referred to them during the advertisement break, followed the two police officers and got into their car.

'What's this all about?' His lawyer, Henry Noble, who was never too far away, was already in the car.

'George,' he said. 'It's Lara. She's been… taken.'

Lazarou's brow jumped to accommodate his now bulging eyes – a reaction infused with confusion, surprise and anger. 'What do you mean, taken?'

'George, as we were arriving here tonight, it appears a man entered your grounds and took Lara.'

He was about to go on but Lazarou interrupted: 'Took her where? What about the security guys?'

'They're… um, they're dead sir. All of them. Muriel knows. She's making her way to the mansion.'

'Fuck Muriel!' Lazarou clenched his fists. 'It's those fucking bleeding hearts, is it? Great timing – as soon as I show up to defend myself, they take the one thing I care about.'

'Please calm down, sir,' one of the officers spoke firmly. 'We'll need to head back to the station now and take some details.'

'Details? Details of fucking what? My daughter's been taken – why aren't you trying to find her?'

'Sir, please just calm down. We believe the crime took place in the last hour and we have a team tracking the trail now. We've got cameras tracing the getaway vehicle, we've got the plate number from a witness, and we're confident this'll be over tonight.'

Lazarou spluttered. 'It better fucking be. It fucking better.'

~~~

Mathers and Danson arrived at the station just about on top of each other. A large group of press photographers and reporters was gathered outside in front of the main steps up to reception. Pete thumbed three times to his right, Mike nodded and the partners backed away and around the back of the building to a security gate usually reserved for taking offenders in and out.

'What the fuck, Mike?'

'Dunno. Must be big though.'

They made their way through the back entrance and in towards the front desk. Mackenzie was waiting.

41

'Hey, guys.' She looked exhausted. 'It's a big one. Child abduction and multiple homicide.'

Danson looked at her blankly and shrugged. He was tired. He'd barely left the station two hours ago, and while his best friend Pete was having dinner with his ex-partner, Mike was sat at home staring at the pill in his palm. He had imagined the pill talking to him, beckoning him closer so it could whisper a soothing secret into his ear. It quickly turned pseudo-sexual – the pill whispering: *Put me in your mouth. Suck on me. I'll make you feel good.*

'Where?'

'George Lazarou, our favourite local peddler of all things smut. His daughter was snatched about an hour ago. His security force have all been killed. It's a bloodbath.'

'Okay!' Mathers had been feeling a little weary himself, half a bottle of wine and a mush of Chinese food sloshing around in his belly, but he felt a second wind coming on. Police work was usually rote – the same things week in, week out, but a tidy package of multiple homicides and an abduction all in one day was perversely appealing to a man who found his thrills in the darkest places.

Mackenzie continued: 'Dave's already on the scene with a team. I don't know what you guys are in for, but it's all hands on deck with this one until further notice.'

Danson felt the pull of the pill again. Sitting in its thin, easily-shed sheath, he could whip it out and into his mouth in a flash. No one would see. But it was going to be a long night and he realised that as much as he'd love to take a hit, right now his attention was needed on the job.

'Let's go find out the deal then.' Danson tugged gently at Mathers' arm and they moved past Mackenzie towards the superintendent's office. The door was open and the chief was in heated conversation with one of the junior beat officers. He blurted: 'Come in, you two. About time.'

'Came as fast as we could, sir,' Mathers responded. 'Where do you need us?'

'Have you been briefed?'

Danson shrugged a little and shook his head. 'Only the nature of the crime, sir.'

Chief Superintendent Gordon Briggs, as the nameplate on his desk gleamed in bold black lettering, briefed his detectives. At roughly eight-fifteen, a man was recorded climbing over the back wall to George

42

Lazarou's estate. It was unclear how he managed to get into the residence without being apprehended by Lazarou's security detail, but once in he had apparently executed three men on the main hall staircase and another in the bedroom of the abducted girl, Lara. She was seventeen-years-old.

'Inside job, then? Definitely a pro with the executions,' Mathers observed.

Danson chipped in. 'If he was an insider, he wouldn't *kill* everyone, would he? We can rule that out.'

Briggs responded sharply: 'I don't want you two sitting here trading theories all night. You're in with the district CID team. I want you out at the Lazarou residence yesterday. Mackenzie's liaison on this one. Now get going and find that girl.'

Danson turned to leave, but Mathers stopped to ask: 'Sir?'

Briggs looked up from the folder he'd just opened and fixed Mathers with a *what now?* glare. Something had been playing on his mind most of the afternoon, and indeed over dinner.

'Did we get any further on the dead girl with the tattoo?'

'The body's been transferred,' Briggs said curtly. 'Out of our hands now. Forget about it. Now move!'

Mathers made an effort to leave the room calmly rather than shout his head off – why had the girl been moved? When he got a case, any case, he took ownership of it. This was like a theft of his personal belongings. Mathers sneered at Danson. He sneered back.

Mackenzie was waiting in the corridor. 'Okay guys. Looks like we're off together. I'll drive.'

Six – Love conquers all

Jez heard his father's bedroom door close – he was due to leave earlier in the morning than Jez was likely to rise – and made sure his was closed too. Although his father was not the sort to invade his privacy, since his mother had caught him masturbating three years ago he was simply careful. It wasn't a matter so much of being caught and embarrassed, but more that he understood it wasn't the sort of thing a parent should ever witness. For the sanity of his father, he kept his solo bedroom activities well to himself and supposed his dad, who had of course been his age once, understood completely – a wankers' handshake.

He had less of an idea about his father's access to his browsing history but assumed if he overstepped any boundaries he'd find out soon enough. He had considered that in the wake of his mother leaving to join the hippies or whatever they were, his father probably had cause to visit some of the same sites anyway. In any case, safety in blissful ignorance.

He reached for his tablet – the PDA screen was just that little bit too small to enjoy the pleasures of internet flesh – and found Col's second-to-last message. He opened it on the larger screen. In the interim Col had sent another, enquiring with a single '?'

Jez responded that he hadn't had a chance to watch the video yet. His chance was now. Col usually didn't send anything run-of-the-mill, preferring as he did the more colourful and amusing content, but he also didn't usually send porn. His interest piqued, Jez clicked *Play* and watched. The blonde woman he'd seen earlier in a loose dress knocking on a door did the same again. The man who answered the door had longish fair hair and was wearing a shirt that seemed a few sizes too large for his build.

So far, so low budget. Jez's eyes closed for a moment. He felt tired. It had been a long day. Some weed, some wine, some sunshine with his friends and some quality time with his beautiful girlfriend. Was she his girlfriend? He hoped so.

He opened his eyes to see the blonde lady speaking in a foreign tongue to the ill-shirted man, who pointed through to another room. The camera followed just behind her, watching her go through an arched doorway and sit down on a couch that barely dented with her form, crossing her legs. Usually with porn Jez could feel the anticipation, a

44

stirring that demanded a little patience, but here he felt a more pressing need for something, anything, to happen. It had been a long day.

Just as his eyes began to narrow again, the camera shifted to the other side of the room. There, in a single armchair not too much unlike Jez's favourite in his own living room, sat a hooded figure – there were no holes cut for eyes, nose or mouth. The hood hung like a petal on a wilting flower, draped rather than tailored. Something about this image made a knot turn in Jez's stomach. The figure was motionless but the camera stayed fixed on it.

From behind the camera an arm appeared, a hand slowly extending towards the hood as if primed to whip it away. It seemed to take ages to get there. Jez found the silence on the video uncomfortable. The hand's thumb and forefinger lifted the hood, again too slowly as if the cameraman had accidentally knocked a slow motion button. As the hood lifted off the face, the knot in his stomach twisted again. It was like a horror movie moment, a scene where a lurking killer edges closer, unseen, to his prey.

The hood raised further and he could see a pair of lips. Pallid, grey, somehow off, Jez thought. Where just a moment ago his eyes had been ready to close, now he was entranced by this very strange scene playing out before him. The nose was revealed, and it seemed between the cheeks to be longer and narrower than one might expect. As the hood came up above the eyeline, Jez felt a punch in his gut – hard enough to take his breath away.

The camera lingered, still but shaky, as the hand drew away, taking the hood with it. He now recognised the girl from the fairground, the one with the strange narrow face and vacant expression. Her eyes were cold and distant, looking – not that she appeared to be *looking* at anything – off to the right.

Jez looked away briefly, feeling his stomach turn again, this time heavier and deeper. The first shot of peristalsis hit his digestive system and he pulled in reactively to stop anything escaping. He closed his eyes to clear the image but it served to strengthen it instead. Opening them again, Strabismus Girl was now looking right at him. The man in his stomach twisted the tubes again.

A thin smile began to form on her mouth, her eyes remaining *somewhere else*. Jez didn't want to watch but – *why the fuck had Col sent this to him?* – he couldn't find the energy to lift his hands off the side of his tablet to press *Stop*. Her smile widened enough to turn another screw in Jez's bowels, forcing him to belch. He had a feeling unlike anything he'd felt before: a sweet, sincere and unexpected flutter of butterflies mixed with some kind of impending inner explosion.

Strabismus Girl – he could see it was definitely her now, the girl he'd observed just hours before – turned her face slightly to her left now, and her smile disappeared as the camera pulled back, blurring slightly. Another hand appeared, holding something, also blurry in close vision. The camera re-focused and Jez felt the explosion coming faster now, as if past the point of no return.

The hand was holding a gun, black and metallic, a dull shine to it. It rotated in the hand, as if floating. Then the gun pointed at Strabismus Girl as the camera twitched back further. Her arms, Jez could now see, were bound tightly around her stomach. Her eyes were fixed straight ahead, staring into the barrel of the gun.

Jez leapt up and rolled off his bed, the tablet tumbling with him and landing askew against the leg of his desk. He was now hyperventilating, his heart pounding, a pool of sweat dripping off his forehead and into his eyes, stinging them. Propping up on one elbow, a messy shape fallen into a pile on his bedroom floor, through burning eyes he caught the denouement – the flash of the gun and a sharp, dull thump as a bullet lodged into the wall just missing the girl.

The camera lingered as Jez felt some wisp of relief, a loosening at once of his bowels and the tension in his whole body and mind. For the first time he could remember in his life, he pissed his pants. A thin, yellow liquid came out of his penis. It escaped the lower edge of his briefs and ran onto the carpet beneath.

He heaved himself around slightly to become upright against his bed, feeling the unpleasantness of a wet, warm undercarriage and the smell of urine gagging him. With his other arm he reached over to the tablet and, his eyes still stinging with sweat, a burning sensation seemingly cooking his brain, he held it out in front of him.

Strabismus Girl hadn't moved an inch but she had that same vacant yet oddly smiling look. Jez was still breathing fast and shallow, the fumes in his mouth, nose and throat now; a ring of hot unpleasantness through his respiratory system. He lifted his arm up to cover his mouth and nose.

At last the camera's focus returned to the other side of the room, to the girl in the loose fitting dress. She stood up quickly, changing the pace

46

of this dreadful film, and walked over to a door in the other corner of the room – a door that hadn't been revealed before. The girl playfully beckoned the camera, and viewer, to follow her as she opened it, revealing only a dark room. Jez's stomach turned again but this time the knot was loose, like an elastic band stretched too many times and losing its properties.

The camera reached the doorway and light began to seep into the room. Jez took a final punch in the gut as the blonde pointed to the other side of this new room, a vision of two girls naked on a single bed, a curtained window behind them, smiling eagerly up at the camera and giggling. The video stopped – from a short, disgusting glimpse of his beloved Maria unclothed in the company of animals, to blackness. He dropped the tablet and grabbed at it again.

He dragged the progress slider back to let the end play again, watching the camera switch across to his girlfriend and her companion, and quickly tapped the *Pause* icon. He stared at the image for a while, Maria smiling at him the same way she'd smiled at him that afternoon. He felt a mixture of fury and heart-wrenching pain and a desire to kill his best friend for sending this sick shit to him.

Thoughts raced through his mind: *I've got to show this to my dad. No... why would he want to see this? There's... nothing. It's just a weird video. He doesn't know about Maria and if I show him this, he'll... fuck it! Fuck fuck fuck. Why why why why? I've got to... save her. I don't understand. Why why why?*

Okay, I'm going to rewind this and look for clues. To the beginning. I can identify the house, or the girl, or the man... Clutching now for some kind of positive action, Jez dragged his finger across, settling the video back to its beginning. Nothing happened for a moment – the loading bar hanging around the half-way mark – until suddenly the page refreshed. A new link opened and the words appeared: *Oops, something went wrong! Please check your network connection or reset your browser.* A sharp bolt hit the front of his brain. Jez was a virtual punchbag, in the boxing ring with some unseen, evil bastard who could make you piss yourself at his will.

'No!' he gasped. 'Fucking no! What?' He clicked the back-arrow on the tablet and got the same screen again. *The link*, he thought. He went back to his message inbox and... *where's the message? Where's the fucking message?* He scrolled up and down manically, entered the 'junk' and 'deleted' folders and saw all but the message he wanted.

~~~

Mack usually hated driving with the sirens wailing and lights flashing, but on this occasion there was no room for self-doubt. A girl had been taken and, aside from the media frenzy which had already begun and could only grow in intensity from here – casting a spotlight on *everyone* involved, she had a singular focus on a moral objective: to protect life. In truth she hadn't had much of an interesting career away from the recent promotion to Detective Sergeant, but in the last year she'd been exposed to the kinds of crimes that promoted insomnia and self-medication.

Now, with the glare of the media about to settle on her and her team, and everything else around them, there was no room to slip up. Pete sat up front with her, Mike in the back. Mack had been grateful in the short time it had crossed her mind that neither of her male companions had caused a fuss about who would sit where – they simply got in the car. She reckoned they felt the same way. No time for bullshit – get the job done, save the girl, and nick the sick, murderous bastard who took her.

Mack didn't relish the proposition of turning up at a bloodbath either, but again this determination, a rush of adrenaline, would do its best to carry her through the ordeal. Besides, whatever she made of the crime scene, it was she who had to call the shots, to determine what happened next, and it paled in comparison to whatever that poor girl was going through.

She'd been so deep in her thoughts and concentrating on following the GPS route that she didn't hear Pete addressing her.

'Mack?' It was the third time he'd said it.

'Sorry, I was miles away,' Mack responded, haste in her response. 'What?'

'Did you know about the body? Our girl's been handed over somewhere.'

'Yeah. Yeah... sorry. I heard. The chief told me. Out of our hands now.'

Pete shot a glance back to Mike, who acknowledged it with a shrug. 'I don't get it. Did he say why?'

'He said Interpol had assumed ownership of the corpse and I asked why. He said it wasn't my business anymore. I didn't push it further.'

'Seems very odd,' Pete said. He looked back at Mike again. 'Doesn't it? Interpol? We barely had her there a day. Interpol would barely have had time to know about it, let alone nick the bones.'

Mike nodded. 'Yeah, seems fishy. But them's the breaks.'

'Wow, such keen insight.' Pete's sarcasm hit a nerve.

'Fuck off, Pete.'

'Okay boys, that's enough.' Mack was firm. With no children of her own, she often saw herself unwittingly parenting her colleagues. 'We're all tired and it's gonna be a long night. So less of the alpha male shit and let's get on with this.'

Mack rounded two lefts and a right, opening out into a wider street bathed in the glow of red and blue lights. 'Okay, let's do this.'

Bruised more than he cared to be by Pete's comment, Mike strode a little faster than usual and reached the assembly first, followed by Mack. A heavy-set officer pushed past Mike and stopped at Mack.

'Mackenzie?'

She nodded. 'That's me.'

He put out his hand. 'Stevens. Forensics are in. I've got five guys out here and two inside. Uniform cars are following witness directions.'

Stevens nodded over at a group of observers, the five aforementioned officers simultaneously attempting to block their view of the Lazarou household and taking statements.

'Okay, thanks, Stevens,' Mack said, shaking his hand firmly. She recognised him from other scenes, but there wasn't time for further pleasantries. 'We're on the clock here. Mike, Pete – you two inside please. Stevens, what's the best lead on the mark?'

Mike and Pete ducked a barrier and headed through the open gate to jog up to the house.

'Mrs Hollister there saw the whole thing. Our man is or was wearing a dark or black tracksuit. She heard shots and saw from her window. The gate was open and he came out with the girl over his shoulder, bundled her into a green carrier and went north, then turned off onto Pike Street.'

'Thanks, Stevens.'

'There's more – she got his registration too.' Stevens handed Mack a sheet of paper, torn from his notepad. It read 'KT169AL'.

Mack's face lit up, a mixture of disbelief and relief. 'Really?'

'Yes, sarge. I know. We've got three cars gone after him and HQ's tracking the cams.'

Mack's mind began to race towards a happy conclusion until she stopped it. 'Well, it's not a done deal.' She smiled unevenly at Stevens and looked beyond him to the gathering. 'Anyone else see anything?'

~~~

Pete looked out of the window, down to the crowd of rubber-neckers eager to see blood and then up to the first floor windows where, he reckoned, no one would be getting any sleep tonight – red and blue lights flickering and dancing off the windows, the curtains and blinds filtering this light show into the rooms beyond with an urgency that would turn dreams to nightmares. Such was the role of the emergency response: *we're here now and to hell with the rest of you.*

Mike was back on the stairs talking to Ed Sharpe. It was a blood bath, he'd said, and there were prints everywhere. Guns lay at angles where they'd clearly spilled out of hands as bodies collapsed against the bannisters. Splashes of blood still dripped from them onto the marble stairs. The gun which lay on the welcome mat just inside the front door was the only anomaly, but as Ed opined, this must be the murder weapon.

Pete turned to the bed, Lara's resting place. To its left, next to the inward-opening bedroom door, was a streak of blood up the wall – thick and darkest at the top, tapering down to a body slumped, the hilt of a knife stuck in its neck. The body's face was down too far to make out its features, but a startled and grim expression emerged from the shadow.

The girl's sheet had been pulled back but rested almost too serenely against this backdrop of horror, as if she'd been taken gently as the body was dealt with harshly. A few drops of blood had made it to the left side of the bed but otherwise it looked like two different rooms in front of him. Death on one side and hope on the other.

Mike appeared in the doorway. 'Fuckin 'ell.'

Pete nodded. 'Fuckin 'ell indeed, mate.' He hesitated. 'Sorry about before.'

'No probs mate. Sharpe and his boys have a task ahead. We can't get anything from there yet apart from the murder weapon.'

'Okay.' Pete had arrived at the same conclusion on the way in. Where some detectives might have moaned that none of this made any sense, to

50

him it was straightforward: someone had broken in, shot everyone up, taken the girl and buggered off. He hadn't wanted to hurt her, not then at least. He just wanted to take her. Figuring out why was Pete's job, and whoever had done this seemed to want to make it easy for him to do that.

Dave Wilson appeared behind Mike. 'Guys, what a day, huh?' Mike turned and went to shake his hand. Dave drew back and put his hands up as if to surrender. They were gloved and bloody. 'No offence, mate. Mack's calling for you.'

Dave led them back to the first floor landing. Pete surveyed the area. Officers in blue uniforms and forensics guys in white busied around the landing, around to a passage that led up and away to the second floor and down to the blood-soaked stairs. Mack stood at the bottom and waved up.

Mike moved down first, a grim descent marked with too much horror. He kept his view up just far enough to avoid the scene. Reaching the third step from the bottom, his left heel caught the edge and he slipped, letting out a cry and falling back onto his arse and elbows. He wriggled up quickly and hurried the rest of the way.

'Oh, for fuck's sake!'

One of the forensics guys stood upright, his voice muffled from behind his mask. 'Be careful, eh?' He shrugged, sneered and looked like he wanted to say more, but didn't and crouched back down. Instead he let out a heavy sigh and surveyed the damage – the clumsy bastard had smudged a blot of blood.

'Fuck it. Sorry. Tits!' Mike's foot and leg hurt the most. The connection of marble stair on his arse was more important to him than the smudge of blood on his left buttock.

'Careful, Mike!' Mack shook her head and looked past him to see Pete mock-slipping on every stair. Wilson shook his head too.

'Sorry, I'm... I'm just knackered.'

'We all are, Mike. Just be careful, please.'

Mack gestured to her colleagues to follow her. 'This way, guys. The father's here.'

'What?' Pete shot an incredulous look at Mike.

Mack continued: 'He's got the whole thing on camera, apparently. Security room.'

Dave patted Mike on the back. 'Hope you kept the receipt, mate.' Mike understood the joke, although his suit wasn't new. Dave broke

51

away and back to the stairs as the three detectives arrived at a room between an enormous kitchen and what looked like a mini cinema set-up.

Mack headed in first. Before she could speak, George Lazarou rasped: 'I've got the bastard right 'ere, the fuckin' bastard. Walking right out the front door clear as day, like it ain't nothin'.'

'Mr Lazarou. I'm Mary Mackenzie. This is Pete Mathers and Mike Danson, detectives from Malton main station.'

Lazarou's companion stepped forward. 'Hello. I'm Noble. Henry. Mr Lazarou's adviser.'

Mack shook his hand. Lazarou looked unimpressed. 'Siddown, Henry. Now look at this – the cheeky bastard's smiling for the cam'ra. Bastard.' He swung a monitor around so the detectives could see. 'There he is. The fuckin' brass of it!'

Mike thought the man on the monitor looked familiar but quickly realised that in his line of work, everyone looked familiar. His arse still hurt and he was carrying around a dead man's blood sample on it.

Pete said: 'Mr Lazarou – thank you for this. A great help. I'm pretty sure given the evidence so far there's no intention to harm your daughter.'

Lazarou spluttered. 'No intention to harm her? Fuckin' brilliant. You can tell that from a house full of dead bodyguards, can you? Some kind of magician, are we?'

Pete recoiled. 'Sir – we'll get him. We've got his face, his car and his fingerprints. It's only a matter of time.'

'Well,' Lazarou shot a piercing eye at Mack. 'Which one of you is going to promise me she comes home, eh? Who's got the balls to stick their neck out on this?'

~~~

Squad car G11 pulled up to the green carrier. Officers Stone and Holding got out and carefully approached the vehicle, their guns off safety and ready to fire. The driver's and rear passenger's doors were open. Stone confirmed there was no one inside. Holding radioed Malton HQ with the location. Stone found an unsealed white envelope on the driver's seat. He opened it.

My name is Piotr Bogdanek. I have taken the devil's spawn. As he stole from me, I take something of his. I am judge, jury and executioner and my justice will be swift. You will not find us.

~~~

'Careful with that!' Jock managed to reach down just far enough to grab the girl's arm and keep her upright. Bleach blinked to clear his vision. It didn't work.

'Shit, sorry. Sorry. I've got something in my eye.'

'You'll have my knuckles in your fuckin' nostrils in a minute mate. Ready?'

Bleach nodded. Pulling back for momentum, they thrust the girl's arms and legs up and out to send her falling into the acid. She splashed in and started fizzing immediately, her body first floating up onto her front and then disappearing into her final resting place, a milky-coloured liquid with the corrosive force of the sun.

Jock watched as the surface settled followed by two eruptions of bubbles that seemed to say *It's all over now. You can go home. I won't be any trouble anymore. Have a great day.*

Bleach didn't witness the scene with as much clarity, his eyes stinging from the vapour. Each time he rubbed his curled finger into his eyelid, it hurt more than before. 'Let's get out of here.'

'Agreed. Now will you agree not to fuck up like this again?'

'Whatever. I said I was sorry. We've done it now anyway. No one's going to find her now.'

'And no one's looking for her either,' nodded Jock. 'A lucky escape.'

'Yeah.' Bleach rubbed his eye again. He winced as it stung. 'Lucky. My dad always said I was lucky.'

'Fascinating. Think I've earned my shit for today. I'll drop you home.'

'Nah. Pub?'

'The pubs are fuckin' shut, mate.'

'The Horse is open all night. Drop me there?'

Jock and Bleach made their way out of the chemical plant, bolted the gate and got in Jock's van. Jock was thankful this was over; thankful that his cousin gave him the key, the code to get into the plant and successfully shut off the cameras remotely. He'd need to pay him ten grand for the privilege but he knew how to get the money to cover that. Besides, family looked after each other.

He drove Bleach to The Horse & Hounds on Beckett Street and almost pushed him out. Bleach blurted out something about seeing him tomorrow but he pulled the door closed quickly and drove off. As Bleach entered the pub for the final time, Jock cursed his name.

~~~

Stanley had little appreciation for the human form, but on this occasion he would make the effort. He always made an effort on his wedding days. It was one of the few pleasures in life, he thought. The grotesque union of the absurd and the beautiful. And today, marrying his two new girls, so human yet so inhuman in their diminished vitality, would be as fine as all the others.

Having witnessed his own fair share of traditional weddings in various cultures, Stanley had been privileged to set his own as he wished. There were no witnesses, not a cake in sight, and no register to sign. These girls belonged to him not legally but deeper than that. The marriage was of souls, not humanity. Flesh mattered but not as much as the bond – the connection of natural and supernatural.

He winced at the word as it formed. Stanley did not recognise himself as supernatural, though, for the simple fact that by his terms he was as natural as it was possible to be. His girls by comparison were neither: unnatural would be more accurate. But that wouldn't stop him from loving them, his eternal companions. He had bought and paid for these artefacts and wasn't about to release them back into the wild.

Stanley buttoned his shirt. Since the first time, he had wondered why he always kept this form, but never really understood. *Everyone likes playing dress-up,* he resolved. *It's nice to play a part and indulge in ceremony.* The white shirt gave him an edge – offsetting the grey of his trousers and brown of his shoes. It also made him look considerably younger, at least in this body. The white seemed to project a bright glow onto his neck and face. He expected his brides to appreciate this a little less than he did. They never seemed to show much appreciation, but that was okay.

There wasn't much for them to say and they wouldn't have been able to say it anyway. 'I do' would be nice, Stanley had thought years before,

54

but they didn't need to give their consent. It was one of the perks of having the girls brought to him. Gifts that, yes, he had paid for, but were still given to him. Just by being there, his brides consented.

He had chuckled before too at the notion of age: where in England he would have been deemed a criminal and a paedophile for taking girls so young as his own, in India he had done the same many times and there wouldn't have been any interest in that.

Cultural difference was another weakness in humanity, and much of the global vocabulary was not only alien but made little sense to Stanley, a true man of the world. How could he be a paedophile when such a concept did not exist? In truth, he realised, his concepts were all his own, unique to him and he could, should he so desire, change them at once.

People were born into doctrines and struggled to break free from them. It was an inorganic process that this species suffered. After all, the simple amoeba was the same wherever it was born. It wasn't forced into any set of rules or told which god to worship.

Stanley pitched his face upwards, eyes focused on the mirror and in particular the reflection of his throat. He had no notion of vanity at least in the way his human counterparts seemed to, but seeing the wrinkles in his neck reminded him of his own form. He visualised his true self – a sinewy network of fluid veins, an amoeba reaching for its next state of evolution.

The door was open behind him, a shifting colourscape seen at his back in the mirror. It could have been anything he wanted, of course. This was Stanley's day and everything would be perfect. He turned from the mirror and walked through the doorway, the colours settling against walls he built as he went.

The stairs formed in front of him, leading up a short way to a door that wasn't yet fully painted on his canvas. As he ascended, it took shape and he edged it open, eager to see his girls. There, arranged around the room, sat his beauties, hooded and lifeless, their bare feet exposing their vulnerability.

Stanley wriggled with expectation, his hot hands clasped together. The fingers seemed to jostle with each other, writhing.

He walked to the first girl on the left, seated as neatly as he had hoped, her hood pulled close against her features. His writhing fingers tugged the hood tight against her face, revealing its curves. Her lips and eyelashes moved against the cloth. He gently pulled the hood up, exposing the girl's vacant yet beautiful face. Stanley always thought they looked like junkies seconds after their euphoric hit – relieved. Full yet somehow empty.

'My darling, it's almost time,' he said softly, running the back of his hand over her cheek and curling off at the ear lobe down to her neck. He leaned in closely. 'Charlie, my beautiful Charlie. The guests will be arriving soon. Today you become my bride.'

Like chicks in a nest reaching up to their mother's mouth, Stanley's tongue came out in black, sinewy trails, reaching into the girl's mouth. Her expression remained still, lifeless yet with *something* there. Two black strands felt their way into her nose, winding their way up and around her sinuses and coming to rest on her eyeballs. They gently pushed and made her eyes dance, rocking slowly from side to side, poking small indents into the white. A rivulet of saliva escaped from her mouth, dripping off Stanley's many-forked, tar-like tongue and into her lap. He could feel the stump of her tongue lolling beneath the strands of his, unable to feed back into his affection but a reminder of her previous personality – the last tool she could have used to communicate before he sliced it away.

His girls didn't need to speak. They communicated everything Stanley needed just by being there. Hopelessly and helplessly plinthed in his trophy room.

Slowly his dark tendrils withdrew, the girl's eyes settling and her mouth closing a little as the last made it back into its host's mouth. 'Sorry, Charlie. That was a bit naughty of me, wasn't it?' He gazed intently into her eyes, imagining a warm response. *That's okay, darling. I'm never happier than when you're inside me.* 'Oh, Charlie.'

~~~

Piotr was in a deep sleep. He deserved it after his ordeal. An hour or so before, he'd jumped awake from another nightmare about his sister. It had been the worst in a while. He'd been standing outside her bedroom door, seeing lights and shadows dancing around on the carpet under it. Muffled cries came from the other side.

He went to push the door open but it was tough – as if made of iron, its hinges creaking with every inch he could manage. He got it far enough open to see his sister's legs kicking out at something. She was on the bed.

56

He saw two large hands appear, each grabbing one of Halina's legs and pulling her up the bed. As her face came into view, something pushed the door back against Piotr.

He pushed harder and could feel something the other side slowly giving way. He was making progress. Halina's cries grew louder and clearer. She called his name. 'Piotr! Piotr! No, stop!'

Piotr didn't want to stop. He heaved himself into the door, which gave way as he fell to the floor, looking up to see a figure with its back to him. A hand in the air held a knife and plunged it down into his sister's stomach.

He leapt to his feet and stumbled to the figure, grabbing its shoulders with both hands but unable to swing the body round. He saw past it to Halina, hanging half off the bed with the knife wedged in her belly, a stream of thick black ooze running from the wound around it. The ooze turned to smoke as it hit the carpet, a dark vapour that seemed to burn on contact, hot as hell.

He pulled at the figure's shoulders but it didn't budge, so he reached to the head and grabbed that, trying to twist it towards him. The figure pulled the knife out, reached up and stabbed it into its own neck. Piotr tumbled backwards as the figure turned around. His own features looked back at him. This dark mirror's reflection of horror shot right into Piotr's chest, a figurative stab that woke him in a flash.

Panting to get his breath back, Piotr trembled, startled and sweating. The nightmares were getting worse, but he had a job to do. The first part of his grand plan had come to bear. The girl was his now. He'd left the irritating safety of his flat and strode into the house of his mark, letting blood as he rescued her from the depravity. Their new subterranean home was very different – colder, damper, darker – and when she woke up she'd want to scream. He knew that. No one would hear her though.

Seven – Question time

'What the fuck was that?' Jez pushed Col's front door hard back against him, sending his friend reeling. Jez didn't notice Col's expression of pure shock. 'Is that supposed to be funny or something? Seriously?'

Col scrambled up to his feet, leaning against the staircase pillar. 'Jez! What? What's going on?'

'You bastard. You fucking bastard!' Jez moved into the hallway, reaching out to grab Col's neck with one hand and readying a punch with the other.

'Stop!' Col shuffled backwards against the stair wall. 'Just wait!'

Jez advanced quickly, scrapped at Col's shirt collar and awkwardly pulled him off balance. Col fell forward into Jez, knocking him over and the two collapsed in a pile. Col struggled up and straddled Jez, managing to pin his arms to his side.

'For fuck's sake, man. What's going on?'

'Oh right,' Jez wheezed. 'It's all very funny, is it?' He pushed against Col's pressure but got nowhere.

'What's funny, Jez? What?'

'That video you sent me last night, you bastard. Why would... you do that?'

'I didn't. I didn't send you any videos, man. What're you talking about?'

Col pushed himself up off Jez and backed away. 'Seriously mate. Seriously. I have no idea what you're on about.'

Jez perched up on his elbows, eyeing Col suspiciously. 'Maria. I saw her in some... in some porno vid or something. A really fucked-up video. It came from your address.'

'What?' Col's expression was pure confusion. 'A video of Maria? I don't know what you're talking about. What video?'

Jez's expression turned from anger to annoyance. 'I can't find it. It's gone.'

'What do you mean, gone?'

'After I saw it, the message disappeared and the website was blank. I can't find it. I was up all night looking.'

'Okay mate.' Col felt a wave of relief mixed with growing unease. 'Okay. You sure it was her? She doesn't strike me as the type.' Jez rolled his eyes. 'Nothing just disappears. Everything leaves a footprint.'

'Yeah, I know that. Look...' Jez sat up. 'I know what I saw. I'm freaked out. It was definitely Maria. That weird looking girl from the fair was in too. She nearly got shot.'

Col laboured on the start of the word: 'Shot?'

'Yeah.' Jez at once realised his best friend really must have been as ignorant as he'd hoped. His shock and awe assault plan had worked and, fortunately, Col had passed the test.

'I think... I think the best thing is to talk to her about it, mate.' Jez stood up and nodded. 'What time is she on today?'

Jez reached out an apologetic hand to Col, who took and clasped it. 'Ten-thirty, I think. Yeah. We should go down there and see what's what.'

The last thing Jez wanted to do was go down there to see what's what.

~~~

Piotr had always been studious. His mother had enforced a strict regime in which he learned to be thorough, focused and determined. Oddly it was only really now, on his new career path, that he would need to employ these traits – where research was much more useful than violence, although there was going to be a great deal of the latter.

He had plotted very carefully last night's abduction, escape and settlement. This teenage girl, Lara, had taken him into her confidence and likewise he had built a bond of trust with his charge. This wasn't your usual abduction, nor was it anything remotely sexual in nature; as her teacher, Piotr had admired Lara's resolve, her intelligence and her humour.

Piotr's plan A had been to take Lara with her consent – feeding on her contempt for her mostly absent, superficial parents. Certainly, with a willing participant things would have been much easier. She was flattered at the intellectual attention and grateful for a friend who treated her as an equal, courtesy she simply did not receive at home.

He had shared with her the disappearance of his sister and the nightmares that had plagued him since. She had told him of her desperation at home: the fighting parents, the destructive divorce, the prostitutes, the parties she was privy to when she should have been shielded. Yes, she wanted revenge on her father, but in the end he realised she also loved him and would never give herself to his own dark plan, which was about so much more.

Piotr admitted that Lara reminded him of Halina, but in only the best ways. His bad dreams had become less frequent as their friendship developed. Of course, keeping this blossoming bond away from the eyes of the establishment, her and other parents and indeed her classmates had been a mixture of skill and luck, but although eyebrows had been raised, Piotr had passed his checks and Lara insisted on his behalf. They would steal five or ten minutes here and there, quietly working together on her own project, and one which her school headmaster approved. Indeed, he had welcomed the idea and seemed to trust Piotr, with his polite manner and smart appearance, as much as anyone else. In any case, she was seventeen and there were safeguards in place.

Lara had undertaken to learn Polish. Few other pupils signed up to the club and over the course of one year the number had whittled down to one. Sometimes they spent the entire forty-five-minute session talking and chuckling, building a friendship. Lara was a quick learner too – enabling the pair of them to communicate fairly well in Piotr's native tongue.

The other parents thought this was sweet, although some simply disliked Lara because of who she was – who her father was. She noticed this contempt and accepted it, even played on it. That she could insult them with a smile in a language they didn't understand made it all the better.

Piotr felt a sense of guardianship and he made sure of this before putting the plan into action. He needed to feel confident of his ability to protect this girl. He hadn't enjoyed killing those men in her house or sedating her but it was all necessary. The man who surprised him in her room was a hiccup but he'd dealt with it swiftly enough.

Emerging from his daydream, Piotr stepped from the alleyway. His heart skipped a beat as a police car came into view and slowly trundled past. The passenger glanced over at him before looking elsewhere. Piotr stopped and watched the car disappear from view, convincing him that his disguise was adequate. He had been surprised at just how easy it was to cover his face with simple items bought at a joke shop. A fake beard,

60

wig and press-on scars gave him the ideal appearance of a vagrant. All but his nose, not a particularly distinctive one, had been transformed.

Lara, the girl he'd spent so much time with, hadn't recognised him in this get-up when he approached her after school one day. Her nanny, Rebecca, had hurried her away from this distasteful remnant of poverty and she too had been a little scared. The test was successful, and very much key to his plan.

The vision of dishevelment crossed the road, reaching his destination with a practised shuffle. The entryway to this block of flats was barred by a keypad, but he'd watched his mark put it in so many times that he knew it well enough. *C4G6.* Only four digits stood between him and justice.

Amanda Higgins, 23. False nails on top of bitten ones, the cuticles distressed but hidden. Her soft finger pads had keyed in this code merely hours before. He knew she was working last night – one of the main attractions in an as yet unnamed feature. Having safely secured Lara, it was now time to unsecure Amanda.

Professionally, Amanda was Bryony Boobs, billed as 'barely legal' – a term Piotr had come to loathe. None of this was legal in his eyes. How could it escape the long arm of the law – this filth; this debasement of everything that is good about people, their souls ripped into pieces for the enjoyment of remote viewers?

Bryony's skill pool was shallow. She knew that as much as everyone else, but big breasts were big money and she had both. Piotr had sat through so many hours of this girl, now lost to the world, lost to herself, and about to take her final breaths. He imagined her heaving bosom, the plastic inside them contorting as he sucked her life away. It could be a simple stabbing, suffocation or some kind of hideous sex crime, but Piotr was no barbarian. He was a scholar and a gentleman, and in seeing justice served on Amanda Higgins, the punishment had to fit the crime.

Her door opened easily with the key he'd had cut. Inside, he closed it gently and put the key back in his wallet. He already knew the layout of the flat well enough. Amanda's bedroom was off the corridor, opposite the bathroom. He found the door open and peered around to the left to see her face down on the bed, the sheets wrapped awkwardly under her. There was a laboured snore, a sleep deep enough for Piotr to shock her out of her wits.

He stepped up to the bed, reaching into his long jacket to pull out his knife. He unsheathed it and reached down to Amanda's shoulder. Before he could grab it, she rolled briskly away from his hand, tugging the sheets over. Piotr flinched backwards. His mark settled, her head pressed into the pillow but cocked as if listening out for something.

For whom the bell tolls, Piotr thought, as he plunged the blade into her throat.

~~~

'Mr and Mrs Lazarou. Thanks for coming. I'm Gordon Briggs, chief inspector here.'

The Lazarous didn't stand to greet their host. George offered a nod and his ex-wife a half-smile. Even her best friends considered her insincere.

'This is Mary Mackenzie, our sergeant in charge of this case.' The chief beckoned Mack to sit down. Again, the Lazarous' courtesy was minimal.

'I don't care who is on the case as long as you find my daughter!' George spluttered. 'So what's going on?'

'Well,' Mack began, 'to start with we're very sorry that the newspapers beat us to it but yes, we know who has Lara and we're doing our best to find him. But we have to ask some questions to help us do that.' Mack's expression was a sympathetic grimace.

'Fine. What do you wanna know?'

Briggs looked to Mack to begin proceedings. The Lazarous joined him. Mack took some papers from a folder. The first was a still of the CCTV capture Mr Lazarou himself had provided. She held it up for him.

'Naturally our first question for you is: do you know this man?'

'It's her Polish tutor,' Muriel offered instantly. 'He's been teaching her for a year. I can't believe the bastard...'

'If I find him before you do, I'm gonna rip his fuckin' face off.'

Muriel let out a laugh, despite the rudeness of her ex-husband talking over her. She agreed with this sentiment.

'Thanks for confirming that, Mrs Lazarou. We also need to know how Mr Bogdanek gained entry to the property.'

'Looks like he just walked in and out,' George said matter-of-factly. 'The bastard strolls into my house and...'

'It seems there was forced entry at the rear of the property, sir,' Briggs chipped in.

62

'How was this man allowed to get so close to Lara?' Muriel's hands were out in front of her; her shoulders moulded into a deep shrug.

'We'll be interviewing the head of the school later, Mrs Lazarou. Please try to remain calm.' Briggs spoke with an authority that seemed to settle her a little. 'For now, working out anything we can about Mr Bogdanek is what we're focused on.'

Mack spoke: 'That's right. How come Lara was left alone last night?'

'Alone? There were four fucking bodyguards in there!' George shouted. 'How dare you!'

'I'm sorry, Mr Lazarou. I meant why were neither of you there last night?'

Muriel: 'His lordship was on the telly. It's his turn to have her. I never set foot in that house now.'

'I see. So Lara was left in the charge of bodyguards and...' Mack saw George's face darken again. '...she was sleeping at the point of abduction?'

'How the fuck should I know?' George blurted.

Briggs: 'Mr Lazarou – we know some of this is irritating for you but we can't proceed without a clear picture. Finding out how, who and when are our keys to finding Lara.'

'Fair enough.' George settled down. Muriel knew her former lover's mood-swings as well as her own. He would fly into a rage in the blink of an eye and out of it in another. 'Just let me tell you what I think.'

'Sure,' Mack smiled empathetically.

'Okay, this bastard's been clawing at my daughter under the nose of people we pay to protect her and now he's made a move. He's strolled in and taken my daughter from her home and he's killed all my men. That's what happened. It's bloody obvious!'

'It appears he wanted us to see him leaving,' Mack said quietly.

'Why?' asked Muriel.

'Well, he is shown on the CCTV leaving – he looks straight up at the camera with no effort to hide his identity. How he got upstairs is unknown. That's why we need to know if there are any other entry points, up on the first or second floor?'

'Sure – there's windows but they're all rigged,' George responded, calmly. 'If one of my boys helped him in, why'd he kill them all? That doesn't wash.'

'Could have been confusion in the firefight,' Mack offered. Briggs nodded. 'There's another angle we need to consider. That Lara let him in.'

'Don't be fucking ridiculous!' George leapt up from his seat. 'Are you mental in the head?'

'Sir!' Briggs shouted, losing his own rag a little. 'Please! Sit down. Shouting at us is not helping anyone. And that's a valid question. If they grew close over a year, it's not unheard of for...'

'That's it!' George pushed up from the table, sending his chair reeling backwards. 'This is not helping anyone.' He started towards the door, Muriel following him, then stopped. 'I am a powerful man. More powerful than you know. Someone takes something of mine, I take it back and then some. If I have to find her my God-damn self, I'll find her. And I'll make sure you lot never make it off the fuckin' minimum wage.'

George and Muriel left the room, slamming the door behind them.

'Erm... interview over,' Mack said, pushing a red button on the console in the middle of the table. 'That was fun.'

Briggs stood, sighed something Mack couldn't hear, and left too.

Mack let her head fall forwards into her hands. 'Arse.'

~~~

Robert pulled his car into the only bay left outside Painsley Forest's tiny police station. His navigation system had sent him the wrong way twice and he was an hour late, the sun beginning to dip below the row of buildings he'd just driven past. The sunset cast an eerie glow on the thatched roof of this station. Robert had been around a bit but he didn't recall ever seeing a police station in such a rustic building.

He smiled as his old friend Jerry Piper stepped out of the station. 'Rob! Thanks for coming.' He held out his hand and grinned. Robert shook it and grinned back.

'Shame it isn't in happier circumstances,' Robert said, his grin settling down to a wince.

'Agreed, mate. Well, we've got quite a rudimentary ops centre here, but I want to take you up to the scene. We'll stop at your hotel first.'

'Okay, so what have we got?'

Jerry got into Robert's car. 'Not much I can tell you that you haven't seen already.'

'Nasty business.' Robert used this term a lot but always meant it. Despite his chosen line of work, or possibly because of it, he didn't find any of it pleasant. Rewarding, yes, but never fun.

'Yeah, nasty,' offered Jerry. 'Don't often see stuff like this round here. Never, in fact.'

'Tell me.'

'It's an odd one. Some signs of possible ritualistic behaviour but overall it seems it was planned, carried out quickly and without fuss. There's spray everywhere. To be honest, it's the worst shit I've ever seen.'

'No witnesses?'

'No. Take a left up here.' Robert swung the car around a corner, passed a short line of houses and stopped outside the Painsley Hotel next to a large police van. Robert remembered he'd been there once before, years ago, on a camping trip with his then wife. The weather had turned bad and at her behest they had checked in to the inn. 'You've been here before, right?'

Robert nodded. 'Where were you when all this went down?'

Jerry laughed. 'To my shame I had nothing to do with it. Maggie and I were in London for the day meeting some friends. I came back especially.'

'Ah, semi-retirement. Can't wait. So... what's left at the scene?'

'We've taken her body to the morgue. The immediate area is cordoned and we've marked points of interest.'

Robert took his suitcase into the hotel and came back out a few minutes later. He got back into the car. 'Let's have a look then.'

Jerry directed Robert to the edge of the forest, parking in a lay-by about five minutes' drive from the hotel.

The men walked for almost an hour before arriving at the crime scene.

Eight – Loose with the juice

'You've checked your facts?'

'Always,' said Marcus confidently. 'You know I stake my reputation on it.'

'You have no reputation, Marc. You're a faceless blogger.'

The joke Marcus Talbot and his editor Jack Drury shared often was worn enough to be comforting rather than insulting. The two weren't just employer and employee but had an edgy friendship – drinks some lunchtimes, possibly even a game of squash sometimes.

'Well, this is good. No, I mean it's great.' Jack shook his head theatrically. 'But it's risky. Very risky. We could get in a lot of trouble for this.'

'Just doing my job, ma'am,' grinned Marcus. 'So can we publish?'

'Yes. Yes... has Suzy seen it?'

'Of course. It's good to go, she said.'

'Subby's the king. Or queen,' the editor chuckled.

'No, Jack. *You're* the queen.'

'Ah, whatever. Okay, I've got to crack on. Stay on top of this, yeah? This is massive, I think. And if we beat the papers, people will remember.'

'Gotcha.'

Marcus turned on his heels and left his boss's office, closing the door behind him. Jack liked the door closed. He walked over to Suzy's desk and slapped the bundle of paper he was carrying down on it. She looked up wearily.

'What?'

'Jack says okay. So let's get it out there.'

Marcus handed Suzy a memory stick, which she turned in her hand a few times, rolling some words around her tongue.

'It's nasty, though, this. Isn't it?'

'Yeah. Damn right it is!'

'I guess... yeah, okay. If Jack says it's okay, it's okay.'

In truth Suzy didn't think it was okay. She thought it was sick, sensational and insensitive to the family of this poor girl. Not only that, it was downright horrible and the image of what had happened to her had stuck in Suzy's mind. It didn't matter what she did for a living. A life was a life and this one was taken horribly.

'Look, I agree,' Marcus said. 'I feel the same way. It's fucking appalling. But we have a job to do. It's not exactly our normal output but it's editorial gold. It's a scoop.'

'I know,' sighed Suzy. 'It'll be good for all of us. *Perversely*. But I don't need to be happy about it.'

She stopped twirling the memory stick and placed its business end into the slot on her computer. A red light flashed every other second and the monitor left its screensaver state, bursting into life. Two clicks of her mouse and an upload screen appeared. She selected the file and clicked again.

'There we go. Five minutes to process and I'll do the titles and pics.'

'Thanks, Suze. Do you want to archive the papers or shall I?'

Suzy looked at the bundle Marcus had dropped on her desk: the police report, a selection of grainy photos which were low-resolution print-outs of those on the memory stick, and Marcus' article printed for his editor's convenience.

'You can, mate. I'm tired.'

Marcus patted Suzy on the head and picked his papers back up. He walked over to his station and put them down again, fishing a large plastic bag out of his drawer. He placed the paper inside and as it cascaded into the bag, he caught sight of one of the more gruesome shots. In low resolution it looked perhaps grimmer than in full colour, he thought. But his name was going on this report. Sure, he wouldn't have got anything like this without the help of the killer or the benevolent police leak, but it was *his* story: he wrote it. The facts were someone else's but the dressing was all his expertise.

This is it, he thought. *An hour away from the big time. Breaking news: Marcus Talbot kicks arse.*

~~~

Robert looked at the alarm clock next to his bed. Three-thirty. He couldn't sleep, which was normally the case when he was trying to make sense of a crime. On the table next to the clock was his notepad, still open on the last page he'd written before nodding off.

67

Something had woken him up – a feeling of unease. His body felt heavy and tight, not unusual for a man in his late forties with a mostly sedentary lifestyle who had just walked five or more miles in the woods – there and back again. The poor girl had been gutted. Her blood covered the ground and leaves around a tall oak tree. The body and clothes had been removed but her essence remained where she had been murdered. Robert seemed to have an affinity for this, for sensing the humanity of a victim spilled on the earth.

The blood on the tree was hers too. It appeared she had been pressed up against it, held in place as a sharp object had ripped her flesh to shreds. Tallying up the bodiless scene with the photographs, he could see the horror unfold in his mind's eye: dragged through the dirt, lifted and thrown, pinned and disembowelled. The blood pattern confirmed his vision.

Jerry had called it a day once the light dimmed and suggested Robert retired for the night. They could resume the next morning. The two police officers who had accompanied them, along with the forensics bods, looked pleased to get away. Places like this simply didn't get murders. It was a country retreat for the wealthy and home to natives who'd never had money but owned land. A crime like this rocked any community, but in the serenity of the countryside and its hills and valleys and forests and paddocks, it was as alien as extra-terrestrials.

Robert decided not to wait. He reasoned it would be light again in two hours and he always liked to visit a scene alone at least once. He could focus better. Insight seemed to come more easily the less human noise there was. This was why he had become a consultant. Leaving the force seemed a big jump but he'd made a lot, financially and reputationally, since doing so.

He got dressed and took care to leave his room and the hotel as quietly as possible. This culture of consideration had been drummed into him as a young boy when his older brother would return from the pub and wake the household up, much to his parents' annoyance. How hard was it to close doors gently, to step lightly? Not particularly, he found. Yet his brother remained a heavy-footed heavy-drinker.

Robert reached his car but decided to head out on foot. It was probably twenty minutes' walk to the edge of the woods and if he was quick he could be at the scene by five-thirty. He opened his boot with care and put some supplies in his backpack: a torch, two bottles of water and a multitool. He'd already placed two apples and the hotel room's packet of biscuits in there. Next he slipped off his laceless shoes and took his hiking boots out. He closed the boot gently but gave it a firm push to lock it.

The hike was uneventful. He navigated easily with only passing glances at his GPS and fewer at his watch. There was a beautiful calm to the woods and his torch had been surplus to requirements, the moonlight giving more than enough guidance. Various animals revealed themselves – squirrels hurrying across and up; birds going about their business and holding their chirpy conferences; and other distant, unseen presences heralded only by the sound of branches and twigs snapping underfoot.

At five-forty-seven he arrived just south of the crime scene, recognising from his earlier visit the birch trees that gave way to the small clearing and the large oak tree soaked in blood. The sun had risen far enough to cast a bright yellow sheen on the forest, its shards piercing the tree canopy and illuminating the ground below in soft, warm spikes.

Standing alone in this setting now, Robert felt the enormity of it. A single life snuffed out in the grand universe but no less meaningful. This was something all police were supposed to learn back at the training academy: that everything, no matter how small, matters. It goes beyond the law and the mores of society. The detail of any case, from a child riding his bike on the pavement to the murder of a wealthy banker, deserved the same attention. Naturally, one was easier to solve than the other, but a crime was a crime and it was, or had been at least, his job to solve them.

Now it had become more of a calling; a passion. It wasn't about the money, but he had a mortgage to pay and a son to put through university and he knew that he could and should charge for his expertise.

He wasn't so interested in viewing the minutiae of the forensic evidence so much as getting a feeling for the event – the beginnings of which had started to creep into his mind hours before. He let his eyes close and spread the fingers on both hands wide, stretching his arms out forwards, as if enticing the truth.

Slowly an image formed of the immediate area. He heard behind him scraping across the earth, following the tracks created two days before by the killer. As the sound passed his head, he angled his ear to follow it. The tracks rounded in front of him and stopped shy of the oak tree, as did the sound. Now the image and sound combined into a blur – a dark mass jerking wildly as it picked something up and forced it against the tree. It started stabbing at it, moving back and forth with violent force.

Robert opened his eyes. This was the easy stuff. He was more concerned with where the killer had gone afterwards. He approached the oak tree, stepping carefully around the marked areas, and stood where the killer must have. There were no footprints here, which was odd given the events that had unfolded in that spot.

The photographs of the girl's body showed lacerations coming from the right, which meant the killer had stabbed down from his or her right hand and had pinned the girl with his or her left. He closed his eyes again and listened, waiting for a snap or a scrape to lead him in the right direction. Of course he knew this was, logically, essentially guesswork but his keen intuition was part of the expertise he charged for.

In his mental image the killer flung the body back with his or her left hand, now facing back towards the village, albeit several miles away. He paused the scene and mentally walked around to confront the killer. The black, distorted mass stood motionless, facing him. The girl's body now to his right, the deed done, the killer would... face the way he or she was intending to go. This seemed to make sense. But with the killer stood still, another thought entered his mind. It was left-field, but worth the consideration.

Perhaps he was not alone. He closed his eyes again and followed the killer's gaze. The line of birch trees which seemed to bracket this clearing began to take on different forms, their branches becoming limbs. Soon it had become a row of silent observers, the hunter standing over his mark and proving his resolve to... to whom?

He walked over to the tree line, training his eyes on the ground around the trunks. The earth was disturbed around one or two but not all. He aligned himself with the trees and noticed they seemed to form a line – in both directions, east to west. This was, to a seasoned hiker, an unusual occurrence. These trees looked planted, he realised. The random natural spread of a forest would not allow for such uniformity. A sense of unease grew in his gut.

He closed his eyes again, viewing the killer facing him once more, motionless between oak tree and freshly cut girl. Unpausing the scene, the black mass moved towards him. The unsettling feeling grew more intense as the dark shadow blocked out the light. Then it turned before it reached the tree line and set off west along it.

70

Robert reached in his pocket for his PDA and took it out. He consulted the GPS app and zoomed out a little. The birch trees did not show up as any different in the satellite view but pinpointing his location and following a line west led to a thickening of the forest for some miles. To the north led out to an expanse of water, some four miles away. East led back towards the motorway about three miles off.

'West it is then.'

~~~

'Shit. This is funny, man.'

Bleach waved his phone under Jock's nose.

'For fuck's sake. I'm driving.' Jock elbowed Bleach's hand, knocking the phone back into his lap. 'What's funny?'

'All right, calm down. No need to be aggressive, mate.' Bleach's eyes were swimming in a glazed haze. The trials of the previous night had been washed away with a couple of hours in the pub and about half an hour of solid piping once he made it home. Now getting on for 11am, he'd had a few hours' sleep and was now in a state somewhere between high-as-a-kite and coming-down-slowly.

'*The Juice*. You ever read it?'

'No.'

'They've got some funny shit. Mostly celeb bollocks but some pretty funny blog stuff.'

'Wow, that's… *amazing*.' Jock's impatience with his colleague had not withered from the night before. His tone was deliberately off.

'Anyway, so there's this story about that porn bloke who lives here. Some guy walks into his house, shoots every fucker in there, steals his kid and walks right out again.'

'Yeah, the Polish teacher. I know. It's all over the news. Papers and TV. But I suppose if you live under a rock like you do…'

'Okay. Fair enough. No need to be rude. I was out last night, wasn't I? I didn't see any of that.'

Jock felt a tiny allowance of sympathy creeping in. 'Yeah, well… it's pretty crazy. I wouldn't have the balls to do that. Mind you, I'd never steal anyone's kid. That's just *wrong*.'

'Yeah, man. Wrong,' Bleach frowned. Jock's irony was lost on him.

71

Jock continued: 'But what we do isn't the same at all, is it? No, we're like saving people. We're heroes.'

Bleach looked over at Jock quizzically. 'What?'

Before he could enquire further, his phone buzzed. It was an alert from *The Juice*. He read the line as he touched the link. 'Exclusive: porn star butchered as murderer speaks.'

'Yeah, sounds like a lot of fun,' Jock said sarcastically. 'Barrel o'laughs, that site.'

Bleach waited as the screen refreshed, the previous story about the child abduction now replaced with the headline and underneath a picture of a pretty looking girl. His eyes were immediately drawn to her chest. *I know this girl*, he thought. *Boobs, something Boobs.*

He scrolled down and read the article aloud: '*The Juice* can exclusively reveal the shocking death of adult actress Amanda Higgins. The 23-year-old Malton girl was discovered this morning in her exclusive flat. With exclusive insight given to *The Juice* by the murderer, Polish fugitive Piotr Bogdanek, we have all the details. Read on to find out about the sickest crime of the century!'

'Wow, this is messed up,' Bleach said. Jock glanced over at the phone, switching his attitude from annoyed to interested.

'The polish guy? Shit!' He felt a surge of admiration and excitement. 'Keep reading. I want to know how many times they can say exclusive.'

Bleach continued to scroll.

Amanda Higgins, aka Bryony Boobs, has been murdered in what killer Piotr Bogdanek claims is the start of a crusade against the porn industry. The Polish teaching assistant, who yesterday claimed responsibility for abducting porn baron George Lazarou's daughter, has contacted Marcus Talbot at The Juice *with exclusive details on his sick crusade.*

Bogdanek told us exclusively: 'Something has to be done about these people. The pornography industry is an abomination against humanity. The internet overflows with disgusting images of girls brutalised by the indecency of men. Porn is not harmless. It destroys the world from within. I am the judge, jury and executioner. My justice will be swift.'

Providing horrifying photos of the scene, Bogdanek told The Juice *that Higgins is his first intended victim and he intends to take more lives in his crusade. We asked him what he's trying to achieve and most importantly, is Lara Lazarou alive?*

'Lara is alive and will come to no harm' is all he would tell us.

In one photo, too distressing to show here but which The Juice *has turned over to police, we see Miss Higgins' decapitated head hanging from her bathroom ceiling. In her bedroom, where the sick killing took place, Bogdanek has removed her breast implants and stuck them on her window. These details, the twisted killer told us, are 'symbolic'.*

We'd like to make it clear that The Juice *in no way endorses these disgusting acts or images.*

Features Editor Marcus Talbot comments: 'We're all completely horrified by this. It was a tough decision how to proceed with this information but in the interests of public safety we couldn't take the risk that Bogdanek might kill again before we had a chance to report. Our thoughts are with Amanda's family now. We urge and hope Bogdanek will hand himself in and ensure the safety of Lara Lazarou.'

Stay tuned to The Juice *for further updates.*

'Fuckin 'ell,' Bleach sighed. 'That's…'

'Yeah,' Jock agreed. 'Mental.' He turned the corner around the back of Stanley's shop and pulled up to the back door, where barely eight hours before they'd left to go pick up the girl's body from the police station. 'I hope they catch the bastard. Nothin' wrong with porn.'

Bleach hopped out of the van and walked up to the door. Over the fence he heard a female voice. It sounded foreign but *pretty*. He backed up to the van and walked to the front, peering around to see a dark-haired girl walking hastily away from the building and sticking her middle finger up behind her. Bleach couldn't see who the finger was aimed at but he heard a door slam.

'Bleach, come on.'

He turned back to see Jock glaring at him. 'She's good. Let's grab her.'

'No,' Jock said, although he thought it wasn't such a bad idea. They had, after all, let Stanley down the day before. This girl was worth fifteen-hundred quid too, and he needed the money to pay for last night's nefarious activities. 'There's plenty of time for that later. Stan wants to see us.'

73

'Stan?' Bleach and Jock jumped at the sudden interruption by their benefactor. Stanley stood in his doorway, hands on hips, with a look that his unofficial employees had come to understand.

'Late night, was it?'

Jock nodded. 'Yes, Stanley.'

'Well, there's much to do.' He turned and disappeared into the dark corridor. Jock and Bleach followed up the short stairs and Bleach shut the door behind himself.

They caught up with Stanley, who led them upstairs to his office. 'Neil.' He motioned to Jock to sit down. 'You're a sensible chap, aren't you?'

'I...'

'Yes, I know. Firstly, never call me Stan. My name is Stanley. You know that, right? *Stan... ley*. Pretty straightforward, isn't it? So let's not make that mistake again! Do I call you Neeeee?' He chuckled, sending a chill up Jock's spine.

'So today, what's left of it, I'll be *neeeeee*ding you to take care of something for me. I'm going to be a little tied up, see? James... you'll be needed here, if that's okay with you?'

Bleach, who was still standing, spoke softly: 'Ye... yes, Stanley. Of course.'

'Good. Okay then. This is wonderful. I'm very happy today. Those girls you brought me are beautiful. Absolutely beautiful.' He threw his hands up above his shoulders. 'I'm in love with them both!'

Stanley sat down. 'Neil, I need you to go next door and talk to a man named Stephen. We have a little arrangement. He broke his side of that arrangement. Silly business, really. I'd like Stephen to understand that I don't like silly business.'

'Okay... sure, Stanley. What did he do?'

Stanley stood up quickly, slamming his fists onto the desk. 'I just told you what he did! You can go now.' He fixed Jock with a piercing glare. Jock got up awkwardly and left the room, disappearing down the stairs.

'Now then, James. I'm getting married today. And you... well, oh happy day. You're my best man.'

~~~

74

Robert followed the bizarre line of trees to its conclusion, a mile-and-a-half from the crime scene. Along the way he took a number of photos on his PDA – of the trees, the ground and the canopy. He'd also checked his phone reception at regular intervals and found it the same as when he entered the woods earlier that morning: zero. When he came to the last birch he stopped abruptly and scanned the area.

There was more light now, the sun well on its way towards the top of the sky. Robert stood silent, waiting for something to inform his next move. His unease had dissolved on this walk but returned in this new scenario of uncertainty.

A blackbird jumped and flew from a branch overhead. Robert jumped a little and watched it swoop across to the north-west. Instinctively he followed. He caught up with the bird soon enough as it perched on a low branch, squawking and looking at him.

'What is it?' he enquired of the bird. It squawked back at him and jumped once more, this time flying up and away through the canopy. 'Thanks a bunch,' he said, drily. A few yards ahead stood a small thicket. He heard a snapping sound somewhere behind him and turned to look. More snaps, one after the other. He supposed Jerry could have come looking for him, but how would he know where he was? He would also have to have arrived just moments after he did. That didn't add up. *Someone is out here.*

The snaps came faster now. Robert scurried over into the thicket, pushing himself through and coming around to a safe spot where he could see a sliver of his previous location. He heard the blackbird squawk and looked around to see it sitting on a branch right behind him. 'What're you looking at?' he whispered.

The snaps were louder now, gaining clarity and sounding to Robert like someone mashing a bag of crisps. He snapped his gaze back to the sound. The crunching was almost upon him now. Then silence. He felt his breathing heavy and for the first time realised his heart was pounding. *The adrenaline rush.* He jumped and fell backwards as the blackbird squawked loudly in his ear. His fall was broken by trees and the noise broke the silence.

The footsteps started again, quicker this time and accompanied by the sound of material rubbing together. Then they stopped again. Robert strained his neck backwards to see a figure just the other side of the thicket. Its eyes looked straight at his.

75

A gloved hand pushed through the thicket, followed by the face of his pursuer. Robert edged back against the trees. A face appeared through the gap. 'Lost, are we?' A large man stepped around the thicket and stood over him. He bent down and grabbed Robert's hand, pulling him up.

'How did you... find me?' Robert brushed his backside, his fear morphing into bewilderment.

'Easy if you know 'ow,' said the man. He was taller than Robert, around six-four, with a full beard on his reddened face. He wore a heavy jacket and carried a dark green bag slung over his shoulder. The barrel of a shotgun poked out of it, pointing upwards.

'Picked up yer trail back a'ways,' he continued. 'Figured yer'd get yerself lost. These woods are...' The man's smile altered to a frown, then back again. 'Unusual.'

'Oh?' Robert finished dusting himself off. 'Unusual how? The trees...'

The man interrupted: 'The name's Red. Got a cabin just up a'ways. There's a phone. Work better than that thing in yer pocket, sure.'

How does he know what I've got in my pocket?

'All you townies got 'em, right? No need of one meself, person'ly speaking.'

Robert's suspicion settled. This man, Red, had effectively offered him a rescue branch. Not that he needed rescuing, but Red might prove a useful informal interview. If he knew these woods, he might know something. But if that were true, surely he'd already been to see the police.

Red started off away from the thicket, west. Robert followed. 'So what are you, uh... hunting out here?'

Red didn't turn around. 'Pheasant, rabbit, mostly. I don't get to the markets often.'

'That gun loaded?'

'Uh-huh.'

Robert walked a couple of paces behind the big man. His pace was plodding but determined. 'What's with that long line of birches?'

Red responded: 'Not far to my cabin. You with those police?'

'Yeah, yeah... I came out to...'

'Dangerous to be out on yer own.'

Robert reached into his backpack and found what he was looking for. 'Really? How so?'

'Not the first time someone's bin got out 'ere either.'

His hand closed around the base of his torch. 'Oh? I didn't know that. Can you...'

Red changed direction a little, heading north. 'Just over here, son.'

Robert wondered how it was that this man could call him son – given he looked maybe in his forties at most. Red's face was, despite his grizzled appearance, young looking. His hands seemed soft when he'd helped Rob up. He would have put him somewhere between twenty-five and forty-three years. In any case, something was wrong here. Another essential ingredient in police work was not taking anything at face value. More often than not people would tell lies and never the whole truth. Everyone had secrets. Everyone was potentially dangerous and Red gave off that vibe loud and clear.

'So... how far is it?'

Red stopped in his tracks and turned back to Robert, who stumbled to a halt. He pulled his hand away from the backpack. Red's hand was too close to his shotgun for comfort. It occurred to Robert that this hulking figure was the black mass he'd visualised.

'I told yer it was just up 'ere, eh?'

Robert hesitated. He could dart off in any direction but forward and probably outrun this guy, but he'd be running for two hours to get out of the woods. Running for his life too. That was not a workable plan.

'Okay, okay. Sorry. I'm just... I'm tired, y'know.'

Red turned away again and started walking. Robert followed. About ten tense minutes later, free of speech but paced with the one-two crunch underfoot, Red stopped and turned again.

'There.' He pointed to the cabin, twenty feet away.

Robert caught up with him. 'Thanks. Wow... big place.'

Red groaned and strode over to the low fence in front of the cabin, hopped over it awkwardly and reached the door. He pulled it open – odd that it wasn't locked, Robert noted – and went inside. Robert followed him in. The cabin's interior was dark. Red set his bag down, taking the shotgun out and putting it next to a lamp on a large wooden table.

'Nice place you've...'

'Phone's over there.' Red gestured towards the far wall. It was too dark for Robert to see. The curtains were drawn over each set of windows and there didn't appear to be any electric lights on the ceiling. The cabin was mainly under tree cover too so although it was bright sunlight outside in theory, inside it was a dark shade of dark. He reached back for his torch and... *what?* It wasn't there. Could Red have taken it out, or had it fallen outside somewhere?

'Could you... turn a light on, please?' Robert inched forward, his hands out. He stopped as his knees connected with an armchair. 'Really, it's very hard to...'

Answer came there none. He turned to face Red but he was gone; perhaps into another room. He stumbled over to the table and noticed the shotgun was gone. He reached for the lamp and took his multitool from his backpack. The flame from his lighter attachment ignited the oil inside easily and he picked the lamp up.

On this side of the room was just the one exit back outside, but he would have heard Red opening the door. He swivelled and held the lamp high. Beyond the armchair he had knocked up against was a bed, a table the other side of it with a telephone, and further over a small kitchenette. *All the mod cons*, he thought. *Now where the hell is Red?*

He made his way over to the bed and stopped with a sharp intake of breath. Lying slumped next to the telephone table was a young boy, the swaying lamp casting a flickering shadow over the pool of blood beneath him. The shotgun lay at his side. The telephone was off the hook.

He didn't need to close his eyes to picture this death scene. Red must have shot the boy. Either that or someone else. There had been no shots fired since he and Red had arrived – no sound at all besides Robert's clumsy footsteps and the clicks of his multitool, so the body must have been there a while.

What the hell is going on? He set the lamp down on the bed behind him and knelt down closer to the body. Maybe Red had led him to this place and exited quietly, leaving him alone in this horrific scene. The thought made him shudder – that Red could be outside, waiting for him as well, or he could have called the police. How could Robert explain himself as a murder suspect? He'd been set up. He was sure of it.

He was just about to stand up when he noticed an odd buzzing sound. He looked around. It sounded electrical, like static. He couldn't see anything electrical – except the phone. He reached for the receiver and pressed it to his ear.

'Hello, Robert. How nice of you to drop in. Would you turn around please?'

Robert went to put the phone receiver down but the voice spoke: 'No. Don't do that. Just turn around, please.'

With the receiver pressed back to his ear, he did as he was told. Standing across the cabin, just enough light from the lamp casting a fiery glow towards it, was the black mass from earlier – the shadow, jutting and wild, shifting jerkily like a car veering out of control.

'So that is what you see? Is that the face of evil?'

'I...' Robert was paralysed – with fear, uncertainty and bewilderment.

'It's okay, Robert. Take your time. We're not going anywhere just yet. You needn't worry about the boy. He's been dead for a very long time.'

Red killed him, Robert thought.

'Yes, yes... But that's not important right now. Do you believe in coincidences?'

How... 'Yes, I guess... yes.'

'Oh good, you're speaking again. How courteous. This really is quite a coincidence, wouldn't you say?'

'I...' *How is this a coincidence? Where the hell am I?*

'You're in Red's cabin. Where else might you be? Are you in control of your own mind?'

Robert looked down to the young corpse, as still and dead and bloody as he'd found it. 'Yes. Yes, I am.' The black mass shifted towards him, stopping just a few feet away. He felt his chest tighten.

'What's the matter, Robert? You were this close in your vision. Does it make you uncomfortable now it is real?'

This isn't real. None of this is real.

'But it is!' The black mass vanished. No puff of smoke, no sound, no disturbance – just gone before his eyes. 'Okay, well *that* wasn't. But let me explain something to you. This incursion is unwelcome. As unlikely a coincidence it may be, it is still a coincidence.'

'I... I don't understand. What coincidence?'

'Isn't it true of a coincidence that one event needs to tie with another? Well in this case, this is such an event.'

A pause – for a time only static came through the phone. He waited. Then: 'Well, Robert, aren't you going to ask me what this coincidence will be?'

'I... okay. What is...'

'That would just be silly!' The voice was light, playful and still deeply unsettling. 'Naturally you have some other, less silly, questions. Allow me to pre-empt. You are Robert Moulder. You live with your son,

Jeremy. He smokes pot and masturbates a lot. Your wife left you to join a cult. She's much happier now. You left a long career in law enforcement to become a criminal science consultant.'

'How do you...'

'We know everything about everything, Robert. You're going to ask who we are and why you're on the phone to us. It's really just for fun. You can put the phone down now. If you like.'

Robert gently placed the receiver back on the table. When he looked back up, a man stood where the black mass had been. Around Robert's height, dressed smartly in a silvery suit, white shirt and purple striped tie, the man appeared in the dim light to be Asian.

'What do you think? Handsome, no?'

No, thought Robert. *Just plain frightening.*

'Oh, for shame!' The Chinese-looking man laughed. 'But no matter. Shall we sit down? Let's make ourselves comfortable.' He walked over to the large table where Red's bag had been. Robert hesitated for a moment and then followed.

'Wait,' *Chinese* said. 'Don't forget the lamp.' Robert swivelled, picked it up and joined him at the table. He pulled a chair out and sat opposite *Chinese*, placing the lamp between them.

'My name is actually Angelo. You're welcome to call me Angelo. I think it's better than a vaguely offensive racial label.'

'Angelo,' Robert said quietly.

'Cheer up, Robert! I don't wish to harm you.' He grinned across the table. 'We were rather impressed by your gumption, following our path there. Not many people have done that over the years. You see, you've somewhat surprised us with this visit. Red had his eye on you. These are Red's woods, see. He saw you following his little path and tagged along.'

The line of birch trees. His path?

'Yes, precisely. That line of trees. You see, where we are now is out of time. When we met Red he was in a bad way. Children, he liked a lot. Not in a good way. Well, that depends on your moral standpoint. But Red used to bring here. He did some really *terrible* things in this cabin. We made an agreement. He could stay in these woods for a price.'

'I'm not really... following you.'

'Yes you are, Robert. There's no need to be rude. It is what it is. I have no reason to lie to you. The body over there marks a point in time. The point at which we made our agreement. You see?

80

'This cabin was built by his grandfather. He used to bring him out here and touch the little boy's winky, see? He'd do whatever he wanted to that boy. So Red inevitably ended up doing the same. And when he did, the juice, the lovely juice flowed back in.'

'What juice?'

Angelo laughed. 'Why, the juice that makes us who we are, of course! For someone who's spent most of their life chasing evil, you're having a hard time spotting it.'

Robert spoke slow and low: 'I know you're evil. I have no trouble coming to terms with that. What I don't know is why I'm sitting here with you. Seeing as you're being so free with information here, would you care to elaborate?'

Angelo leaned over the table, his face lit up by the lamp. 'You'll soon know more than you ever dreamed of.'

~~~

'She was one of the best. Real solid worker, she was. Didn't fancy her personally but I know some of the guys loved getting inside her.'

Skip Standings folded his newspaper and looked over at his right-hand man, Geoff Kirton. He was scrolling on his PDA.

'Yeah, she was good. You don't get girls like her all the time. Bit of glamour to that one. Nice tits, too.'

'Aye,' Skip nodded. 'Lovely tits. Now she'll be buried without them.' He chuckled. 'Or they'll stick 'em in a bag next to 'er.'

'Nice!' Geoff looked up from his PDA, smiling. 'Unless she's being burned up. Those funbags don't burn properly so they chuck 'em away with the leftovers.'

Skip laughed again. 'I bet there's all sortsa shit leaked out of her. Hard worker...'

'At least she wasn't one of ours,' Geoff said, his smile widening to a grin. 'Lazarou, the fat wanker... he's got it coming.'

'That's the business we're in,' Skip said, also now grinning. He opened one of his desk drawers and took a bottle of dark rum out, then reached back to a shelf and grabbed two glasses. He poured each a shot.

'Here's to Miss Boobs.'

'To Miss Boobs.'

81

As they clinked glasses, Skip wondered if Lazarou would give a shit anyway. He was all about the money. He never seemed to care about the girls.

~~~

Jez and Col waited for forty-five minutes at the fairground. There was no sign of Maria and, Jez found on several attempts, her phone went straight to voicemail. This had done nothing to relieve his sense of unease. Although he was now convinced of his friend's innocence, the fact remained that he had seen a terrifying and disturbing video the night before and it was all he could think about.

'Just take some deep breaths, mate,' Col said, putting a reassuring hand on Jez's shoulder. 'What do you wanna do?'

Jez knew what he wanted to do. Kill someone. Grab that gun-wielding bastard by the neck and squeeze the life out of him. Find Maria. Kiss her. Pretend he never saw that video.

'Think I'll just go home, mate. See you later.' He gently slapped Col's back and started off towards the road away from the fairground. He turned back: 'I'll call you later, okay? Sorry mate.' Col nodded and smiled but felt a queasy mixture of sympathy and sadness.

Despite feeling emotionally exhausted, Jez was still high on adrenaline and walked briskly up the hill away from Malton seafront and the half-mile to his house. He felt hazy, a daze as the sunlight seemed brighter than usual and the noises around him were clearer, louder... heightened senses that he rationalised were the result of a nasty shock and a lack of sleep. He felt strangely powerful though; some kind of urgency to do something.

He turned the corner into Prince Charles Avenue and walked along to his house. 'Jez! Oh my God, Jez.'

Maria sat on the porch step and jumped up to her feet, her handbag falling to the ground as she ran to him. Jez wrapped his arms around her tight and wedged his head against hers, withdrawing back to lock lips.

'Maria.' He stopped to catch his breath. 'You're okay? I thought...'

'Yeah, I'm fine. I'm fine now. It was Steve. I had to get away.'

It was Steve? What was? Jez bent to pick Maria's bag up and led her back to the front door.

'What do you mean? What did he do to you?'

82

'Ah, he was a little rough, that's all.'

'Rough?' He opened the door and they went in, checking no one was lurking outside as he closed the door. 'Steve was rough with you? Are you okay?'

I'm gonna kill the bastard.

'Yeah, he... sometimes he loses his temper. But it wasn't about you, honey.'

'Did you call the police?'

'Huh?' Maria looked confused. 'Why?'

'He hit you, right?'

'No... no, I mean... no, he didn't *hit* me. Forget about it. I could really use a drink.'

Jez suddenly remembered Maria hadn't been to his house before. How had she known where he lived? 'Sure, yeah, come through.' The initial sense of relief was gradually losing out to a niggling sense of danger.

'Really, forget it. I'm fine. I just missed you and didn't want to go to work today or back to the house, so...'

Jez led Maria to the kitchen. He swung the fridge open and grabbed a small bottle of lemonade. 'This okay?'

'Sure, yes. Thanks. Is your dad here?'

'No, he's away on business.' He was about to say what kind of business but thought better of it. 'You sure you're okay?'

'I'm fine.' Maria took the bottle from Jez's hand and placed it on the kitchen top, then wrapped her arms around him. 'Everything's fine now,' she whispered, leaning in and kissing him.

Still kissing, they moved haphazardly into the lounge and fell back together onto the sofa. Jez's negative thoughts dissipated as Maria moved one hand down to his crotch. He moaned and pushed his tongue deeper into her mouth. She began unbuckling his belt, then loosening the zip on his jeans. He shifted a little to help, feeling his cock hardening further still and ready to burst out.

The image jumped into his brain – Maria and another girl, giggling for the cameraman – and he pulled away from the kiss, startled.

'What's wrong?' Maria said, still fumbling on his zipper. His hand met hers, pulling it off his crotch gently.

'No... nothing's wrong,' he lied.

'Good.'

Maria went back to her task and managed to undo the zip, slipping her hand inside and wrapping it around his shaft. Jez moaned as he threw his head back against the sofa. He could feel his pulse quickening. These amazing feelings rushing through him... he could ask Maria about the video later. After *this*.

He opened his eyes and reached down to grab Maria's top, a loose blue silky vest, and pulled it up over her head. *Wow*, he thought. *She's beautiful. This is the best day of my life.* He went back to kiss her again but Maria dropped her head to bend down, settling on the tip of his penis and kissing it. *Oh shit*, he thought. *Oh shit, this is good.*

He spread his hands over her shoulders, pulling her closer to him as her mouth went to work. He glanced down at the back of her head and grinned, rubbing his hands now over her back. He let his gaze shift to her bra strap, and started to undo it. As he eased the material away he saw a dark smudge of something underneath – a bruise perhaps – and let his head fall back again, reaching around to her chest and cupping her left breast in his hand. Maria moaned as her head began to bob faster.

Jez felt his scrotum tighten and leaned his head forward again, moving his left hand to grab Maria's hair while the right squeezed at her breast. He looked down and saw the smudge wasn't a bruise at all. He opened his eyes wider to see it with greater clarity, feeling his genitals almost at the point of no return. The tattoo seemed to form in time with his urgent breaths, a few moments later revealing itself.

'Oh shit!' Jez's hips bucked up as Maria's head did the same, moving out of the way of his ejaculate just in time.

PP. It says PP. The same as the murdered girl. Oh shit. PP. No. Why has she got PP on her back? Oh shit shit shit shit...

Maria smiled up at Jez, her expression changing to match his. 'What's wrong?'

Jez was still panting, trying to catch his breath. He felt like he'd been kicked in the balls. 'Uh... uh... no. Nothing... nothing's wrong.' As Maria sat back upright and the tattoo disappeared, he wanted to believe he'd just imagined it. But something was definitely wrong. *Everything* was wrong.

'No, you don't look happy. Did I do something wrong?'

'No... of... course not,' he panted. 'Just give me a minute.'

Jez fell back against the sofa and closed his eyes. *This can't be happening. This can't be happening. PP. What the fuck is PP?*

84

Maria got up and put her bra and top back on. She walked to the kitchen and picked up the bottle of lemonade. Jez heard the fizz of the bottle and opened his eyes, looking straight at the wall and somehow through it, staring into the abyss. Maria downed the lemonade and put the bottle back on the surface.

'Honey? You want something?'

'No, I'm good thanks.' Jez felt his breath coming back and pulse slowing a little. He looked down at the mess on his jeans and slipped them off, pulling his briefs back over his cock. It was still semi-hard and, he thought, he looked a lot bigger down there than usual.

Joining her in the kitchen, he opened the fridge again, then closed it and went to a cupboard. He took out a glass and poured filtered water into it.

'Wow,' he said, managing a smile over another heavy breath. 'Just wow. Where did that come from?'

Maria giggled. 'I keep one in my bag just in case.'

Jez chuckled too. 'Only one?' He wanted to ask about the tattoo but thought better of it.

'Oh, I can make new ones whenever I need them,' Maria said. She turned and walked to the back of the kitchen, taking in the view of Jez's large garden. 'It's nice here,' she said. 'Much nicer than my place.'

'Yeah, it is nice here. You can stay as long as you like.' Jez couldn't stop himself now. 'So... what's with the tattoo?'

Maria pirouetted. 'My tattoo? Oh, that... yeah. It's a thing I had years ago. Back home.'

'What is it then – PP?'

'It's a Polish thing.' Maria paused. 'Hey. Did you see about that crazy guy who took that girl? He is Polish too.'

Jez did see that. Indeed, it happened just around the corner from his house, apparently. The Lazarous lived a stone's throw from the Moulders but it didn't mean anything. People's neighbours were usually nameless faces coming and going. They weren't exactly neighbours anyway. The Lazarous lived in Malton's most exclusive street, all gated mansions; the Moulders lived in a nice house with a nice garden, but a few streets over – comfortable but worlds apart in reality.

'You know that girl who was found yesterday?' Jez changed the subject back. 'She had a PP tattoo too. The same thing.'

Maria's face darkened. 'How'd you know that?'

85

'My father... he's in the police, remember?'

'Oh?'

'Yeah... his friend came over last night and they were discussing it. They're trying to figure out what PP stands for.'

Maria turned back to the window. 'That's... that's my old life.'

Jez wanted to say *Sure, no worries, let's forget all about that and go to bed*. But he found himself unable to suppress his line of enquiry. 'If you can help... could you? She *was* murdered...'

Maria fell silent for a minute. Jez deliberately backed away. The last twenty-four hours had been weird enough.

Eventually, she said: 'Okay. You're right.'

Jez moved beside Maria and gently coaxed her into his arms. 'Can you... tell me?'

She sighed heavily. 'It's... it's Po Polnocy. It means, I guess... After Midnight?'

Jez repeated it back to her. 'After Midnight?'

'It is all in the past,' she said, pulling away from Jez. 'My previous life.'

'It's okay,' Jez said. It wasn't okay but he was beginning to see where this was going. It had to be porn, or escorts, or something like that. Something sexual. It shouldn't have come as much of a surprise, he realised, as most of the porn he watched seemed to come from Eastern Europe. Girls with names like Annika and Paola helped him do what a man's got to do.

'We should go tell the police.'

'Your father?'

'No, he's retired. He doesn't work for them anymore. But I know who we need to talk to.'

'Okay.' Maria pecked Jez on the cheek. 'I'm sorry,' she said. 'It's... I'm sorry.'

~~~

'Good morning.' The pretty blonde, bespectacled and tidily assembled, smiled up from the reception desk at Standings Room Only. 'How can I help you?'

A slight yet handsome gentleman in a light silver suit, his shirt open and tieless, smiled back. 'Gut morning...' He peered at the name on the girl's desk. 'Megan. I am here to see Mr Skip Standings, please.'

Megan pushed her glasses down to rest on the tip of her nose and eyed the diary open on her desk. She traced a finger down the short list of four entries and looked up at the man.

'I don't have any appointments in for Mr Standings today. What's your name, please, sir?'

'No, he's not expecting me,' he smiled. 'Please tell Mr Standings that I am here. Mine name is Assman. Herr Assman. I am come from Chermany.'

Megan giggled playfully at Hairy Assman. She pushed her glasses back up to the bridge of her nose and wrote the man's name in the diary. Then she reached for the phone, picked up the receiver and pressed 0.

'No. It's one S and two Ns. A...s......m...a...n...n.' The man leaned over the desk and picked Megan's pen up, thrusting it towards her. She recoiled, a look of confusion crossing her face.

'Please,' he said, 'My name is Asmann. One S and two Ns.'

She put the receiver down. 'I... I'm... it's not an official document, it's just for my...'

'Please.' He thrust the pen closer. 'It may not matter to you but it matters werry much to me.'

Megan jumped in her seat as the phone rang. She picked it up quickly. 'Y... yes, sir. Yes. It's... there's a Mr Asmann here to see you.' She very carefully pronounced the name and flashed a nervous smile at him. 'Okay. I'll bring him through.'

She stood up and, it appeared, was the same height standing as when sitting down. Asmann regarded her with renewed interest.

'This way please, Mr Asmann.' This time she attempted to relay the second syllable with Germanic precision. He found this amusing.

'Vait!'

Megan jumped again. Asmann leant over the desk and picked the diary up. In both hands he tore at it, ripping the pages from the binding and dropping them. Once all the pages were out, he calmly folded the cover over and reached over to Megan. He grabbed her by the hair and yanked her down onto the desk face-first. Her glasses shattered with the impact. She moaned, her voice muffled by the desk pressing against her mouth.

87

'Lizzen to me, Megan. You are an imbecile. Vorthless. Does your brain reset every time you blink? You can go home now.' He yanked her head back up and pinned her to the wall behind the desk. 'You can call your police if you like. I vill be gone in tventy mints.'

Megan slid down the wall into an awkward squat, her heart racing and her head throbbing.

Herr Asmann bent down, picked up his briefcase and stooped down. He located the door release button on the underside of the desk and then turned back to Megan. 'I meet a lot of people in my vork. Not many like you, I am happy to say. You fahucking shit-for-brains. Learn some fahucking manners.' He slapped her hard, knocking her face against the wall. Then he stood up, pushed the security door open and disappeared through it.

Nine – Strange encounters

Bleach opened his eyes. It felt difficult – like waking up after a hard night on his chosen substances, and as if his eyelashes were stuck together with something. He felt something *hard* in his head too, kind of central. As his eyes widened, the stickiness coming loose like the petals of a flower opening out to the sunlight, a blur of colours gradually formed into shapes and he could see Stanley again.

'Ah, James, good to have you back.'

Back from where? Bleach had the faint recollection of coming to Stanley's with Jock, then going up to his ornate office and... that was all. The feeling of something hard in the centre of his head grew. There was some kind of pressure. It seemed to resonate further down too, but he couldn't follow the line down.

Stanley was a vision of light in the darkness. In fact, he was the only light in the room, a glow around and on him. Bleach realised he couldn't move his head or anything below it. It was as if his head was disembodied, floating somehow but immovable in this dark room. And it hurt like hell.

'We are gathered here today,' Stanley began, 'to witness the joyous union of one man and his women, to celebrate the love we share in the eyes of James, our welcoming host.'

Stanley clicked his fingers and a light appeared from over his shoulder. It shone immediately on the figure of a young girl, stood motionless beside him. Bleach gasped inwardly and felt a surge of pain from the blockage in his head.

'Quiet, James. Today is not about *you*. You'll get your turn. This is *my* day, mine and beautiful Charlie's. Oh, Charlie honey...' Stanley turned to the girl and grabbed her throat firmly, twisting her head to face his. There was no force pushing against his grip. 'Your beautiful eyes and your skin... is so delicate. James, isn't she just so *delicate*? Oh, my word. I could just eat her up!'

Bleach swallowed hard. The air was thick with something – something warm and intoxicating. He vaguely recalled this was always how he felt at Stanley's. *I can't breathe. Why can't I breathe?*

Stanley clicked his fingers again. 'And here, on my left...' A second spotlight beamed down onto another girl. 'This is the delectable

Stephanie. My darling Stephanie. Going to give herself... all of herself to me today! Isn't she *precious*, James?'

Bleach tried to nod. He didn't exactly want to but it seemed like he didn't have a choice. In any case, his head wouldn't budge at all. The *whatever-it-was* in his brain started to throb. An itch appeared on his forehead and he went to scratch it but again nothing moved. It seemed as if the blackness in the rest of the room was somehow enveloping him from the neck down.

'Come on, James!' Stanley barked, shocking him out of his wonder. 'Show a little enthusiasm!'

Stanley clicked his fingers a third time and music began. *Laaaaa, laaaa, la-la-la-laaaaaaaaaa...* It sounded to Bleach like something you'd hear in an old film, all sweeping strings and a slow, brushed beat. *Laaaa, laaaaaaa, la-la laaaaaaaaaaa...* Stanley swept Stephanie up in his arms and began to dance around with her, sweeping from side to side and around Charlie too as the spotlight followed them. He kept looking back over his shoulder, maintaining eye contact with Bleach all the way.

The pain in his head throbbed harder now. He wanted to scream, but there was no voice in his throat. It was a *nothingness* – like the blackness in the room, he couldn't *feel* anything there at all. He could just about *think* the scream – to form it in his mind but not to vocalise it.

Laaaaaa, laaaaaal, la-la-laaaaaaaaaaa...

He watched in only imagined horror as Stanley stopped and the music followed. Stanley gently replaced Stephanie under her spotlight and went to stand behind her.

'Do you, beautiful Stephanie, take Stanley to be your unlawfully wedded husband?' he giggled.

The girl's face remained lifeless. Bleach approximated a feeling of sickness.

'Of course you do! And James, we have you to thank for bringing this incredible specimen to me, you bringer of beauty! The most wonderful gift in the world!'

The throb turned to a thud.

Stanley crouched down, his hands reaching under the girl's dress and with a mute cry his fingers penetrated her skin. 'Ooh, squishy!' Stanley called from behind the girl. His fingers stretched out from pink wrinkly skin into black, sinewy tendrils, reaching into her body and wrapping around the flesh inside, poking and consuming, working their way up and around everything in their path.

Bleach imagined a scream again, louder than before, as he watched Stanley's face and head bleed into the back of the girl's, an oily bundle of worms bulging through her skin, up to her temples and eventually filling her lifeless yet pretty eyes with pure darkness.

Her lips started to move. 'Hey James, what do you think of this?' Stanley laughed through his new bride's mouth. 'We're married! Someone throw some confetti!' He laughed harder. 'Oh James, look what we've become. We are the joyous union!'

Bleach's head started to heat up, the throb now a thump. He tried in vain to make sense of the images before him. Thoughts were swimming over each other, grasping for traction in a brain set to explode.

Stanley's voice came from the lips of the girl: 'Now it's your turn, Charlie.' The laughter grew more hysterical as the body of the girl, semi-consumed by Stanley's writhing, horrible form hobbled over to the other girl, the spotlight following this monster's every move. The puppet girl clicked her fingers and the music started up again, the same tune but this time faster and pitched up at least two octaves. Her eyes swam with black fluid, tendrils bulging out of her skin.

Leeeeee, leeeeee, le-le-leeeeeeee...

'Come on James, clap along!' Stanley knelt down behind the puppet girl, his body half-melded with hers and juddering across the floor towards his other new bride. It appeared to James something like a giant black slug consuming a mound of human flesh.

'Time to make you an honest woman!' Stanley laughed. He stopped behind her and placed his back against hers. 'Oh Charlie, you are beautiful. I hope you don't mind us consummating our marriage with an audience.' As he said this, his half-head and back began seeping out into further black tendrils, melding into the second girl and with the same squelchy, squishy sounds that made Bleach's head start to pop. *Leeeee, leeeee, le-le-leeeeeeeeeaaaaaaaaaoooooo...* the music became deafening, screeching in Bleach's head and threatening to explode it like a sledgehammer on a watermelon.

Then the music stopped. The spotlights dimmed and disappeared.

~~~

'So you're going to kill me? I'll take my chances.'

Angelo laughed heartily. 'Kill you? Of course not, Robert. Why would I do that? I couldn't even if I wanted to. Let me explain. You have intruded – in the back door, I suppose. There are certain areas in the world which we have closed off to you.'

'What do you mean by *you*?'

'To humans. We're not human, Robert. We are the ordinary.'

'*The ordinary*?'

'How could I be? You've seen it for yourself. You can't deny what you've seen.'

'I haven't seen much. But... carry on.'

'Thank you. This is our planet, you see. Well, not strictly, but we're at the core of it while you humans bounce around on the surface. It might be a bit tricky for you to grasp.'

'Try me.' Robert was now more interested than frightened. He no longer felt threatened but wasn't sure why.

'We are born of you. For that we owe you a great gratitude. We grew and keep on growing. Are you religious?'

'Not really.'

'Well... it's what some religions refer to as sin. The blackness of the heart and soul. It feeds us. You think of evil as a concept rather than an entity, and there you are wrong. But...' Angelo drew back into his chair. 'You must understand that we are not evil. Like in any battle, both sides believe themselves to be fighting for the true cause. Sometimes there are factions fighting within those sides too, possibly against the benefit of the many. Your view of right and wrong is dictated by the directors of your society. Likewise so is mine.'

'I don't need to be taught the semantics of moral distinction.'

'Ah, but you do. To understand that we are just what we are is essential for your next step.'

'What next step?' Unease began to creep back in.

'It's just simple evolution, dear Robert. Nobody asked you to come here, but you did so anyway. That's the coincidence, see.' Angelo paused. 'I can see that you *don't* see. This cabin sits on something of a hot spot. Red's grandfather kept it moist, Red's father died too soon to do much, and Red himself kept our lifeblood running very nicely, but now it's drying out. That girl, the murdered girl... are you getting it now?'

Robert shook his head.

'I'm surprised how slow you are considering your line of work.' Angelo frowned. 'Still, your intelligence is about to take a huge upgrade.'

'How so?'

'You know we can read your thoughts. We can manipulate certain things. It's a great trick! We can place images inside your brain. And you... you have come to this place of your own will. Red may have led you here but you had already crossed over, so to speak. Our way in, as yours, is to follow the line.'

'So the girl was... filling the pipeline?'

'In a manner of speaking, yes.'

'Her blood...'

'No, not the blood. Blood is just liquid that keeps you alive. Our power comes from the fear, the sadness, the sin. We rule this Earth with fear and sadness. Haven't you ever wondered why the media is so full of such darkness? Why television shows play on common human anxieties? Why the justice system is so inefficient? We control it all.

'It is a product of humans' arrogance – their assumption that in the vast continuum of space and time their lives have any meaning. Perhaps it is difficult for the human psyche to comprehend, that you are just specks of existence in an infinite universe.'

Angelo was being economical with the truth and overplaying the extent of his reach, but the task was clear: Robert needed to accept these claims as truth in order to join the pack. Angelo was very good at making people believe him.

'This is just hippy psychology. If you are what you say you are, why are you sitting here talking to me?'

'Well... I was getting around to that. I suppose I don't really have to tell you anything, but one of the things I've picked up from you humans is good manners. Despite everything I've told you, we don't dislike humans. We *need* you, in fact. Without humans, we wouldn't exist.'

'You live by... our darkness?' Robert could understand this concept. He'd thought about it many times before, how evil could proliferate and spread like a virus.

'That's right! Now you're getting it. I could have just walked in here, devoured you and set you on your merry way, but as we're about to assimilate I thought we should get to know each other. Manners, see?'

'I'm honoured. How do you intend to assimilate me?' As he said this, he wondered: *can I say no?*

Angelo leant forward again. He smiled. 'It's already begun. I'll tell you why. Your human self is dead. I found your darkness right away. Like a beacon!'

Robert felt a painful twitch in his brain, knotting down into his throat and chest. 'I don't feel dead. My darkness? What darkness?' He did a good job of sifting through his memories and settled on the one that punched him in the gut.

'You crossed over, Robert. You walked a path you shouldn't have. You're one of us now. You're *ordinary*. Ironically for such an inquisitive man whose entire career has been based on finding answers to questions, this time you've actually outdone yourself.'

Robert felt his hands tingling. Something was pushing under his shirt and his legs felt heavier. Angelo's voice entered his mind: *Don't fight it. This is happening. Now.*

Wait... the veins in his fingers bubbled and bulged. He could feel his head expanding as if shedding its skin. *What was the coincidence?*

Oh, that? Angelo stood up. His clothes seemed to evaporate away as his skin turned from pale olive to black, revealing a mound of fluid, dark flesh. The shiny blackness spread up to his chest and neck, then the back of his head, leaving just Angelo's thin flap of Asian face hanging from the front like a paper mask. Then like a dark, wet mouth the head folded over the face, the mass now writhing, squelching, consuming itself over and over.

You see, we were going to come and get you anyway.

~~~

The lights came on quickly this time. Bleach opened his eyes to feel completely different to moments before. It seemed like an instant, as if he'd just blinked and found himself here, but he couldn't be sure. The popping, bubbling and thumping feelings in his head had gone, although some kind of blockage remained.

'Ah, you're back. Good.'

Bleach looked up and saw Stanley, now dressed not in his wedding suit but his usual embroidered red gown.

'Everything okay?'

Bleach struggled to find the answer. 'Y... yes, Stanley.' He was surprised to find he could speak again. This room seemed not to have the

94

intoxicating effect of the last. He found he could look around freely now too.

'Wh... where are we?'

'Don't worry about that, James. We're just where we need to be.'

Bleach realised his own voice sounded a little muffled. His hand was pressed up against his nose. He looked down to see his other arm out of view.

'Stanley, what's...'

'We need to have a talk, James. That's all. You've been such a good boy for me, and I want you to know I appreciate that. There're certain things you do for me that I cannot do for myself. I'll be eternally grateful. Really I will.'

Bleach wondered why his hand was stuck against his face and attempted to move it. His arm and wrist budged but the fingers were stuck in place.

'Don't fight it, James. This is your last call. I know that sounds harsh but you've become a bit too loose for my tastes recently. You pump yourself full of these drugs and what good does that do? You've been making mistakes, haven't you?'

Bleach tried to shift his hands again. Nothing at the back at all. He tugged his right arm down and a pain shot from his nose into the centre of his brain.

'Oh, are you looking for this?' Stanley held up an arm – *fuck, that's my arm!* Bleach swallowed hard and gagged on his tongue. He could feel his face reddening and swelling. He looked left and realised he couldn't feel it because it wasn't there. No wound in its place, just gone – sheared at the shoulder.

'I'm so sorry, James. I never like ending things like this. Well,' he laughed, 'not always. But with you, I thought this might be quite fun.' Stanley clicked his fingers and a long mirror appeared in front of Bleach – emerging from the ether. He gagged again as he saw in the reflection his legs were gone too – a stump of a body sat on a pike; his only remaining limb free at the elbow but his fingers rooted into his nostrils.

I can't breathe. Can't breathe. Oh shit shit shit.

'Really, James. It's best if you don't fight it. There's no choice really.' Stanley stepped up to James' side and raised the dismembered arm up. 'Are you hungry, James?' Bleach gagged again and started trying to shake free, but there was nothing to move. Stanley stood and leaned over

95

Bleach, bringing the arm level with his mouth and forcing it in. Bleach felt his teeth spiking through its flesh, his eyes wide with horror and again, unable to scream as he watched events unfolding in the mirror.

'There we go!' Stanley gave the arm a final pull to wedge it further in and stepped back. 'Did you say you can't breathe?'

Bleach started desperately trying to push the arm out, his tongue flat against the flesh of his arm.

'Maybe you should just blow your nose?'

Bleach's arm shook violently, pulling down and down and down… his fingers were jammed in and wouldn't budge.

'Come on, James! Put some effort into it, man!'

The left side of his mouth tore open, sending a thin spray of blood onto Stanley's gown.

'Oh dear. That just won't do!' Stanley started laughing. 'What a mess!'

Bleach tried gasping but still nothing came. He pulled down hard on his fingers and something tore in his nose. It hurt like hell and the pain shot right through all that remained. He pulled again, the tear becoming greater as he felt his nose running. Blood ran down his fingers and onto his top lip, breaking into rivulets over the flesh protruding from his mouth. He tugged again and this time the fingers came free as a gush of blood followed.

'We're going to need a big mop for this!' laughed Stanley, the glee on his face the last thing James Bleach saw as his life bled out of his nose.

The room faded to black.

~~~

Jock stood for a while watching the house from the back. Having left Stanley's establishment as he always did by the back door, he'd casually trotted down the steps, through the gated fence at the back and settled against a wall running the length of the alley to get a good view of the neighbour. If someone came out, he'd just be a nobody lurking in an alley, minding his own business. They'd seen him down there often enough, making his grim deliveries.

Stanley had asked him to teach Stephen a lesson; at least that's how he interpreted the instruction. But he didn't know what to expect. Over the time he'd been working for Stanley he'd seen people coming and going through this rear entrance. He knew that around the front it was a nondescript office frontage, and assumed that the girls going in and out the back door must have worked there. Stephen must have been a manager of some sort. Jock wondered what he could have done to rile his neighbour but knew full well that Stanley could rile pretty easily.

The door swung open. A pretty girl came out and Jock saw a sliver of red corridor behind her as the door closed. She flashed him a suspicious look and quickened her pace, going past him by just a few feet and scurrying up the alley towards the main road. The door clicked as it closed. It wasn't a light click, Jock thought, like a simple latch lock but more like an electronic lock.

He waited some more. *I can't stand here all day. Got to do something.* Jock realised he was lacking the confidence to barge into a four-storey residence with an unknown number of people inside and start raising merry hell. He imagined Stanley knew that too – usually Jock's jobs involved bundling girls into the back of his van, tying them up and delivering them. Actual heavy work involving violence was rare. But he knew Stanley had *implied* violence here. Stephen, whoever he was and however prepared he was, was an unknown quantity. Would Jock just kick the door in and ask everyone, 'Where's Stephen?' *No, I'll go round the front.*

He was just about to when the door swung open again. A heavy-set man wearing a fairground worker's T-shirt stood behind another girl. She was not as pretty as the last, Jock thought. The man immediately clocked Jock but kept his focus on the girl. He spoke sternly but Jock didn't understand the language. The girl shouted something back as she turned away from the man and walked off in the same direction as the previous girl.

Jock fixed the man in his gaze.

'Help you with something, mate?'

'Yes,' Jock said, rising to stand upright. 'I'm looking for Stephen.'

'*Stephen*? Who are *you*?'

Jock realised Stephen, if this was he, was eastern European. His accent was tinged with that Eastern Bloc quality. Polish, Czech or Hungarian, he thought, but it didn't matter where the guy was from.

'I'm a friend of Stanley. He asked me to give you a message.'

The man raised his brow. 'Who?'

'He's upset. You have an arrangement.'

97

'What arrangement?'

Jock wondered why Stanley had been sending him and Bleach all over the place to pick his girls up when there were so many living the other side of his wall. Could that be the nature of this arrangement?

'You need to honour your side of the arrangement.'

'There is no arrangement.' Stephen looked like he was losing patience. 'I don't know what you're talking about.'

Jock found himself in a quandary: would he return to his boss and give him this inevitably unsatisfactory news or would he push this man further? The latter option seemed best. He walked towards Stephen.

'What are you doing?'

'If Stanley says you have an arrangement, you have an arrangement.'

Stephen walked down the three steps to meet Jock in the small yard, folding his arms. 'I told you. There isn't one. You are mistaken.'

Jock leaned in so their noses were almost touching, his chest pressing against Stephen's arms. Although Jock was not of a slight build, Stephen's body mass was far greater.

'I don't think so, Stephen.'

'Last chance mate. Fuck off. And it's Steve. No one calls me Stephen.'

Jock put his hand in his pocket, grabbing for his small, sharp flick-knife. Steve saw the movement, unfolded his arms and pushed Jock back. He stumbled but remained upright, taking the knife out and flicking it open.

Over the small fence into Stanley's yard, the camera above his door whirred a little as it turned to focus on the fracas. Neither man noticed. The camera over Steve's door stayed fixed on the action.

'Serious?' Steve shook his head. 'Come on then.' He reached around to his back and pulled a gun out of his belt, pointing it right at Jock's face. Jock backed up.

'Hey, look... I... I'm sorry. You're right. A mistake. I'll tell Stanley. Sorry, okay?' He stumbled back into the wall where moments earlier he'd been a casual, unconfident observer. Now he was skittering away like leaves in a wind trap, his legs flailing for grip.

Steve kept the gun trained on Jock's head, walking towards him. The cameras followed his movement. 'Who the fuck is Stanley and who the fuck are you?'

'I...'

Steve used his other hand to grab Jock's shirt, pulling him up and back towards the door. 'Get in,' he barked, forcing Jock up the steps. Once they were both inside, he glanced cautiously left and right and slammed the door shut.

~~~

The sign on the door ahead of Herr Asmann read: 'Skip Standings – CEO.' He knocked once and pushed it open.

Skip instantly jumped from his seat. 'Mr Asmann. Hi. Skip... Standings.' He had just watched his receptionist take a beating from this man and didn't fancy taking one too.

'Gut morning,' he smiled back. 'I haff come from Chermany speshly today. Ve haff some business, yah?'

Skip nodded, slowly, his face pure confusion. 'We... do?'

'Off course. Zis man, the one you haff helped childnap the girl. We need him.'

'Okay...' Skip had no idea how this man knew he had helped Piotr Bogdanek take the girl. 'How did you...'

'Not your business, misster.' Asmann strode forward and put his briefcase on Skip's desk. 'You haff two choices. Vun: you can tell me vair ze man iss or I can open zis case and make you vish you had choshen option vun.'

Skip smiled uneasily. 'I... don't know where...'

Asmann thumped his first down on the desk, sending everything but his heavy briefcase skittering across its surface. 'Don't fuck wiff me. Where iss he?'

'I... honestly...' Skip was frightened more than he'd been in a long time. He had never been the type to enjoy confrontations. 'I don't know where he's gone. He didn't tell me.' Asmann reached for his case. 'Wait! I... I can get in touch with him. I'll find out!'

The German leaned back from the table and sat in the larger of two leather armchairs across the desk from Skip's even larger one. He pointed at him with his hands fashioned as guns.

Pc-choo. 'Go on then.'

~~~

Piotr was in a deep sleep. Having returned back to his and Lara's makeshift home after setting up a crime scene no one would forget in a hurry, at least until his next one, he'd spent some time with Lara.

He empathised with her, even though she couldn't speak through the duct tape over her mouth. He explained how he knew she had been exposed to so much filth in her family home, the one place she was supposed to feel safe. They even used to shoot porn in the upstairs guest rooms – he'd recognised them when scouting the house. He told her how much that sickened him.

Piotr knew there was no way Lara would approve of killing anyone, but it was the only way. He knew that. Sometimes tough decisions had to be made. Lazarou was effectively killing these girls anyway, profiting from their degradation. Anyone who watched that stuff was feeding him too, feeding the hungry, greedy lion. It sickened Piotr almost as much as the action he had decided to take.

But here, in their bare but comfortable-enough residence in a forgotten storm drain on a golf course on the outskirts of Malton, where no one would ever find them or even think to look, Lara was shielded from the truth. He knew she would find out eventually, but by then the job would be done. Once he let her go, she would come to appreciate his actions. He was sure of it.

Piotr's legs twitched and he rolled over onto his side. Lara couldn't sleep. Her hands and feet were bound to a tall steel pole set in the foundations of the storm drain. She was trapped. The only indicator of her state was the fear in her eyes. She watched him toss and turn and hoped it was a nightmare.

She was right. Piotr was walking towards a house, his childhood home. But the exterior walls were grey, not cream as they had always been. The door was a darker slab. On the porch was a single chair with something on it. He drew nearer to the house and walked up the steps to the porch, seeing Halina's old doll on the chair. It seemed to be smiling at him, rocking back and forth.

Piotr… Piotr…

The voice came from inside, behind the dark door, hollow and distant. He went to open it but there was no handle. As he pushed against it he realised the door was not a door but just darkness. His hand felt cold as he pushed it further in.

Piotr…

The voice came from his side, clearer and louder. He looked down and saw the doll. It had Halina's face – the smile turning to a face of fear as its eyes and nose came closer together. He felt something tug his hand from the blackness and let it take him through.

'Halina?'

There was no answer. In the house the walls were grey too. It was like all the colour of the place had been sucked out.

Piotr…

Distant and hollow again, the voice seemed to come from upstairs. He walked to the staircase and peered up. Halina stood at the top, holding out her hands. *Piotr*. Thick liquid dripped from her fingers, merging into a puddle on the top step.

'Halina.'

He began to walk up the stairs but on every step another one joined – he was going nowhere, treading on the spot. As he looked down he saw something small and black on his foot. It looked like a spider. He raised his head a little and saw a procession of these small spiders coming down the stairs, emerging from the puddle at Halina's feet. Looking further up he could see they were coming from her mouth too – wide open, pouring out like water and separating as they cascaded down her chest.

Piotr turned to run down the stairs. He got to the bottom and felt tiny legs on his back, running up into his hair and over his shirt, down inside and over his shoulders. He tried to scream as he made it to the front door, the thick dark fog. The spiders quickly covered his face, climbing into his mouth and nostrils and clawing at his eyelids. He felt them slip into his ears until he could no longer hear their scurrying but just feel his body filling up.

He turned one last time to see Halina, his beloved sister, standing behind him, her body on fire and her head stripped of its flesh, melting down into the fire. Her fiery hands reached out and grabbed his neck.

Back in the real world, Lara hoped it was the worst nightmare he'd ever had. Piotr was a bad man, she thought, and deserved the fire of hell upon him.

~~~

Skip knew he'd made a mistake, but he wanted badly to hurt Lazarou's business. It was a simple case of 'this town ain't big enough for the both of us and you're a ruthless fat bastard'. While the internet had become saturated with amateur pornography, finding material that people would pay for had become more difficult.

Switching to a model where only a handful of girls were responsible for a lot of revenue, and cutting down on syndicating their performances elsewhere, had worked for both Standings and Lazarou very nicely indeed. They still had the volume though from other avenues, syndicating back and forth and paying small beans for the relatively tame content.

As their girls had become superstars, the media had gradually come to open up a little more to the porno concept, with late-night strip shows on terrestrial TV replacing most of the gambling programmes that had proved so popular before. Porn had become bigger than gambling – and this proved the turning point.

Skip himself had come through the ranks. Starting as a hard cock in a wet world, he soon went behind the camera, then into casting and commissioning, and then when he saw his chance to strike out, he set up the business. Taking a few of the girls with him and keeping an eye on the marketing gurus bashing out free advice in the trade papers, he went from the low thousands to the several millions in just a few months.

Although Skip had been in films around the same time as Piotr Bogdanek, they hadn't starred together and first met when Skip was directing a shoot. Piotr hadn't been much in the size department but his features were good. Not quite handsome, but a chiselled, rough and sexy guy. They hadn't really talked much until Piotr got weird with one of the girls during a scene.

The girl was prone on the bed while Piotr went at her like an oil drill. The camera panned smoothly over their bodies and then up to their faces. Piotr's was manic – panicked, even. As the camera came to face him, he broke the fourth wall and looked straight into it, his eyes fiery red and his grin monstrous. Skip had stopped filming as they all erupted in laughter. From that moment they'd become friends.

Piotr left the porn industry to train as a school teacher, appearing in subsequent films with a mask on so as not to jeopardise his chances. This puzzled Skip at the time but as Piotr had explained, Polish teachers were in demand and highly paid, and he didn't want to spend his whole life as a sex machine or risk turning up in the newspapers.

Then something had happened. Having found a job at a school down on the south coast, sixty-plus miles from Skip's headquarters back in south London, he'd gone quiet for some time and didn't answer his calls or acknowledge his messages. Skip, concerned for his friend, had driven down to Malton and found Piotr in a bad way in his flat.

Piotr had been honest with him. His mother had died since he moved and in a low groove he'd become obsessed with a woman he met on the net. It turned out she was a young glamour actress attempting to break into the porn industry. Although it had got off to a good start, she had spurned his advances and the situation had escalated to a point where it could get dangerous. He'd asked then for Skip's help. He was watching her amateur videos over and over – given perverted access to a girl he had fallen for but who in other circumstances wouldn't have shared her body with him.

The obsession had gone well beyond the sexual and now he was ready to hurt her. This worried Piotr, aware he had crossed the line and could go further, and Skip told him to break away from it completely, to concentrate on his role at the school. Piotr had smiled ruefully as no matter where he went, he couldn't escape from the sex industry – now he was tutoring the daughter of porn baron George Lazarou.

Skip and George had worked together for years before going their separate ways. While Skip built up his experience at George's SkinFlix company, he came to realise he didn't particularly like working for other people. But as he broke away, George had seemed to bend over backwards to make business difficult for Skip. They were always pleasant to each other in public, but privately their formerly friendly relationship had devolved to mutual contempt.

This was when Skip and Piotr had talked about finding a way to upset George's business. Access to his daughter, who Skip had watched growing up on the sidelines of this mucky industry, seemed too good to be true. It was Piotr who suggested he could kidnap Lara. He thought even she might go along with it, knowing she wasn't exactly enamoured with her father's chosen career or indeed her mother's behaviour.

Skip had returned to London feeling confused – unsure of where they'd left this plan, uncertain of Piotr's mental well-being but also convinced that an opportunity to get back at that fat bastard George Lazarou was not to be missed.

Ten – The flow of information

Subject G. Day thirty-five. PM. Observations: subject remains coherent. No dyspraxia following increased positive charge and introduction of free electrons. Suggest increasing magnetic force and ampere rate.

~~~

'Right then, where are we?'

Mack slipped her hands together, kneading her fingers over each other. Facing a room full of her peers, early in the morning after the first good night's sleep she'd had in days, she answered Chief Briggs' question: 'Basically we're where we were yesterday. Everyone in this room knows as much as anyone else. And that's the problem.'

Briggs clenched his fists and snorted. 'This isn't good enough.'

'No, sir, it isn't,' Mack agreed. She surveyed the conference room. Her closest colleagues leaned against the far wall, in quiet conversation. Briggs sat alongside her, in front of sixteen assorted officers from the plain clothes brigade, a couple of detectives from another station who were there to *liaise*, and a number of 'uniforms'.

'The problem we have here is flow of information. Unfortunately our prime suspect is controlling it. We know he has the girl, and he says there's no intention to harm her, but we can't trust that. That trail has gone cold. Frozen. We know, or we think, he bears a grudge against Lara's father, and we know he plans to keep on killing.'

'What's his motivation?' A uniformed officer shifted in his seat as he asked the question. He didn't seem too interested in hearing the response.

'He says porn is evil. Girls who go into it willingly are his targets. Unfortunately that makes his potential target base somewhere in the hundreds of thousands. Millions.'

'But isn't it restricted to Lazarou's output?' asked another. 'If he's trying to hurt Lazarou. Higgins was one of his.'

'We don't know that. It's assumed but that still gives us several thousand targets. He's been making movies for over twenty years. In any case, we have a team working on possible connections between Bogdanek and Lazarou.'

Danson put his hand up. Mack nodded. 'But we know he's operating locally. There's no evidence to suggest he's working outside of the immediate area, not yet anyway. And besides, his note said Lazarou had taken something from him. We need to work that angle.'

'That's right,' Mack agreed. 'We're going through Lazarou's records now to cross-reference. Another problem is many of his films are not logged centrally – they're put out under the SkinFlix banner but actually produced by all sorts of people. We're tracking those down. At least this stuff is semi-organised.'

'Yes,' Briggs said. 'Have we got the report on his home?'

'Sir,' said one of the detectives. 'Home address is rented. We found nothing useful there. Some clothes, toiletries, a few books. The landlord said he always paid on time and was a good tenant – if a little weird.'

'This stuff *would* be useful if we didn't know who he is,' Danson volunteered. 'He doesn't care about that. This guy wants us to know all about him. Everyone at the school's shocked and scared, but they liked him. We've got zilch to go on here. We know he's from Wroclaw and we're talking to them.'

Briggs clapped his hands together and pursed his lips. He let out a long, heavy sigh. 'Okay. He's got her somewhere. We need to sweep the town, fields, farms... everywhere. I am not waiting for this maniac to kill again. Everyone clear on that?'

~~~

'Hey.' Piotr stroked the back of his hand down Lara's cheek. She opened her eyes and moaned into the duct tape.

Piotr had originally told her they'd be in the drain for a week. He thought that would be long enough to punish Lazarou. Lara had looked fearful but he put that down to nerves. The plan had been to return Lara to her mother. After all, her father would be in jail, or dead. As far as Piotr was concerned, he could quite happily kill the bastard for what he did to his sister.

Halina, taken from him before she was a woman. Taken to England to work for Lazarou's evil empire; to take her clothes off and let men rape her on camera. Taken against her will, her soul sucked out through the monitors of men who needed a quick fix of pleasure. A life, and those around it, destroyed for hollow, solo humiliation.

105

Piotr's own death wish was as clear as his intentions for Lara's father, not that the girl could see or understand that. As intuitive as she had proved to be in learning a foreign language, certain emotional charges were beyond the comprehension of one so young. This was the way it had to be. He knew she would despise him for it, once she learned the truth of his campaign, but there was no other way.

'Not long now. I promise.'

Lara screamed into the tape again.

'You must be hungry. Breakfast?'

It was almost too easy for Piotr to come and go from this place. A storm drain angled conveniently towards a hedgerow, out on the far outskirts of Malton's largest golf course, where no golf balls ever suffered a slice bad enough to end up, it was both secluded and accessible. Hopping over the low hedgerow, there was a short and largely hidden route back into Malton, coming over the top of a ridge to view the sea, cliffs and the town below.

Fitting out their makeshift holiday home had been straightforward too. Piotr had taken a van load of various camping equipment and driven it off-road to the drain, using a double-sided step ladder to carry it all over the hedgerow. Once he'd prised open the drain cover, sliding down was the hardest part. He'd even had the good sense to bring a rope ladder. It wasn't quite long enough for Lara to scramble up, which he decided was a happy accident, but it was lengthy enough for him, a good six inches taller than her, to get in and out without incident.

A pile of sandbags stood at each area which could get wet if it rained, although that had been one of the main reasons Piotr had waited until a run of good weather to put the plan into action. Behind the sandbags, Piotr had managed to hang some sheets from ceiling to floor, providing a modicum of privacy between them and the outside world. Not that anyone would go looking down there. Indeed, Piotr had spent a good month walking that secluded path at different times of day to see what kind of human traffic he might expect.

Examining the sewer system and drainage tunnels had taken longer – finding this place had not been easy in that respect. But it was ideal: out of general use, it was a remnant from the original golf course landscape, built into the original design but not required. The two tunnels coming off it led nowhere. They were alone, apart from the insects, mice and spiders.

106

Piotr strode over to his makeshift kitchen. The 'living area', as an estate agent might have put it, was cosy. With his mattress taking up the majority of the space, heading down further into one tunnel was the 'bathroom', which comprised a cassette toilet and two large containers of water. A battery pack connected to a heating element in one of the containers provided enough hot water to last up to a month for simple washing purposes.

Back down the other tunnel was Piotr's gear. He had put a lamp by the bathroom, casting enough light to disperse the darkness into small curves of shadow against the tunnel wall. It still wasn't pleasant but it was good enough.

Piotr did not like leaving her alone for very long, and he only left for a few hours at a time. He had bought a number of books for her as well as a tablet and a portable charger. The network functions were permanently disabled. Even so, he was yet to present her with these items. She seemed what he considered a little frosty. He could at least keep her comfortable.

Killing Amanda and staging her remains had taken a little over two hours, from door to door and back again. The second murder had to be done at night. She'd put up a fight, which Piotr had not expected. He only had two more girls he knew of in Malton anyway. As long as he could get that far, that would be enough. His job would be done. And moving Lara wasn't worth the trouble. He needed to keep her hidden throughout all of this. If they caught him first, he'd tell them where she was.

Piotr knelt down next to Lara and placed a bowl of cornflakes by her feet. She looked him in the eye, attempting sympathy. He ripped the tape from her mouth and unbound one of her hands. She coughed for some time, sputum dribbling down her chin and onto her nightdress. 'Water,' she croaked. 'Please.'

He went back to the small table he kept the food on and picked up a bottle of water. He unscrewed the cap and gave it to her. She drank it all and gasped.

'Please let me go. Please. You don't have to do this.'

'Eat your breakfast,' he said. 'I have to do some things on the computer.'

~~~

Marcus sat opposite his boss. They both felt triumphant. In just twenty-four hours their stats had gone through the roof – almost fifteen million hits, and not just on the murder stories. This was just the shot in the arm *The Juice* needed.

Jack had enjoyed a career twice as long as Marcus', but it was now Marcus on the brink, he felt, of something bigger. Jack's career took in the national dailies – broadsheet and tabloid – and he'd only struck out on his own and founded *The Juice* website with a nice redundancy package when one of the country's most successful publishers, NewsWorld, ran into trouble. Print had been on the way out for decades, or so the experts claimed, yet it was still going strong for some. Over on the web, however, although it was harder to attract advertising revenue, securing sponsors was the key.

The Juice had broken even in its first year, amazing not only Jack but key observers too. From there it had been steady, earning him a good living although the hours were long. Marcus went home with a lot less but always with a glimmer of light at the end of the tunnel. Now, emerging from that tunnel with the scoop he'd go down in history for, he was sure better things were on the way, if not at *The Juice* then anywhere... the world could be his oyster at last.

Jack switched the sound up on his monitor. 'This should be funny.'

Marcus looked up from his PDA. He'd been monitoring his messages ever since the story broke. 'Ah... that Lazarou's a character.'

'Feel for the bloke though. If anyone took, even touched my daughters, I'd fuckin' kill 'em.'

The TV show, *Daytime*, had just finished its opening jingle. The words 'EXCLUSIVE: The Lazarous speak for the first time about missing Lara' heralded the producers' best scoop in ages.

Good morning. I'm Kate Hardiman.

And I'm John Butterworth. Welcome to Daylight.

The dazzling duo smiled at the camera, then each other, as the studio went dark. The camera panned around and then zoomed back in on the presenters. The lights faded back in.

Today we've got full coverage of the Lazarou-Bogdanek story, with the world's first exclusive interview with La-La's parents, George and Muriel Lazarou.

The camera switched from Kate's face on close-up to a shot of the Lazarous sat on a light red sofa across the studio. They sat closer than they had in the last five years.

But first, the headlines.

Marcus spoke over them. 'La-La? Seriously? Fucking La-La?'

'The whole thing's la-la, mate. It's a media circus.'

'Yeah, and we're the ringmasters.' Marcus leaned over Jack's desk for a high-five. Jack met his hand with a satisfying slap. Photos of Lara and her captor overlaid the screen, carefully placed so as not to obscure either presenter. It was one of those masterful practices of TV designed to preserve the egos of its stars.

Two days ago, Lara Lazarou was abducted from her family home. Four men were killed. The police are now hunting Polish immigrant Piotr Bogdanek, an ex-school teacher who was last seen leaving the residence with the teenager. It's already being called the most audacious kidnapping of the last fifty years.

That's right, Katie. He's also admitted to the murder of actress Amanda Higgins, a twenty-three-year-old from Malton on the Hampshire coast.

Today we're speaking to Lara's parents as they make a plea for Bogdanek to return their daughter unharmed and to turn himself in. We'll be back right after the break.

'A break already? This is why I stopped watching TV.'

Jack laughed. 'You're glued to that fucking PDA though, mate. You're still *plugged in* all the time. I just prefer my news vomit splashed on a big screen.'

Marcus had never been into TV much but he was keen to watch this interview. He'd put in his own bid for the exclusive. Within a day of the abduction the PR firms had stepped in to 'help' the Lazarous with their profile – naturally a means to the end of getting their daughter back. George was the rough and ready one. TV didn't phase him at all, but Muriel was different. Part of the reason their marriage had failed was a marked disparity in confidence levels.

On the light red *Daytime* sofa though, with the studio's safe pastel décor and soft lighting creating a sense of calm, she seemed fairly relaxed. This was, Marcus suspected, the result of some hasty acclimatisation work – cosmetic psychological conditioning for the TV-shy.

109

It hadn't taken long for Marcus as a young reporter to grasp the way the media worked. Shows like *Daytime*, while puffy and pointless in his opinion, served a purpose and a demographic. Building a sympathetic media profile was all part of the process.

Jack typed an email throughout the ad break while Marcus glazed over, staring through the commercial messages and deep in thought. Then the short jingle came back on and the two autocue-robot presenters, with their tidy faces and colourful clothes, introduced the next segment. They were now on the sofa, shaped in a crescent for convenience, with the Lazarous.

George, Muriel. Thanks so much for coming in today. We can only imagine the pain you're going through right now.

'She's quite fit, that Katie.' Jack grinned at Marcus. 'Nice tits.'

Marcus shushed him: 'Hey. I want to hear this.'

The Lazarous nodded and smiled weakly in close-up. A school photo of Lara hung in a digital inset next to them.

We just want our daughter back. Muriel, my wife, and I... this is our plea to you. Please bring Lara home. We miss her so much. We'll do anything. Please. Please don't hurt her.

The camera pulled out of close-up and back to presenter John.

Do you have any idea what this man wants with your daughter? He said you stole something from him. What could he mean?

What's he mean? I've no idea. I run a legitimate business. I've never 'eard of this man before. I don't even know any Polish.

Muriel's face changed and she awkwardly glanced at her feet. She knew. Glossing over the negative side of her husband's vocation with the word 'legitimate' didn't excuse the fact that it did ruin lives. Beyond the glossy, more acceptable side of porn – although that acceptance was by no means as wide as its peddlers believed – there was a deep well of depravity.

She had seen it all. George's business, legitimate though it might be on the surface, extended much further than popcorn pornography. Clearly Bogdanek's vendetta against her husband was connected to a girl – someone he cared about, a friend or a family member. In some respect she could understand that pain might drive someone to drastic action. But not this drastic, and not with her daughter.

Katie leaned towards Muriel sympathetically.

Muriel, you two have been separated now for a few years. Has this tragedy brought you closer together?

Her expression changed off camera back to her coached, practised smile just in time.

Oh, absolutely. You never stop loving someone, y'know. When we get our daughter back, we'll provide a safe and stable home for her. That's all we care about.

Her eyes began to water.

People want to think they know about us. We know we're in the media spotlight, but this isn't... this isn't about us. It's just... we just want Lara back safe. Please...

The camera capitalised on the melodrama.

...we just need her back. She's just... just a child. She's our child.

Katie passed a tissue to Muriel. 'This is bollocks,' Jack said, gleefully. 'They've clearly done a deal here not to mention the *P* word. He's a fucking pornographer!'

Marcus nodded. 'I bet they're getting an appearance fee too.'

The presenters thanked the Lazarous for coming on. It was, Marcus continued, exactly as expected: a brief PR exercise designed and plotted to a tee. He'd watched enough of Lazarou's output to know what kind of a man he was and yet, in the soft focus of early morning television, it was as if this reality didn't exist. Even though the newspapers reminded readers at every turn that he was a dirty bastard – and they had not held back visually in that regard – Lazarou's *Daytime* persona was of wounded animal and head of a family beset with tragedy. Maybe this was so, but Marcus didn't see that image tally with the man's willingness to publish videos of young girls having their anal passages inspected by old men.

~~~

'Hello.' The desk sergeant looked tired, his expression not welcoming but beckoning the boy in front of him to say what he wanted.

'Hi... I'm... my girlfriend needs to speak to someone about the murder.'

The sergeant's demeanour changed from bored to mildly interested. 'Right.' He looked past Jez to see a nervous Maria a few feet behind him.

111

He motioned for her to come forward. 'Okay, hang on. Let me take some details.'

Jez moved over.

'Good morning. What's your name, please?'

'Maria. Maria Sierska.'

'Okay, Maria. You're... what, Polish?'

'Y-yes,' she replied, shifting on her feet.

'And you have information about yesterday's murder?'

Maria hesitated. *Yesterday?* The murder had been the day before. Or had it?

'Erm... yes. Yes, I think so.'

'You think so? Or you know so?'

For fuck's sake, Jez thought. *Get on with it.* His mind was preoccupied – he and Maria had spent the night together at his house, and it had been *amazing*. After settling down following the revelation of her tattoo, which had come as something of a gut punch on top of the previous night's gut punch where he watched her giggling away in the freakiest video on the planet, they'd had a heart-to-heart.

Maria told Jez she loved him. She felt safe with him. She revealed details of the fairground set-up and her relationship with Supervisor Steve – how the girls who worked on the fairground were shipped in from Poland and other parts of Europe, how they all stayed in that house on the other side of town, and how they made some extra money from doing soft porn. She said she hated doing it but it was part of the deal, part of the bargain for coming to England to earn good money and be looked after.

Jez felt sick, his stomach uneasy with nervous energy, for most of this revelatory session. But perversely he wanted to know more, to go deeper, to understand what was happening to this girl he loved.

'I know so,' Maria said, confidently. 'Please, I have information that might help.'

The desk sergeant picked up a phone handset and turned away as he spoke. Maria couldn't hear what he said.

Jez recalled images of Maria's body on top of his – how soft she had felt, her legs wrapped around his as he reached up to her breasts with one hand and steadied her hip with the other. He felt the lump in his pants stiffen further.

A door opened behind the desk and a lady came out, lifting the hinged desk end. 'Miss Sierska?' Maria nodded. 'I'm Sergeant Mary Mackenzie. How can I help you?'

Jez looked the lady up and down. She was pretty. A little bit taller than Maria, with a slim and sporty build. Aware his cock was hardening in his pants, he wilted back a little and let Maria give this lady her full attention before she gave him hers.

'The girl who was murdered?' Maria fashioned the statement as a question. Mack nodded a few times, her eyes widening to coax out the next bit. 'Her tattoo... my boyfriend told me. I have one too.'

Mack's expression indicated confusion. They hadn't released any details of the girl yet and as far as she knew, unless the killer had issued more photos elsewhere, there weren't any tattoos released to the press.

'Miss Sierska. Did you know the victim – Amanda Higgins?'

'No, I didn't,' Maria replied, her expression confused now too. It didn't sound like a Polish name at all. There must have been a mistake. 'But my tattoo...'

'Thanks for coming in, Miss Sierska,' Mack said, her tone irritated. 'If you leave your details at the desk, we'll be in touch if we need to.'

Maria looked quickly back at Jez and shrugged. He ignored his boner and strode forward. Mack turned back and closed the desk flap behind her. She was about to disappear through the door.

'Excuse me!' Jez called. The desk sergeant looked over, startled. 'Mrs Mackenzie?'

Mack turned back and half-smiled through her annoyance. 'Yes?'

'Aren't you even going to look at the tattoo?'

'The girl didn't have any tattoos we're investigating. If you really have any information, I'm all ears.'

'But my dad and Pete Mathers were talking about it. It was one of the only leads, he said. The tattoo. PP?' Jez shrugged, his face pleading and sneering with impatience.

Mack turned fully to face Jez. 'PP?'

'Yes,' Maria said. 'It's up here.' She pointed to her shoulder.

'Okay,' Mack said, striding over to Maria. 'Come with me.'

~~~

'Pete.' Mack tried to get her colleague's attention. 'Interview room two.'

He looked up from his desk but Mack was gone. He stood up and walked out into the corridor, just to see her entering the interview room and closing the door behind her. He looked back into his and Danson's office. Mike wasn't back yet from the toilet. Pete walked the length of the corridor and pushed the toilet door open. 'You in here, Mike?'

'Yep. Two mins.'

'Get on with it, and don't forget to wipe. Mack wants us in room two. We all remember the last time you forgot to wipe.'

He went back and let himself in. A pretty young girl with dark hair and eyes sat nervously across from Mack.

Mack looked up at him and smiled. 'Detective Pete Mathers. This is Maria Sierska. She's come in with information about the girl – the PP tattoo.'

He leaned in and blocked the young girl's view with his shoulder. 'Does Briggs know?'

Mack shook her head.

The door opened again. 'Sorry, guys.'

Mack took care of the introductions. Maria explained who she was, where she got her PP tattoo and how the PP girls back in Poland were offered opportunities in England. They worked on the fairground by day and did other things at night and on their days off. The PP girl who had died – she didn't know who she was, but then it was a big house with several dorms, and girls came and went all the time. No one had gone missing, as far as she knew.

She told them about Steve, who became 'acquainted' with some of the girls. But at the same time he looked after them. Although in England it wasn't as usual for girls to do this kind of thing, back in Poland there was a different attitude to porn, she said.

Mack showed Maria out and back to Jez, who looked concerned. She thanked them both for coming and returned to meet Mathers and Danson in their office.

'We can't follow this up, anyway,' she said. 'Briggs has forbidden it.'

'But there's new evidence,' Danson protested. 'That's got to mean...'

'I'm sorry, guys. I'll take it to Briggs, see what he says. But the case has moved up and out. He'll probably pass her statement on to Interpol.'

Half an hour later, Briggs came out of a meeting of the district police chiefs. Mack gave him the new information. He said he'd pass it on. He never did.

~~~

Robert's assimilation had been painless and quick. The world around him simply melted away: the cabin, the woods, the earth beneath and the sky above. It was as if this furniture in his sight had been torn down like a curtain, and all that remained was his sentience. He reached out for Angelo, physically. As he had seen the Asian man's skin evaporate into a black fog, his had done the same, and he watched in wonder as all that he knew of himself gave way to a mass of thin, dark tendrils, swimming in and out of each other; writhing like so many snakes.

As Angelo's tendrils snaked over and under, making their way across towards him, his responded. One of his final human thoughts was how much this reminded him of worms feeling out of the soil, searching for food. Now Robert had found his food and it tasted of Angelo.

Once assimilated, the clarity of thought was absolute. Robert existed no longer and it had only a sense that he ever had. As the world was peeled away, it felt something guiding it as it began to reconstruct. Somewhere in this new consciousness it witnessed a depth that as a human he had never imagined. This new form could rise and sink at once. Images began to form but not as the human mind might interpret them. Rather than colour there was essence; in the place of solidity was fluidity. As a human he might have felt emotion at this, but in this new state there was nothing in those terms.

Something guided the consciousness again, peeling back another curtain and revealing a vision of such potency that would have destroyed the human brain: a giant, pulsating miasma from which came a sound no ear could process – as loud as the sun was hot. Within this fluid, shifting cloud were the thickest tendrils, lashing against each other, melding and consuming and thrashing and shrieking.

With full understanding, the world began to bleed back in. These thick tendrils propelled it up and down and in all directions at once as the birth came to completion. Of nothing came Robert's previous form, humanoid but still fluid, and in its consciousness images formed again, this time of shifting colours, shapes and lumps of flesh floating, drawn together by a

115

core. Robert's tendrils stopped thrashing and calmed, now weaving and forming again. The cabin lurched back into view and stopped in place, with the final piece of the puzzle appearing from the ether.

The Asian face remained. The man formerly known as Angelo spoke: 'We are one. Did you see?'

'Yes.' Ex-Robert could see himself in the consciousness, the human form still shifting, his face unset like sand in the wind. The humanoid stood close by was connected. Its thoughts and hunger swam around with ex-Robert's in an ocean of others.

He was whole again – indeed, greater than the whole; created from the DNA of his human self but supercharged. New Robert felt great.

Eleven – Births, deaths and marriages

Subject F, control group. Day fourteen. AM. Subject has responded as hypothesised to increased electromagnetic charge. However, co-operation has been markedly reduced. See annex document folder for full analysis.

~~~

As Robert's human form reconstituted, he had surveyed his new network. At first it was a cacophony of a million voices, noise over noise. Then, as if falling from a tree and grabbing a branch to break one's fall, he caught one and hung onto it. Other branches seemed to thrash around it, weakening his focus, but he held fast and they calmed, backing off.

It was almost an afterthought now that he understood the 'coincidence' Angelo had alluded to. It was pure logic. Robert's old friend Jerry had asked for help to solve a murder. Ergo, Jerry could not solve it on his own – at least not yet. The ordinary didn't want this murder solved. The reasons for that were obvious now. They knew Robert was coming to help and they knew his reputation. They had planned to assimilate him anyway because of his brother. He had just made it much easier for them. Humans would call it serendipity.

Despite their abilities and *supra*human essence, the ordinary were just as fragile, only in different ways. The last thing they needed was human interest, especially now they were so close to completing their dark circle. Typically the human response would be hysterical; the ordinary were to take the planet at last. It had been a long time coming – but the proliferation of darkness in the world had escalated so much in the twentieth and twenty-first centuries and this was finally bringing it to bear.

Much of this had been by deliberate intervention, yet humanity had done its worst all by itself. As the ordinary grew, so did the number of humans falling into its mass, although in population terms it was a tiny minority. In the ordinary's own measure, it was a beautiful thing.

But the human psyche and physiology varied greatly. Humanity's capacity for variance was a constant concern for the ordinary. While this race, connected by the dark heart of humanity, thrived on fear and hate

117

and sin yet had no capacity for true emotional connection, humans' ace in the hole was love and its many seeds: compassion, kindness, hope, kinship and friendship.

This was the one key advantage the human race had over the ordinary, who were, indeed, ordinary – each as all. They all fed from the same bowl. The collective consciousness saw and heard the same sights and sounds, to varying degrees. At Robert's end of the spectrum, he was like a foot soldier. There were only around a hundred of his type on the planet, manipulating and harvesting. Higher up were the true alphas, but he couldn't sense them, let alone wonder what their deal was.

There was, Robert found, some room for individual expression. There were blotches in the consciousness. Surveying his world map with its stems and spikes and thrashing, lashing tendrils, he could sense through the conduit faint glimmers of hatred, depravity and sorrow. The globe had opened up in a way no human could imagine – an ability to feel around its surface and to pick and poke.

Robert felt, reached out and grabbed hold of a thread that seemed to thrash more than any other in the region.

'That is Stanley,' Angelo said.

Robert understood immediately before the question arose: why, if we can all hear each other and everything else, do you address me directly? The answer was clear: singling out one thread in the huge mass relied somewhat on guidance. Finding a needle in a haystack was much easier if that needle stuck itself out and waved, as Stanley's did now.

'Stanley is a problem?'

'Perhaps, but one we cannot solve.'

Again, Robert didn't need to ask. The consciousness could not attack itself. It was not in the DNA of this beast to chew its own tail but Stanley's actions seemed to be acting against it. Stanley had become too noisy, possibly too powerful – sticking his neck out and attracting attention, too close to the final event they had been working towards. The last thing the ordinary needed was exposure. Despite their capacity for hatred of others, humanity could also band together and it was imperative that that didn't happen.

Stanley liked to collect trophies. He had a fascination with the young female form. This was not in itself acting against the consciousness but his largesse implied he had, perhaps, evolved in some manner. That this was beyond the comprehension of the consciousness, with its collective

118

intelligence, was a crease in the fabric that required immediate attention. With only Angelo and his new protégé Robert in the area, it fell to them to investigate.

'We should pay Stanley a visit then.'

Robert's naturally enquiring mind was in overdrive. Reborn as the ordinary, it was as if all his career to that point had been hard-won. Now, with access to people's hearts and minds, he wasn't only going to be privy to previously private information but he would be able to manipulate it too. He understood that humans were not generally recruited like he had been – and indeed, effectively by coincidence; the small number of assimilations were usually by invitation – a moment of pure darkness opening a door. He had no sense of regret though. It was what it was. Sorrow was now something he could create but not feel.

He reached out again. Gradually the images settled into something not too unlike a graph, points along it sticking up. He knew why this was: years of analysing criminal data. His old mind was not intact but his memories remained somewhere in his new make-up. Recalling these was instant. Superpowered, dehumanised Robert would have been a credit to the force.

As he latched onto one point on his graph of despair, he felt a strain. He couldn't reach it. *Closer*, he thought. He felt the distance almost measurable. Another strand seemed within reach. Bringing it in was like fishing in reverse – he being reeled in by the target. He felt a rush towards it, hundreds of thousands of much shorter stems passing at imperceptible speed.

The darkness swelled into view and he was there, inside it. His body in the cabin but his intellect swirling around someone else's. The sensation was entirely ordinary. The consciousness had been doing this forever and so, by extension, had he.

The girl was slouched beside her bed, a cloth tied tight around her upper arm. Her body was bruised by violence and pierced by the delivery of the medicine she injected to escape. Downstairs, two further clouds hung, on opposite sides of the room but connected by heavy despair. Robert felt energised. He skipped out and tried to grab one of the short stems but couldn't. *We can't get those. There's nothing for us there.*

He could sense Stanley's area – and indeed Stanley, but distantly. He realised the mechanics naturally and understood he had been heading the wrong way. Now he latched onto something south of the cabin. It seemed not just to transmit but to call to him, to the consciousness.

Robert understood why this action was happening now. Stanley had become a problem not by taking humans for his own pleasure but by drawing attention to it. The police local to Stanley – Robert acknowledged his ties to them with no hint of sentimentality – were aware of it. One in power there had visited Stanley especially to deal with this problem, but now he had taken another life, almost defiantly. He was not assimilating but destroying the ordinary's very lifeblood.

In order for the circle to complete, it all had to happen at once. The alphas in America would call when it was time, but the feeling was that the time was very close now.

The world had darkened. In all areas the consciousness had spread, coming ever closer to completing the circle. As it had spread, its coverage had thinned, leaving patches untouched and others rampant. The alphas were tying up loose ends in the lead-up to the final, glorious event.

Even a human could have understood the logic: sickness, terrorism and random acts of extreme violence had increased so much that fear pervaded much of the western world, and the east had its own set of problems brought about by over-population, a series of major earthquakes and an economic collapse, all of these flowing into the ordinary's pool. In the four corners of the Earth, it had been written:

Jet, Ebony, Raven, Sable
For one and for all
When the circle is fulfilled

Angelo and Robert left the cabin and the forest. He could come back for his old belongings and his car later – in the meantime, it would be another mystery for his old friend Jerry not to solve; to feed the fear, sorrow and uncertainty. They entered the vein which Robert had walked along hours before and now he shot through it, covering the distance in the blink of an eye. This travel was different to reaching out for the spikes: rushing along micro and radio waves, feeling the currents energising their disembodied structures.

They headed further north and around, reaching the banks of the motorway and hitting a row of pylons. They zipped along the wires to Malton in seconds. This new mode of travel was ideal and Robert liked it.

~~~

'Marc,' Suzy called. 'Come and see this. Oh fuck.'

Marcus got up from his desk and joined Suzy at hers. 'What's up?'

'He's done it again. Look. He's just sent me a link. I don't believe this. Why me? Fuck!'

Suzy clicked her mouse and scrolled the page up. At its top was a single line of text: 'In death she is free.' Underneath it was the frame of a video player, ready to go.

'Oh my God.' Marcus took a deep breath. 'Press play then.'

Bogdanek spoke calmly as his head-mounted camera reflected in the mirror. His face was clear and his expression earnest. 'This girl is barely old enough to drink alcohol, but every day Lazarou rapes her for the pleasure of men. She is complicit. As she breaks the heart of her mother, I will break hers.'

The view swivelled quickly and jerkily away from the mirror. It headed out into a short corridor and then stopped in front of an open door. Suzy clicked her mouse and the video paused. She looked pale.

'I don't want to see this. I don't want to see this shit.'

Marcus shrugged inwardly. 'We don't know what it is yet.'

'Of course we fucking do!' Suzy raised her voice. She felt a wave of hysteria. 'He's about to butcher some poor girl. We need to call the police. Now!' She pushed away from her desk and walked quickly to the nearest window.

'We can scoop this,' Marcus said. 'Yes... yes, we call the police, but let's scoop it first.' He joined Suzy at the window. 'First things first, we'll see what Jack thinks.'

~~~

Jez stroked his hand down Maria's cheek. He lay across the sofa, one leg dangling off the side. Maria lay next to him, folded into his side. He wanted to ask her about that video – the one he'd pissed himself

121

watching, but at that point in time it wasn't appropriate. This was a loving moment with the girl of his dreams. That was all that mattered.

He jumped a little, disturbing the peaceful embrace, as he heard the front door open. *That's odd*, he thought. *Dad's back already?*

The door closed and he heard a thump on the floor. Maria stirred, lifting her face up to his. 'Your dad?'

'I... I guess so. That's weird though. He said he'd be gone for a while.'

Jez unhooked his arm from behind Maria's back and swung himself off the sofa. He stood up and walked out towards the entrance hall. A few seconds later Maria heard muffled cries of happiness. Jez walked back in.

'Maria – this is my mother, Sue.' He shrugged and smiled. 'Mum – meet Maria.'

~~~

'Okay, put it on.' Jack stood behind Suzy, back at her desk.

'From the start,' Marcus said.

They watched until the point Suzy had stopped it before. 'I don't want to see what's in that room,' she said. 'I really, really don't.'

'Close your eyes then. Go on.' Jack's arms were folded. He drummed his fingers on his chest impatiently. 'It can't be any worse than those torture porn movies. All sorts of grim shit in those.'

Marcus nodded. The inexplicable acceptance of what used to be called 'video nasties' years ago had puzzled him, although what they were back then was nothing compared to the movies of his time. These days it was perfectly acceptable to see limbs and heads being hacked off – *gruesome* wasn't really covering it. He didn't watch those movies anyway. Sure, he'd seen some when his friends had shown him clips here and there, but he was much more into slow-burning psychodramas. Like his colleague, Suzy, he didn't want to see what was in that room.

Suzy clicked the mouse and got ready to hide behind her hand.

Bogdanek's head-mounted camera caught it all, albeit in a frenzied, jarring manner. The girl was tied up. Her head had been shaved, with clumps of her blonde hair on her lap. She was gagged with duct tape, her raw terror screaming only through her eyes, wet and red and ready to pop out of her skull.

Jack's stomach turned. Suzy's heart began to pound. Marcus felt his legs weakening.

'Selena. You have given your heart to the devil,' Bogdanek spoke. He held up a tablet and steadied it between the camera and the girl in her chair. He pressed the screen and a video played. It was her, naked and smiling and reclining on a bed, around which stood a group of six men, naked but for their tent-poled briefs.

'As the devil drinks your blood, I drink yours.' He placed the tablet down in front of her. 'Today I deliver you from evil.'

Suzy covered her eyes with both hands as Bogdanek held up a blade. He drew it back and then sliced across the girl's throat, sending a spray of dark red onto his camera lens. Marcus stepped back as if it had hit him. The camera, having jerked with the motion, settled back on the girl. Her head was taken mostly off at the neck, hanging lopsided by a hinge of flesh. Blood dribbled from the wound onto her lap, staining her cut hair. The video finished, fading to black.

'Oh fuck. Fuck,' Marcus breathed, a thought amusing and disgusting him in an instant: *she always gave good head*. He looked over at Jack, who had shut his eyes and clutched his hands to his chest.

The majority of a minute passed. 'Okay,' Jack said, opening his eyes at last. 'That's fucking disgusting. Let's publish.'

~~~

'Of course I'm pleased to see you.' Jez hugged his mother again. Despite the fact she had left them and moved away to join some kind of cult, he did love her. She had always been a colourful character – all beads and crystals and holistic therapies and friends called Tarquin-Gulliver and Persephone-Wild. His friends had always adored her: one of the yummiest mummies in town. Her loose crop-tops, leggings and jean skirts earned her lean figure a good deal of attention. This, combined with a failing marriage due to her husband being 'married to the job', eventually led to her taking off.

Sue smiled past her son to his girlfriend. 'You're gorgeous!' She nudged Jez gently out of her way and rushed to Maria, embracing her warmly. 'Gorgeous!'

Maria grinned. 'You are... gorchus too!'

His mother turned around: 'Jeremy – you dark horse. So tell me. How long?'

Jez thought for a moment. 'Er… just a few days?'

His mother danced a little and clapped her hands together. 'Oh, yes. It's so exciting.'

'So… to what do we owe the pleasure?'

'Well, that's a good question,' his mother said, skipping lightly over to the long bay window that looked out to the street. 'I'm… I need to speak to your father. Is he… here?'

Jez shook his head as he spoke. 'Sorry mum, no. He's away on a case.'

'Oh dear,' she said, still grinning. 'I'll hang around until he gets back then. Okay?'

'Of course. It's your house too.' Jez looked over at Maria and smiled, then back to his mother. 'What's up? Is everything okay?'

'Yes, honey. Yes, of course. It's just… I've met someone. He's… asked me to marry him!'

Twelve – Into the funhouse

Mike Danson was not a complicated man, or at least he assumed he wasn't. At forty-two-years-old he had, he thought, accomplished very little. He'd been a detective for coming up sixteen years, rising early in his career from regular uniform to plain clothes.

Mike had proven himself a sharp tool in the CID armoury; maybe not the hardest worker and lacking a little in motivation. Much of his mental acuity had come from his little friends: those tiny rounded clumps of powder. He used to roll them between his thumb and forefinger, eyeing them up as a sniper does its target, willing each to be the one that would break his mind into the next level.

He recognised this for what it was. An addiction. Those pills he'd read about on the net. Those pills that had no side-effects – or any long-term use data to support that claim. Since the government had ordered trials of these increasingly popular 'nootropics' years ago, nothing much had been reported since, aside from the occasional reminder they existed and that a couple of users in the States had died from brain haemorrhages.

Mike wasn't interested in dying of a brain haemorrhage, or anything else for that matter, but his continued struggle to stop taking these beautiful little spheres had, if anything, seen an escalation in his usage. He was, ironically, smart enough without the drugs to know what they were doing to him – his skills blunting, his eyesight blurring, his headaches worsening... but those headaches only seemed to go away when he popped one into his mouth.

At least there was enough of him left underneath the drug to keep an even keel. No one knew about his habit. Police drug tests didn't search for nootropics – they weren't an official threat, after all. Perhaps, he thought, it was assumed that police hopped up on these enhancers would be at the top of their game, so penalising their consumption would be counterproductive. But as far as he had read up on the subject, they just weren't considered dangerous. He knew – and it was a thought he tried to ignore – that nootropics were definitely dangerous. It wasn't all that different to cocaine in some respects, but an addiction to intelligence was much better than being a slave to unfounded arrogance.

Now, though, as he rolled this awesome orb in his finger and thumb, he felt another rush of anxiety. How could he have been so stupid, letting his supply run out? Two a day, sometimes more, for all these years, and down to his last one. The online store he'd been using for at least two years had closed down, and his local dealer had managed to give him a good stock of two hundred but that was about six months ago. Now his 'brand' had gone out of production too. *Just one left.*

These simple facts put together had given him the motivation to get out of this habitual groove, but this last pill weighed on his shoulders a thousand times more than the couple of grams in his hand. If he took this last one, that rush could be the last. The anxiety was almost too much to bear at times – he could only imagine it would be far worse if his little friends never came around again.

Mike stood up, put the pill on his coffee table and grabbed his coat off a peg next to the front door. He closed his eyes and took a couple of deep breaths, telling himself, 'Just leave, get out of here, and we'll deal with this later.' He put his coat on and left, auto-piloting down to the ground floor of his block.

Five minutes later he pulled up and parked his car opposite a row of shops, only one of which was open. A large convenience store, its lights were the brightest beacon on the strip. The buildings on this block, between Prince Street and Cutler Street, were all four storeys, the shop fronts on the ground and then a few dimly-lit windows dotting the other floors.

To the left of 'Fosters' 24-hour' was a dry cleaning shop, its frontage on an incline of about five degrees, as the road bent away further left, following the curvature of the beach promenade opposite. A strong breeze rode over Mike's car bonnet and he felt the chill over his jacket, the cold air finding the opening at the top and diving down to his chest. He knew he was still anxious, on edge as he had been for days but hiding it well.

To the right was first an antique furniture shop, named Beds and Bits, then a charity shop, a bakery, a hardware store, and finally what appeared to be an office – a plaque over the door and blinds drawn over the single window. It looked odd on the end of a row of large shop windows, inviting people in. This was the property Mike was interested in.

Mack had been told to leave it alone and she had passed on her dissatisfaction to Mike and Pete. Pete had been taken in on another team to work up some angles on Lara's abduction but Mike had been given the evening to himself.

126

His inquisitive mind, enhanced or not, couldn't allow a genuine lead to go cold. A dead girl in a beach hut and then on the coroner's table had given him all the excuses he needed to defy his boss. Besides, having gone way over his overtime limit in the last two days gave him a little freedom to act on his own intuition.

Waiting to cross the road as the traffic edged past, held up by a van turning right just up ahead, he checked his watch. It was just after ten. Mike found his path through and skipped across and up onto the pavement outside the hardware store. The large sign proudly declared 'Stanley's'. He peered absently into the shop and saw nothing remarkable as he continued to the next frontage.

Mike stopped at the door and read the plaque. 'Davies Consulting'. To the left was a button on a panel and a blank field where usually some details would be inscribed.

A sudden noise made him jump. Turning to see the source, three teenagers were staring at the ground and mumbling to each other. Mike realised what had happened straight away: a bottle had fallen through the bottom of a flimsy bag and smashed. Judging by the lack of other bags, he could confidently assume they had no more bottles and so, taking into account that none of them had ventured back into the shop, it was likely all they could afford. Therefore they must be students, or just poor, jobless, aimless youths.

He snapped back to the matter at hand and followed his gaze to the window. The blinds were drawn tight although Mike could just make out a glimmer of light beyond. He rounded the end of the terrace and came to an angled break in the road. The length of the side of the building sat a row of parked cars, meeting a right-angle and beginning the next road. At the back of this building was a long fence, bracketing off the yards of the shops out front and giving residential access to the flats on top.

Reaching the end of the fence, Mike angled his head around it to see the hundred-metre stretch – an alley bolstered by a tall cliff at its back, rising up in natural rock until it began a new synthetic layer just about level with the third storey of the buildings at Mike's level. He felt a little queasy looking at this tall, jagged wall, resembling a wave about to crash down. Vertigo was probably another side-effect of his mental enhancements seeing as it had developed over the last year or so, but this wall was imposing and foreboding somehow.

A sharp snap jerked him back once more as a figure entered the alley at the other end. Mike withdrew quickly and then eased forwards again to get one eye on the figure. It was female, probably early twenties. Her walk was bold and purposeful, much like the gait of any woman walking alone in the dark.

He pulled back a little more as the girl drew nearer, then nearer still, eventually forcing him to retreat fully behind the fence as she came within ten feet and entered the rear of the property he was interested in. He heard a loud knock at the door, then a beep, and took that as his cue to make a move. Slipping around the fence post smoothly and keeping low, he saw a glimpse of red light as the door closed, a hand pulling it closed as the girl's legs disappeared in the sliver he could see.

Shit, he thought. *A camera.* They would see him coming. It was a little late to knock and expect a warm welcome.

Mike stayed low and out of the camera's view, moving sideways to the next yard. Another camera was focused on a short flight of steps up to the back door. To its left was a goods delivery entrance, obviously for the hardware store out front. He felt a little self-conscious out here at night, hiding in the shadows from no one in particular.

The door opened again and Mike shuffled silently forwards, this time ready to... he wasn't sure. He watched the back of another girl – this one walked with more vulnerability than the last – and managed to round the fence and hug it all the way to stand under the camera. The door closed just as he got there, clicking and sounding a faint beep. He looked up at the camera. A small black wire went from the camera casing and into the wall, confirming it wasn't just for show.

Estimating the angle of the camera as he kept tight against the door, he managed to get the other side of it and crouched, now leaning his front and face against the door. This felt even more ridiculous, as if he was twenty floors up on the outside of a skyscraper and hanging on for dear life.

Still pressed against the door, he examined the lock – or lack of it. With no handle or keypad on the outside, he had even less chance of getting in.

He slid against the door and wall and made it over to the light shadow of the fence-wall intersection, just as the door swung open.

His jaw fell and eyes widened in true shock as the familiar physique of his boss emerged from the red light, turning back to nod at the unseen body in the doorway as he walked away and exited the alley. Just as the door was about to snap shut again, Mike pulled a pen from his jacket pocket and stopped it, the metal of the door just tapping against the plastic casing. It was a technique he'd used many times before.

Withdrawing the pen as he replaced it with his hand, he eased the door open, grateful that this time the door had been allowed to close by itself instead of deliberately. This registered as a hypothesis that the girl was concerned for her safety, alone in this dark alley, and so felt an urgency to secure the door, while his chief – *what was Briggs doing there?* – had seemed far more casual. He was leaving. *Shit – what was Briggs doing there?*

This thought unnerved him a great deal as he peered into the slowly opening doorway. The red light opened out onto his face and cut a shape into the yard outside, widening its cone as Mike leaned in, then narrowing again as the door began to close softly behind him.

'Mike!' The call startled him. He whirled around and stopped the door with his shoulder. Pete strolled towards him.

'For fuck's sake, Pete. I've just spent ten minutes sneaking in here and – look, see that camera? Avoiding that!'

~~~

'I didn't know to expect visitors.' Stanley was delighted to have some ordinary company. It had been some time since any of his kind had entered his domain.

'You didn't sense us?'

'No... I didn't sense that. My mind has been on other things. Beautiful things.' He waved his hand ceremoniously. 'Besides, I never was any good at multi-tasking.'

Robert and Angelo had jumped straight into Stanley's office, a room he almost always kept just so. He would change the décor periodically but it was the single room where he felt singular satisfaction; where everything was as it should be. He realised this was an echo of his past life, that of Stanley the shop owner. These days, though, he didn't often venture onto the shop floor. He paid well and maintained a business-like relationship with his staff. They only used the lower rear entrance, which led through to the stock room at the back and then through to the large retail area.

129

Stanley's living quarters, a four-storey house with a basement, were strictly off limits except to invited guests. Chief Briggs, the police patsy, was a regular visitor. He'd competently helped Stanley build up his collection of wives just by looking the other way.

The hold he'd taken over Briggs was organic: by putting images in his brain; images of cause and effect – a simple road from A to B which, if travelled, would end up in the removal from existence of the Briggs family. And he very much believed this would happen. He had seen Stanley's natural form once. That was enough. In his usual day job, Briggs was the chief for sure, but when Stanley called, it was clear where the authority lay.

They all sensed it. As the camera spotted Pete Mathers entering the residence next door, it shone into the consciousness – electrical frequencies carrying the images to them.

Angelo smiled. 'Let me take care of this.'

~~~

Pete darted inside. Mike let the door rest against its lock and pulled it slowly but firmly enough to sound the beep.

They were in a corridor of about twenty feet. There were two doors – one first on the left and another further up on the right, before the corridor right-angled off into darkness. The single red lightbulb on the ceiling just ahead of them cast just enough light to see. The walls were lighter – a washed out pink, although not distressed. It reminded Mike of a strip club – this moment in time, the light and the shadows, the hum of music coming from somewhere beyond.

'So you changed your mind.'

'Yep. Data analysis isn't really my bag so I thought I'd come along for the ride. Just in time, it seems.'

Pete walked to the door on the left and tried the handle. It turned easily and he edged it open to allow a quick recon of the room. It was too dark inside to see anything. He took out his torch. The door closed behind him.

'Mike?'

Mike moved up to the next door, opening a storage room lit only by the thin, weak light in the corridor. He could see a bicycle leaning against a bench. There were some buckets and mops and bottles of various

130

detergents around it. He sealed the room again and walked around the corner, straight into a dead end. His pulse quickened a little.

'Pete.'

Nothing.

'Pete?'

A feeling rushed in. There was something behind him. He froze, staring ahead at the pinkish wall, somehow lit brightly now despite the only lightbulb being ninety degrees and several metres away. His skin prickled as his heart began to pound.

His breathing noisy and shallow, he turned around slowly. 'Help me.' A girl with rope around her neck was tied to a hook on the ceiling, her head covered in a woven hood with just her lips visible underneath.

'Help me.' The voice was muffled. The red light behind her began to flicker, *on-off on-off on-off*... the wall seemed to curve away from her too, not straight anymore but somehow tapering off. As her left arm came up he felt something at his back – something cold, damp... and a sound, a crunching sound like slowed down, erratic clapping. The girl's hand reached up to her hood, grabbing at it with bloody fingers. A dark brown, thick liquid appeared from under the hood, cascading over her lips and down to the rope and onto her chest, following its curves.

'Peeeeete!'

The hood came forward and her arm snapped down, dropping it to the floor. The sound in Mike's head grew louder, his body frozen on the spot as he witnessed this pure horror. The girl's face was a mess – this dark liquid seeping out of her eyes, mouth and nose. She tried to say 'help' again but her tongue was suppressed by the flow, lapping at this treacly spring but going nowhere.

Mike let his eyes drop, as if in slow motion – each frame of this video nasty more intense than the last – and saw the liquid pooling at her feet and flowing towards his. He looked back to her face. The liquid flowed still but not from her eyes now. Flesh was ripped around the sockets, fanned out, but her eyeballs met his with burning intensity.

The coldness rose up his back now, a sheet of frozen air beginning to envelope him. From below the girl the liquid began to rise, tentacles feeling out and others growing from those. It pooled now around his feet, snaking up around his ankles and into his shoes. It should have felt wet but there was nothing.

'Peeeeeeeeeeeeeete!'

He looked back to the girl's face again. Her eyes had gone, replaced by black holes leaking more of this terrifying liquid. Then the flow stopped immediately as her body dropped from the rope, coming to stand right in front of him. Her mouth opened again, dripping. 'Bad things…' Her voice was croaky and wet.

Mike stood slack-jawed, his mouth dry and gasping, his body dripping in cold fear. She said again, 'Bad things.' Mike felt something against his chest but didn't look. The girl tore at his shirt, finding a way in. She started to scrape on his skin but he couldn't locate the sense of touch. Her mouth widened to reveal another black hole. This time her words were broken and formed without teeth or tongue.

'Baa… fin…'

The words echoed in his mind: *baafin baafin baafin bad things badfings baa fin fin baa*, as a hand closed around his right shoulder, yanking him around. A bright flash blinded him for an instant as the horror vanished and he found himself back in the dimly lit corridor. His breath heavy and fast, Mike hesitantly looked back and saw only an empty space.

The apparition, or whatever it was, was gone. His shirt was still open though, marks visible across his chest. He felt his stomach turn, a rush of vomit shooting up into his mouth. He let nature take its course, bending over as a thin spray splashed onto the floor and his feet.

Footsteps. A door closing. Footsteps getting closer. Mike felt exhausted. His mouth sagged open, specks of vomit around his lips and threatening to drip from his chin. He wiped them away and pushed his hands into his knees and stood up. Now the footsteps were behind him. His breathing had become more laboured, accompanied by an increasing ache in his forehead.

Looking back over his shoulder, a shadow appeared at the edge of the turn in the corridor. It stopped as the footsteps did too. The feeling of nausea rushed back. The shadow seemed to twitch, as if a lightbulb was swinging from side to side in tiny movements. Now footsteps started again, this time in front. He turned his head forward, surveying the corridor through exhausted eyes.

Where there had been blank walls, a dark red was bleeding into them, like wine pouring into a glass. Mike looked back over his shoulder again, catching a glimpse of something dark pulling back around the corner, where its shadow settled again. He felt his feet propel him towards the bleeding walls, towards the footsteps. Now the walls were red all around him, moving as if organic.

Brownish chunks seemed to bulge out towards him, this bloody pulp pumping around him as if he was a fleshy morsel moving down into the digestive tract of hell. The walls came closer at his sides and he reached out his arms to push them away. They met with nothing – as if his hands were just floating in air.

He walked faster and saw some kind of opening – *a mouth?* The feeling of travelling through a body intensified. Some kind of fleshy lips seemed to pulsate around the opening with a dim light beyond. He could hear no footsteps now, just sounds of rushing air, a dull thumping in his head, and something squelching under his feet. And then, as he tried to push his arms against these pulsating lips, he felt something behind him, pushing him through, and he emerged from the fleshy nightmare.

Ahead of him now stood a single black door, stark against the white borders. Behind him was no sign of his ordeal, just brightness. Now there was no lighting, no right angle or any other kind of boundary in this space. It was as if he stood suspended in light, only the darkness of the door in front of him offering any escape.

But did he want to escape? As sickened and frightened he had felt seconds before, he was now somehow at peace: spat from the succubus into a serene void. The most bizarre, horrifying experience of his life had left him numb. He opened the door.

~~~

Piotr was exhausted, physically and emotionally. A day spent uploading his video through the back channels of the DarkNet and waiting to see the results had left him in need of some fresh air. It didn't help that he kept losing his signal and had to start all over again several times. He'd gone for a walk into town and decided to scout his next victim. She would probably be his last, he decided. He had never intended to grow up to be an angel of death. It wasn't at the top of his list of career choices.

Now, as he climbed down into the storm drain and the makeshift home he'd built for his guest, he slipped and cracked his ankle against the cold, hard stone, his wrist catching painfully on the rope ladder as he tried to slow his fall.

'Kurwa!' He slid down the rest of the way uneasily and came to rest on the ground. 'Ty skurwysynu!'

He hobbled over the twenty or so feet to the sheeting and brushed it aside. One of the portable lamps had gone out, leaving much of the 'room' cast in shadow. He limped over to it and knelt down. His knee cracked and shot a bolt of pain up his leg.

He pushed a switch on its side. Nothing happened. 'My poor Halina. I'm sorry. This should have stayed on.' He got up again, his knee cracking again, and looked back to the first light, then over to the small table. His portable charger sat there. He picked it up and took it over to the lamp. A minute later it came back on with a flicker.

Now he could see Lara, bound as he left her to the pole on the wall. Her head was hung against her left shoulder. Without standing, he shuffled towards her. 'It's okay, Halina. I'm back. It's you and me now. I don't like to leave you. I'm sorry.'

Lara didn't respond. She was awake but didn't want him to know that. Piotr gently raised her chin up and looked her over, then relaxed it back into place. 'I'm sorry. It will all be over soon. I promise you, my beautiful Halina.'

~~~

Mike fell through the opening onto his hands and knees. *Where the fuck is Pete?* He blinked to adjust his vision. His exhaustion was both mental and physical, the former similar to one of his worst hangovers and the latter reminding him very much of being beaten up – a feeling distant but starkly memorable.

He looked at the floor inches from his face: a light wooden, polished surface. He let his gaze wander up to see he was in what appeared to be an office. Certainly it was nicer than his own, back at the station. He crawled over to the desk on his right and used it to pull himself up. A dizzy wave knocked his balance but he managed to take stock: a room about sixteen by twenty-five feet, the desk sat back towards a wall and central along it. On the opposite side of the room was a small round table, a telephone in its centre, and to the left of the table an armchair. It looked uncomfortable to Mike; uninviting.

He looked over at the space he had landed on when he fell into this room. The door was gone. Taking a spin, he saw there were no windows;

just light purple-pink painted walls. The desk also had a telephone on it, the same bland, utilitarian design as the other, as well as a single sheet of paper and a pen.

Mike gasped and jumped as the phone on the little table began to ring. A second later the phone on the desk did too. He stood in limbo between the two, a choice he couldn't understand presented to him in alien circumstances. The desk phone seemed more insistent somehow, louder and sharper; but the other had a greater clarity to it, the rings shorter by a shave.

He opted for the closest one. Reaching across, his foot left the ground as his hand grabbed the receiver. Both phones stopped ringing. He flopped awkwardly, his side sprawling on the desk. The receiver made it to his ear.

'Hello, Michael. How's tricks?' The voice at the other end was jolly, bright. Mike was silent but for his laboured breathing.

'I said hello, Michael. It's terribly rude not to present some measure of acknowledgement.' Each word was pronounced crisply.

'Oh... hello.'

Mike was a fish out of water, figuratively gasping for some kind of reality, or an explanation of the last two minutes.

'That's better. Well now, let me introduce myself. I'm Angelo. Say hello, Angelo.'

Mike obliged, the pain in his side growing. 'Hello, Angelo.' His sideways view of the room seemed to flicker, to oscillate.

'Thank you,' the voice continued, crisp and excited. 'First I'd like to apologise for all the theatrics. We weren't... expecting you, see. We're not used to people snooping about.'

Mike had nothing to say.

'You must have some questions. Hmm?'

'What... what is this place?'

'Oh, it's nothing important. You don't need to worry about that. You're... Well, you're not *anywhere*, really. Strictly speaking.'

'Oh?' Mike elbowed himself up off the desk and came to rest on both feet again. 'I must be... somewhere.' The room continued to vibrate, almost imperceptibly. It wasn't just the walls – it was everything. The very air seemed to warp.

'You'd like to think so!' the voice chuckled. 'You know where you think you are, I'm sure. But that's not quite right. You're where... people

135

don't often go. You're not the first, no. Just the latest to take the wrong turn. What did you want, anyway?'

'I'm following a lead. About a missing girl. A dead girl.'

'Dead girls!' the voice shrieked. 'Oh my. That sounds so... dramatic!' More chuckling. 'Why, there are dead girls all over town. Why did you decide to come looking here?'

A spear of rationality pierced Mike's brain. He hung up the phone and closed his eyes. *There's no way any of this is real. Just the worst dream. The absolute worst dream anyone can have. I'm having it.* He stood motionless in the oscillating, bland yet functional room, his sense of space dissipating in the silence.

Mike wondered if he opened his eyes, would the room be the same? Regardless, would the phone ring again? If he kept his eyes closed, would he be free of this waking nightmare?

He felt a rush of air across his face. No, not air. *Breath*. His stomach knotted and a lump rose into his throat. He felt his face somehow retreat into his skull.

Another breath on his face. It was warm and odourless. He stumbled backwards onto the floor, opening his eyes instinctively. The blue walls were gone, replaced by bright white in every direction. The vibrations in the 'room' seemed more intense.

'No, it's not a dream.' A man now stood over Mike, smiling. His face seemed almost a caricature, pale and pencil-drawn. Mike recognised him as Asian, possibly Chinese or Korean. 'I can hear all that, you know. In your head. It's just electricity. Brain waves.'

Mike thought: *you can fuck off then*.

'How amusing!' Angelo cried with delight. 'What a developed vocabulary. Anyway, before you so rudely hung up the phone, I asked you a question. Why are you here?' The crisp voice was as before, but deeper now it was delivered in the flesh.

Still fairly paralysed with fear, Mike spoke uneasily. 'If you can already hear my thoughts, why are you asking me?'

The Asian man sneered. '*Why are you here?*'

'The girl. PP. I'm looking for PP.'

'Ah, PP. Yes. After Midnight. You know about that then. But we don't have any dead girls here. Not *here*.'

136

Mike detected a divergence in his voice, from mock sincerity to something more sinister. 'Okay. No dead girls. That's fine. Can I... can I go then?'

Angelo chuckled again. Now Mike could see his face, it was a pure laugh – not edged with malice but somehow trustworthiness. In spite of his young appearance, the laughter rose from his cheeks and pressed a web of wrinkles around his eyes.

The man leaned slightly forward and winked playfully. 'Not just yet, Mikey-boy. Not just yet.'

~~~

Lara snapped awake – a pain rising in her torso. She moaned as loud as she could through the duct tape. Piotr snapped awake too and looked over at her from his mattress.

'Toilet?'

She nodded. As humiliating as it was, using the lavatory at gunpoint, Lara had got used to Piotr's rules over the last few days. He kept saying he wasn't going to hurt her and that they were all alone down there, yet he kept her gagged and watched her like a hawk at every turn once she was let off the pole. He never pointed the gun directly at her, which led her to believe he really wasn't going to shoot her, but she felt that it was time to try to find out more about her situation.

Piotr got up and unbound her, then stood back. He smiled weakly. 'Are you okay?'

Lara nodded. She really didn't know what other response would be acceptable to this man – a man who she thought was her friend. She went to pull the duct tape from her mouth and shrugged at him.

'Okay,' he said.

Although he hadn't been applying the tape tightly, it still hurt each time it was ripped off. Lara winced.

'Piotr. How much longer...'

'Not long now,' he said. 'It's almost over.' He looked at his feet and back at her. 'You must understand I am sorry to do this. What your father did to my sister. I cannot let that be any longer.'

Lara shifted on her feet, the pain in her bladder growing stronger. 'I just want to go home. I just...' She turned and walked unevenly down the passage to the toilet, her bare feet scraping along the stone floor. Piotr followed her.

'Why can't you let me go? I'll lay low somewhere. It's really painful being... tied up here. It's so painful.'

'I know. I know.'

'What are you going to do to my father?'

'He will pay. An eye for an eye.'

Lara looked up from the toilet, the sound of heavy rain echoing off the curved walls. 'You're... you mean you're going to kill me?'

Piotr looked at the gun in his hand. He had no intention of hurting this beautiful girl. This girl who reminded him so much of Halina, who Lazarou raped and raped and raped and raped.

'I'm sorry,' he said. 'It will all be over soon.'

Lara wiped herself and closed the cassette toilet. She started walking back to her pole. 'Please, Piotr. Please. I'm begging you. Don't tie me up. There's nowhere I can go. I don't even know where we are. *Please*.'

Piotr put the gun down on his mattress. He was too tired to overthink it. What could this girl do in the middle of the night? She was as worn out as him, or so it seemed. And he felt that she had empathised – her initial expression of cold fear had morphed into one of emotional appeal. He'd read about a syndrome where a hostage came to sympathise with their captor. Could this be it?

'Okay,' he sighed. 'Just don't... don't try anything. I don't want to hurt you.' He motioned to his mattress. Lara looked at him gratefully and shrugged, as if to say *really?* He nodded. 'It's fine. Just... I'll be watching. Here...' He leaned over and pulled a bottle of water out of a plastic bag. 'Have this.'

Lara drank the water and sat on the mattress. She smiled weakly up at him. Something caught in her throat as she saw the gun at the end of the bed. He saw her looking at it.

'Don't...'

'I wouldn't,' she said. 'Piotr, you're my friend. Aren't you?'

He frowned and bent down to get the gun. 'Yes. Of course.'

~~~

'You *should* take this personally, Michael. We don't often reveal ourselves, but then once in a while we happen on someone like you.

138

You're not quite as shit-brained as most of them. You have qualities. You think about things. We admire that.

'Frankly it's easier to tell you the truth than make up some lie and have you sniffing around here again, so I'll lay it all out for you. We don't kill girls. They're no use to us dead.'

Mike felt himself relaxing a little. 'Use the girls for what?'

'That's not really any of your business, see. But we don't kill them.' Angelo paused. 'We like you guys in law enforcement. You've got the right idea. You know what's right and what's wrong and all that. You're especially good at appreciating the stakes in a situation.

'So here's the thing. You have no jurisdiction here. We're going to let you walk out of here. Your superior told us there wouldn't be anyone coming round here, but *here you are*. That's intuition. We love it when you show intuition, but there's a time and a place, and neither of those are now or here.

'So we're going to let you go home, have a stiff drink, and get a good night's sleep. Tomorrow you forget all about this lead of yours and get back to finding that poor little girl who's been kidnapped. We like intuition. Free thinking. If you think about this situation, you'll appreciate how close you just came to the end of your life.'

The only thoughts Mike had were of the girl hanging from the ceiling then scratching at his chest.

'Her? Of course, you're wondering who that girl was! She's no one. Unreal. Just a projection. Once we're inside your head we can put anything there. Art has no boundaries! All that imagery is already in your head so we know what frightens you.

'But back to business. It's simple. We're in your head now. You popped up on our radar and forced us to deal with you. It's pretty likely you could have gone through your whole life never finding out about us. Hardly anyone does. It's a hoot!'

Mike didn't think it was a hoot. He didn't have any opinion yet on any of this. He'd stumbled into a paranormal or supernatural or whatever the fuck it was nightmare and his only solid conclusion was that he'd be delighted to take the offered reprieve.

'The wise choice, my good man. But let me be clear. You put yourself in front of us. Now you know us. We know each other. You won't feel us watching but we most certainly are. And there's a cost. We do things for our friends, and we expect the same back from you.'

139

The unanswered question which had been fizzing in Mike's brain throughout this incredible monologue – *who's we?* – remained. He knew his well-spoken, diction-to-die-for host could hear his thoughts just as clearly as his voice, so why wasn't he answering this?

'If you must insist, we are the ordinary, Michael. There's no need for you to put a label on us. We are not really within your comprehension. We don't want to tell you too much because... well, as you are fond of saying, we'd have to kill you!'

He paused, smiled and pointed to a doorway. 'Goodbye, Michael.'

Having taken his eyes off Angelo for just a second or two, he was now gone. Mike surveyed the room. It was empty, a white-walled room too small for any of the previous events to have happened in. He moved towards the doorway and found himself back in the corridor. Just a few feet away was the back door he had snuck into minutes earlier. He pushed against it and walked out into the yard, turning to watch it close. He felt as raw as he ever had.

His head lazily turned back to the fence as two girls appeared from the alley, giggling together. They shot him an awkward glance but walked past him and up to the door. One girl knocked. The door beeped and clicked open. Mike watched as they went into the building, the corridor back to its original red colour, the sound of music close inside. He sensed the camera watching him, turned away and left.

Thirteen – Comings and goings

Maria fell asleep quickly. Jez's mother opened three bottles of wine over dinner. Maria insisted on cooking and found a good selection of ingredients in the kitchen. By the time dinner was over, the three of them were full and, Sue said, 'fabulous'. She had become instantly enchanted with Maria. Jez wondered how different it might have been if his dad had been there.

Jez sat on his sofa rolling a joint. His mother had taken the spare room while Maria slept in his. As he rolled it, a family photo on the fireplace mantelpiece caught his eye. He found his gaze shifting to it, pulling his concentration from the reefer. There was his mother, just months away from announcing her departure. His father looked happier than he must have felt. Their marriage had been disintegrating for ages when the photo was taken. And there was Jez, in the middle, smiling as he always did, apparently untouched by the heartache in the house.

His fingers rolled at the paper as he felt drawn in. *Something isn't right*, his photo self said. *You know something is wrong.* He looked away from the photo, suddenly feeling very self-conscious. *What kind of prick stares at his own picture?* He looked back to the reefer-in-progress and finished the roll, then licked the paper and twisted the end.

The photo pulled him in again. *You still haven't got to the bottom of the video, Jez. What was all that about? Who made it and why did it vanish? Who was behind that camera?*

He snapped himself away and walked through the kitchen, opened the back door and shut it gently behind him. The first drag was strong – Col always got good weed and Jez always rolled them loose. About half way down the joint, its effects kicked in like a warm fog settling over his brain. He felt his face heat up slightly as the warmth spread throughout his body.

A noise behind startled him but it barely registered. The back door opened and his mother stepped out. She wore a dressing gown and slippers, just like she would have done before she left. It reminded Jez of happier times.

'Any of that going spare?' she asked, smiling.

Jez held the joint aloft and regarded it with satisfaction.

'Sure.' He passed it over. 'So... you really love this guy, huh?'

141

His mother took a shallow drag and did a good job of disguising her gag reflex. 'Yes, I do. It's nothing personal, honey. Just didn't work out with your dad and I. Life is never simple. With your dad, it... it was like we were two batteries powering a torch, and mine just ran out of juice first.'

Jez smiled ruefully. 'So I'm getting a stepdad. Cool.'

~~~

Piotr sat watching Lara as long as he could before his eyes closed to sleep. He'd been fighting it for over an hour, the gun in his hand growing heavier in tandem with his eyelids.

Lara rode it out – despite her exhaustion, she stayed awake, waiting... and when she was sure Piotr was asleep, she made her move.

As his eyelids flickered, Piotr's dream began. He was on a train, sitting opposite Lara. Next to her was Amanda, and next to him Selena – his latest victim. Their heads were hung, the three of them praying.

Lord give us the strength to stand up to the devil and rebuke him in your name. Lord Jesus the Father we bless you and stand up in your name...

Piotr felt himself compelled to stand, to distance himself from this holy trio. The carriage was full of replicas – him, the three girls praying, all the way ahead of him. He moved up the carriage, hearing their whispers as he went, blending in and out of each other, like wind through a treetop.

As he got closer to the next carriage, he could see a figure moving towards him. Further still and he realised it was his reflection. He felt something wrapping around him and looked down. Limbs twisted and slithered like snakes around his legs, binding him in place. But even as he stopped, his reflection advanced. He tried to push and pull against the slithering mass but they were too many; too strong.

The limbs filled his view now, writhing over each other and forming some giant fluid mass of arms and legs. His reflection pushed through them, unbothered, and came to stand right in front of him.

When will you wake up? Look at what you've done. When will you...

Lara knew she wouldn't be able to make a run for it, at least not yet. Her body was knackered: dehydrated, underfed and as tired as it had ever been.

'Wake up!' This time she kicked him, jumped back and levelled the gun at him. Piotr stirred and leapt up to a squat, his eyes fixed on the gun.

'Lara. Don't. Please put it down.'

'No... no way. Tell me where we are. I promise... I'll shoot you. I fucking will.'

Her face looked grim in the meagre light of the almost discharged lamp Piotr had left on for the night. The moonlight cast a shard down the slope of the drain and across the ground to her feet.

Piotr got up to his feet as Lara trained the gun on his head. He started to move towards her.

'Stop! I will... I'll fucking shoot you!' Her voice was shrill, fearful and shaky.

Piotr stopped right in front of her, the gun pressing against his face.

'I'm not stupid.' He put his hands up in mock surrender. 'Go on. Shoot me.'

Lara buckled. She shouted: 'How do I get out of here?'

'Pull the trigger!' Piotr thought how it would be wonderful if the gun was loaded; to end it all. But he still had work to do. 'It isn't loaded,' he sneered.

Lara let out a scream as she kicked down into Piotr's ankle, the one she'd seen him sprain earlier. He howled in pain and reeled back, tripping over the edge of the mattress and falling onto it. She threw the gun and it bounced off his shoulder, skittering across the floor until it came to rest against the wall she'd been up against for days.

She looked around for something else to hit him with but couldn't find anything. Piotr looked up from the mattress, a wave of concern appearing on his face. Lara followed his gaze towards the slope of the drain.

'Fuuuuck!' Piotr struggled up and started after her. 'No!'

The horrible realisation hit him in the gut. He had been so tired and pre-occupied when he got back and slipped down the slope, he'd forgotten to secure the rope ladder and lock the grating. 'No!' He scrambled up to his feet and ran towards her.

Lara jumped onto the slope, just catching the rope enough to pull herself up. She missed Piotr's grabbing hand by less than an inch as she shimmied up. He reached again and this time caught the end of the rope. He tugged at it and tried to pull himself up. 'Owwwww.' His ankle twisted and gave way as he fell back onto his arse.

Lara stopped for a brief look back and saw him awkwardly rising up from the fall, pushing up from his side to get on his knees.

'You were supposed to be my fucking friend!' she screamed at him. 'You bastard. You fucking bastard!'

She made it to the top and climbed out of the grating, pulling the ladder up and out. She laid it on the grass behind her and turned back to the hole.

Piotr stood at the foot of the slope, the shard of moonlight painting his face with a serene glow. 'Please,' he said through a heavy breath. 'I never meant to...'

'Shut up. Just shut up! Where are we? Where is this place?'

Lara looked across the field for clues but saw just grass bathed in a soft glow. 'Tell me!' Her voice was raspy and hysterical.

Piotr put his hands up again, his breathing still heavy and laboured. 'I can't get out of here. That ladder... is the only way. Please don't leave me here.'

'You've got to be fucking joking!' Lara exhaled theatrically and shook her head. 'No! What I am going to do right now is go to the police and lead them back here so they can lock you fucking up and throw away the key and...'

'Please!' Piotr looked genuinely distraught. 'You have to understand. I was doing this for you, for Halina.'

'Doing this for me? How exactly was this for me? What have you done for me?'

Piotr put his arms down, his expression pleading. 'The girls. I've been... setting them free.'

'What girls?'

'You know what he makes them do. Your father. He is the devil. I am the angel.'

'You're out of your fucking mind!' Lara screamed. 'You've killed people?'

'I did it for you!'

Lara felt a rush of dizziness, stumbled backwards and fell. She didn't attempt to get up but stared up at the night sky. The Moon was bright and the stars all seemed to be out, staring down at her in this field. She breathed deeply, calming herself, and got back to her feet.

Piotr disappeared from her view back into the darkness of his prison. 'You can fucking rot in there.'

144

Lara realised she was cold – and lost. At least in the storm drain she'd been warm. Now, in this alien place, with no sense of direction to safety, for a moment she contemplated the wisdom of going back in. *No. Don't be stupid. No.*

She was stood pretty close to a hedgerow which seemed to go on forever in both directions, tapering into the darkness of the night. She walked over to it and noted she was too short to see over it, so she reached up to gain some leverage in the hope of climbing at least up and hopefully over. *It could be someone's back garden. It could be anything.*

Her fingertips pushed into the hedge and she recoiled instantly. A splinter had gone into her middle finger and hurt like hell. She heard a clanging sound coming from the storm drain and went back to the hole, clutching her injured finger tightly.

Oh shit. Piotr was half way up an unfolded step ladder, climbing quickly. Lara leant in to push the ladder backwards but recoiled when she saw the gun in his hand. She quickly got her foot under the grating and kicked it over to cover the hole. The sturdy padlock which was loosely hanging off the grate came off completely and she went for it. Leaning back out of Piotr's line of sight, she managed to hook the padlock around the grate and closed it just as he got to the top.

'Kurwa!' Piotr slammed his palm against the grate. It budged a little but nowhere near enough. He slid down the ladder a little and pointed his gun at the padlock. A shot rang out but the bullet missed the target. 'Kurwa!'

Lara sprang away from the drain, panting. *Oh shit oh shit oh shit oh shit oh...* She turned back to the hedgerow and realised it was her only chance of escape. If she ran across the field, Piotr would easily be able to shoot her down, or worse. Getting over the hedge would give her new options.

Another shot rang out. 'Fuck it. You'd better run, Lara. You'd better fucking run!'

She did. Heading straight for the hedge, she leapt up it and jammed her feet into the side, managing to get her elbows on the top ridge. She howled as her bare left foot split on a thorn but pushed as hard as she could. Her right knee joined her arm and she pushed harder still with her left foot, now spurting a thin spray of blood. She didn't feel it.

Another shot. This time it hit and ricocheted out of the grating. The padlock broken, Piotr slammed his palm once again and the hatch flew open. 'I'm coming!'

Lara swung her right hand over the top of the hedge and flailed desperately trying to grab onto anything she could use to lever herself over completely. Her face was pressed hard into the hedge, scratching against the spiky protrusions as she edged over. Then Piotr came into view, his face furious. She knew at that moment he was going to kill her. He raised the gun, slowly, as if to relish this moment of finality.

'Please,' she said, her voice weak and scared. 'Please.'

Piotr levelled the barrel at her face, steadying the butt in two hands. 'I'm sorry,' he said. 'It was not supposed to…'

Lara's hand found something and she gripped it with all her might and just as Piotr let out his last shot, she swung her left leg up and over, rolling off and landing on the hard earth the other side of the hedgerow. She had no idea the bullet missed her head by less than an inch before it disappeared into the darkness.

As she scrambled up to her feet, a shooting pain ran up from her left foot, piercing her brain just as the bullet almost did. She screamed in pain. *Fuck fuck fuck fuck…* Now she had three options: run straight ahead across this new, but much safer field and vanish into the night or go right or left along the hedgerow. She looked both ways along it and jumped backwards as she heard Piotr clattering on the other side.

Shit. The ladder. He's getting the ladder!

She chose left and ran as fast as she could into the darkness, her pace frenzied, her heart ready to explode from her chest and her feet now both shooting raw pain all the way up her body.

By the time Piotr had re-assembled the step ladder and hobbled with his sprained ankle over the hedgerow, Lara was long gone.

~~~

Everything was moving along nicely. Stanley poured himself and each of his guests a glass of water. It had always seemed to him perverse that beings with such mastery of electricity as they had could interact so freely with water. Its purity and clarity fascinated him. They could travel with electricity, their dark essence breaking down into an almost microscopic physicality. They could manipulate it and send messages via electrical frequencies and microwaves in the air. These channels of electrical activity criss-crossed the globe, and with their exquisite ability to hop between hot spots along these lines, the ordinary were free to roam – sharing with humans, as they did, the limitations of stamina.

Certainly, as Robert had found since his assimilation, one could not travel very far using these methods – a good deal of footwork was involved too. Indeed, the distances covered were relatively short in global terms yet finding these energising hot-spots kept fatigue at bay. It was not something the consciousness seemed to understand; it just was what it was. What the consciousness definitely did understand was its weaknesses, however, and this potential fatigue figured highly on that short list.

With that concern, born of a heightened sense in the consciousness that it was indeed concerning, the ordinary had over time become almost lazy in approach, like a sloth slowly feeding and only when it needed to; in the ordinary's case this manifested very similarly.

Stanley was quite the opposite. He had found himself with a thirst for the black stuff, relishing in his abilities and the flow he could create with a good push of effort. He had much enjoyed manipulating certain personalities in his home town and had never felt much need to leave or explore. In his previous human existence he had been well travelled, his thirst then for knowledge and experience. Now none of that was necessary. His urge was primal rather than ruled by potential.

Assimilations had been growing in frequency as the ordinary's goal came ever closer. The nerve centre in America had spiked just days ago, its warmth spreading among the consciousness. Some business with a rogue agent at large following the fiery destruction of a coastal town had invigorated Stanley, his feelers attuned perhaps more than those of his brethren to the bigger picture. As his previously human intelligence had been high, and more essentially inquisitive, these traits had carried over with his rebirth.

That business in America had made the news in the UK six months previously. Three police officers had been accused of starting a fire that killed thousands, but with the dearth of evidence to prove such, they had walked. This of course was handled expertly by the ordinary but also what followed was caused by their relative incompetence and inability to control certain variables that hinged on free will.

The main agent, a man named Joe, had found himself wandering around in the hallowed corridors of Raven – the place they affectionately called the House of Pigs. Joe had been assimilated as a child following a family tragedy, but due to a gross oversight by some particular ordinary his fragmented echo personality had walked out of their domain. The 'real' Joe, somehow, had been mislaid.

Stanley could have expended much effort in entering the domain himself, but this was not something the ordinary's foot soldiers – effectively what he and his dark colleagues were – ordinarily did. It would be a long and exhausting journey and he would not be welcomed anyway. The thousands of deaths that day had fuelled the dark harvest so much, and although Stanley had never directly experienced the consumption of a human soul, he felt some sense of it through the consciousness, along with the satisfying payoff.

This man, Joe, had been pivotal. Assimilated children had qualities that would have been ironed out in adulthood, but Joe's development was rapid and he was a very useful puppet for the ordinary. When he had returned as an echo to the domain and been assimilated back in, the balance had been restored. This was as much to do with careful manipulation of a potentially explosive rogue ingredient as it was the supervision of friends in high places.

What really mattered was the ultimate goal. Scorched earth and souls devoured was a voluminous shot in the arm for the ordinary and with it came the greater sense of urgency to devour more, to spread and to fulfil the circle. As clear as all this was in Stanley's mind, so it was in Robert and Angelo's, the clarity coming from close proximity. It reminded Robert of a passage in the *Bible* – something about fellowship making the faith stronger.

As Robert experienced in his new form, trying to latch on to distant frequency spikes resulted in muffled, confused feedback. Now, sitting with his brethren in Stanley's very own hot-spot, in the delightfully understated environs of his office, some of the more distant frequencies came through crisp and clear.

Stanley, Robert and Angelo sat in silence, swirling around each other's thoughts. Angelo could have assimilated the policeman, Michael Danson, very easily, but the consciousness had not demanded it. He could prove useful in the coming hours and days. Taking his colleague, Peter Mathers, was not a wise move either. Steve and his minions had seen to it that an arrangement was made as to his future leanings – unwittingly taking part in a movie that humans might die watching.

148

Although the future of humanity was now so short that it hardly mattered what any of them were doing, keeping the balance was more important than ever. Mere hours away, in this terrible event the ordinary were about to become extraordinary.

Fourteen – One last job

Good morning and welcome to Daytime. *Today's major headline: internet magazine* The Juice *releases porn actress killer's sick video of second killing. Analysis and comment later in this programme. Also this morning: Bangladeshi terrorist sect vows to 'get revenge' on Iranian head of state; disgraced former MP Paul Johnson denies drink and drug driving charges; and Chancellor Eric Simons touches down on the first day of his European financial summit tour.*

'That's another shot in the arm!' Jack rubbed his hands together while grinning over his desk at Marcus. 'I know it's a bit sick but if I ever get to meet this bastard, I'm gonna shake his hand.'

'Me too.' Marcus didn't mean that. Although he was now in demand as a direct result of the killer's benevolence, he didn't share Jack's apparent ambivalence towards these disgusting, unthinkable crimes.

'I've got a lot of meetings today, and by the looks of things so have you. I've got a stack of emails here asking if you're available for comment. Rather you than me. I'll forward them in a bit.'

The news broadcast continued with pixellated footage of the second video with a voiceover explaining that the victim this time was adult actress Selena Clark, aka Keira Sweet. The video stopped just short of the decapitation.

~~~

'Get up.'

Jock pushed up against the wall and managed to get onto his feet. Dazed and confused, he began to recall the events which led to this point. He remembered his confrontation with Steve outside, then being dragged into the building at gunpoint. He'd been marched up a corridor, up a flight of stairs, and then shoved into a room – a dormitory of sorts. A group of girls had been told to get out. That was the last thing he remembered.

Steve, whoever Steve was, had been replaced by a stocky boy who Jock assumed was barely out of school. He spoke with an eastern European accent: 'Come with me.'

150

Jock followed the manchild out of the room and up another flight of stairs. He climbed the stairs uneasily, fatigued by whatever they'd put in his system the night – he thought it had been just one night – before. The manchild waited at the top and pointed down a corridor. 'There.'

Jock got to the top and followed his gesture. Across from the stairs was an open door where he could see girls sitting on a bed and giggling. Up from that was another door, ajar. Muffled laughter came from within.

He felt a push from behind and stumbled forward. 'Now. Get in.'

His head fuzzier from the forced exercise, Jock made his way to the end of the corridor. The two doors he passed on the other side were both open, showing larger rooms made up like movie sets. He'd seen many of the kinds of movies filmed in such places.

The manchild brushed past him and rapped twice on the door. A voice called from the other side. He pushed the door open and nudged Jock inside.

'Sit down, Neil.' Steve smiled. He seemed completely different to the man who had overcome Jock in the yard. 'How you doing today?'

Jock's mouth curled to one side as he sat down opposite his host. The room reminded him of somewhere. It was a plush office – dark red walls and leather furnishings, a classical wooden desk that looked like it cost thousands, and soft lighting in the corners. He realised then it looked very much like Stanley's. He'd been in that office several times and this one didn't only look like it, it felt like Stanley's.

'I'm dandy, thanks mate. And it's Jock.' His expression was calm and cold.

'Good, good. *Jock*. Sorry about all that yesterday. Nothing personal. Just Stanley gets a little tired sometimes and we needed you for a bit.'

'Needed... me?'

'Yes, yes. A little insurance.' Steve smiled broadly and opened his palms out gratefully. 'I have a job for you.'

'What's your name, pal?' Jock sat up straight.

Steve's face dropped a little. 'You know my name, pal.'

'Okay, Steve... or whatever the fuck your name is. Listen to me. I don't work for you. I don't know what you've done to me here, but I'm out. I'm gonna stand up and go down the fuckin' stairs and that's it. Okay?'

Steve stood up and put his hands on the desk, leaning onto it. He laughed. 'No, pal. *You* listen to *me*.' Jock stood up, ready to have a go.

151

'Sit the fuck down!' Hands grabbed Jock's shoulders from behind and forced him back into the seat.

'Stanley told me you're capable. That's why he sent you round here. Just having a bit of fun, he was. You enjoyed our little joke, yes?'

With this information came the dawning of a thought – he'd been in that room, drugged and unconscious for hours in the house that porn built.

'I'm not seeing the funny side, mate. No.'

'That's fine. It was more for us anyway.' Steve grinned. 'Let's not waste any more time then.'

Jock shrugged the hands off his shoulders and sensed the man back away behind him. 'What've you got on me then? And...' He hesitated. 'Where's Bleach?'

'Ah,' Steve started. 'Well... let's just say we've got a great distribution network and a few good scenes of you with some ladies in demand. We think the authorities might want a word if they ever saw this stuff. Bleach is... your friend? Sorry, he didn't make it.'

Jock's stomach turned as the hazy recollection faded into his mind's eye. He saw a corpse, lying out in front of him. He had a long... kitchen knife in his right hand and he was plunging it down into the corpse, blood spraying up and all around. *What is this what am I doing what is going on...*

Steve noted Jock's pained expression. 'Oh, good. You remember a little, yes? As I said, we have a job for you.'

Jock opened his eyes, not realising he had shut them in the first place, and noticed on his wristwatch it was just gone six AM. He felt an uneasy mixture of relief and horror at the thought of Bleach being gone. Although he didn't exactly *like* the bloke, there was a soft spot. 'For fuck's sake... okay. So what do you need? Y'know, Stanley could've asked me himself if...'

Steve bolted around the desk and shot his hand around Jock's throat. It happened so quickly that Jock had no time to move. Steve's other arm joined his leg across Jock's lap, restraining his hands. He gripped the throat hard as he thrust Jock's head back against the head of the armchair and leaned in until they were nose to nose.

'You fucking *runt*.'

Jock's breathing was restricted. He couldn't speak. Steve withdrew by a foot and fixed his eyes on Jock's. *He's having a nosebleed*, Jock

152

thought. A thin dark strand of blood seemed to drip from his assailant's nostril and then onto his top lip. But the strand didn't stop and began to curl upwards from his lip as it was joined by another and then another. They writhed around each other and came closer to Jock's face as he found he was pushing his head back into the chair more than Steve's fist was, terrified.

The strands touched his skin and his body seized up in fear, his eyes bulging with raw terror. They slithered over his mouth and cheeks and were joined by more, these finding their way into his own nostrils and snaking their way up. He felt them entering his sinuses, spreading out over the ridges of his cheeks and curling up towards his eyes, holding his face in place. Steve's eyes were liquid black, a fog swirling around his pupils. Then in a flash the snakes were whipped out of Jock's head, disappearing back around Steve's septum.

He released his grip on Jock and stood back up. Jock hurled himself forward and vomited, falling to his hands and knees. He gasped for breath a few times and looked up at Steve, his face still contorted with abject fear.

Steve smiled down at him. 'Do I have your attention now, pal? First thing: you can clear that shit up.'

~~~

Lara awoke suddenly. Immediately discombobulated by her surroundings and shivering, she instinctively wrapped her arms tightly around her chest. She had found a small hollow set into a group of bushes, which in the night had appeared close to something like a public park. She felt like she had made it back close to town but this escape had run her down completely. The safest thing to do, she reasoned, was hide. She had fallen to her knees and crawled into the bush and within moments had passed out.

Now, with the light of a new day streaming down, but too early for its warmth to heat the earth and air, Lara was conscious and in excruciating pain. She immediately localised this to her left foot and twisted it around so she could see. A short but solid protrusion was surrounded by cracks in the skin, spattered with caked blood. She reached down and carefully pinched the top of the splinter. The pain hit her straight in the forehead.

153

She recoiled back against the branches as motion to her right startled her back into consciousness, then calmed as she saw two human legs followed by four animal legs – a man walking his dog. Relief set in right away. She was somewhere safe, potentially at least, and reasoned – as she had over and over in Piotr's prison – that people would know who she was if she ever made it out alive.

Lara tugged at the splinter and it came out a little, accompanied with another blast of pain. Gritting her teeth and inwardly screaming, she pulled and twisted and it came out, followed by a trickle of blood. She raised this miniature death trap up to eye level and focused on its sharp point. *Bastard. You sharp little bastard.*

She rolled forwards onto her knees and crawled back out of the bush, slowly, keeping an eye out for any psychopathic Polish teachers. The dog walker was about a hundred feet away now, disappearing around a pavilion next to some tennis courts. Now she realised where she was – Prince's Park, at the far end of the promenade from where she needed to be. She had no idea how far she'd run or for how long, but she'd made it.

She turned around and could see the rest of the park, stretching off towards town, and hobbled in that direction, looking over her shoulder as she went.

~~~

Stanley reached his back door and opened it.

'Ah, Neil! How wonderful! I trust you enjoyed your stay next door?' He chuckled and beckoned Jock in with his index finger – *come hither.*

Jock stepped in and closed the door behind him. He didn't feel like talking.

'It's just in here. There you go...' Stanley pushed the door open and Jock shuffled around him to go inside. It was the same room he and Bleach always took the body bags into. Now there was a single body bag in the middle of the room.

He bent over and picked it up, the ends folding over his arms as whatever was inside rolled to the extremities. 'Shit,' he muttered, looking back at Stanley in the doorway.

'It's just a few... bits.' Stanley laughed again. 'I'm afraid your friend... came to bits rather easily.'

154

Jock's stomach twisted further, the horrors of the last few days building the tension in his temples. He knew it was Bleach inside – Steve had explained that – but he hadn't been prepared to find him in scraps. He let the bag drop and held it up in one hand. The lumps inside all dropped to one end. He felt momentarily like he was carrying Santa's sack, making his final delivery to the home of young Master James Bleach, who really, really had not been a good boy this year.

Reinforcing the image, he slung the bag over his shoulder and made his way out of the room.

'Goodbye, Neil,' Stanley smiled smugly.

Jock's van was still parked outside. He loaded Bleach's mercifully concealed remains into the back and set off.

~~~

Piotr's alarm woke him up quickly. He'd gone to sleep knowing he wouldn't have much time to make his own escape. If Lara had made contact with anyone, the police would be all over that storm drain very soon. He had to hope that in the heat of it all she wouldn't have had any bearings. She might even not have made it back to town, but he had no way of knowing.

In his own heated moment, Piotr had gone back into the drain to take care of some loose ends. He didn't need to cover his tracks anymore. They knew who he was, just not – hopefully – *where* he was. He turned his mobile phone on and listened to several messages, two of which were from his friend Skip.

Skip had helped him with his plan but he hadn't told him where he was going to keep the girl. That information was exclusive. Now, though, what he really needed was a friend. He'd called Skip back before going to sleep at about four AM. Skip was awake anyway, it turned out. He told Piotr to sit tight while he got his shit together and he'd follow Piotr's directions and be there by seven.

What Piotr didn't realise was Skip's offer of help was quite the opposite. Herr Asmann had given him twenty-four hours to locate Piotr, and he had been entirely fortunate to take that phone call while preparing for his own imminent demise. His time was almost up when the phone beeped. Even while he sympathised with fake sincerity, Skip felt only relief at his own promised stay of execution rather than any emotional response to what he knew was about to happen to his old friend.

Asmann had seen this in his face as he relayed the information. He thanked Skip for his co-operation and left. Not much later he was standing in the field, mere feet from the hatch where he could hear Piotr's alarm going off.

~~~

Jock arrived at Bleach's block and parked as close as he could. Taking the girls in and out had always been under cover of darkness but now he had to sneak this bag of bones back in without anyone seeing. Seizing the moment, he swung the van door open and pulled the body bag out and slung it over his shoulder. He kicked the door shut and strode quickly over to the building. The lobby door, as always, was propped open. He headed inside and pressed the 'tradesman's button' – the notion crossing his mind as it always did that this button entirely sidestepped the whole point of having a security door in the first place – and pulled it as it clicked open.

He hurried up the stairs. It was a far more private option than waiting for the lift, potentially having to share the ride with someone. The bag felt heavier with every step and by the time he reached Bleach's floor he was out of breath. After all, despite being in pieces now, he still weighed the same. Something appeared to be sloshing around in there too. Jock did not want to see, and he wouldn't have to.

He'd got his instructions and knew full well he had to carry them out. Steve, and Stanley by association, had him over a barrel. Do this or die. He didn't want to die.

Jock dropped the body bag outside Bleach's door and reached in his pocket for his multitool. It was one of his favourite possessions – a sturdy wedge of five by two inches with an assortment of attachments, one of which would be perfect for prising the door open.

He found it, drew out what was effectively a mini crowbar and wedged it hard into the door frame. He pulled against it with a good deal of force and the door sprang open. Jock wondered why it was still so easy to force someone's front door open. Having built up experience in the home-raiding-and-taking-anything-valuable-corps when growing up in Scotland, it was as easy now as it had ever been. For all the advances in

156

technology, home security remained a luxury that only the wealthy could really afford or be bothered with. Still, he reasoned, Bleach owned nothing of value anyway.

He dragged the bag into the flat and shut the door, resting the bag against it to hold it shut against the broken lock. The living room was messy from the night before. Three presumably empty cans of lager, a half-full bottle of gin and assorted drug paraphernalia sat on the coffee table next to an open A4 notepad. The duvet and pillow Jock had seen on the couch a couple of days earlier were still there.

The room was silent – an eerie atmosphere Jock had not experienced in that flat before. Bleach always had plenty to say. Jock used to mock his verbal diarrhoea, but they'd had some fairly deep conversations over the years.

He recalled one they'd had about patriotism a while back. Bleach had been raised in Kent in a particularly rough area. He'd grown up among what anthropologists might consider akin to a pack of wolves. It was a harsh introduction to society and his rare glimpses of the greener grass elsewhere would pull him out of that reality. Naturally then, Bleach was a daydreamer.

In the vicious circle of social security payments, drug abuse, a seemingly genetic predisposition to alcoholism and a general community feeling of celebrated hopelessness, he was merely a product of the system but he had risen above it intellectually at least, if not necessarily in terms of lifestyle or chosen profession.

Jock was staunchly Scottish. His patriotism was ingrained, something Bleach would continually rib him about. While Bleach claimed that patriotism was always misplaced given that everyone was born into a place and raised within its prescribed customs, Jock maintained that Scotland was the greatest country on Earth.

Bleach maintained he would say that no matter where he was from – if he was born in a toilet it would be the greatest toilet on the planet – but Jock didn't want to hear that argument. As far as he was concerned, Scotland was the greatest country, full stop. On occasion he found his mind drifting towards the subject and always stopped it, acknowledging the fear of losing his national pride. Subconsciously he knew it was a ridiculous notion and realised it really was all random, but he wouldn't admit this officially. It wasn't the only time Bleach's philosophical ramblings had opened Jock's mind a little.

He opened each bedroom door and then the bathroom door. He draped the body bag across the couch on Bleach's duvet and stopped for a moment to look at this odd sight: almost as if he could tuck it in and kiss it goodnight. He went out of the flat onto the landing and smashed the butt of his multitool against the fire alarm. It started ringing immediately.

Back in the flat, the gas hob came on easily and Jock held a wad of newspaper against the edge of the flame. As it burned he saw the remnants of a large photo of the Polish kidnapper looking up at George Lazarou's security camera, the teenage daughter slung over his shoulder just as Bleach's ripped up body had been over his. It was a powerful image to put on a newspaper. At least Jock had his anonymity, as long as he did this job properly. If he didn't, a very nasty movie starring him as a sick bastard with two girls and a bloody blade would be released on the world's largest stage.

He walked with the burning paper past the couch and to the window, holding it under the drawn curtains. They caught fire quickly. Next he took the gin bottle and poured the remainder over the body bag and then on the carpet towards the fire. The room wasn't silent now – the sound of fire rolling over the material and lapping at the ceiling competing with the fire alarm outside, loud and insistent. He could also hear doors slamming and excited voices.

Jock went over to the curtain and quickly pulled at it. The textile fell and spread ash over the carpet. The fire was going out. He found the flamer attachment on his multitool and started waving it over the gin-soaked carpet. It caught right away and snaked across and up to the couch and then on to Bleach's final resting place.

We are gathered here today... he mixed up the metaphor... *to witness the...*

He fell back with shock as the phone rang on the coffee table just behind him, only a couple of feet from the fire which was growing in intensity. He went to grab it but stopped himself. After five rings the answerphone kicked in.

'Hi. This is Bleach. State yer fuckin' business.'

For a few seconds after the beep he heard only static. Then: 'James, it's yer mum. You were s'posed to take me to the shops today. Didya forget? Is everything okay honey?'

158

The fire hot on his face, Jock got up and walked back to the kitchen, taking the notepad from the coffee table with him. Bleach's mother continued delivering her final message to a son who would never hear it.

'Just give me a call, will ya? I miss ya. We can go shopping later or tomorrow. It's okay. Okay... well, love you, James. Give me a ring, eh. Love you. Bye love. Bye.'

The line went dead again as Jock opened the undersink cupboard and emptied its contents onto the kitchen floor. Among the meagre assortment of cleaning materials, he found a bottle simply marked 'Bleach'. He smiled a little as he twisted the cap open and soaked the paper in it, then went into the first bedroom. He could still see where that dead girl had been – a dark stain on the carpet, a spent needle and syringe and her holdall, the one they would have presented to Stanley had she been alive. That explained why Bleach was sleeping on the couch, he realised.

Jock threw the soaked paper onto the bed and noticed ink bleeding through as he leaned in with his multitool flamer, ready to light it. Before he did, he flipped the pad up and saw pages of notes – this was Bleach's book. It never stood any chance of being published anyway, he thought, not now anyway. That ship had sailed when Stanley put him in a bag in pieces. The pad caught fire quickly and within seconds the bed was ablaze.

Jock went back out into the living room, now filling with smoke – the main plumes coming from Bleach's bag. The odour was intoxicating – flesh, plastic, carpet and curtain – and disgusting.

He managed to repeat the arson in the second bedroom but much quicker. The room was smaller than the bedroom Bleach used – at least when it wasn't populated with unconscious or deceased teenagers – but crammed with his stuff. Years of accumulated old records, clothes and bedding, a couple of photo albums, an old bicycle and much more besides were engulfed in the thick flames and smoke within seconds.

Jock was satisfied he'd done enough. He would leave the flat, run down the stairs coughing and looking hurt and emerge into the street below where he would explain how he was a workman doing some plumbing in a flat and then he'd heard the fire alarm and went to check everyone was okay but found a man asleep on his couch and... he just *couldn't* save him. While they discussed this among themselves he would slip away and never be seen again.

An almighty bang came from the kitchen and Jock was knocked to the floor with force. Two saucepans which had been sitting next to the sink flew straight at him, one catching his temple and dropping to the floor as the other caught his chin and rebounded. *Good shot.*

He lifted his head quickly as his left sleeve caught fire. *Oh shit, no.* He rolled over away from the couch and scrambled up, frantically patting his arm to put the flames out. *Shit shit shit.* Another blast came from the kitchen and a moment later he heard the sound of approaching sirens outside.

I've got to get out of...

Another blast ripped through the bedroom wall and sent Jock flying across the room, hitting his back on the lip of the couch and ending up behind it. He got up to his feet and found himself stuck in a ring of fire, from the curtains and wallpaper to his right and Bleach's half-arsed cremation-in-progress in front. The flames licked across the ceiling now and anywhere to his left promised instant death. Back over the couch was the only option.

Jock tried to leap forwards but his foot caught on the lip and he fell flatly onto the burning body bag and slid onto the floor, the bag slipping with him. A slit created by the flames spewed its contents out, spilling underneath Jock and pooling around his head on the floor. A large ball of red hot flesh rolled out and stopped inches from his eyes as he felt his trousers catch fire. He knew exactly what it was, despite never having come this close to Bleach's testicles.

He tried to pull himself forwards, towards the front door – pretty much the only area of the flat that wasn't engulfed in flames – but something held him in place. He was welded now to the couch and body bag, the heat joining his skin and the leather of the couch in a happy, horrific union. As he tried in vain to prise his shoes off, his feet frantically nudging at the soles, no one outside heard his screams above the sirens and gossip.

~~~

'Where ze girl?'

As Piotr emerged from his bunker, Asmann stood calmly a few feet from the hatch. Piotr stopped dead, his bag hanging loosely from his hand.

160

'Are you... with Skip?'

Asmann smiled. 'Yes... and no.'

Piotr shrugged. 'Who are you then?'

'I am Asmann. Get back in ze hole.'

Piotr hesitated before laughing arrogantly. 'What? No. I'm done in there.'

'No, you're not.' Asmann strode towards him. Piotr backed away. His hand twitched as he remembered where his gun was – in the bag.

'I just need to get out of here,' he began, 'so can we...'

Asmann strode closer still, stopping just a foot from Piotr. 'So can we... what? I said get back in ze hole.'

Piotr stepped back. 'Who are you? Where's Skip?'

'Skip isn't my business. You are.'

Piotr reached down with his other hand and started cautiously pulling the slack of his bag up, keeping his gaze fixed on Asmann. He reached inside and felt the butt of the gun.

Asmann grabbed the bag with one hand and Piotr's throat with the other. He whipped the bag away as his other hand lifted Piotr up off the ground. Piotr's hand was still on the gun as it slipped out of the bag. In a flash he pointed it at Asmann's chest and pulled the trigger. Asmann swatted his hand just in time to knock the shot off course, grabbed the barrel and wrenched it from Piotr's grasp.

He smiled up at Piotr as he let his own shot off. This time the bullet hit its target, shattering Piotr's kneecap and embedding in the joint. Piotr howled. Asmann took out the other kneecap, followed by a *click click click click click click* as the chamber failed to refill.

He turned back towards the hatch and effortlessly threw Piotr down onto the grating. Blood sprayed from his knees onto Asmann's polished brogues as he stepped forward and stamped on Piotr's torso, sending him down onto the storm drain's slope. He slid down quickly and, unable to slow himself down against the metal ladder, thumped into the hard concrete surface at the bottom. He howled again, looking down at his knees and the red volcanoes erupting from them.

'You bastard... Wh... who... Who are you? Who the fuck are you?'

Asmann stood at the top of the hatch, his tall frame peering down at his helpless prey. 'I'm Asmann.'

~~~

161

'Mike!' Pete called down the corridor. 'What the hell happened to you last night? Where'd you disappear to?'

Mike wondered the same thing, although he wasn't about to reveal his truth considering the warnings he'd received at the hands of his new boss, Angelo.

'You shut me in that room and what... just left?'

'Uh, yeah. Sorry. Just messing about... I thought you'd see the funny side. Anyway, I got called away.'

Pete shrugged. 'Er... okay. What happened to me was I spent about half-a-fucking-hour banging on that door until someone let me out. And I did your bloody job for you!'

Mike looked at him as if to say: *go on*.

'It's a boarding house. The girl Sierska was right about that. Well, she lives there so that's not a surprise but... I spoke to this Steve guy. He was pretty co-operative actually. He said he did know the girl...'

Chief Briggs appeared outside his office and stopped to observe them for a moment. Pete stopped talking and smiled over at him. 'Guv?'

Briggs shook his head as if irritated and went off towards the front desk.

'Anyway, so the girl, and all those girls, they're PP. As Sierska said. They work on the fairground during the day and get rogered on their days off. It's pretty weird. But...' He looked ruefully at Mike. 'It all looks legal. No evidence of prostitution. Not at first glance, anyway. The girls. Well, they seemed pretty happy. You don't usually see that in a pimp set-up.'

Mike shifted his weight. 'We can't follow it up anyway. There's no case to follow up.' He smiled weakly. 'I am sorry about that last night. And *you* spoiled my stealthy approach!'

Pete laughed. 'Mate. We've been in some hairy situations. That was... a bold approach. They didn't seem to mind though, like they're used to having guys just coming and going. I could've been anyone. And some of those guys in there were built like brick shithouses.'

Mike recalled the events of the previous evening. He hadn't met any burly men or this Steve guy. He'd met a girl spewing brown shit out of her head and pushed his way through a giant pulsating vagina into a doorless office to speak to a charming evil bastard who gave him an easy choice to make.

When he'd found himself back in the yard, he'd reached straight into his pocket and grabbed the wrap, then torn it apart to get at the pill inside. He swallowed it straight away. His last pill. No more. Finito. As he walked back around the front to his car, physically and emotionally wrecked, the pill kicked in, sending warmth rushing inside him and spreading all over. He settled into the driver's seat and processed the events as his drug-induced ultra-clarity set in. They were not, he surmised, the thoughts of a sane man, yet he could recall them in detail. He knew they had really happened because he still *felt* them.

Mack joined them in the corridor. 'Guys. We've got a team raiding *The Juice* in twenty-five. But we've also got this.' She waved a piece of paper under their noses. 'Jackpot.'

'Jackpot?' Pete's face lit up. 'What?'

Mack turned on her heels and opened the ops room door behind her. She beckoned the boys to follow.

'Here. Interpol returned a match on Bogdanek. Although that's not his real name, apparently.'

'Sur... prise!' Pete grinned. 'Of course that's not his real name. Duh.'

Mack continued: 'Here – he's Gabriel Pomorski. Thirty-one years of age. He served a few short sentences back in Poland, let's see... two counts of indecent exposure, two sexual assault and... one aggravated assault. Three years total.'

'Fits his own profile then,' Mike chipped in. 'Have we got anything from the scene?'

Mack sighed. 'It's a bloodbath over there. I'm not going anywhere near it. Poor girl. Unbelievable.'

Pete nodded. 'Is that it then?'

'No.' Mack handed Pete the document. 'On the back there's a précis of a psychological assessment he had after the second sexual assault.'

Pete scanned the assessment. 'It says he's got an obsessive personality and mild paranoid schizophrenia. Okay... and he refers often to a sister, although the doc notes he's an only child.'

'That'll be the schizo,' Mike said. 'Probably another of his personalities. A bit like that case we had last year, where that guy had multiple splits and he'd act very differently depending on which one he was at the time.'

Pete chuckled: 'You've been stuck in your feeble little girl persona for years mate.' He passed the document to Mike.

'It doesn't bring us any closer to finding him,' said Mack. 'Handy information to have though. At least we'll be able to charge him under his real name.'

'What's with the raid on *The Juice*?' Pete asked as Mike scanned the Interpol notes for himself.

'Briggs reckons they might have more than they're letting on. Especially considering they've announced both murders. It also sends a message. Hardly the right channel to be breaking news like that.'

'So what are we doing?' Mike passed the paper back to Mack. Given the events of the previous night, he just wanted to do something – *anything*. 'Is it lunchtime yet?'

~~~

Asmann stood with one foot on Piotr, pressing down on his chest hard. Piotr grunted under the weight, certain a couple of his ribs were cracked and some more were dangerously close to giving way. He'd lost most of the feeling in his legs and couldn't move his arms.

'You look pale, misster. Chall I call you a doctor?'

Piotr grunted but couldn't find the lung capacity to answer.

'Is zis vat you do to ze girls? You stand on zem and butcher zem and make your sick mooviss?' He increased the pressure on Piotr's chest and felt a couple of crunches under his foot. Piotr squirmed and groaned again.

'Really. You made some pretty stupid mistakes here. You know who I am?'

Piotr shook his head. Asmann took his foot away. Piotr let out a loud belch and convulsed in his new freedom. His hands instinctively came up to his chest and clutched it.

'It izzy message,' Asmann said. 'I work for Mr Lazarou. This izzy justice. You do not mess with a man like Lazarou.'

Piotr croaked as he tried to speak. 'I can... I can pay... you... for...'

Asmann reached around under his jacket and produced a pistol with a silencer fitted to the end. 'I have already been paid, my friend. You cannot pay me what Lazarou pay me. He told me make you suffer. But you know what? I need to piss. I see there is a toilet down there, yah?'

Piotr nodded and croaked again. 'Please. I do... need a doctor.'

Asmann said nothing and put his gun down on the floor a few feet from Piotr, then strode over to the toilet tunnel. 'I'll be back... in a tick!'

Piotr eyed the gun desperately. He knew it was a trick. The only reason this man would put it there was to... to give him false hope. He tested his ability in any case and found his body simply unwilling to reach for it. Asmann was coming back.

'Would you like zumthing to drink?' Piotr looked up as Asmann tipped the contents of the cassette toilet over his head. He snapped his mouth shut before much could go in, but his nostrils were less fortunate. After a few seconds he opened his eyes to see Asmann standing over him once more, now pointing the gun straight at his head.

'Do you think you have suffered enough?'

Piotr stared blankly up at him, his face wet and foul with excrement. He was done.

'I am not so sure.'

Fifteen – Love bites

Subject K. Day nine. AM. Subject has stayed in liquid state following ionic balancing. Increased static charge has made no difference. Note: speculation point. It almost seems as if the subject is deliberately refusing to co-operate. Will monitor closely and suggest approval to make subject priority case.

~~~

Jez woke up gently to the sound of Maria humming. He opened his eyes and saw her sitting on the end of his bed, putting her vest on as he stretched. She felt the movement behind her and turned, smiling.

'Hello. Good morning!' she beamed.

Jez beamed back at her and lifted the duvet up a little to beckon her back in.

'Oh, baby. I would love to but I have to do some stuff. I have to go to work.'

Jez sat up quickly. 'Work? No, no, no. Bed!'

'I'm sorry.' Maria stood up and walked over to Jez's dresser. She opened her make-up bag and sat down in front of the mirror. 'I need to get back and get my things. Then I can find somewhere to stay.'

'You can stay here as long as you want,' Jez said excitedly. 'My dad won't mind. He'll like you. Besides, he's not here anyway.'

Maria thought about it all: getting away from the PP house, away from Steve, away from the soft porn before it became hard. It was the right time. She'd been involved with PP for almost two years, first back home in Poland and then for about the last nine months in England. Steve had been understanding and patient with her as she gradually became more adventurous on video, but she hadn't done anything she didn't want to.

She'd felt an odd compulsion to take part at times; something hidden coercing her into things she didn't exactly feel comfortable with. There was a lot of lesbian kissing, a little bit of breast play, and she'd done one scene with a man but no penetration. She knew it was the lower end of porn but it was all part of the market. People paid for all sorts of things.

166

Some of the girls had gone way beyond. Although they had come from all over Poland, she did recognise a few of the girls from back home. One, Anka, had given her whole self over to it in such a destructive way that it made Maria feel sick to think about it. Anka was using hard drugs too. Her soul wasn't in her eyes anymore. She let the men do whatever they wanted. Steve had been relaxed in his approach but he wasn't calling the shots; Maria knew that. He laid down a few ground rules and made it clear that the girls were the property of PP. He would look after them, and in most cases he had done. There were other PP houses too.

Maria knew it was all part of the SkinFlix empire and that some of the girls were called up to work in London and Manchester and some were taken back to Poland. But the distance between what she was prepared to do and what some of the girls ended up in – rape and torture scenes, sadomasochism and bondage, and some really freaky stuff beyond even that – was as far as it could be.

In truth she had never minded exposing her body. She knew boys found her attractive and she could play on that. The movies were easy money too. She'd occasionally joined in with the drugs but never gone harder than cocaine and she'd always felt a little bad doing it, but there was something about the whole world of it that could sweep a girl up.

Although she wasn't really unhappy, Jez was the brightest light to shine on her life in a long time. He was good looking, but not arrogant with it, funny and smart and considerate. Over just a few months she had grown to love him and she knew he felt the same. Being in his house, playing happy families with his mother, brought thoughts of starting some kind of future.

'I'm serious,' Jez said, hooking his legs over the side of the bed. 'You can get your stuff and bring it here. I'll come with you.'

Maria smiled broadly. 'Okay. You better wait outside though. We'll go after breakfast?'

Jez kissed her on the cheek and put his dressing gown on, then left the room. His mother was standing at the bottom of the stairs in her gown, looking distressed.

'Mum? What's wrong?'

'Don't you listen to the messages, Jez?'

'No. Not usually.' He hurried down the stairs. His mother hugged him.

167

'Here. Listen to these.' She pressed the *Play* button on the answer machine. The first message was for Robert – his colleague Jerry asking if he'd gone home for something. The second was Jerry again, sounding cautious. Then the third: 'Hi, Jeremy. It's Jerry, your dad's friend. I'm just checking on something. Give me a ring when you get this message? It's 17652 566466. Cheers.'

'Didn't you say he was with Jerry?'

Jez had said that. It's what his dad told him. He nodded as a lump rose in his throat. He felt like he'd done something wrong.

'So where is he then? Have you got his number?'

Jez nodded again, the lump growing. 'Yes, it's... I've got it on my PDA.' He rushed through to the living room and picked up his PDA, scrolled down his list of contacts and found his father's number. His mother appeared behind him.

'Go on then. What're you waiting for? Ring him!'

It was unusual for his mother to get flustered like this. Even though he hadn't seen her for a while, her easy-going way was consistent. He did remember times when he'd heard his parents arguing, but this was different. She seemed genuinely concerned, like something bad had happened. His mother had always seemed attuned to such things – the good and bad vibes.

Jez paced towards the front door, the phone ringing at the other end. Maria appeared at the top of the stairs, looking concerned too.

'Jez? What's wrong?'

He flashed her a weak smile, all he could muster as his stomach turned. He'd seen it on TV so many times, when a loved parent who happened to be a policeman didn't come home on a fateful day, leaving the family to pick up the pieces. But that was fiction. This was real. He clicked his PDA off the call.

'Answerphone,' he announced. 'I've got a bad feeling.'

Maria ran downstairs and hugged him. She didn't know what to say so she kissed his cheek softly.

~~~

Robert had stood at the back of his garden for hours, concealed in the darkness. For the first time since his rebirth, he had become confused. He had met some kind of mental obstacle when sitting with Stanley and

Angelo, as if he suddenly wasn't able to read them, as if the consciousness had shut him out.

His new form had given him incredible reach but now rather than absolute clarity there was a fog. He tried to reach into it and found nothing, just some kind of void. It was disconcerting.

Angelo had left Stanley's office with a parting suggestion that Robert should go home. While he had perhaps assumed that his new form would not need a home, he was corrected – again, an unexpected sensation that seemed to defy the 'open book' nature of the consciousness. Now he questioned that; he wondered why he now felt disconnected and why he had been effectively dropped in at the deep end.

His home remained his home and his family and friends likewise, although they had no idea of what he had become. They would soon enough though. He would break it to them gently. He realised the Painsley Forest and Jerry situation was unresolved. Jerry would be looking for him and now, as he picked up the frequencies coming from inside his house, he 'heard' Jerry's answerphone messages. He sensed the people in the house and their feelings – of worry and uncertainty. It energised him.

The last thing Stanley had said to him back in his office was that he needed to sort out his family affairs, specifically those of his son, and then his brother. So he had travelled to his old home and waited in the cold, feeling it but not minding at all. He had mentally eavesdropped on his son and this girl, the girl he knew was promised to the ordinary; a girl who had so little darkness in her and yet therefore had immense capacity for it.

Turning someone like Maria into a hopeless, desperate wreck was exactly how the ordinary made progress. Sure, taking hold of those already pushed over the edge was bread and butter, but almost like the old religious concepts of virginity equalling purity, girls like Maria were a prize worth winning.

It made sense then – the coincidence Angelo had alluded to in the cabin: Robert had entirely unwittingly become a key player because of his job on one hand and his family ties on the other. By those measures it was nothing but a coincidence. But still he couldn't read Stanley like he could before and although his human intellect had been replaced, there remained a capacity for doubt.

169

Had Angelo lied to him? How could he even do that within a collective consciousness? He reached out for an answer as he stood in his garden, venturing further than the concern of his son and ex-wife, and the realisation came to him organically: if the ordinary could manipulate frequencies, these were the very same frequencies he was picking up. How could there be, therefore, a one hundred per cent reality?

The world is fluid, he realised. *All we ever see is frequencies*. Brains interpret these colours, sounds and liquids and solids as messages processed along nerves and neurones. The consciousness was no different. This explained how Stanley could act on his own volition and how Angelo could hold back on information. If one could learn to alter or stifle these frequencies – these thoughts, ideas and desires – then the world would be entirely what one made of it.

Robert enjoyed this introspection, far deeper than he had ever gone as a human. His mind, eyes and ears were open. Still, he snapped back to the situation at hand. The ordinary needed to solve this little problem. He needed to solve this little problem.

~~~

'It iss done.' Asmann delivered this single statement and clicked the call off.

George pressed the speaker button on his desk and clapped. 'See, Henry? I told you.'

Henry nodded and smiled. 'So you did.'

'Drink?' George poured himself a full glass of whiskey.

Henry shook his head, still smiling. 'No, thank you.'

'Suit yerself. Now that fucker's dealt with, we can get back to business.'

'Yes, sir. Should I fetch Muriel?'

'She won't give a shit, Henry. All she cares about is little Lara. It's all *La-La* this and *Laralaz* that. Media circus's what she enjoys. She always bought into all that shit.'

Henry returned a blank expression. In the years he had worked for the Lazarous he had never seen any affection in this family. The girl, Lara, had been his favourite – a youthful innocence but with a plucky, knowing streak. He tried to persuade George not to use her in his videos by listing the potential risks to his business. She had no idea. Her intermittent history of blackouts was investigated to a point – neurological and

170

psychological assessment in particular, but never a hint of sexual assault. She was never penetrated anyway – that would be too risky, and George knew that only too well for in his vast, sprawling network was the most base kind of filth. Anything people would pay for, he would provide. Those people liked young flesh, and when Lazarou needed some he had it right in his own home.

At least, as his daughter, he had managed to use her as a puppet master would but with never a question of sending her the way of the other young girls who might've ended up sold as sex slaves to the highest bidders. George had no love for his daughter, Henry knew that, but he put a price on his possessions. Lara belonged to him just as his house did. Allowing that cheeky Polish bastard to walk out of his home with his actual flesh and blood could not go unpunished, and now his version of justice had been served.

'As you wish.' Henry stood up and straightened his jacket. 'I'll be off then. See you tomorrow?'

'Have a few days off, nobby. We've got some cameras to smile for. Take a holiday.'

~~~

Lara made it down to the promenade quickly, drawing stares as she did. Her clothes were filthy and her long hair wild. Her boho chic look was rounded off with a limp that hurt every time. A few people pointed and called out, but Lara didn't hear them over her inner voice, chanting over and over. *You're safe now, you're safe. Just a little further. You're safe now, you're safe. Just a little further.*

She crossed over the road and saw the top of the helter-skelter slide in the distance, knowing if she headed for that she'd be at her friend's kiosk in about a minute. As she rounded the mini golf course and hut, her path was clear.

'Oh my God. Lara! Oh my God!' Her friend came running out of the kiosk and wrapped her arms tightly around Lara, who used her final spurt of energy to reciprocate.

'Jenny.' It came weakly but full of relief.

'Lara, my God. Where've you been?'

Jenny looked round and called to a rotund lady who was cleaning plastic tables and shooing seagulls away. The lady looked up, her face the definition of surprised, and then hurriedly took her phone from her apron pocket.

'Come in, Lara. Oh my God. Come in and sit down.' Jenny led Lara around to the back of the kiosk and then inside. She gently helped her down onto a plastic chair. 'Betty's calling the police. It's okay now. Everyone's been so worried.' She put her hands on Lara's face, stroking her cheeks softly. 'I've been so worried.'

~~~

Skip hung up the phone. It was done. His plan, as ropey as it was, had backfired and got his old friend killed. But it had been Piotr's responsibility. If anything, Skip believed he had kept his hands clean.

George wanted to meet. *I know what you did*, he said. He had recognised Piotr the first time he saw him on his security monitor. If George knew anything, it was porn. Despite there being thousands of films in his stable, he'd seen them all. It was his business. Asmann was an old acquaintance who guaranteed to get things done. Over the years George had used him several times. He never asked Asmann about his methods or questioned the results. Now Piotr was dead. Asmann said so, and so it was.

Following his own ordeal with Asmann, Skip realised it could have been him instead and after George called to suggest a meeting, he knew well that he could have had him killed too. He wondered why he was still alive and supposed George must have a good reason. He was, at that moment, grateful for that unknown reason.

He would meet George in twenty-four hours. In the meantime, he would make sure he'd deleted all of Piotr's porn appearances. He'd done that a year ago but now rather than saving a friend's face he was protecting himself. Besides, deleting the files from his own servers was no guarantee – porn was shared and re-published so much, it could be anywhere. The last thing he needed was the police or the media sniffing around, but if they'd found Piotr's phone and computer it was bound to link back to Skip. It was a matter of time.

Lost in thought, Skip scrolled disinterestedly down George's main site's homepage. It was a seemingly infinite tapestry of flesh and faces and fat, thin or curvy bodies solo or writhing over each other. His eyes flitted between the thumbnails of promise, and within a minute he had scrolled past nearly four hundred such images, each registering in his

172

brain. He continued to scroll, his trained eye darting between the majority but lingering on the few that caught his attention: big girls with big tits. Absent-mindedly he chose one, scrolled past the first couple of minutes and let it play.

A curvy blonde girl, nineteen-years-old according to the video's title, sat on a bed pleasuring the naked man standing in front of her. After a while he grabbed her by the hair and bucked against her. The scene changed to the girl playing with herself and then again to the man pumping her from behind. The camera panned into close-up on the girl's face.

Poor girl, Skip thought. *And George hasn't even removed her videos. She's just had her head cut off and here she is with her head back on, wrapped around some guy's dick. Tasteful.*

His own site's homepage was similar to George's. It had been standard practice on these porn preview sites to break the sections down in the menus but just let it all flow out like titillating diarrhoea for browsers to get right to it. The only way to avoid seeing some of the more extreme images was to select from the categories menu. He clicked on the BBW tag and spent the next ten minutes in his own company.

~~~

The giant in the garden had stood still for a long time. A garden spider crossed the length of the lawn towards it. The night before, the same spider had unwittingly hitched a ride across the garden. Two giants had been creating thick smoke in the air and one of them had walked to the end of the garden to dispose of a white stub of paper with an orange, fiery end. The spider had been hanging from a branch overhead and not noticed the giant below which moved into its web-in-progress, catching the web and hooking the spider's new thread onto its rough frame.

When the giant got back to the building it flicked at the spider, which was frantically trying to detach itself from the giant anyway. It was knocked off by the giant's hand and fell to the hard ground, where it stayed in some state of shock. Hours later, it came to and decided to head back to its web. On this lengthy journey over rough, uneven terrain it observed this new, larger giant standing at its destination.

The spider reached the giant just as it transformed. In its short existence, it had never witnessed such a defiance of science but now, as the giant in an instant dissolved into tiny black molecules, like a dark mist, and disappeared just as quickly, it carried on as if nothing had happened.

~~~

Robert could easily have walked up to the house and let himself in, but there was no need to hide his new abilities. He found he was able to hover in place, his ultra-fine mist of no fixed size or shape sitting within a current of sorts. There were electrical currents all around – overhead and underneath, and radio and microwaves just in the air. They were all accessible, buzzing and fizzing and almost beckoning him. It felt good to hover in the mist – satisfying some kind of primal urge he didn't quite understand.

Here again was this fog in the, or rather *his*, consciousness. He didn't feel like he'd been told the whole story. Something was absent from the big picture but the picture was indeed so big that he couldn't grab all the threads and pull them together.

Maybe, he thought, Angelo and Stanley had been straight with him after all. Perhaps there was no effort made to conceal details. He had been sent to kill his son, and after that his brother, and he understood that the human reaction to this would be entirely different to his need now to carry out this task. The remnants of his old mind sat at odds with his urges.

Sensing the three humans inside the house together, Robert reconstituted right in the middle of them.

~~~

Piotr's final breath was a long time coming since Asmann had left the scene. Once he was satisfied that Piotr was left in a position that would cause him a great deal of suffering, he calmly went up the stepladder and pulled it up after him, closing the hatch. As Piotr now hung on the pole where Lara had been bound, he heard movement above and then suddenly the light was gone. Asmann had covered the hatch with something. Piotr couldn't see any of it anyway.

Asmann had pistol-whipped Piotr to knock him out then hoisted him up and, using Piotr's own materials, bound him to the pole with his wrists

174

criss-crossed behind it. He'd done the same with his feet, taking care to tighten the electrical cable-ties just so as to ensure the wounds on his knees were open, exposed and likely to tear further should he move.

When Piotr came to, he was in confused agony. Having lost consciousness horizontally on the hard floor and now getting it back vertically was an odd sensation but it didn't even slightly mask his pain or the smell of excrement stuck on his clothes and in his hair. Every movement sent exquisite shots of pain through his body. His knees had stopped spurting blood, at least. Small, shiny pools of coagulated plasma settled in the wounds but as he tried to shuffle on the pole to a more comfortable position he opened the wounds again.

It was then he felt something at his left side, but his head was too tight against the pole to get a good look. He shifted it just enough and gritted his teeth through the fresh pain to see something trailing from his armpit. It looked like a red piece of cord. As he stared intently at it, he realised the inside of the cord was moving. He shifted his head a little more to the left, opening the wounds on his knees further. A thin spray of blood erupted from his right knee and settled into a dribble.

He managed to follow the cord down to the ground, drawing his knee up just enough to see a drip pooling onto the stone floor. The drips were slow and regular. He understood now: Asmann had made a surgical incision in his armpit and fashioned a slow drip which would bleed him out.

He hung there for hours, his eyes closed; unable to pass out, to sleep or to free himself. As he became even weaker, he opened his eyes and let them close again. His dreams had not come. His sister, the one he made up as a child while becoming obsessed with the female form, obsessed with the depravity of men, was not here to haunt him. It had all been for nought. Piotr was dead. He would die as Gabriel.

~~~

'What the hell?' Sue fell back onto the couch as her ex-husband materialised in front of her. 'How…'

Jez immediately put himself in front of Maria and shielded her with his arms out.

Robert swivelled round, his face a contorted mess of black worm-like tendrils lashing around and his human flesh appearing within it, coming

175

into form. Sue watched in astonishment as Robert's back and sides and hair appeared to weld together out of this black, throbbing mass. She screamed.

'Maria, run!' No sooner had Jez pushed her away than Maria escaped through the arched doorway into the hall and towards the front door. Robert went to push Jez out of the way but then in an instant disappeared into a thin mist and shot past him to reconstitute right in front of Maria.

She screamed and fell backwards as Jez ran towards his father, now reconstituting again from the same fleshy and slithering worm mass. Jez put his arms out and stepped over Maria, then stopped to watch his father come back into form. His mouth fell open as he saw the shapes shift into each other, the physical jigsaw pieces almost making a whole.

Robert's expression was blank and indifferent as he moved towards Jez, a thick tendril emerging from his mouth and shooting towards his son. Jez instinctively dropped away from it and ran at his father with his right shoulder proud, then slammed himself into the monster, thumping it into the door.

Robert howled out, feeling this pain but not in the human sense. It was more like frustration. Again he vapourised himself and found the nearest point of conduction to jump to.

What is this? I do not understand. His fine mist, imperceptible to the eye, hovered around a double socket in his bedroom upstairs.

The consciousness seemed to speak to him: *You cannot do this. There are better ways to fulfil your obligations. You must overcome any obstacles.*

Is this some kind of a test?

Their minds. Use their minds against them.

Robert refocused on the spikes in the house, finding his ex-wife's the strongest. He tried to grab hold of it and couldn't.

You are not strong enough like this. Re-form.

He pulled himself back together and stood in his room, expressionless and still, as he reached out again. Sue screamed as her world altered around her, the walls closing in and turning blood-red. Robert latched onto her fears and amplified them.

Jez appeared from the bloody wall and loped across the room towards her, his body covered in blood and his throat slit open, his head lurching from side to side. He tried to speak... *mummy... mummy...* as blood gurgled out of his mouth, and then...

Jez ran to the couch and yanked his mother up by her arms, pulling her close. 'Mum! Come on! Come on!' She was rigid against him. Maria had scrambled up and run through from the hall.

Robert, standing serenely upstairs, tried to divide his manipulation. *I can't...*

Sue snapped out of the vision in an instant and now saw the real face of her son and Maria behind him. Maria screamed and reeled backwards as Sue's face exploded into a ball of flame, spreading down her body fast and engulfing her entirely.

Sue watched and Jez turned to see Maria fall onto her back, her hands up to her mouth and her eyes shut tight as she howled with terror.

I can't do them all at once. I can only do one. I need to separate them.

Robert walked calmly out of his room and down the stairs, maintaining the vision in Maria's mind. He caught glimpses of the origin of her fear, of witnessing a fire as a child and seeing her own mother burned to death. It might not have been real, but it was in her head for him to play with. He got back to the living room to find Jez and Sue kneeling with Maria, trying in vain to comfort her.

'Shit!' Jez charged at him once more and just at the point of impact Robert dematerialised again. Jez went straight through the mist and into the wall, crunching his shoulder and face hard against it. Sue got up to her feet and faced the monstrous mass as it came back together.

'Robert. What is this? What are you doing?'

His mouth reformed: 'Hello, Sue. How've you been? Let's catch up.' He advanced on her and passed Maria, who was still lying on the floor screaming and holding her head in both hands.

Maria's horrible vision disappeared as Jez thumped into his father from behind, sending him hurtling past his ex-wife. He seemed to splash against the wall as his blackness reformed but now facing the room again.

I didn't know that was coming. I cannot see everything now. This is... confusing. Robert felt something pulling at him as he misted up again and rushed out of the scene. Jez and his mother watched it trail away and disappear.

'Where'd he go?' Jez held his mother tightly around her back and chest. 'What the fuck just happened?' He looked at Maria, lying down and gasping, her face a picture of terror.

Sue wrangled free of Jez and ran out to the hall. Jez followed her. 'What're you doing, mum?'

She screamed: 'We have to call the police!'

Jez covered the phone receiver before she could grab it. 'The police? The police? What're you gonna tell 'em?'

Sue fell back against the stair wall. 'I... don't know. I don't know. What if he comes back?'

'That wasn't dad.' Jez's voice was trembling and high-pitched. 'That wasn't him. That was some kind of...'

'We need to get out of here,' his mother said. 'Right now. Come on.'

Jez went back to the living room and picked Maria up. 'It's okay now. It's okay. We have to get away from here. Come on.'

The three of them stumbled out and across the front garden to Sue's car. It unlocked automatically as she drew nearer and they got in, Jez ushering Maria into the front with Sue.

As she sped off up the road, looking frantically in her rear-view mirror, Sue's mind went round and round: what do we do now what do we do now what do we do now....

~~~

Robert found himself settling down from what was the ordinary's version of a rush of adrenaline. His focus had been scattered and now his connection to the consciousness was bleeding back in.

The realisation, as always now, came quickly. The stems and spikes were stationary. Those which were moving were some levels below these. On the move, it was far harder if not just impossible to latch on to those. He imagined some kind of speed-matching, but it didn't make sense.

He reached for his family but it was moving too fast. He realised he had missed his chance – and it would be difficult to search their stems now they weren't where he expected to find them. All of a sudden Robert realised he was not quite as powerful as he'd originally felt and he struggled still to find answers to all his questions.

He reached out again. *Can they hurt us?* Answer came there none. For the first time since he'd changed, Robert *didn't* understand. His rush into the consciousness at the start had been overwhelming and now, settling into it, he felt the power and the wonder diminished, reduced even. It was becoming, he thought, too ordinary.

~~~

'Nothing – they're clean.' Mack shrugged. 'Bastards for doing it, but we can't prosecute the free press.'

Pete shrugged too. 'Can't blame them, I s'pose. But it was pretty pointless anyway.' The raid had been officially sanctioned by the government, not the police. They merely had to do as they were told. In any case, the officers who carried it out were nothing to do with the small CID units which made up a relatively small part of the force. Those kinds of ops were always handled by specialists, not jobbing detectives.

Mack smiled ruefully. 'And we're still no closer to finding the...'

The door swung open, stopping Mack mid-sentence. Mike burst in, looking more excited than he had in months. Mack and Pete looked up at him expectantly.

'It's the girl.' He pointed to the TV on the wall. 'Lara. She's back!'

Mike ran to his desk and picked up the TV remote, which always seemed to be on his side of the room, and flicked it on excitedly. The rolling news channel came on in seconds and there she was, flanked by her parents outside Malton District Hospital. She looked, Mike thought, a lot like the girl he'd seen swinging from the ceiling just before he met Angelo.

'We needn't bother coming in!' Pete elbowed Mack playfully and laughed to release the huge relief he felt welling inside him. 'It's all happening despite us. Pub, anyone?'

'Not so fast... we've still got a killer on the loose.' Mack elbowed him back.

'Not necessarily, mate. If she got away from that sick bastard then maybe she got the better of him.'

'Shut up, will you?' Mike looked annoyed. His last pill had kept him alert and happy and comforted but now it was wearing off. His final shot – fizzing down to nothing. Although it had been burning a hole in his pocket for days, the simple fact that it was now gone was hurting.

His colleagues did as they were told, exchanging a look of mock concern. On the TV, a spokesman stepped forward. It was Briggs.

'We are delighted to see Miss Lazarou safe from any further harm and we trust you will all respect the privacy her family needs at this emotional time.'

179

Briggs stepped forward into the crowd of photographers and reporters, confidently shouldering them out of his way. One reporter managed to get his microphone into Briggs' path.

'Sir... sir! Can you comment on the whereabouts of Piotr Bogdanek?'

Briggs stopped and frowned deeply. As he hesitated, the noise in the crowd dissolved. He fixed his gaze straight at the camera. 'Although I cannot comment on this in any official capacity, Miss Lazarou's escape and the circumstances thereof lead us to believe he is still at large. I have nothing else to say right now. Thank you.'

He began to push forwards again and the camera panned back up the steps to the hospital entrance, where the backs of the Lazarous could be seen disappearing into the lobby.

'See?' Mack poked Pete in the cheek. 'You *are* as dumb as you look.'

'We'd better get over there.' Mike flicked the TV off. 'If she can tell us where she was...'

'We'd know already,' Mack finished. 'We'll wait for Briggs. If she told him, he'll tell us.'

~~~

The analysis was as expected. Simon turned the monitor by a few degrees so his colleagues could see. Caitlin was the first to comment: 'Yes, Dr M. Yet *again* you've hypothesised correctly.' She smiled.

'Not exactly difficult,' retorted Anthony. 'Perhaps if we changed the...'

Simon interrupted. He wasn't particularly interested in his colleagues' opinions anyway. 'There's still no discernible pattern. We need a pattern!'

Caitlin saw the passion in her mentor's eyes. 'I know we'll find it, Dr M. The stakes are too high not to. We will. I *know* it.'

Anthony turned to the console behind the cabinet and pushed the red button. The shutters came down on the windows and once more covered the compact dwelling of their captive – the label above stating simply 'Subject K'.

'Why are you so sure there is?'

Simon Moulder, a holder of two doctorates and professor of physics, knew the answer only too well: 'There is always a pattern.'

Sixteen – Revelations

'So are we dead?'

'No, I don't think so. We're just in... some place. Some different place.'

'How did you find me?'

'Louise. She found you.'

'Frank. What about Frank? Didn't he make it out too?'

'I didn't see him. It all happened so fast. I'm not even sure how we got in and out anyway.'

The fog cleared a little further, pushing out away from the two escapees, floating in some kind of void but strangely on some kind of solid ground.

'I remember looking at you, but it wasn't you. At least you *said* it wasn't you. I knew it was all wrong, like I shouldn't have been there, although I felt like maybe I was wrong about that too.'

'No, it wasn't me. *This* is me. Everyone in that place was grinning. I felt it too, a feeling creeping in like it was exactly where I was supposed to be. It was warm and welcoming and perfect but it was an illusion. It felt like it wasn't real.'

'But it was real. I know it's real. I've been there before, many times.'

Joe was certain of only one thing at that moment – that he'd been close to fulfilling a destiny he never asked for. The realisation that he'd been used since childhood left a gash in his soul. Once his forgotten past was revealed to him, it would have been too much to bear but for where he was when the revelations came. He had been in the womb of evil, dancing and drinking and grinning like an idiot as the comforting, blanketing warmth of darkness settled over him.

'That explains a lot.'

'So what do we do now?'

Joe had no idea. His life as he knew it had been false, or at least in terms of what had gone before. He now realised this descent into the bowels of lost humanity had informed his journey entirely. From the fire he had helped to cause, killing hundreds of people, to his being shepherded back to this place which didn't belong on Earth, it all had been orchestrated for him – and there was much more besides; earlier than the fire, back in Chicago, and even further back than that. He could now recall clearly the terrifying moment his mother shot herself on the boat, driven to suicide by an abusive, drunk husband; and then the kindly suited gentleman taking him from there, taking him to this place, the place they called the waiting room.

He now also understood why it was called that and what they had been waiting for. His career had been spent manipulating the innate lightness and darkness of people. These detestable beings in the belly, born of the core – the slippery, searching blackness, always in control. He had become intoxicated with the drug of darkness and done their bidding, but now through some kind of opportunity of salvation he was released. Free, but now trapped in a new prison of uncertainty.

He knew he had come so close to the next stage of evolution, to become one of those *things*; to lose his humanity altogether and achieve great power in its place. But he didn't want that at all.

'What we do now depends on *where* we are now.' Tom had always been pragmatic. 'Can you still do that... fast travel thing?'

'No, I don't think so. I can't feel any of that. I want to find Louise. Where is she?'

'That, I don't know.' Tom put his arm around Joe's shoulders. 'She was there and then she wasn't, but she saved you. She saved us. She came to get me and explained... I mean she tried to explain. What in hell is that place?' Tom thought it actually *was* hell.

Joe surveyed the area and the fog, hovering ominously and shifting in place. 'It is the waiting room. It is where the ordinary gather. There are a few ways in. Pathways. That's what all the shit at the farm was about. It was a lure, for me. I'm so sorry. They were after me.'

Tom's grip on Joe's shoulder tightened. 'Hey, fella. We made it out of there just fine. And you... you're one of the good guys.'

'I'm not,' Joe said quickly. 'I'm really not. The things I've done.'

'It doesn't matter what you've done but what you're gonna do now, son.'

'It does matter. Those things. They're not human, Tom. You can see that. The things you've seen. I was a part of that. They didn't force me to do anything. I just forgot I'd done it. Like there were fragments of me here and there and the whole...'

Tom knelt in front of Joe and put a hand on each of his arms. 'We're not going to get anywhere if we don't get up. Come on.'

He lifted Joe to his feet and for a moment they just stared into the fog. The ground had been the only solid thing in that place and as Tom stood

182

on it he realised it was indeed ground, of some sort. He took Joe's hand and stepped forward. Joe pulled him back hesitantly.

'Thanks, Tom.' He smiled weakly. The transition from drowning in that oily pool, its tentacles having woven into his flesh and blood in the dark baptism, to being pulled out and rushed back through that ornate red and white room, the people with their pig masks standing and staring, was like being pulled from drunkenness into sobriety in the blink of an eye. It was hard to grasp the reality of the situation, or even to contemplate if there was any reality left in this situation.

Tom led Joe forward and as they walked the fog dissipated before them, edging away with each step as if they were magnets opposed. The ground remained hard and even underfoot, yet their steps on it were discomfortingly silent. They stopped suddenly as the fog lifted entirely.

'Well, lookee here.' Tom let go of Joe's hand and edged forward, putting his arm out to touch the wall in front of him. He looked back at Joe, seeing the fog lapping behind him, following them, enveloping their progress. It looked awesome – this giant mass hovering, concealing and promising nothing.

'What... that's a wall?'

'Sure looks like one.' Tom pressed both hands against it and pushed. 'Feels like one too.'

Joe joined him, unaware of the fog behind following each inch of progress he made.

'You go that way and I'll go this way?'

Tom nodded. Joe kept his right shoulder against the wall as he took small steps along it. Now he could see the fog all along his left side and in front but the wall was his safety – his touchpoint. Tom went the other way. When he turned back, all he could see was the fog creeping along the wall behind him. It turned a knot in his stomach.

'Joe?' His voice sounded dead in the air. This time louder: 'Joe?' He turned and followed the wall back in the other direction, his pulse quickening. Eventually the fog began to thin until he saw him.

'Look.' Joe had found some kind of opening. 'There.' Tom nudged close to him. The wall had softened. It resembled a silk curtain. There was something on the other side – a dim light. Joe slowly put his hand into the curtain and it went through.

'Shit,' muttered Tom as he did the same. 'This is how we got into the waiting room. Through one of these.'

Tom's bowels had loosened the first time he experienced this. It wasn't all that different to some of the stuff that'd happened to him on that fateful night at the farm months ago – multiple versions of himself crossing over and strange forays into fantastic dimensions – but entering the waiting room was an altogether unsettling experience.

Louise had gone looking for him and when she got to his house had explained why she hadn't been able to phone. She'd waited there all day for him to get back from work. Joe had gone missing, she'd said. Some old, shifty guy calling himself Nel seemed to have double-crossed them and sealed the entrance. The trapdoor Joe had disappeared down had disappeared too. The barn – everything. She and Tom went back to Shenbury to decide what to do and hired a trailer in the camp that had been set up there after the great fire.

Although some months had passed and they'd been moved on, they were recognised. Tom, in particular, had been on the national news for a time when the fire was being investigated. He'd been cleared of involvement but had taken a new post some miles away 'for the best'. Some of the older folk living in the camp smiled and waved to him.

Two teenagers saw Louise and asked to speak to her privately. They told her they'd been out in the woods and seen someone take their friend into a thicket. He'd just vanished there, but no one would believe them. A couple of days had passed and no one seemed to think it significant – he was one of the local stoners and had gone walkabout before. Louise asked them to take her there, so she and Tom followed them to the spot and found this portal – almost something that wasn't there unless you looked at it right; a warped perspective.

They went inside and found themselves in some kind of narrow, dark tunnel which led to one of these thin, meshy curtains. Looking back, the way they had come in was now gone. It was just darkness and neither of them wanted to venture into it. Louise went through the mesh first and Tom stayed the other side, just watching. The sound from inside was muffled but musical, drunken melodies and sedated rhythms washing over each other. The kid sitting at the piano matched the description of the missing stoner.

Louise had walked among these finely dressed creatures, cautiously at first and then with great haste, looking at their masked faces, one by one, trying to find Joe. She walked past the band and started to draw attention as people stopped dancing. At one side of the room was a single white door. She opened it and closed it again quickly, and as she went to cross the room some of these grinning monsters tried to block her way, their hands grabbing at her. Tom had pushed through then, striding over to Louise and pulling her away from the scrum. She pointed at a set of doors on the other side of the room and shouted something which didn't reach Tom's ears with any clarity. They reached the double doors and pulled them open.

That sight had almost knocked him dead – a vast, voluminous sea of black; shades of darkness in thick and thin strands, reaching up and around and over each other, a visual and aural cacophony bleeding out. There, barely visible in this mass, was Joe, face down in it, naked and floating, the strands like tendrils soaked into his body, limbs and head. Tom leapt into the mass. The thick liquid reacted against the impact with an unearthly howl and lunged, pushing him forward like a wave would a surfer. He grabbed for Joe and caught his arm, then fell back, slipping against the oily mass and pulling Joe up and out with him. He came out with a little resistance, the tendrils retreating with a sickly, high-pitched scream like fingernails on a chalkboard.

Still pulling on Joe's arm, dragging him closer, Tom turned back to Louise who was lashing out against the smartly-dressed, masked accosters. He tried to call for her but the sound coming from the mass was now deafening, its tentacles thrashing against each other and trying to pull Joe back in.

Joe tugged at his arm and Tom pulled him forward, getting up to his knees and using his other arm to swat the tentacles out of the way. He pulled Joe again and pushed him to the door. At first Joe had just stood there, watching Louise getting smothered by the suited bastards. Then in an instant he began pushing against the people too, putting himself between them and Louise. Tom got up to the doorway and took one look back at the writhing, squealing mass and shut the doors fast against the thrashing snakes of darkness. The cacophony disappeared behind the closed doors.

The throng of people had then parted as one of them came through to stand in front of the defiant trio. In the new silence of the room, its voice was clear and crisp, its expression blank: 'You belong here, Joe. They do not. Your cleansing is not over.' It smiled. 'These people don't know you like *I* do. They don't care for you like *we* care for you.'

Joe said nothing. Louise took Joe's hand and squeezed it tightly.

'You should go back in now, Joe. It is calling for you.'

Tom had looked beyond this charming, well-spoken sinister minister and saw the band taking their seats again, ready to play. It had seemed an ideal opportunity to do... something. He stepped towards the man and slugged him in the jaw.

'Now! Run!' As the man reeled from Tom's punch, Louise had yanked Joe around him and led him over to the other door with Tom right behind them. She opened the door and shoved Joe through and then as Tom made it through as well she was suddenly pulled back. Tom could see the gloved hands on her head and shoulders. He reached back out to her but the door slammed against him, sending him stumbling back into Joe and they both fell down. An almighty sound had crashed around them, like wind thumping against a mountain, and Tom's world had gone dark.

There was no explanation he could conjure up for any of this. Now, his hand reaching through another of those thin curtains separating this foggy void from God-knew-what-else, he felt no fear. It was an entirely different emotion, raw and hollow and uncertain.

Joe was first to get completely through. 'Holy shit, Tom. Look. Holy shit.' They had come out into a forest, with woods stretching down a slight gradient one way and up the other.

Tom stood next to him. 'We've done it. We're out.' They looked at each other as Tom let out a weary sigh with a tentative smile.

'We have to go back for Louise. I can't leave her there.'

They turned back to see the curtain they'd slipped through. Now there were just trees in its place; the thick forest cast in twilight.

'What...' Joe trailed off. He knew the answer already. Nothing was ever what it seemed. Perhaps there was no way back in now, but he didn't think that was true. If Tom and Louise had managed to get in, so he and Tom could do the same. *Somehow*.

'There is no way back, Joe. Not here anyway. I don't wanna leave her there either.'

Tom put his hand on Joe's shoulder. 'Right now, we should move. And...' He grimaced at Joe's nudity. 'We need to find you some clothes. Which way do you fancy?'

Joe didn't care. The place seemed familiar though. He pointed up the hill. 'That way.

~~~

Sue pulled the car with a swerve into the forecourt, slammed the brakes on and skidded to a halt, the front bumper knocking into and felling a standing sign.

'Mum! Was that really necessary?' shouted Jez. Maria turned to look at him, her expression unsettled. 'We've been going for an hour. I'm sure we're far enough away...'

'How can you be sure of that?' Jez's mother eyed him in the rear-view mirror, her voice hysterical. 'After *that*, I'm not sure about anything!'

The car journey had been strained at best and downright painful at worst. Sue had driven way faster than the law would allow, slowing only in built-up areas but on one occasion doing seventy past a primary school and receiving a tirade of righteous abuse from a crowd of parents waiting outside, not that she noticed. Maria and Jez had spent most of the trip holding hands, he leaning forward to take hers. They hadn't said much but had briefly discussed the ordeal. Then Sue had put the radio on and turned it up *loud*.

Now Sue almost aggressively exited the car and stomped towards the café entrance. The sign on the door confirmed it was open and she pushed it, disappearing inside.

'I'm sorry.' Jez got out of the car and opened Maria's door for her.

'It's not your fault. It was that thing. I don't even know what that was.' She got out too and shut the door gently. Maria felt drained; in shock. It was, she couldn't stop herself thinking, the worst day of her life.

~~~

'Subject G is sedate.' Caitlin finished her audio report and emailed it to her superior. It was a close-knit group, and rightly so. The circle of trust simply had to be a very small circle given what the team had learnt in these last few months. The research had finally yielded positive results. For a potential biological threat which thrived on electricity and seemed to be able to move freely through it, precautionary measures were the only essential measures: render safe, examine, render safe again, and analyse.

Caitlin's years of experience in studiously following the instructions of her superiors had instilled in her a steadfast commitment to authority. In this post, one she had fallen into easily but could never leave, she was as useful as every other cog in the machine, and that made her feel like a champion every day.

Dr Moulder was a rare case, in Caitlin's experience at least, of a scientist who had as much heart as logical resolve. His family tree read like a random list of vagabonds, under-achievers, and at the other end of the spectrum some highly intellectual beings who had left marks in some of the more detailed history books.

Caitlin handed the tablet to Anthony. She didn't notice his apprehension. The previous two days had taken their toll on him but, given Caitlin's narrower field of empathy, she failed to read the signs that her colleague was experiencing something of a tear in his fabric.

Although the experiments had been going on for decades, Anthony and Caitlin were the first civilians to witness the controlled behaviour of these *things*. They didn't have a name for them because they had no idea what they were. In isolation it was an entity that defied existing scientific principles: how could these entities de- and re-constitute at will?

When Caitlin had answered the call to be Dr M's assistant, she hadn't hesitated at all. That would be madness, postponing or throwing away the opportunity to work with the eminent physicist. Regardless, he could take her places. A recommendation from the esteemed Simon Moulder was priceless.

Anthony had considered himself even luckier to get on the team. It seemed that keen intelligence ran in his family and they'd understood when he told them, even though at the time he didn't know why, he'd be unable to see them at all or even keep in touch while working in this team. The money was poor in comparison to some of the earlier pharmaceutical research jobs he'd had, but to get to work with one of the greatest names in the field of physics was a dream come true.

Caitlin and Anthony had full board and were looked after. Simon didn't choose to socialise with them and had explained that keeping such things separate was best. In any case, he said, there wouldn't be much time for socialising. He was right: with over twenty subjects that needed almost constant monitoring, their small team had a lot to keep on top of.

The team had previously been much smaller as Simon himself had struck out from his previous position at the Institute of Applied Science in Manchester to pursue this research on his own. He had set up a small but well-appointed facility, secured funding – much of which came from his own accumulated wealth – and managed to keep it almost entirely secret from the scientific fraternity.

Speculation had been rife at the time but since died down as people assumed he had simply become a recluse as part of some kind of high-pressure nervous breakdown or that his research was too early to publicise. Either way, he was by no means under anyone's spotlight, or so he thought.

~~~

'Sir.' Mack opened the chief's door, Mike and Pete standing out in the corridor behind her. Briggs waved her in.

'Right.' He closed the folder he'd been perusing on his desk and slid it over to Mack. 'It's all in there. The girl doesn't have any idea on location but we're widening the search area. Chances are he's gone and he's got a good head-start on us.'

Mack flipped the folder open and scanned through it, then turned and handed it to Pete.

'Yes sir. So what do you need us to do?'

Briggs eyed the trio wearily. 'House fire. Arson. In the Old Town. Judy's got the info.'

Mack nodded and followed Pete out of the room, pushing past Mike and flashing him an *aren't you coming?* glance. Mike shook his head and smiled, closing Briggs' door behind them.

'Chief.'

Briggs' weary expression grew more pronounced. 'Hmm? What is it?'

'I wondered if we could have a chat about… something.'

'Spit it out.'

'Oh. It's just… the other night. I saw you up at that house on the promenade. Round the back of that, er… Davies Consulting. I was there too. I just wondered…'

Briggs stood up and slammed his palms down onto the desk, facing Mike with an intense glare.

'Do I follow you around the fucking place and…'

Mike leaned back from the aggression and interrupted: 'Chief – I was there following up a lead. Not following y–'

189

'You need to learn to mind your own business.' Briggs stood upright without taking his eyes off Mike's. 'There aren't any leads to follow up there. Is that clear? You go where I say and...'

'Actually, sir, it was my night off.'

Briggs' face looked ready to explode. He skirted the desk and came around to stand toe to toe with Mike. 'If it was your fucking night off, why were you wasting your time following up a lead that doesn't exist? Get out!'

Mike backed away slowly, thinking: *okay, that was a little unexpected... what's his problem?* He hesitated at the door.

'I said get out!'

~~~

Stanley had been looking forward to sharing his hobby with someone and now, taking advantage of a rare visit from a non-human colleague, led Angelo to his trophy room. He promised it would be fun to see.

'Which one is your favourite?' Angelo stood in the doorway, licking his lips. 'They all look the same from here. There's nothing... *inside*. But I can still *feel* them.'

Stanley clapped and grinned with glee. 'I think on their behalf. My beautiful wives. I love them all the same.'

Angelo felt compelled to investigate one of these lovelies but hesitated. Stanley noticed. 'Oh, it's fine. Help yourself!' Stanley put a hand on Angelo's shoulder. He liked the solidity he felt there. It was unlike the fluidity of the ordinary's form, something more dependable. Although an ordinary was part of a giant collective and living from the same consciousness, there was a certain solitude that went with it. Simply put, these supranatural creatures were beyond the need to socialise and seek validation of their lives from others, and as they were relatively few and far between globally speaking, it was a rare occurrence for two to be in the same place, except those who were honoured enough to be invited into the core, the place where the dark heart beat loudest.

'It is quite the collection. How many years have you been collecting?'

'Oh,' Stanley grinned, rubbing his hands together. 'A while. They're beautiful, aren't they? I think of them as my wives, my daughters, and my best friends. We play all the time. They truly understand me. We are one and the same.'

Angelo nodded. He knelt down next to the girl closest to the door. 'What do you do with them?'

'We go dancing together. Dancing to the most sweet, beautiful music.'

He could create these melodic frequencies with such ease, as if his head itself was the ultimate musical instrument – a true one-man orchestra. He walked straight to the girl sitting in the middle of the row on the far wall.

'This is Candy. It was easy to name her. She's so sweet!' He turned and grinned at Angelo. 'I can just taste her!' A shot of black came out of his mouth and worked its way into Candy's, followed by more strands until his and her faces were joined by an oily bridge. He sucked her towards him until they were touching nose to nose, then dissolved his eyeballs into more tendrils. They reached into her eye sockets and carefully felt their way around the outsides, rounding the balls and cushioning them. The tendrils reached further inside as more erupted from his torso and legs.

Angelo watched with interest. *I want to do this too.* He felt a surge of desire and let his sinewy self reach out to the girl in front of him, enveloping her face and drawing it towards his. Strands came out of his neck and chest and penetrated her skin, sending trickles of blood down her chest and stomach.

'No!' Stanley had re-arranged himself with his face now where the back of his head had been before his loving assault on Candy. 'Don't do that to Rosa. She is perfect. I am always very careful with my girls.'

Angelo withdrew his tendrils, caressing Rosa's face and neck as they lapped back into him. He saw why she was called Rosa – a rosy complexion and light red hair.

'This is a distraction,' Angelo said as he watched Stanley's mouth move back around to face him.

'We don't have much time,' Stanley said, now immersing himself back into Candy. 'I need to make the most of them. They're all I have.'

'Okay. A little longer.' Angelo continued to probe but not penetrate Rosa. His feelers curved along her hip bones, jutting out like little mountains and then around and under her buttocks, pooling around her anus and settling, then gently feeling up and into her digestive tract. It was a sensual experience, for him at least. The girl didn't react; she just

191

sat still, her hood hanging askew on the crown of her head as this monster defiled her.

'Shall we have some music then?' Stanley was ready to dance. He clicked his fingers and the unseen band started, hijacking the radio waves and playing the best show of their lives. Stanley, melded with Candy, a sixteen-year-old from Hungary who had originally been called Katya, leapt up and began to sway, his arms folded around his partner and settling into the flesh.

Angelo joined in, taking Rosa up with him in a flourish that echoed his days back in university when he took ballroom dance classes once a week. He hadn't lost his natural rhythm, it seemed; he imagined he was even better now he wasn't restrained by physicality.

Stanley swept Candy around the room, organically following the nuances of the music as it came from his being. He swooped her around Angelo and Rosa and the two leading men exchanged a contented smile. Angelo withdrew a little, his tendrils stretching between them as he began to swing Rosa in a graceful arc. He then held her in place and called loudly to Stanley: 'May I dance with Candy?'

Stanley stopped the music and gently backed his tendrils out of Candy, replacing her softly onto the chair. 'We have things to take care of, don't we?'

Angelo nodded as he did the same with Rosa. 'Yes. But that was... satisfying. It would be... satisfying to taste some more of your girls.'

Stanley felt something he had not felt in a very long time. It was a sensation of want, of need, and of jealousy. He had often considered how humans would view his collection and indeed had enjoyed testing Jock and Bleach – giving them a glimpse; and he had considered their emotional response untypical of the average human. They had not been repulsed but interested. Bleach had tipped slightly into sentimental territory but Jock could have stayed in there and had his way if he wanted. How he loved toying with these simple folk, driven by primal urges, although it was never as fun as playing with his wives.

His own, ex-human opinion of his behaviour was that he could appreciate a point of view driven by human instincts but he simply didn't care. Why should he have to? After all, what he was doing shared much with the way humans took possession of each other, just as any husband would take a wife and consider her his. Humans' obsession with celebrity

192

had them worship and idolise trophy people, attempting to adopt their ideals and appearances. How was that any different to what Stanley did?

They were *his* girls. He didn't like the thought of Angelo playing with them anymore.

~~~

Mike caught up with Mack and Pete at the front desk. They were talking to Judy, a part-time desk sergeant who had just uploaded the details of the suspected arson case to their PDAs. Mike's buzzed in his pocket at the same time. He'd always viewed this process with mixed feelings. In the old days, it was all paper files in cardboard folders but now, getting a case was more like taking a ticket and waiting for your turn.

They left through the front entrance and were met with a wall of photographers. After an initial wave of expectant excitement, they realised they were just looking at three average officers and nothing worth snapping and lowered their cameras, muttering amongst themselves.

Pete caught the eye of a pretty brunette carrying a camera case and smiled at her, then shrugged apologetically. She smiled back and did the same.

'Pete.' Mack knocked her knee into the back of his leg. 'Quit flirting. We're working.'

Pete stumbled a little. 'Oi!' He turned to playfully slap Mack on the arm. 'You're just jealous. *All* the ladies love me.'

'No,' Mike jumped in. 'They wonder why they see a child in a man's clothes. And they're wincing at the idea of having to wipe your arse for you.'

Pete raised an eyebrow. 'That's one of your worst putdowns, mate. Off your game?' He stopped to fix on Mike's face. 'And mate, you don't look so good yourself.'

Once out of the station forecourt, they got into Mack's car which was parked out front. 'Okay,' she said. 'Where are we going?'

Pete flicked his PDA open. 'Viper Court. It's off Turpin's Parade. Head up to the high street and it's off up towards the old church up there.'

193

Viper Court... why do I know Viper Court? Mike's come-down brain tried to grab hold of a memory which refused to settle. *Viper... oh shit. Where do I...?*

'Hey, Mike?' Mack glanced back to look at him. 'What were you and Briggs talking about?'

'Oh. Er... not a lot. I wanted to... just asking about something personal. Some time off. It's... uh, private.'

Pete scoffed: 'Time off for what? *We* are your private life! Got a lump on your bollocks or something?' He too turned to see Mike in the back. 'You know you can confide in me for your... *personal* stuff, right?'

Mike wished it was as simple as a lump on his balls. 'If you must know, Briggs asked to see me.' The lie was deepening, but he couldn't tell them what had happened to him. They'd think he was batshit crazy. At times they said he was anyway, so adding to that was a bad idea.

'See you about what?'

'Can we just leave it, please?'

Mack and Pete exchanged shrugs and moved on. 'So...' Mack started. 'Any plans for the weekend? Now this shit is over.'

It's not over, Mike thought. *None of the shit is over. The old shit might be but there's a whole lot of new shit coming down.*

Pete spoke cheerfully. 'Nothing I'd call interesting. A bit of work on the house. Might have a barbie. Anyone fancy some meat and two veg at my place?'

Mike didn't answer. He was lost now in his thoughts. Thoughts of little round pills that he might never see again; of Viper Court and why he couldn't recall its significance; of the dead girl telling him bad things happen to good people; and of Angelo, this sinister Chinese bastard who could have killed him but loaded him with cold fear instead.

'Sure, I'm in.' Mack smiled. She was relieved just as she was in every interval in casework. It didn't matter that they hadn't really done anything to solve the crimes. Someone else would deal with Gabriel Pomorski. The media circus was over for them. Now, heading to a suspected arson, expectation was low. The fire brigade would be sifting through the wreckage looking for cause, and really all they needed to do was have a look, shake a few hands, cut some cheese with the fire chaps and head to the pub to round off an insignificant day.

Mack's general outlook was one of acceptance that although they were small fry in a giant universal ocean, they had the means to make a

194

difference in micro situations, to people's lives, to make them feel safe and to know that someone was fighting for justice. She knew this was one of the ingrained mores of the police force but she felt strongly about it all the same. Pete had a similar positive outlook.

Mike, meanwhile, could only think about the cloud of uncertainty in his head. As Pete and Mack exchanged barbecue puns up front, he could feel his face reddening as his temples started to ache. Mack turned the car off Turpin's Parade, past a row of shops and came to a stop just down from the cordon of fire engines. Mike looked out of the window and felt the wind rush out of his stomach. *Oh shit fuck shit fuck... Viper Court. Viper fucking Court.*

He couldn't remember the guy's name but some chap calling himself Jock had taken him here from the King's Head at his request. *It must have been... three years ago. Maybe four. Jock. Definitely Jock.* He remembered the man approaching him in the pub, saying he could get anything he needed. Mike saw it as an opportunity to make a bust but it didn't go as planned. Instead of arresting the guys, which he easily could have, in a moment of weakness he simply joined in the fun. And the guy really did have *everything*.

Mack and Pete had got out of the car and were talking to the uniformed officer on duty. Pete looked back at Mike and gesticulated as if to say *get on with it!*

Leach. Was that it? Yes, Leach. He recalled the guy opening a suitcase with scores of wraps and baggies and pill pots and cellophane. He knew he should have cuffed him there and then but there was something likable about these fellows. They seemed kindred – on opposite sides of the law, in theory at least – but Jock had been a typically charming, poetic Scot and this Leach guy had been earnest.

Mike got out of the car, taking the sunlight on his face as hostile. *What are the chances of it being the same flat? One in... what, twenty? Good odds.* He joined the others, squinting against the light. The flat was a few floors up and burning out. Glass and embers lay on the pavement, across the road and on top of a couple of expensive looking cars. Further up the road past the cordon was a group of people being ushered by two policewomen.

'Can we go up then?' Pete asked the uniform.

He nodded. 'Just go easy. It's still pretty hot up there and the fire forensics team are in charge for now.'

Mike followed Pete and Mack and caught a little of their banter between his micro panic attacks as they took the same steps he'd taken on that night, which he could now recall much more clearly. When they arrived at the flat he got another psychological punch in the gut.

The doorway was burnt out and the interior showed only patches of what was there before, but he recognised the layout of the place. Dave and Ed from forensics were already on the scene and marking an area around what used to be the sofa where two piles of flesh and bone lay. The smell was intoxicating.

'Two bodies,' Dave said. 'But one of them's in pieces.'

Pete stepped over a pile of debris and squatted next to Dave. 'Pieces?'

'That's right, mate. Far as we can tell we had a body bag with the pieces and the other body might have been trying to burn the place out. Looks like he got caught up in his own escape plan. Fire team's found a few hot-spots.'

Mike could almost see the scenario playing out. *The suitcase.* An argument and one of them getting carried away and... that wouldn't explain the body bag. Maybe Leach had got himself into trouble and had to dispose of a body for some reason or somebody. He didn't seem the killing type. *Where's the suitcase? It could still be here.* Maybe the other guy had been Jock.

'Flat's registered to a James Bleach.' Mack flicked her PDA off. 'Can we ascertain identity on either of the bodies yet?'

Wilson shook his head. 'A lot of damage here – especially in *there.*' He pointed his gloved finger at the remains on the sofa, a pile of barely recognisable bones.

Bleach! That's it. Bleach. He kept the case under the bed. That's where they'd opened it and looked through the contents and chosen their delicious, delightful poisons that night. Mike moved across to the open doorway of the first of two bedrooms and ducked inside. One of the fire forensics guys was kneeling down next to a hole in the wall, which looked like it had exploded through. A length of distressed copper pipe – gas, Mike registered – was poking out of the wall.

The bed was mostly gone apart from a segment of the base which seemed to have escaped the fingers of fire. *It might still be under there. If only... it could be there.* Mike had paid for and taken a supply of pills from Bleach. They'd been stronger than his usual brand and he wasn't sure they even did the same thing but they'd filled a hole. *There might be some in there. I've got to see.*

The forensics man glanced back at Mike curiously and turned back to what he was doing. Mike squatted down and lifted the bed base up to save him having to lie down. *It's there! It's fucking there!* He felt his pulse quickening as his prize drew nearer.

'What you found, Mikey?'

Mike lost his balance and fell onto his back. 'Fuckin'ell, Pete.' He looked up at his partner with angered annoyance. Pete returned the expression with pure confusion. The fire forensics man did the same.

'Something under the bed? Why are you looking under *there*?'

'No... no reason.' He was still visibly angry. 'It just looked, you know, more intact than the rest of the room so I thought I'd check it out.'

Pete nodded. 'Good idea. Off your arse then! Let's have a look.'

'No!' Mike scrambled back up to a kneeling position, blocking Pete's view of the case. 'I mean, no... it's fine. There's another bedroom next door I think. I can handle this.'

He watched Pete leave the room and sneered at Mr Nosey Fire Forensics Fucker then slid his hand under the bed again and gripped the handle of the case. It was hot but not too much. He gently pulled it out and settled his other hand on the lid. *Please please please please...*

He took the case around the side of the bed and out of sight and settled it on the floor. The locking catch was warped and came apart easily. He flipped the lid up slowly and grinned at its contents.

~~~

'Robert! Thank God. We were worried sick!' Jerry Piper jogged over to Robert, standing by the boot of his car. Robert regarded him with a fresh view. His old friend was, he supposed, still his old friend, yet he felt no empathy towards him. But this was a loose end and one he was sure he could deal with. His assault on his son, his ex-wife and a girl he didn't recognise but could sense his son's attachment to, had failed. Getting his car and taking it away from this conspicuous spot would be much easier.

'Where've you been?' Jerry put his hand on Robert's shoulder. 'Are you okay? You look... different.'

'I'm fine.' Robert's expression was blank and indifferent. 'I got lost in the woods, of all things.'

197

'Lost? Out there? We couldn't get you on your PDA. You've been gone for almost two days!'

'Yes, I...' He forced a smile. 'I know. I'm a bit shell-shocked to be honest. I lost track of time and... well, I'm here now. So did you...' For a moment he struggled to remember why he'd gone there in the first place. 'Get any further on the murder?'

As Jerry spoke, Robert imagined how fun it would be to inject some imagery into proceedings, to alter the frequencies in the immediate area and to create something more memorable than this dull human yapping at him about actions of no consequence. He could kill Jerry and just vanish into the air if he wanted. He could kill all of them and no one would ever know.

He knew Jerry's answer anyway. No – they'd got no further with the murder of the poor girl; that sorry bag of flesh torn open for the gratification of those beasts. Robert's disappearing act had slowed them down even further. He was, in fact, the only one who would ever know who killed that girl. Jerry was a loose end, one he felt he should tie up before moving on to his brother.

Again, here he felt in the dark. It frustrated him more than anything else. Why, in this big ball of coincidences, did he have to visit his brother? This nagging feeling of doubt, of deception by his new friends, wouldn't go away. What did his brother, an eminent physicist based two hundred miles away in Sheffield, have to do with anything? It wasn't as if there was a stem he couldn't grasp – it was simply a giant void in his interpretation of the consciousness.

It was making him angry. Angry enough to kill his old mate Jerry, a friend he'd made in the Harlow police academy all those years ago. He'd been there at the hospital when Jeremy was born. He'd been best man at his wedding to Sue. His next duty as a friend would be to die horribly.

~~~

'Gabriel. Wake up.' He gently tilted the dying man's head up to meet his. 'Wake up. It is time.'

Gabriel opened his eyes just a sliver. It was all he could manage. No one had called him by his real name in such a long time.

'Come on, Gabriel. It is time to go.'

His eyes opened a little wider. He recognised the face before him as if he'd seen it yesterday. 'Ber... Bernard?'

'That's right, Gabriel. Come on.'

Gabriel felt out of place. Something was very different. He tried to recall. *I was dead. Bleeding out. That man. Asmann. He... tied me up and left me for dead. How am I not dead?*

Bernard helped him up to his feet. 'Got yourself in a bit of a pickle here, huh?'

'How am I still alive?'

'We keep an eye on our flock, dear boy. You rather messed it all up, didn't you? But that's not really important right now.'

Gabriel remembered the first time he met Bernard. After the last time he'd been released from prison in Wroclaw, he'd gone straight out to a bar. It had always been easy for him to pick up girls with his easy-going charm. Beata was pretty but large. He just wanted someone to lose himself in. They'd gone back to her apartment and as things were heating up, Beata had backed off and asked him to leave. He didn't want to. Instead, he caved her head in with an iron. A man had appeared next to him as he knelt over the body, sobbing. He introduced himself as Bernard and said everything would be okay. He could leave with Bernard and he'd take care of the mess.

From then on Bernard would visit from time to time and ask Gabriel to do things. One of those was to move to England, and when he got there Bernard set him up with a job in adult movies and helped find him a place to live.

And here he was again, just in time, offering his hand – a guardian angel for someone who deserved nothing more than death.

'I'm sorry. I just... I lost track of things. I took my eye off the ball.'

'There, there.' Bernard put his palm flat on Gabriel's forehead. 'We just need you to do something for us. Before your lights go out for good. Just one final thing.'

~~~

'I really want to get my stuff. That's all the stuff I have, in the world.'

Jez closed his hands tightly around Maria's. 'We can go back there, can't we, mum?'

Sue was happy being as far away from Malton and her monstrous ex-husband as possible and had no intention of driving back there, let alone making house calls.

'Please? How will he know where we are?'

'I still think we should call the police.' Sue took a mouthful of coffee and swallowed it hard.

'And what do we tell them?' Jez threw his hands up. '999, what service do you need? Oh yeah, my dad has turned into a raging lunatic monster and tried to kill us all. What does he look like? A giant black worm with a thousand arms that come out of his bloody eyes!'

Sue shot him a look of displeasure. 'So who do we call?'

'Ghostbusters?' Jez grinned. His mother's frown deepened.

'I promise we can just grab my stuff and get out of here and go wherever.' Maria's insistence was grating on Sue. Jez noticed.

'Mum – we can take the car. You can stay here and we'll be back in two hours.'

Sue took her phone from her bag and started thumbing the screen. 'I'll call Geoff. He'll know what to do. He's very... resourceful.'

Although Geoff could be, as she said, resourceful, she had no idea if he'd know what to do in this situation. Letting her son take the initiative seemed the best idea. Then she remembered – obstacle number one.

'But Jez, you can't drive.'

'I can.' Maria said. 'I got my licence back home. It's good anywhere in Europe.'

'Are you insured?'

'Oh... no.' Maria shrugged, disheartened. 'But who cares?'

~~~

Robert stood over Jerry's body, his face blank and Jerry's frozen in a state of terror. He had effectively fried his old friend's brain: filling it with stark fear, the imagery of his years working horrific cases from murder to child abuse and everything in between. Robert felt so powerful – the energy of Jerry's pain bleeding into his fabric.

'It doesn't matter.' Angelo's voice came from behind. Robert had been so caught up in destroying Jerry from the inside-out, he hadn't sensed his new best friends joining him. 'Nothing matters now.'

'Oh, you make it sound so morbid!' Stanley chuckled, stepping forward to stand next to Jerry's corpse. He stuck his foot in the open mouth, waggling his foot gently from side to side. 'Oh look! Jaw-dropping!'

Robert smiled. He felt better than he ever had. Getting Jerry alone had been easy. He hadn't suspected a thing. 'Come with me, Jerry. Over here. No, a bit further. Just over here. Now, close your eyes. No peeking. Don't open them until I've sliced your wrists, stomach and throat apart. There you go, old friend. Oh, are you okay? Is that blood? I think I might have some tissues in the car. Oh? You're dying? Oh dear. Oh very dear.'

'It's time to go, Robert.' Angelo seemed to be the only one taking anything seriously. 'Can you feel it?'

Robert could. Something to the north-east, miles away from Painsley Forest and the birthplace of New Robert, was tugging at him, beckoning him onwards. He hadn't noticed while he was ending Jerry's life, but he had the sense that it was okay to do so. After all, as Angelo had said, it didn't matter now. None of the details had any meaning now. The circle was complete.

Strength in numbers. That was the human way of looking at it. Bringing the key players together in the House would consolidate it all. They'd be able to dive into the pool, take the dark baptism all together and spread their poison... *wait... poison?* Robert felt contradicted. *Why would it be poison? We are not the bad guys here. This is our planet. It belongs to us more than those beings who kill each other for pleasure, who exist in a vacuum of lies, who destroy their environment for financial gain, who...*

Robert's clarity returned. He understood once more. Where ethnic cleansing had proved so ineffective in the wars that had come before, this planetary cleansing was a safe bet. It was, simply, necessary. There were still some variables but the consciousness was so powerful now, it couldn't fail. Strength in numbers would prevail.

'First, Robert. Your brother. You need to pay Simon a visit, don't you?'

The frustration rushed back as Robert couldn't push beyond the question. The answer seemed not to exist at all. He looked at Angelo, then Stanley, and frowned. 'I do not understand.'

'Neither do we,' Stanley smiled. 'That's the problem. That's why you have to find out what's going on. We'll go together. It will be quicker that way. Then after that, we can join everyone else. Okay?'

Robert nodded, not knowing what he was agreeing to.

Seventeen – Electric dreams

It didn't take long for Stanley, Angelo and Robert to travel two hundred miles to their destination, a small town a few miles outside Sheffield. Dranhill was quiet and secluded, situated within a valley cut out of rolling countryside leading back to the city. A small boutique precinct built of lime and sandstone led up from the railway station along a windy street to the centre of town, with its handful of restaurants and a couple of cafés and pubs, a bank and a supermarket. Further up the hill the main residential area spread out and then back down into another valley, heading north and further away from the city.

Dranhill was a reasonably wealthy area considering its proximity to some less salubrious settlements, and it was where Simon Moulder had decided to base his research laboratory because, located in a field about half a mile from the main drag, he didn't think he'd ever be bothered there.

So far, that had been true. On occasions when he ventured out of the lab and living quarters, no one seemed very interested in him. He had supplies delivered to a location close by and would pick them up without fanfare. It was a lonely existence but one he knew he had to live considering the potential of his hypothesis. Years before he had acquired an entity. This entity had properties he had never witnessed before.

They had run into each other during one of Simon's experiments. He was testing a hypothesis on the superconduction of negative ions. As he increased the charge beyond levels that would have been meaningful within the controlled variables, something very odd occurred: an object appeared to be forming out of the current. Although his instinct was to keep going, the expensive specialised lab equipment was dangerously close to overheating, a risk he couldn't take.

Simon had recorded his findings and slept on what to do next. It was years later when the technology caught up with his ambition, and he set to work on creating a lab with the single purpose of recreating and intensifying the earlier experiment. It hadn't taken long at all with his new equipment, made much safer with multiple cooling sources and thermal insulation.

The first experiment yielded Subject A. Incredibly this sample could be altered depending on the current and type of charge, from a fine mist of particles to a solid. This, Simon believed, could have huge implications in healthcare and manufacturing, as well as any number of other sectors. He knew he was onto something massive, but he didn't know what.

This, it transpired, was the same for the ordinary, who too had been unable to latch onto the meaning of Simon's discoveries. They could not, in fact, seem to get anywhere near the research laboratory. All they knew about it was that one Simon Moulder was running the lab. They had attempted to read him and also to get inside the lab, but each time had failed. The closer they came to it or him, the foggier their consciousness became. It was a hugely frustrating mystery but one they had largely given up on.

Now, however, with the circle so close to completion and at last a sense of urgency, it was an unknown variable that had to be ironed out. Perhaps, they thought, Robert stood a chance of getting close to his brother.

The three of them stood across the field from the lab's entrance. It was a blur for all of them and each step closer only deepened the density of the fuzz. Robert stepped forward and turned back. *Go on*, Stanley and Angelo said.

As he walked towards the small opening of the bunker, he felt his thoughts scattering, spreading and impossible to read. His strength was draining and about three hundred yards away he collapsed to his knees. Using his last wave of current to look around at his colleagues, before his head could turn he fell fully onto the grass.

~~~

'Oh God.' Simon had been watching the men on the field intently through his security system since the alarm was tripped. The system was calibrated to detect anything larger than a fox and, powered by his proprietary technology – the same that he was using to experiment on the entity – the cameras operated on a closed loop, feeding back to a single set of monitors. 'Is that... Robert?'

As the figure came closer and dropped to its knees, he zoomed in and froze the frame. It *was* his brother. 'What the hell's he doing out here? I've never told him about this place.'

Anthony and Caitlin joined him at the bank of security monitors. Caitlin recalled the name Robert from a previous conversation. 'Your brother? What's he doing here?'

'He just fell over,' Anthony volunteered, quietly. 'Weird.'

Simon had made sure his installation remained as protected as possible. Corporate espionage was rife in the science industry and letting anyone from the outside get close would almost certainly be a mistake. Now, seeing his brother collapsed in his field with two onlookers in the distance, he was more confused than worried.

'Yes, weird,' he said. 'Very, very weird.'

'Shall we let him in?' Caitlin began to back away from the monitors.

'No!' Simon shouted. 'No, wait. Something about this... it's wrong.'

Anthony agreed inwardly. He wasn't the most confident of people and moments like this ramped up his anxiety.

'Just watch. Watch and wait.' Simon smiled apologetically but insincerely at Caitlin.

The two figures standing far away didn't move.

Caitlin hesitated but said it anyway: 'Aren't you going to let him in? He might be hurt.'

'No. We observe and analyse. That's what we do. So: observe and analyse.'

'But he's your brother.'

'I know that well enough and I know what he's like, and this is not like my brother. Observe: what do you see?'

Anthony answered confidently: 'A man – *your brother* – is lying face down in our field. There are two men... *presumed* men, watching him from a distance.'

'So what does that tell us?'

'Your brother needs help?'

Simon sighed. 'Well... yes, perhaps. But more crucially, it tells us our secret is out. For whatever reason my brother is face down in our field, it can't be a positive one.'

'So what do we do?' Anthony's nerves had returned. Moments of suspense did not agree with his meagre emotional constitution. 'Just sit here... and watch?'

'Yes, exactly that. Life is a game, my esteemed colleagues. A game of few steadfast rules. And it's their move.'

Maria kept to the speed limit on the way back to the house. Getting nicked for having no insurance would scupper their plan entirely. The car would be confiscated for starters, and questions would be asked. And, as Jez's father, or rather his previous self, was tied to the police it was too risky to stick out. Careful, law-abiding driving won out.

On the way they talked – about Jez's quiet devastation, drowned out by the sheer fear of the unknown, and whether or not his dad was still his dad. Maria told him that no matter what, she was there for him. She said there were some things in life that could bring people together with a bond that could never be broken. This, as mad as it was, was one of them. This softened Jez somewhat and for the last quarter of the journey he let himself forget the events of that day so far.

They arrived back just after one PM. Jez parked along the side of the terrace end and Maria said she'd back in five minutes. He didn't feel good about her going in alone, being separated for the first time since his father's rampage. Together they were safe, or so he liked to think. Apart, they could be picked off.

Jez turned on the radio and caught the end of a news preview: '… and the army have been called in to cordon off a large spillage on the east coast of America. They now believe it to be a biological weapon. We'll be back with the full story in three…'

He pushed a button on the console and then another to settle on a station playing music. *That's better. Why do grown-ups listen to that talking shit all the time?*

The car door opened. 'Jez, come on.' He flicked the radio off and got out of the car.

'What's wrong?'

'Nothing!' Maria said. 'The house. It is empty. Come and see.'

'Empty? Seriously?'

'Yes! Come on!' Maria was whisper-shouting. Jez wondered why people spoke like that. Whispering had never made much sense to him.

They rounded the back fence together. The back door to Steve's stronghold was open. Jez followed Maria inside. 'Look,' she said. 'It is empty.'

'Oh,' he said, looking around. 'No, it's not empty. What you mean to say is it's deserted.'

Maria eyed him a little crossly. 'Okay. It's *dee*-serted. Whatever.'

Jez imagined a corridor full of girls waiting to giggle on a bed with his girlfriend, lining up outside and waiting their turn. As she led him up the first flight of stairs, he felt what his mother would call bad vibes.

'This is my room, up here.'

As Maria went into the room, Jez poked his head into the one opposite. There in the middle of the room was a bed, a long mirror on the wall behind it, and an assortment of camera and lighting equipment. A suitcase lay open on the bed and he went closer to investigate. Handcuffs, wet wipes, unmarked bottles of liquid and some industrial looking sex toys sat in the case. He felt sick looking at them, wondering which of these items his girlfriend had become intimate with.

'Jez?' Maria appeared at the door, a large suitcase at her side and a big cloth bag slung over her shoulder. 'I have my stuff. Let's go.'

'I don't get it,' he said. 'Where's everyone gone, do you think?'

Maria shrugged, looking uncomfortable with the weight of the bag. She saw he was standing next to the suitcase of sex. 'Don't look at all this stuff. I hate it. It's horrible.'

'Do all the rooms look like this?'

Maria nodded. 'Yes, there are some more upstairs. They are all the same. It is for the branding.' She fixed him impatiently. 'Come on. Let's go!'

Jez thought for a moment. 'And you did all your... video stuff here?'

'Please, Jez. I feel bad about something. We need to go now.'

'Hold on. Just a moment. You never went outside, like to... someone's house, or anything like that?'

'No.' Maria dropped the bag to the floor. 'Never. You can carry this for me. Why are you asking all these questions?'

'That girl at the fairground. You work with her. Her face is all... narrow, kinda weird looking. Did you ever do anything with her?'

'No... what girl? I don't know who you mean. Please, Jez. Please!'

Jez grabbed the top of the suitcase and closed it. 'Okay,' he said, more confused than ever. He felt like he should apologise but he didn't know what for. 'Have you looked upstairs?'

'No! There's nobody here.'

'We should take a look.'

'Why?'

'I just have a feeling. I want to see. If no one's here, we're safe, right? Two minutes, that's all. Two minutes.'

~~~

The first occurrence had been reported in Australia. A group of surfers hitting the beach at Bondi early in the morning caught some footage on video: the sand seemed to be leaking some kind of oil. It was dark and gloopy, flopping out from underneath and onto the sand, where it spread like an ink blot on paper before coming to settle in a pool about five metres across.

The Australian national news picked up on this right away and blamed an oil spill from a pipeline. Environmentalists were called in and the area was cordoned off.

Thailand's beaches were next, or at least they were in terms of news coverage. A beach on the east side of the island of Koh Samui became fairly saturated with the oil. A British documentary team making a film about the sea life there had happened to witness this odd phenomenon and sent footage back to the BBC, which ran it as a short segment in its lunchtime broadcast but without reference to the Australian spill.

Further west and Kazakhstan in its afternoon national bulletin screened a number of amateur recordings capturing these odd spillages, followed by the same in Finland. Back in the UK, a group of scientists plotted a line and hypothesised these spills were occurring from south-east to north-west, which meant the north of Greenland would likely be next. The BBC ran an info-graphic. This speculation was disproved within hours as the east coast of America reported the next sightings.

The Americans reacted quickly and classed it as a potentially biological weapon of unknown origin. As the army set up a cordon around a small area of New York, more sightings occurred in Boston, down in Jacksonville and then the Bahamas. Within hours, activity on social media networks had declared it 'an attack on US soil'. The US Senate called an emergency meeting and an assortment of highly-decorated colonels and generals and eminent advisers convened with President Davis Peters to discuss targets for retaliation.

The spills were relatively small in isolation but as the media began to pin the world map it became accepted that it was more likely a natural rather than man-made phenomenon. Anti-fracking campaigners joined

208

the circus, claiming the eruptions were the consequence of drilling far below towns and cities, resulting in irreparable cracks in the core. Oil companies were quick to defend themselves and pointed out that no fracking had occurred in Finland or Jamaica, the latter of which was the most recent to report a sighting. The campaigners' retort was that the structural damage to the core had been so bad that large geological shifts were occurring as a result.

The first sighting in the UK was next.

~~~

'Seriously, Mike. What the hell's wrong with you?' Pete had Mike pressed up against the wall. 'Drugs? Fucking drugs? Seriously?'

Mike had almost got away with his haul. Having miraculously discovered among the rubble the dead dealer's unsold stash, he'd spent a little too much time deliberating over what to take for himself. Caught up in the moment, he was slow to notice Pete coming back into the burnt out bedroom and he hurriedly shoved the suitcase back under the bed.

When they got back to the station, Pete had stayed close and when Mike went into the toilets, Pete followed him. Mike clearly looked shifty when he went into a cubicle. Pete went into the one next to Mike's and stood on the toilet to peer over, whereupon he found Mike staring at a baggie in his hand.

'It isn't what you think!'

'Yeah, I bet. Cause I'm thick, right? I've never seen a drug addict before...'

Pete pressed Mike firmly across the chest with one arm and thrust his hand into Mike's trouser pocket.

'I suppose I'm imagining this too, yeah?' Considering the events of the week that far, it was the first real adrenaline rush Pete had experienced in a while.

'Let's just turn 'em all out then.' Pete backed off and gestured to Mike to empty his pockets on the surface next to the sinks at the far end of the room.

'Bollocks, no. No!'

'You don't really have a choice, mate!'

Mike turned back towards the exit and went to push past Pete, who grabbed at his jacket and shoved him back against the wall. Mike pushed back this time and managed to overpower Pete. He ran for the exit and punched the door open.

'Mike!' Pete rushed out after him and saw him heading down the corridor towards the front desk. His progress was halted by a wall of people, staring up at the television hung over the reception desk.

On the screen was Piotr Bogdanek, the man at the centre of the media circus for that week. The police hadn't released details of his real name, his psychiatric assessment, or anything else that might lead to further speculation on his crimes. At the foot of the screen, in bold digits, two timers counted down:

01:54:14

03:54:14

Pete grabbed Mike's arm and followed his gaze. 'What the…' Mack was in the crowd of about fifteen people. She turned quickly, trying to spy one of her colleagues, and met Mike's eyes. She thought he looked half-dead. Then she slipped back through the mire to reach her friends.

'It just came on by itself.'

'Huh?' Pete kept his eyes on the screen, mesmerised by the digits flicking on and off with each passing second.

'Really. I was standing out here filing the report with Judy and the TV just sparked up. And that was on it.'

'I guess we know what happened to that bastard then.' Pete, his grip still tight on Mike's arm, felt nauseous examining the image of the Polish kidnapper and murderer, his face devoid of colour, his pores dry and exposed, his eyes red and sunken. The killer's eyes were barely open but there was a hollow, lights-out dullness to them.

More staff arrived in the lobby behind them, muttering that the TVs in their offices had come on by themselves too, showing the same image.

Mack noticed Pete's grip on Mike. 'What's up with you two?'

'Never mind,' Pete answered quickly. He let go of Mike's arm. 'So we've got about two hours until… *something* happens.' He looked around the lobby. 'Where's Briggs?'

The crowd turned as one as a uniformed officer burst through the front door. 'It's everywhere! All up the street!'

Mack pushed her way through to him and made it outside, followed closely by Pete. An electrical shop a few doors down had a similar gathering outside, all fixed on the screens in the window. In the other direction, a newsagent's façade showed the same broadcast.

Back inside, as Mike snaked off away from the crowd towards the rear exit of the police station, Judy tried changing the channel. She flicked through twenty or so before realising it was the only thing on. Next she turned the volume up. The muttering in the room died down as the sound on the TV became louder. It was music – slow, drunken jazz, a buzzing sound behind it, buzzing like wasps. Judy put the remote control down on the desk and kept her eyes on the enigmatic, terrifying image.

One woman in the lobby, who had popped in that afternoon to hand in a wallet she'd found on the south pier, began to scream. Mike heard this only faintly as he took his car key out of his pocket and left the building.

~~~

There was a different show taking place in Dranhill. The two figures on the far side of Simon's field had gone, with only his brother remaining, still face down. Caitlin had spat out her coffee when the figures just vanished into the air. Anthony was in the way of the blast and swore when the spray landed on his back and neck.

They all knew what they'd just seen. It was the same physically impossible behaviour they'd seen in their laboratory; these entities shifting between solid and some kind of liquid or gas at will or by force. For several minutes Simon kept his focus on the spot where those figures had stood. He then checked the full radius around the hatch to see if they'd just shifted their viewpoint, but it appeared that now it was just them and his brother.

'Okay,' he said at last. 'I'm going out. Whatever is going on, sitting in here isn't going to reveal any answers.'

He stood up and was about to leave the security room.

'Shit! Dr M!' He turned back to see Anthony pointing at the central monitor. 'Look!'

Around Robert's prone body, some kind of dark gloop was pooling, spreading out and snaking across the grass. Simon watched it intently as it came out from underneath his brother and then seemed to vaporise and disappear.

Caitlin stood clutching her empty coffee mug tightly in both hands. 'Dr... M... I'm scared. I'm really scared.'

Simon put his arm around her and brought her close to his side. 'Me too, Katie. I'm pretty scared too.'

Anthony's adrenaline rush took him over the line of sensibility. 'I'll go out with you.'

Across the field, Angelo and Stanley communicated through the consciousness, their forms forced away from the humanoid solidity into their basic particular constitution. Robert's collapse had as good as proven their fears about this place.

'We are stronger than him.'

'But it is killing us even now.'

'No, not killing. Reducing.'

'Then there is no point. We are needed elsewhere.'

'What about him?'

'There is nothing we can do. He was always expendable.'

A spike hit them both.

'We need to go.'

'My girls.'

'You can't bring them with you.'

'They are all I have. All I had.'

'Soon you will have so much more.'

~~~

Mike hadn't got far in his car and had to ditch it half-way up the promenade. He had intended to go home and pack a bag but after leaving the station he'd run into traffic that just wasn't moving. All he had was two pockets full of Bleach's drugs. Bleach was dead, so they held no monetary value. Mike felt good about acquiring them. At least they'd be put to good use.

Crowds of people ran past, some of them screaming. A voice in his head told him to run too – to get as far away from there as possible. It occurred to him that as this seemed to be happening everywhere, it wouldn't matter where he ran to, but the voice was more compelling.

He snaked his way up through the cobbled street parallel to the promenade and headed down to the beach, figuring he'd escape a lot faster away from the crowds. When he got down to the pathway he saw another crowd, rolling a lifeboat out of a warehouse and down a concrete slope into the water. He jogged over to them and could then see a number of them already out in the water.

'Room for one more?' He flashed his badge at a middle-aged couple in clothes befitting faux sailing enthusiasts and smiled.

'We'll be safer at sea,' the man said. 'Whatever's coming, we'll be safe out there.' The lady with him nodded sternly. 'Give us a hand then, son.'

~~~

'Can you hear that?' Jez stopped fast as the sound startled him. 'I thought you said it was… empty.'

Maria was two steps behind him. 'It was. I checked.' She heard the music too – faint, coming from not just one place, a stereo effect.

Jez angled his head, trying to locate the source. 'It's up here.' He strode up the rest of the stairs and towards a door across the landing. He opened it cautiously, the sound widening with it. Across the room, at the end of a line of beds and assorted furniture, a TV stood on top of a dresser. Maria gasped as she came up behind him.

'What is that? That's creepy.' Jez recognised the man's face from the news reports. 'That music – like lift music. Weird.'

'Why are there two clocks?' Maria tugged on Jez's arm.

Jez shook his head as he went to turn the TV off. He pressed the red button on the lower right of the unit and it flashed off. 'Whatever it was, it's fucking creeping me right…' The TV flicked back on, the sound bleeding back into the room. Jez turned back to it and pushed the button again, believing he hadn't connected with it properly the first time.

'Let's get out of here,' he said. Maria nodded. As they left the room, the TV came on again. 'Jez.' She wrapped her arms around him tightly. 'Jez. I want to go.'

'What's that room up there?'

Maria followed his gaze. 'Oh, that's the office. Steve's office.'

He unbound himself from Maria's arms and headed towards it, the sound of drunken jazz getting louder the closer he came to the door. He felt like he should knock. Maria scuttled up close behind him. He grabbed the handle, twisted it and pushed the door open.

The music was louder this time – almost distorting in the TV's shallow speakers, and still coming from the dorm they'd just left. Jez quickly surveyed the room: a dark red colour scheme and good looking

213

wooden and leather furnishings. A couple of abstract paintings hung on the wall past the desk and the only window in the room was partially covered with a burgundy velvet curtain. Off to the other side was another door. The TV on the wall was large and from the doorway Jez couldn't see the image clearly.

'Just leave it!' Maria called. She was now facing back down the corridor, feeling more upset by the second. She felt like something was coming for them, or maybe waiting at the bottom of the stairs. The distance to their getaway vehicle was lengthening in her mind. The concept of safety was slipping away.

Jez walked over to the desk and picked up the controller. He pointed it at the TV and pushed the red button. It flicked off and in three seconds came back on. He flicked the channel selector up, then again, and again, and put the controller down. 'It's on every channel! Every fucking channel!'

'Jez, I just want to leave. Come on!'

He didn't hear her over the sickly music. He walked up to the TV and reached up to take each side as firmly as he could. There was no cable visible and as he looked up to see behind it he saw the cabling had been built into the wall. He tugged at the set and it budged a little, twisting slightly against the wall bracket. He tried to wrench it from the other side and this time it gave more.

'Oh. Fuck this.' He turned away from the TV and went back to the desk. He yanked a small lamp off it, freeing the power cord from underneath it, and launched the lamp at the TV. It smashed the screen and the image disappeared. The music continued to play, but quickly became quieter and then went off altogether. Maria had picked up the remote control and manually turned the sound down.

'I didn't think of that!' Jez was on fire inside – something raging through him, the pain of the day pooling in his core and forcing some kind of vengeful aggression. He was irritated too that his control over something as benign as a television had been taken away.

'Let's just get out of here. Please Jez.'

He nodded, following Maria out of the room with some kind of extra weight behind his steps, his body feeling primed for action. The sound of the TV in the dorm grew louder then quieter as they hurried down the stairs. Maria took her suitcase by the handle and Jez slung her cloth bag over his shoulder. It was, as she had warned, heavy.

They got down to the ground floor and ran out of the open door, out through the back yard and around to the street. Maria dropped the suitcase on the pavement and fumbled in her jacket pocket for the car key.

'It's fine. Look…' Jez tried the door but it didn't open. 'It usually opens automatically.' He tugged at it again, this time with so much force that it hurt his fingers. 'It won't open! It won't fucking open!' He thumped his fist onto the car roof.

'Hey!' Maria found the key and opened the car manually. 'What's got into you?'

Jez sneered. 'Into me? What the hell was all that? That was your house!'

Maria looked wounded. 'I haven't been there for two days, Jez. Two days. I've been with you.' She got into the car. Jez put his hands on the bonnet and leaned onto it.

'Just give me a minute, okay? I'm sorry. I feel… I feel really angry. Two minutes.'

Maria slammed the door more than she'd intended to and stared out of her window. Down the street were groups of people blocking the road and pavement. She leaned forward and switched the radio on. At first she didn't realise it was the same music they'd just run away from. The realisation punched her in the gut and she flung her door open.

Jez pushed himself back up off the bonnet. 'What…'

'Look…' She pointed to the crowds. 'Over there. Something's going on.'

Jez jogged up the street and Maria followed at walking speed then stopped, not wanting to get too far away from the car. She watched Jez reach the gathering. He turned to look back at her and shrugged. Moments later he jogged back to her.

'It's everywhere. The TVs – everyone's TV is showing that guy and playing that music. They think it's a terrorist attack or something.'

'We need to get out of here.'

Jez nodded and put his hand on Maria's shoulder, leading her back to the car. They got in and Jez immediately poked at the console, cutting the radio amplifier. Maria started the engine and reversed up just enough to make a U-turn. Facing the promenade, she drove to the junction and stopped.

Both ways stood masses of people lining the streets. Jez opened his window. That music – drunken jazz; a skittery, lazy beat lolloping behind sickly brass tones and a piano played underwater – was carried in. He closed the window.

'What the fuck is going on?' Maria was all fright in her face and her voice and her posture.

'Just drive.'

'Where?'

'I don't know. Just drive!'

~~~

Simon opened the hatch carefully and stepped out into the field. Anthony followed him out and left the hatch open. Caitlin was ready to lock it down on her employer's instruction. As she sat in front of the bank of monitors, her left foot tapped an irregular, nervous rhythm.

Robert's body seemed even more lifeless as the men came closer to it. The strange pool had gone without a trace and all that remained was the silence of the countryside. Simon knelt down cautiously and put his hand on his brother's head. It was hot.

'Robert? It's Simon. Robert?'

Anthony squatted on his other side. 'Maybe he's just passed out.'

Simon nodded. 'He's burning up.' He put both hands under his brother and rolled him onto his back. Robert's face was red, his eyes closed. Simon tapped the back of his hand on Robert's cheek and checked the horizon. The spot where those figures had stood still seemed *off*.

'He's alive at least. Let's get him inside.'

~~~

'Okay? Are we online?'

'Hold on.' Suzy scrolled back up the server diagnostics page. 'Yes. Now. We are online!'

Marcus fixed his eyes on the camera. *The Juice*'s resident video blogger, Johann, steadied the unit in his palms.

'Live from *The Juice*, this is Marcus Talbot bringing you the news as it happens.'

216

Suzy glanced at her monitor to check the feed was coming through. She'd turned the sound down to avoid feedback. Johann had insisted on it. Everything Johann said was taken as gospel in the office.

'As Britain's media is besieged by an unknown hijacker, here at *The Juice* we are pleased to report it's business as usual. Stay tuned for regular updates from around the world.'

Johann paused the feed. Marcus' body language invited a response.

'That's a good start,' Jack said. He'd been watching the timers counting down. The top one was down to 01:17:23. 'Okay, so let's pull the data together and get back on in five.'

Suzy's monitor showed *The Juice* logo static in the feed window. She brought up the analytics window. 'It's up to 289,076 now. That's doubled right off the bat.'

'Right,' Jack said. 'Marcus. For the next shot let's get the TV in the background.' He gestured to Ian, a media intern they'd taken on just a week ago, to help set the shot up. 'After this shot we'll hit the street, and I want as little downtime as poss so let's get down there – no delays. Okay?'

General agreement murmured through the office. Marcus sidled up next to Johann, who was fiddling with a setting on the camera. 'How come this works?'

'You mean the TV? Yeah, that's easy. The TV broadcast is not the same as a web broadcast. Same goes for radio. TVs are plugged in. Wireless stuff isn't affected. I mean, in theory whoever's doing this could tap the web but there's like millions of servers around the world. However they're doing the TV, that's different.'

Marcus nodded. He understood the basics of plug-and-play and at the least was grateful that he was in an office full of wireless devices. The camera ran on a battery which was fully charged in readiness for whatever they would need to film, and several backups were available. The wireless connection would work anywhere in London, so it would be straightforward to keep the feed going as long as they needed to.

'Shit!' Suzy eyed the stats again. 'Up to a million now. And rising.'

'We might be the only ones doing this,' Jack said.

'Doubtful.' Johann shook his head. '*The Juice* isn't the centre of the universe. There're others with *much* better equipment than us.'

Jack sighed and rolled his eyes. 'Okay, well let's just make sure we do it the best then.' He turned towards his office. 'Jay – where are those figures? Come on. Chop-chop!'

'Coming!' Jay Bance skipped around the desks and handed Jack a pile of paper. 'Hot off the press, sir!'

Jack flicked through the printouts. 'This is…' His expression turned from focus to disbelief. 'Okay. There's reports on the wire from Asia, America, all over Europe. The oil spills and now this music. It's global! Fuck me, it's *global*.'

Suzy looked over at Jack, concerned. 'Yeah. That's what I'm seeing here too.'

Jack handed the top sheet to Marcus. 'It's all there. Keep your PDA open and we'll run the latest stuff through to you. Okay?'

Marcus nodded. 'I'm ready when you are. Johann?'

'Sure.' He motioned for Marcus to stand in a spot just ahead of the TV on the wall. 'On five.' Marcus took position. 'Okay, we're on one, two, three, four…'

'You're with us live from *The Juice*. I'm Marcus Talbot. As you can see behind me, the UK is reeling from some kind of attack on our broadcast networks and we are now able to confirm the attack is global. From Australia to India and including the American networks, we're seeing the biggest media attack of all time unfolding right now.'

Suzy added the timers in a close-up inset. Johann had only just shown her how to do this but she did it well.

'With two countdowns overlaying this image and just over one hour to go on the first, the world is watching the same clock regardless of time zone and we've just had further confirmation that the British cabinet has set up an emergency convention. Reports coming in on the global newswire are officially linking the hijack to the international oil spills of the last twenty-four hours. We can also confirm that many flights are being grounded as this chaos ensues.'

Marcus swiped his hand out of shot and Johann paused the feed again. 'Right, let's get outside.'

~~~

'Dr M. He's waking up.' Caitlin's voice was quiet and withdrawn.

Simon clicked the communicator. 'Okay. I'm coming.' He hurried out of the security room, leaving Anthony in charge, and jogged down the short corridor to the first aid room. Caitlin was leaning back against the wall, looking like she wanted to be as far away from the red-faced man as possible.

'It's okay. He can't get up, see?' Simon pointed to the straps around his brother's wrists and ankles on the stretcher.

'Robert? It's Simon. Can you hear me?' Robert's eyelids twitched.

'It's your brother, Simon. Can you hear me?' He tapped his fingers on Robert's cheeks. 'Come on, Rob. Come on. Open those eyes. We need to make sure you're okay, okay?'

One eye opened, its movement laboured as if pulled from the other side. It looked up at Simon. The other eye followed.

'Hey, Rob. It's Simon. We've got you on a stretcher here. You were collapsed outside. Can you hear me okay?'

Robert nodded painfully. He felt entirely drained but his head seemed primed to explode. The pressure in his ears and temples made it hard to hear.

'Great. Okay. Do you know where you are?'

Robert struggled to look around the room. He shook his head. Simon flashed a glance at Caitlin.

'You're in my research lab.' Simon reached to the trolley behind him and picked up a small black box. He held it over Robert's body and moved it the length from his head to his feet. 'Nothing,' he said to Caitlin. 'Nothing at all.'

'Who brought you here, Rob? Why are you here?'

Robert couldn't find the answer. He blinked at Simon. He wanted to speak but couldn't find the connection between his mouth and brain.

The room's communicator beeped. 'Dr M. You'd better come and see this.'

'Caitlin, you go.' She was pleased to have a valid reason to leave and did so without hesitation, getting back to the security room in seconds.

'Hey, check this out.' Anthony swivelled the laptop so Caitlin could see. 'The TV signals – they've been hijacked. Everywhere.'

'That's okay. We don't have a TV in here.'

'No, look. Watch this.' Anthony dabbed his index finger on the touchpad. The feed started. '... and as you can see, it's chaos on the streets of London...'

219

'What is this?' Caitlin had never been very interested in online exploits. Books were much better. Anthony was well aware of her preference for paper over ones and zeroes.

'It's *The Juice*. It's like a news site. Mainly celeb stuff. Sensational. Well, anyway, the other day they published a couple of stories straight from this murderer on the south coast.' He looked up at Caitlin and confirmed she had no idea what he was referring to. 'Okay, so he also kidnapped this girl and the girl got away and now he's here, on everyone's TV, and there's a timer counting down, and there's like *forty minutes left*!'

Anthony's expression was more excited than frightened. Caitlin didn't know how to feel about this odd revelation. They turned their attention back to the live feed. The camera was struggling to follow the presenter as he made his way through a noisy crowd of people. His voice was just loud enough to hear: '... we now have confirmation that the image of Piotr Bogdanek is unique to the UK...'

An inset appeared showing four faces, with the text underneath reading 'Yuri Lenbedev – Moscow. Darius Phelps – Washington. Peter Johannsen – Denmark. Paul Figgins – Sydney.'

'It appears the regions are broadcasting the same music but the personalities are local to those regions...'

The presenter lost his footing as the crowd overwhelmed him. Seconds later the live feed went dead, replaced by the logo and a separate window showing the grim countdown.

'Shit. Dr M. He needs to know this.' Caitlin ran back out and down the corridor to the first aid room. Simon was bent over his brother's body.

'He's dead. He was there and his face went redder and then... that's it.'

Caitlin stopped in her tracks. 'Dr M. I'm so sorry. I'm so sorry. But you've got to see this. On the computer. The world's gone crazy.'

Simon forced himself to sit up. He looked at his late brother's face, the rosy glow now softening back to its natural colour. In the last few hours he had kept his thoughts to himself and he had no desire to utter them aloud. The circumstances all pointed to his research – his electrical noodlings, which somehow had killed his brother. What else could it have been? That something had happened to Robert that brought him to this place was not in doubt; whatever that might have been was though.

220

As Anthony re-played *The Juice*'s feed from that afternoon, Simon gradually began to form an opinion. Electricity: just as he had sought to harness it for his own scientific gratification, someone somewhere had gone *all-in*. He knew how they could do it in theory, and it would mean whoever was behind it had global power he couldn't remember a precedent for.

TV, the drug of the nation, was doing what some people warned it would. Where fear and control were manipulated by faceless bastards in boardrooms, now they had been taken to the nth degree. A simple image, some jaunty music and a couple of ominous countdowns were all they needed to plunge the world into chaos. Those timers ticking down towards who-knows-what might have been just as effective on their own.

There, in Dranhill, in the quiet of his research lab, with his two pseudo-children safe in his bunker, Simon knew the only option was to wait and see. To watch the timer. To pray.

~~~

'Try up there.' Jez pointed to the left as he keyed in his mother's number. Maria turned right. He looked up. 'No, that's where we've come from!'

'You fucking drive then!' Maria slammed the brakes on and quickly got out of the car. Jez looked back at his phone and pressed the *Call* button, then clicked the speaker on. It rang four times.

'Jez? Jez? Is that you?'

'Yes!' The line was very faint. 'Can you hear me?'

'Oh, Jez. Can you speak up? I can hardly hear you.'

'Mum. We're trying to get out of here but all the roads are blocked. It's manic.'

'What did you say?' It sounded like his mother was running. 'Say that again?'

'We can't get out of Malton. There's traffic everywhere.'

'Jez?' Her voice was barely audible, competing with the sound of heavy wind and the rustling of clothes. 'Jez? Just get away from there. Just go! Go!'

'Mum? Muuuum!' The line went dead. Jez got out of the car and shook his head at Maria. 'She was running. Why would she be running?'

'Look around, Jez.' Her voice was flat. 'Everyone is running. Maybe we should run too.'

'But what are they running from?'

Maria looked around.

Jez thumbed his PDA screen up, his eyes darting between the icons. He selected *News360* and waited for the app to launch. It didn't. Next he tried *The Juice*. That wasn't working either, just hanging as a loading bar refused to fill. He tried *News360* again and this time the bar slowly crept up. *Come on come on come on come on...* eventually it loaded and the top story filled the page.

Oil spreads as countdown nears zero...

Underneath the headline was a rough photo of a beach completely saturated in the oil, partially covering the road alongside. It appeared to be reaching, like a worm or slug, its antennae leading it forward.

'Fuckin'ell.' Jez felt a rush of cold in his chest as his stomach twisted. 'This is real. This is actually happening.'

'What is?' Maria had stopped looking hurt and was now just a picture of worry.

'Oil spills. Didn't you hear on the radio earlier? There's oil coming out of the ground, all over.'

'Let me see.' Maria skipped round the car and joined Jez. 'Oh shit. Really? That's not possible though.'

'Nothing that's happened today is possible. None of it.'

Jez scrolled down further and beneath the photo and its caption, which stated it was taken just an hour before on the south-west coast of France, was the timer: 00:05:09.

'We've got five minutes,' said Jez, quietly.

'What happens then?'

'How should I know?'

~~~

Simon didn't know what else to do with his brother: he fetched a sheet from the laundry cupboard and draped it over him, turning the first aid room into a makeshift morgue. He felt bereft; everything had happened too fast and he'd had no time to come up with any conclusions. To a scientist that was the worst thing: a result with no accompanying explanation or identifiable cause.

For a while he just sat with his elbows on the stretcher and his head in his hands. He thought about the global broadcast and the timer. People could just turn their TVs off, he thought, but they were probably too transfixed by the countdown to do that. Ignoring it wouldn't make it go away. If anything, it would heighten the anxiety; the fear of the unknown. The whole thing appeared to be an exercise in propagating fear – but why? The how was fairly straightforward, he knew. Hackers could get into just about anything and if the effort was co-ordinated enough, and timed just right, he could visualise a scenario in which it would work. Indeed, it was working right at that moment.

Hacking had become so rife that several governments had signed treaties to crack down on the perpetrators, and to all intents and purposes it had worked. Very few cases had occurred in recent years and those that did were punished quickly and severely. It seemed odd to Simon that the sentence for hacking could be longer than one for murder, but he wasn't particularly interested in justice. After all, justice was subjective and as a scientist he had to deal only in facts.

The facts as he understood them were simple: his self-sufficient facility was out of the loop. Whoever had got themselves in control of the world's broadcasts would not be able to hack into his little set-up. He was entirely off the grid. An internet connection to the outside world, hidden behind an advanced firewall, was the only tether and if that went off, it wouldn't be the end of the world. A single cable connected to the rest of the world was not of concern simply because it was isolated.

The timer played on his mind the most. There seemed to be no significance as once the first timer reached zero it would be just coming up to half-past six. The second would stop at a few minutes before eight-thirty. He reasoned that time zones would make this even less significant. If the Americans had the same timer, which according to the news websites was true, there was no point trying to guess the reason anyway. In some parts of the world it was the middle of the night though, and if every TV in every house had turned itself on to that creepy vision, it really would be a waking nightmare.

Eventually Simon got up and left his brother's warm corpse. As he walked away he latched onto the most important thought: how did his brother become charged up with the entity he had in his lab, or something very close to it? As he had drawn closer, the charge in the lab's self-sufficient network had floored him, and seemed to have wiped the charge out. That suggested it was a positive-negative reaction. But it also meant the subjects in the lab were different. They reacted in various ways but they remained vital. He had not, however, seen the entity interact with a human.

He joined Caitlin and Anthony by the laptop in the security room. The light was dimming outside as the sun started to descend behind the tree line.

'How long is it now?'

'Four minutes.'

'Four minutes.'

They sat in silence and watched the timer count down together.

~~~

Jet, Ebony, Raven, Sable
For one and for all
When the circle is fulfilled

Gabriel's face was gone from the screens, replaced by just these cryptic lines and the second countdown timer. As the first had hit zero, what happened next was not instant. Relatively few would have noticed it anyway. Those who had kept their distance deliberately or fortuitously from a television set were none the wiser; entire villages in rural Africa and cave dwellers in Afghanistan avoided the hysteria, as did many in the slums of Nigeria and the Scottish Highlands, deep in the mines of Western Australia and in the glacial environs of southern New Zealand.

They could not, however, avoid the effect. The oil spilled out from the earth in many hundreds of thousands of gallons, following the geography of the lands it covered, from mountain tops to the depths of valleys. And from the oil came these beings, these shadows emerging from it, growing out of the very ground before the sheltered and exposed alike, enveloping them and turning them to dust, swept away in the flood of primordial sludge.

Julia Bugden, a retired anthropologist living on the outskirts of Seattle in the USA, kept horses but her family didn't own a TV or radio. She walked about half way back from the stables to her house, across a crisp green lawn, when the oil spilled out in front of her. She stopped in her

224

tracks and by the time she realised what was happening it was too late for her to get away. The figure rose up right in front of her, forming from the oil, tendrils reaching out of it and piercing Julia's skin. It reached into her skull and tore her brain apart.

More figures formed from that one and began to spread out, some entering the house to take Julia's husband and two daughters and others flowing off the property to devour her neighbours.

It was Kirsty Davies' ninth birthday. She was waiting for her friends to turn up for her party. Her parents' bedroom window, on the second floor, provided a wide view of the street below. As she hopped up onto her mother's dresser she nearly fell back off it with the force of her scream. A horde of beings, trailing a thick oily river, were making their way up the street. She watched in horror as the figures, liquid but upright, tall and terrifying, took her neighbours' doors down so easily and entered their houses. Her parents joined her at the window, concerned and affectionate, and then they saw it too, just as their front door was taken off its hinges downstairs.

Kirsty heard the screams outside and added hers. Her parents – Don, a thirty-two-year-old postman and Susie, twenty-nine and a hairdresser – leaned up against their bedroom door. The oil came rushing underneath, pooling between them and their daughter. It rose up and split into three, then devoured the family.

Olufemi Johnson, a bank clerk living in Johannesburg, ran home after leaving work in a hurry. He sat down on the couch and began to eat his salad sandwich as he flicked on the TV. He was fascinated by the countdown, the image of the Cape Town Butcher who had gone missing, and wanted to be safe at home when the first timer reached zero. He'd had a compelling feeling to go, to run, but he fought it with the greater urge to get home. There were crowds everywhere, and that awful music bleeding from every building and car. He found the pull lessen and almost go entirely once he'd got away from that music, and with the sound off on his TV he found his thoughts clearer.

Then the words came up – the riddle. It was somehow creepier than the image it had replaced, the cold and dead eyes of the murderer who had taken over ten lives in South Africa – young men and women – in his quest for infamy. A knock on his door jolted him from his thoughts and he almost tripped while running to it. As the door opened, the nice lady from down the hall at number 5 told him to run, to get away from there as fast as possible. She was screaming and waving her arms about – out of her mind. He could hear that music coming from her flat, drifting out into the hallway and joining the others in a grim chorus.

As she tugged at Olufemi's clothes, pulling him out of his flat, the oil appeared behind her. She saw Olufemi's face drop and turned to scream one last time before it consumed her. He ran back inside, slamming the door, then took a kitchen knife and crouched down by his kitchen cabinets. He heard the door slam down onto the floor and pressed himself tighter against the surface, desperate not to be seen. He could almost feel the oil slithering across his lounge when the urge came back – a voice in his head, telling him to stand up. As soon as he did, the oil formed into a column and shot right through his face and out the other side, his brain pulped and splattering against the cupboards on the kitchen wall.

The oil spread through the favelas in Brazil's Sao Paolo, the cobbled streets of Split in Croatia, the landscape gardens at Wisley in south-east England and the red light district in Amsterdam – and everywhere in between. By the time the second clock had clicked down by twenty minutes, the global death toll was over two million.

~~~

Pete and Mack had caught up with Mike just as he boarded the boat. They'd tracked his PDA and fought through the chaos to get to him, but it was too late. He shrugged as the lifeboat sped away from the jetty, leaving his colleagues stranded and dumbfounded. The constant mantra in his head, *just run just get away just run just get away*, kept him on that boat. He felt he should go back to them but his desire to satisfy the urge in his brain was stronger. He could still hear that music, going round and round in his head but also coming from the town like a cloud of sound.

Pete and Mack's desire to find their friend was replaced with the same as his – to escape, to go quickly. They ran around the side of the lifeboat building and in through the large double gate. There were bags of inflatable dinghies and snap-together oars. They quickly unwrapped a dinghy and were relieved to find it was self-inflating. Two minutes later they were on the water, sporting expensive borrowed lifejackets, paddling as fast as possible. The shoreline and horizon were dotted with people doing the same thing.

A large wave knocked their dinghy back toward the shore. Pete took both oars and tried to dig in, his back to the beach as he jammed the oars into the sand below and frantically tried to push back out. Mack screamed as the oil appeared at the top of the beach and flooded down it, heading straight for them.

'Get out and swim!' Pete stopped pushing and turned to see the oil rising up and forming into some kind of tall figure. It looked to him like the grim reaper. He swung his body over and fell sideways into the water, then got enough purchase on the sand at his feet to launch himself backwards, taking the dinghy in his hand and pushing it out with him.

The oil stopped fast against the water, its tendrils snaking over each other. Pete made it about twenty feet out, pushing Mack in the dinghy and all the time watching the oil spreading across but not forward, and stopped.

'Pete! For fuck's sake, what are you doing? Move!'

He stood his ground, the water lapping up against his face. 'Look! It's stopped. It's not following us.'

Mack leaned forward and scrambled to Pete's end of the dinghy. Several hundred yards further out to sea, Mike's lifeboat had stopped too, bobbing in the waves as its passengers watched with terrified fascination.

'You're right,' she said. 'What's it doing? And what the fuck is it, anyway?'

Pete struggled to stand upright and realised they were being sucked further out to sea. He grabbed a handle on the side of the dinghy and swung up into it, soaking Mack in the process.

He picked the paddles up again and began to row just hard enough against the force of the sea to maintain the distance. The oil had almost covered the whole beach before it withdrew from the shore, retreating back up to the pathway, where it seemed to gather itself and rush over the concrete lip and out of sight.

'It must hate water,' Mack called. 'We might actually be safe!'

Pete shook his head. 'If you're happy to die out here, then yeah, we're safe.'

'Oh my God.' Pete saw Mack's relieved expression disintegrate as a massive shadow appeared over them. The oil had formed a huge canopy, coming over from the promenade in the shape of a giant wave but hovering there in mid-air, strands lurching from all over it. 'Row faster! Go!'

Pete put everything he had into it, plunging the oars into the water as deep as he could and going nowhere fast.

'No, Pete! Shallow – keep your strokes shallow!'

He changed tack and started making headway. Mack could see the huge tsunami of grey death edging forward and back, suspended but gearing up to pounce.

'Get in the water!' She grabbed Pete by his lifejacket and they tumbled in. Pete grabbed the handle and managed to flip the boat over. They ducked into the water and came up underneath it, each taking a handle to stay afloat under the protective shell.

'What the fuck is that thing?'

Mack was worn out and struggling to speak. It took her three attempts through shallow breaths to say: 'I'm hungry, Pete. I'm really hungry.'

~~~

'What is that stuff?'

'I don't know. It looks like some kind of liquid, but it has to be carbon-based.'

'Because electricity wouldn't travel in water?'

'No. You know better than that! It most definitely would. But it would also not carry whatever this thing is, as once the ions connect with it there's no separating the two until the charge is released. Either that or in theory this mass charge, if controlled in water, could do a lot of damage. A lot.'

'But it doesn't *look* like water.'

'Exactly. That's what I'm saying. Whatever that substance is, it appears to be liquid carbon. Whatever that may be. It leaked out of Robert before he collapsed so whatever it was, it brought him here in some capacity.'

'Okay, so by doing this, we're...'

'Careful!' Simon put his hand on the stretcher to stop Caitlin pushing it too far. 'We're not quite ready.'

Caitlin pulled herself in. She hadn't really understood her employer's instructions. Why they were about to fuse his dead brother with Subject K was not entirely clear. She felt as nervous then as she had on her first day in the lab.

'That's it. Pressure, temperature and atmosphere now equal to subject base levels. Zero charge confirmed in chamber.' Simon confirmed the calibration and gestured for Caitlin to push the stretcher all the way in. She did so.

'Closing screen now.' Anthony had just this single job to do, and he did it well. His colleague had been given the slightly more awkward task of putting the stretcher inside, but he supposed sealing the chamber properly was of equal importance.

'Can this even work?' Caitlin looked at Simon with wide, inquisitive eyes. 'I just don't see how it can.'

'There's only one way to find out.' Simon's focus on the console was intense. 'Okay. Which one of you wants to get subject K in there?'

After a brief silence, Anthony volunteered. He walked to the end of the row of cabinets and stopped at K's, then pressed a button to withdraw the shutters. Hovering inside was a fine mist. K had been the easiest to work with and had yielded the best results, so it made sense, Simon had explained, to use K on his brother. Years earlier than he had envisaged doing such a thing, now was the time. Although the science behind what they were about to do was dumbfounding and well beyond anything they could comprehend at that point, it seemed worth a try at least.

Anthony keyed the console. 'Charge chamber is clear.' He waited a few seconds for the on-screen confirmation. 'Done,' he called. 'K is in the hole.'

He went back to Robert's cabinet. 'It's okay. I'll do it.' Simon released the charge into the chamber. It came through like a swarm, hovered briefly over Robert's body and then darted into it, disappearing into the open mouth and nose.

'Wow,' Caitlin and Anthony chorused. Anthony glanced back at Simon, who was watching the monitor on the console intently. 'That's *insane*.'

Almost immediately, Robert's body twitched and then leapt forward off the stretcher to stand up against the screen.

Caitlin fell back onto Simon just as he did the same onto her. Anthony remained rooted to his spot.

'Simon?'

His brother pushed Caitlin behind him protectively. 'Robert, I...'

'Yes, me too.'

Simon felt something warm in his head; pushing into the centre of his brain. The quasi-parasitic behaviour of subject K was at once fascinating, impossible and downright frightening.

'How did you...'

'It looks like you figured it out, brother.'

'I don't really know how.'

Robert's voice was flat and muffled inside the cabinet.

'You should.'

'Should what?'

'Let me out of here. That's what you're thinking.'

It was. Simon couldn't think about anything else. He'd just brought his brother back to life. He already felt inhumane, keeping this actual real human subject captive. He'd never done anything like that before. That was for the pharma testers, not his gentle probing into extreme electricity.

'Please don't.' Caitlin clung on to Simon's waist.

'You should be scared. I would be. But right now, we don't have much time. I can't help you from in here.'

'Help us what?' Anthony had been waiting to participate. 'The world's falling apart.'

Robert laughed, sending a chill down his observers' spines. 'No. No, it isn't. It's bad, but it's not *that* bad.'

Simon's expression was puzzled. He couldn't believe he was talking to his brother after weeping over his dead body just minutes before. 'We've seen it all online.'

'No, no, no. You've seen what they want you to see.' Robert backed away from the screen and hopped back onto the stretcher. 'Here. I'll show you.' He pointed at Caitlin and smiled, then after a few seconds asked: 'Do you see?'

Caitlin's jaw dropped. 'I... yes. How? *Yes.*' She looked wounded. 'How did you do that?'

'Never mind how, but if I can do that, then you'd better believe they can do it too.'

'They?' Simon shrugged.

'Of course you don't know. You have this great research facility and you mess around day after day and ultimately you know nothing.'

Simon frowned. 'And you do?'

Robert stood up against the screen again. 'They took me a couple of days ago. I didn't realise it at first but it was all about you. Well, mostly about you. They needed me to get to you. These things are taking over. They do it every few thousand years.'

Anthony shot a sly glance at Simon and muttered: 'Bollocks.'

'Oh dear, no. Not bollocks at all. History is a myth, mostly. But excuse my tangent. What is crucial here is that the longer this goes on, the more damage there will be. And I cannot do anything in here.'

'Okay, Rob.' Simon looked at his feet, then to Caitlin, and back to his brother. 'I'll let you out if you can give me a decent explanation of how the hell I'm talking to a dead man. And why did you need to get to me?'

'You were right, brother!' He smiled. 'Now listen. They brought me here to test me, and to test you. You've been a worry for some time. What you're working on, in here. Well, you've just proven it works.'

'I wasn't trying...'

'Of course you were. You just didn't know it. You can hurt them. They don't know that for sure, or rather they didn't. Those two who came with me... they know now.'

'I can hurt... you? I'm not sure what you...'

'Yes!' Robert's expression changed for the first time since his second rebirth. 'I guess you can. But there's no need for that. You are my brother.'

'I don't... I don't trust you.'

'I know. Hey, that's as obvious as anything. But you do *have* to trust me.'

Simon wanted another burning questioned answered: 'What was that liquid that leaked out of you?'

'That was *them*. That was the ordinary.'

Anthony fancied another crack at the interrogation. 'The ordinary what?'

Robert laughed again, his grin widening across his face. 'That's what they call themselves, and right now they are harvesting.'

'Harves...' Simon started.

Robert fixed his gaze on each of his captors in turn. 'Easier to show you than to explain it all.'

'Oh, my God.' Caitlin's knees felt ready to give way. She'd imagined some kind of apocalypse scenario but seeing it in full crystal-clear colour was overwhelming, amplified by the fact that this thing, this man, could invade her mind so easily.

Anthony already felt sickly and on edge from the ups and downs of his anxious psyche and various internal injections of adrenaline.

Simon keyed the console and the screen lifted. Robert stepped clear of the cabinet and stood facing his brother.

231

'One hour, your computer says.'

Simon turned out his palms. 'One hour? How did you...'

'What can we do in an hour?' Caitlin's practical brain told her they were too far away from anywhere to be useful, unless Sheffield was somehow ground zero. Besides, they were a good thirty minutes from there anyway.

'You don't need to do anything. You've done what you needed to do.' Robert smiled, broadly. 'It's just simple mind control, albeit on a grand scale. Quite clever, really.'

Anthony was beginning to harness his anxiety. Now the fear had become attached to something real – those images Robert had put in his mind; images of people running, heading for nowhere in particular, the goal seemingly to create chaos.

'I'm going to put myself in the middle of it. Wish me luck.'

'But I don't understand,' Simon said. 'What just happened? How are you doing these things?'

'There are some things science cannot understand, brother. And while you may not understand why, you might just have saved the world. You most definitely saved me. I was connected to them, but that is lost now – they have a shared consciousness. When they bled out of me, so too did that connection. But now, this thing you've put inside me... it's neutral, untainted. Synthetic purity.'

'Are you still... Robert?'

'Yes. No. Maybe. I'm not the man I was last week, that's for sure. But my mind is my own. There's a lot more stuff in it now, but it's still... *me*. And right now I *really* need to go.'

'Will you come back?'

'I don't know.'

~~~

By the time Joe and Tom made it back to Shenbury it was early morning. They made their way out of the woods to hit the highway linking Shenbury and Bostwick out to the north. They both recognised the road but didn't appreciate how far it was back into town on foot. As they followed the edge of the forest, they were surprised to see cars shooting past them way faster than the speed limit. Their drivers and passengers barely registered them on the side of the road, until one car stopped.

'You don't wanna head that way, sirs. Whole town's gone to shit! Come on, jump in.' The kindly stranger opened his door but Joe and Tom politely declined. Then he opened the holdall on his passenger seat and threw some clothes out to Joe. He muttered something as he drove off, his tyres squealing on the road.

Joe got dressed. The stranger had given him some shorts, which were a little tight around his thighs, and a green T-shirt. Tom said he knew the way back to the curtain from there. He explained again to Joe how his rescue had gone down. If Louise was still in there, the way they'd gone in to grab him was a worthy plan to get her out the same way. That was assuming she was in that black, slithering pool too.

When they arrived back into the shanty town of New Shenbury, Joe felt a rush of horror. He remembered it all so clearly now. Those people. All those people. Burned alive in their homes, while he was out of town fighting the inevitable. For the first time since that night, he now felt in control of his own actions, as if the puppet masters had stopped pulling his strings. His memories were clearer, confirmed. His conviction was solid.

The shanty town was buzzing with activity. Slow, plodding jazz music seemed to be playing all over and Tom instantly recognised it as the song from the waiting room. People stood mostly in crowds while others were broken off into smaller groups packing cars and caravans.

'It's happening. We need to hurry.'

Joe had seen it all. For years to all intents and purposes a puppet, he'd at last been thrown into the upgrade tank and given a glimpse of the event horizon. He had felt the hunger in that thing, reaching in and out and just needing to consume, to grow. He didn't know how long he'd been in there but the realisation of the truth came through almost immediately as the tendrils sunk into him, probing into his core and weaving around his spine, holding him there and feeding off him while simultaneously giving him a surge of its own revealing nutrients. He'd been pulled out too early though, withdrawing prematurely and unable to tap into the power he had felt so closely within his reach. He felt like he'd been on the cusp of something both terrifying and tempting.

As they walked away from the town and skirted around the trailer park which had become home to the privileged but which was now all but

233

vacated, they spied a large oily protrusion, spilling out from underneath a tree trunk. Joe had seen this from the comfort of the black pool. He knew what it was.

He stopped Tom. 'How far is it now?'

Tom couldn't take his eyes off the dark spring, bubbling and spreading out over the roots of the tree. 'Not far. Fifteen minutes, tops.'

Joe tugged his arm. 'Come on then.'

Eighteen – Full circle

When Robert left the hatch and zipped into nature's own speed travel system, he had just minutes to ponder his situation before he reached the other side of the world. It was the greatest rush, literally: a hundred times the speed of sound, and the most efficient routes taken. He calculated these routes in seconds, almost subconsciously, feeling them out and crossing vast distances swimming in these frequencies.

Before he had bled out in Simon's field, he'd received a flash of information, like somehow in that final moment of ordinariness the blocks in the consciousness had been lifted. He felt the entrances, four of them.

Now, on his super-speed travels he recognised from the hundreds of thousands of TV broadcasts the names of those entrances: Jet, Ebony, Raven and Sable. Four ways in; the black gates of hell. He had seen the mass in the middle of it all, the giant throbbing and writhing primordial soup, but now in his born again, evil-subtracted but supercharged self he couldn't access the consciousness anymore.

His detective brain had pinpointed one of the locations though: as the ordinary seeped out and evaporated into Dranhill's mild atmosphere, he caught it just briefly but long enough to take a mental picture because he'd seen it before. The town that was destroyed by the fire. It wasn't the sort of story one could forget in a hurry, especially in the enquiring mind of a police consultant. He remembered it was called Shenbury and it was towards the east coast of America, and armed with that information he knew he would find it easily.

Across the ocean from Wales to Northern Ireland, he swept over and picked up a wave that took him to just inside the border of Mexico, then snaked his way up, passing hundreds of these oily rivers and their wakes of death. As he rushed through those areas the rivers stopped mid-flow as if startled by his presence. Then he followed a short bundle of frequencies up the coast and headed a little way inland to reach Shenbury. It was exhilarating but not the same as before.

The town was mostly gone, so much of it burned away bar the neighbourhoods which were too far for the flames to have reached. Robert observed this in a flash as he headed north-west over the railway line and entered the woods, homing in on the beacon which became stronger with every thousandth of a second.

235

Robert arrived and stopped at the Raven entrance. It was invisible to the eye but he felt it there, some kind of tunnel through reality and out the other side. For a few moments he listened, the hum of clashing frequencies filling his new, clean consciousness with clarity but no deeper meaning. He knew this was the time. He had passed so many corpses, their bodies brutalised and their souls catapulted towards a giant spider's web, and it had to stop. He would stop it.

~~~

Even through the mesh curtain, the music was loud, coming through to Joe and Tom like they were in the front row at a jazz concert, the rhythm intensifying and intoxicating, each lazy beat folding over the next.

'I can't see her.'

'I'm not getting used to this.' Tom looked on grimly through the curtain, the dancers faster and more numerous than the last time he'd seen them. The room seemed to be much larger too since his last visit and was apparently growing as they looked in.

'Me neither. All we have to do is get in and out, just like you did with me.'

The physical process of walking through this curtain into the room was entirely alien to Joe and Tom; an inhuman, unnatural crime against physics that made no sense to either of them. Once through, that curtain would be gone, and the exits were not exactly signposted. The idea of going back in there was as nauseating as the sounds coming from the other side. Joe remembered the last time he had gone in, led there by his keepers, eager to have him back in the fold. He remembered his revelation, the flooding in of the past making his memories and personality whole again, and the husk of his tortured human body hanging from a hook like a dirty rag.

He had glimpsed their true essence and power during his time in that disgusting, consuming mass, cooking him and feeding him at once. The more of them who came together, the more power was in there, pulsating and reaching and leeching from the earth.

It was all about strength in numbers and now, having reached the point where the circle could finally be completed, covering the globe in the veil of the ordinary was all that mattered. But not to Joe, whose informal resignation had spurred them into some kind of action. Whatever was happening with that oil oozing out and the citizens of Shenbury making a run for it, he wondered why it all had kicked off at just that moment. Was he as important as he had been made to feel? He had some sense of it while in the House, that his power was great, but now he felt none of it, and didn't understand quite why that was.

'Okay. You first.' Joe smiled uneasily at Tom.

'Well,' he replied. 'It's got to be one of us.' Tom stretched his arm into the curtain and pulled it back sharply. 'Holy fuck!' He grabbed at his hand and stared at it, pain shooting up the arm into the shoulder. 'It won't...'

Joe went to do the same. Tom stopped him. 'Shit, Joe. Just leave it. Hold on a second. Something's not right here.' Joe got his face as close to the mesh as he could without touching it. *Something's not right? Something? How about everything?*

He watched as the room continued to grow, its perspectives stretching from all sides. Shapes appeared to be forming from the centre of it, pulling towards each other as their clothes weaved around the oil, solidifying and consolidating their ghastly figures into faux human structures.

Joe realised then just how much of his life had been spent in there, just sitting and grinning and spinning and playing. The man who had 'saved' him as a child, Edward; the pairing with their other chief puppet Paul Motta, the good cop who had disappeared without a trace. Everything he had done since his pubescence was following someone else's agenda. And Frank, his friend and colleague, could be in there somewhere. But most importantly, Louise. Finding her was all that mattered.

'Shit. Shit, that hurts.' Tom flapped his injured, hot hand at his side, symbolically shaking the pain out of it.

'We have to get in there.'

Tom leaned closer too, his face next to Joe's. 'It's different. When did that happen?'

'It's growing.' Their eyes met. 'We'll never find her.'

'I will.'

Joe and Tom swivelled, nearly clashing skulls.

'Excuse me, gentlemen. I need to get in there.'

Tom put himself between the man and Joe. 'Who the hell are you?'

'I'm Robert. Please, get out of the way.'

~~~

Jez thought he'd never held anyone so tightly as he was holding on to Maria. She was freezing, as was he, but the adrenaline had coped with his rapidly falling body temperature up to a point. Now the two of them were just cold, and getting colder.

The supermarket had been the only option. After they'd abandoned the car, they were on the run just like everyone else. The oil came right at them, spilling out of the drains and pooling before a large group of terrified people. As it began to rise up, forming some kind of giant wave, they dashed the only way they could.

Jez and Maria only just made it in before one of the staff hit the failsafe button and closed the automatic doors, leaving a still fair-sized crowd hopeless outside, screaming as they were devoured by the encroaching mass. It splashed up against the doors then seeped underneath, through a gap of just millimetres, and began to rise up inside the market.

There were eleven people left inside the store and one of them called something about following her. The survivors did and snaked through the aisles before reaching the back end, where they entered the warehouse. She kept saying it was the safest place in there. She'd seen that oily nightmare stop at the water's edge and rise up, as if frightened by the wet, and figured the freezer might act in the same way as the sea.

In the assumed safety of the freezer was a microcosm of society. Jez and Maria had fallen into a corner, his back against the wall as she let herself mould into his dwindling warmth. In the opposite corner, up against the large freezer door and leaning against it for her life, was a girl in her staff uniform, her spotty face red and sore, almost cracking in the cold.

'This is the worst place we could possibly be.' A woman of about forty, stood up against the back of the freezer, volunteered her opinion, directed keenly at the uniformed girl. 'Seriously. We'll all *die in here*.'

'You woulda fuckin' died oot there, ye twat.' A darkly-dressed man pushed himself off the opposite wall. 'Leave 'er aloon.'

The woman stepped forward too, avoiding the hands of the people on the floor beneath her and the gathering of bewildered bodies standing

238

around her. Her cropped black hair clung close to her scalp, complementing her leather jacket and skinny blue jeans. 'I wasn't having a go at anyone,' she said, her voice only slightly louder this time. 'But I'm just saying: now we're cornered. We've nowhere to run. Open that door and we're dead. Don't and we're dead.'

Jez nuzzled his face into Maria's neck. She looked around the freezer. Around its perimeter were numerous shelves, each stocked with an assortment of meat packages, cheese and some unlabelled boxes, more of which were scattered across the cold floor. She couldn't see much of anything really, considering all the people in there with her, and for eleven people it was far too cosy for comfort. Adding the fact it was a freezer into the equation, Maria was already feeling petulant.

Another woman, slight but confident, spoke up: 'I'm not dying in a fucking freezer.'

Maria startled Jez when she stood up, quickly. He fell back into the corner and looked up at her.

'She's right. We can't stay in here.'

The large Scotsman blocked Maria's path to the freezer door handle. 'Doon't even thank aboot it.'

Maria tried to push past him and Jez jumped to his feet. 'Hey...'

The Scot pushed Maria hard, sending her reeling back into two other survivors who hadn't felt the need to stick their necks out. 'No one's opening that fuckin' door. Okay?'

Jez helped Maria up, his eyes on the Scot. He noticed the man was wearing a belt buckle with *BENSON* emblazoned on it. 'Let's just calm down here.' He looked around the room to faces terrified, blank or ambivalent. 'We have no idea what that is. I mean, does anyone have any idea what that is?'

A young boy took his opportunity: 'I've seen it in my comic!' His mother smiled down at him and patted his head. *Shhhh.*

'An' I've been fed that shit for thirty years but it doesn't mean I want to eat anymore.' Most of the room turned to see the old man, his face pale and worn, the cold setting a layer of mist over his wizened features. 'By which I mean to say, I'm with *him*.'

Benson checked behind himself to make sure he was blocking the handle as effectively as possible. 'We've nay idea what's oot there,' he said. 'An' I nominate meself to keep an eye on this door.'

Jez replaced his firm grip on Maria, folding her into his arms and wanting to make sure she wouldn't get away again and anger the volatile Scot by the only exit from the cold coffin.

'How long can we stay in here?' *Benson* turned to the staff girl, hovering uneasily next to him. 'How much air have we got?'

'I don't know.' She looked apologetic yet hurt. 'Not very long.'

~~~

'I don't want to go out there!' Caitlin screamed, her head in her hands. When Simon had remotely angled his cameras to look not at his field but over towards the main town, the three of them had gasped, sat and stared at the horrifying images on the monitors and Anthony, particularly, had almost fainted in shock.

The images were distant but clear enough. Some kind of creeping, fluid shadow was marauding and enveloping everyone in its path – and those people were running but not getting away. It was then that Simon's eureka moment came. He'd watched his manufactured, hyper-electricity work a miracle on his brother, just as moments before he'd watched it destroy whatever was inside him.

Subject K was gone but there were nineteen others they could use. Anthony had cleared the central chamber each time as Caitlin operated the shutters and Simon zeroed the static. Without the three of them working together, the plan never would have had a chance. It was shaky enough anyway.

The test chambers were modular in design and although it took some wrangling out of position, once all the subjects were isolated in the same chamber, they were forced with an electromagnetic charge into one of the delivery tubes. Simon sealed each end and the three of them detached the tube.

'We've got to try. We can't just sit in here and watch.'

'But you said our job is to observe and analyse!' Caitlin sat up straight, her expression pleading and frightened.

Simon put his hand on her shoulder. 'If you stay here, I can't guarantee your safety, Katie. Together we stand a chance.'

Anthony looked at the supercharged electric torpedo on the table. 'He's right. We have to try.'

~~~

'Be our guest.' Tom shrugged at Joe. 'We're right behind you.'

Robert was determined. He had no idea what might happen when he went through the curtain but that didn't matter. He wanted to kill those bastards who'd killed him. All he'd done was his job. That dogshit Angelo had taken his life and poisoned him with some kind of faux superiority he never asked for. He may have still been upright, but his core had been raped and left in shreds. As human as he looked, his humanity was mostly gone, replaced by a primal, animalistic desire to hurt those who hurt him.

Tom watched intently to see what might happen to their new ally once he tried to cross over. Robert wasted no time and walked right in, the extreme force and heat leaving no trace on him. He turned back to see the curtain gone, in its place a wall of figures that seemed to stretch forever in all directions. They danced around him, the music loud and punchy, having somewhere along the line lost the laziness of its beat and gained an even more sickening urgency. Robert looked around, trying to catch sight of a familiar face, and realised they were all wearing masks; thin, white and cracked, otherworldly and unsettling.

He felt a surge of power in his arms and hands, tightening his palms and bringing his fists together. In his vision he'd seen doors. He felt their importance but had forgotten why. Now they were nowhere; out of sight behind hundreds or thousands of dancing lunatics, detached from their lives. He reached for the strongest frequencies and pulled himself towards one. As he homed in on it, he realised it was pulling him in all by itself.

'Robert.' Angelo stood before him, his Asian features curled into a soft smile. 'Look around. You have nothing to do here.' The dancers brushed up against them, their lifeless masks coming in and out of view. 'Think about it, Robert. Nothing you can do but go home.'

Robert laughed, the sound barely audible in the stuffy atmosphere. Where Angelo's voice was clear, his was muffled: 'You left me for dead.'

Angelo smiled warmly although behind his expression lurked pure confusion. 'Settle down. Get yourself a drink.'

Robert thrust his hand around Angelo's throat. Angelo convulsed as an almighty roar came from all around. Robert tightened his grip and felt the oil bubbling up in his palm, pressed up against Angelo's throat. It came out fast in a fine haze and imploded, its particles crashing into and cancelling each other. The body slumped to the floor, knocking a group of masked dancers back, and then dissolved into a dark grey fluid before disappearing altogether.

Robert felt for the other major spikes in the room. It was growing all the time, expanding outwards and upwards and pulling his focus in all directions. Joe and Tom appeared at his side, their clothes and hair singed and smoking, their minds already filled with the warmth and comfort of the place.

The music stopped dead, replaced by a strong murmur, sounding like a storm of bees and wasps and flies all at once. They stood and scanned the sea of masks, lips just showing beneath some of them; lips turned up into sickly broad grins. These figures were not hostile but they just stood there, staring from dead eyes.

'How did you...'

'You should've stayed back.'

Joe stepped up to face Robert. 'Louise. We have to find Louise.'

'Good luck with that.'

Robert pushed past Joe and put his hands in the air, then down on two figures standing before him. The dark matter emerged from their mouths and clashed into a cloud of vapour. He felt something surging within him, some kind of otherworldly version of bloodlust. As he worked his way through the crowd, the murmur became stronger and was joined by a high-pitched shriek, piercing the aural atmosphere.

Tom shouted in Joe's ear. 'I can't see the doors.'

Joe shrugged and called back: 'We need to keep moving! I'm not leaving without her!'

Ahead of them, Robert was cutting through the swathe like lawnmower blades, working faster and faster as the figures dropped like sacks of coal, their essence reduced to nothing. With each one he felt more powerful, surges running through his veins and filling his core with contented weight.

~~~

Stanley found it easier than expected to slip away, shrouded in the chaos within Raven. He saw Robert rip through Angelo and that was enough to make his mind up. He channelled himself out and quickly

242

away, riding the waves back. At one point he stopped to admire the carnage in a small suburb just outside Miami.

A large car park leading up to an out-of-town shopping paradise was overrun with the gloop and he stood in the middle of it, watching it cascading and lurching and consuming. He caught the eye of a woman cowering behind a minivan about a hundred feet away, hoping to escape the doom. He smiled as he pointed over to her, guiding the oil right to her position. It tipped the van over with ease and muffled her screams as it sucked her life away.

He left the scene in a flash and got back to business – getting home to his girls. He felt alone in the consciousness but aware of it all. Globally the effect of their purge had been huge: millions taken, devoured and reduced to nothing; towns and cities destroyed; lives and bloodlines wiped away and their memories gone with them.

Those who had made it out to sea were safe. Indeed the ordinary had made sure people did escape. They didn't take everyone. There always had to be some survivors. Those who were helped, intelligent or just plain lucky enough to take to the water would rebuild just as they always had. That was one of the keys to fulfilling the circle.

It reminded him of the *Bible* story about Noah. Those scriptures had been so fanciful, the great bearded man rescuing all those animals on his giant boat. But Stanley knew the truth. At Sunday School all those years ago as a trusting child he had believed those stories. Since being truly born again he'd seen the reality of it all; the cycle of life and the manipulation of the masses.

He made it back quickly, feeding off the buzz in the consciousness. He had never travelled so quickly and where previously such distances would have been impossible, he was in the sweet spot, energising and feeding as he went.

He stopped just shy of his building, still wanting to see his girls more than anything but also curious to see what had become of the town where he'd made a name for himself, where he'd gone beyond his place in the ranks of the ordinary to become, in his own mind, truly *extraordinary*.

Stanley surveyed the scene with his typically inhuman eye. The last global refreshment had been so different, years before even Jesus had walked the Earth. There were no cars or electronics, no fancy clothes or handbags spilling out their contents, just emaciated bodies lining the streets as they did now, without the modern distractions and detritus.

243

He stood in front of his hardware shop. The large window panes on the frontage were smashed. Inside, the bodies of his staff lay prone, their features sucked inwards from the implosions, pools of blood among the destroyed shelves and furniture displays. He liked those people, as much as the ordinary would like any human, but his empathy with the cattle was one of those things that made him extraordinary.

He'd created so many happy memories in this place: feasting on each new girl, tasting them from the inside, becoming one with them – sometimes two or three at a time. Even deciding which ones to keep had been a joy, poring over their relative merits and sending those with certain qualities next door to Steve.

It had been a fine arrangement. Stanley would do his little thing to them: the ordinary's version of a frontal lobotomy. It left them looking simple and withered – the lights would be on but no one would be home. Steve would put them to work at the fairground just like the normal girls he brought in by his own means, but there was a special clientele for those girls whose souls had been taken. Their eyes were so dead, more so even than the junkies'. And there were plenty of those.

Stanley had admired Steve's approach immensely. But Steve had left, taking the girls with him. Now there was no fairground to work at. Malton's breath had been taken away. Its social structure had been all but destroyed, as had most of the world's. The buildings stood but their lights were out. The sun was going down and when it rose again the world would be born again too.

His treasured, precious girls were still there, waiting as they always did and would. Untouched since his last dance with Angelo. He was pleased Angelo was dead. Committing sacrilege against one of his beautiful wives was certainly punishable by death. He'd been upset that he couldn't do it himself but that didn't matter now. Justice was served.

He knelt down in the centre of the room, drawing spotlights onto each of the girls, sat hooded and docile on their identical wooden chairs, their hands neatly folded in their laps. The warmth surged through him as his body shifted into long, black, oily snakes of love.

~~~

Robert had made his way through hundreds of the masked, smartly-dressed figures when he encountered the double doors. Joe and Tom were right behind him, having followed in his wake as he swept through. For every one he vanquished, another appeared elsewhere. It was like a wellspring and Tom and Joe weighed up the risks in seconds, opting to treat their ally as a shield. The noise was overwhelming – a cacophony of shrieking death and thumping like a heartbeat. Now, on the other side of those doors, the heart was beating louder than ever.

'She's in there. I know it.'

Tom pushed past a group of dancers, knocking them out of the way, and grabbed both door handles. Joe stood right behind him. Tom threw the doors open as the black mass crashed through, cascading over them and everything in its path like a tsunami attacking the rocks on a seashore. In the middle of it, rising up to the front as the mass reared up, was Louise, the tendrils bolted into her, consuming her completely. Her eyes swam with the dark oil as they stared down at Robert.

An almighty, deafening screech came as Louise opened her mouth wide and the blackness shot out at Robert, grabbing at his head and pulling at it. He swatted it away with ease.

Joe had managed to crawl out to the side, the mass flopping over him as he escaped its feelers, poking and nudging at him and trying to stop his progress. But the mass was focused elsewhere, as Louise raised her arms up, the tendrils fanning out like a bat's wings as she prepared to pounce on Robert and suck his life away. Another screech came, shrieking over the thump of her heartbeat as she surged forward.

Robert put his palms up towards the mass and they collided, sending a massive pulse into it. It lurched backwards, Louise screaming as some of the tendrils fell away from her, retreating back into the mass.

'Tom!' Joe shouted as loud as he could but no sound seemed to come. 'Tom!'

Robert focused on the mass as it started back towards him. It was twenty times his size in front and stretched back as far as he could see through those doors. Behind him the throng of beautifully dressed, soulless husks continued to grow. He could *feel* them there, dancing around and squirming and folding over each other just like the black stuff he was planning to pulverise.

The enormity all around him, incomprehensible and all-encompassing, at once shocked him out of his bloodlust as he realised it would be, if anything, a war of attrition. These two lost souls, the men looking for the woman he was now confronting, would be no help.

245

Louise reared up once more – the fallen tendrils reaching back into her and giving her a shot of strength. Her face lurched forward from her skull, stretching out black sinew as her jaw opened to let out another shriek. Robert stepped back like an athlete about to attempt a victorious feat and sprang forward. He threw himself with all his power into the mass beneath Louise's wrapped, oily torso, burying himself in it.

The mass began to vibrate and scream violently as Robert pushed further inside. His sight was gone – just darkness all around, writhing over and suffocating him. He clenched his fists and hunched down, drawing all his power into his core. Then he let it out.

~~~

'Maria, please don't…'

She turned back to face Jez. 'You need to grow some fucking balls!'

'We're probably safe now, anyway,' said the lady with the cropped dark hair, speaking with forced confidence. 'That… whatever it was… it's probably gone now.'

Benson exerted his assumed authority once more. 'And what if it's not? Eh?'

The woman with the child threw her hands up. 'We'll never know if we don't look. And she's right…' She waved her hand at Maria and looked down at her shivering boy, his teeth chattering. 'We're all freezing. I've got my son to think about. I do not want to die in here!'

'Just open the door!' Maria strode over to *Benson*. 'Open it!'

'Noo fuckin' way, mate.' *Benson* leaned forward off the freezer door and pushed Maria hard. She fell back and collapsed on top of the young boy.

'You bastard!' His mother leapt at *Benson* and managed to scratch his face with one hand while the other tugged at his belt buckle, trying to pull him off the door. 'You fucking bastard!'

The girl in uniform edged away from the fracas, while Jez scampered over to Maria and helped her up off the young boy. *Benson* punched the mother in the jaw, sending her flying back into her son, who shielded himself with his arms. As she fell on top of him, his left arm broke at the wrist and he howled.

246

One of the group of three sitting just left of the middle of the freezer floor jumped up and confronted *Benson*. 'That's enough!' He was larger than *Benson* and a few years older, wearing a chequered short-sleeved shirt and jeans. He pushed Benson back against the freezer door. 'We'll take a vote. Okay?' *Benson* pushed back against him as Jez joined him and countered his weight. 'Everyone who votes to open, stick a hand up.'

Maria made it back to her feet and bent down to pick up a large slab of beef that had been knocked off the shelf.

As the man in the shirt turned to see how many people had stuck their hands up, Maria slammed the frozen beef joint into the side of *Benson*'s head. The impact knocked him out immediately and his body slumped down against the door. Jez and the man stepped back in shock and Maria bent down again, grabbing *Benson*'s arm and dragging him out of the way.

'Yes. I vote we open the fucking door.'

Once they'd made it to the other side of the field, Caitlin had a stitch from running. She doubled over as Anthony vaulted over the fence.

'Wait,' she panted. 'Hold up.'

Simon turned back. He was carrying the tube under his arm. 'Come on, Katie. We've got to keep moving.'

Anthony climbed back over and helped her up. 'It's not far now.' She knew just how far it was, and couldn't escape the dreadful feeling – in just a couple of minutes they would run into that stuff, that deathly liquid.

'Okay.' She stood up, clutching her right side and panting. 'I'm fine. I can do this. Okay.'

Anthony helped Caitlin over the fence and vaulted it again, enjoying the extra spring he'd gained from the burst of adrenaline. He felt like something between a superhero and a stuntman, as if all eyes were on him, the audience on the edge of their seats as they waited to see what he would do next; how he would save the world.

Simon was far less fanciful. As they made their way down the short but secluded lane that would take them to the main Dranhill road, his focus was absolute: before he'd decided to settle his laboratory there, in his research he had completed a thorough survey of the area. He knew where the power was coming from, and where the telephone lines ran to.

They would head first up the short hill to the top of town and then down towards the railway station. In a siding there, protected only by a padlocked gate and a couple of large 'danger of death' signs, was not the main local power station but a satellite unit. It represented, as far as he could tell, their best opportunity to do anything.

Once on the main road, the carnage was sickening. Bodies lay strewn across the tarmac. Although some were untouched, most of the shops and residential frontages were distressed. Windows and doors were smashed out; cars were abandoned or crashed into buildings. The peace and serenity of this rural jewel had been shattered entirely. What they were seeing was pure aftermath though. They headed up the hill.

'Oh shit.' At the top of the hill, next to a boarded up pub, they could see the shadow clearly. They stopped and watched as it rolled down and followed the corner, wrapping itself around the sandstone buildings as protrusions leapt out of it, reaching and moulding itself into the contours of the brickwork.

Caitlin had never heard her boss swear. She looked at him, the fear in her face now intense. He looked back at her. 'This is it.'

Anthony felt truly pumped. 'I'll do it.'

Simon turned to face him. 'No. We'll all do it. Come on.' He started walking then eased into a jog, carrying the tube in both arms in front of him as Caitlin and Anthony flanked. As they rounded the corner, they stumbled to a stop. The grey, lumpen sheet of death rose up before them, as if ready to strike. Then Simon's tube began to vibrate and the shadow reared away from them, letting out a fierce shriek as it fizzed and flopped back down, zipping back into itself and vaporising.

'It's working! Oh, man. It's working!' As the grey mass vanished entirely, beyond it they could now see a group of people – some standing, screaming; others on their knees, praying.

'Come on!' Simon set off again and this time his jog went nearer to a sprint as he made it to the gap in the wall which led down to the station. As they passed the remaining townsfolk, Anthony raised a hand to wave, expecting a cheer. All he got was screams and sobs.

They ran along the narrow stone-lined pathway and made it to the unit. Caitlin looked over to the railway bridge and beyond. The shadow was still rampant there. She watched as it rose up and then shot forward, enveloping a group of people who put up no credible resistance. She gasped and doubled over. 'Hurry up!'

Anthony grabbed the padlock and pulled at it aggressively. 'How do we...'

'Like this,' Simon said. He handed the tube to Anthony and slung the backpack off his shoulders, then reached into it and pulled out a gun. Anthony's eyes widened as he felt a mixture of renewed fear and wonder at the thought of his mentor being armed with a deadly weapon. Those 'danger of death' signs seemed more relevant than ever.

Simon took aim with both hands and pulled the trigger. The first shot missed. The second connected. He kicked the gate open as the broken lock and chain fell to the ground, then turned to Anthony.

'Here.' Anthony passed the tube back to Simon. He reached into his backpack again and pulled out a mass of cables and wires. Back at the lab he'd deliberated over which connections to bring but then realised it wouldn't matter. Metal-to-metal contact would do the trick.

'Okay then. This is it.' Simon turned back to his junior colleagues. 'You'd better stand back.'

Caitlin looked up. 'No! Dr M!' She knew what would happen. 'Danger of death' was a warning loaded with authentic dread. Anthony grabbed her and wrestled her back up the path towards town. She screamed again. 'No!'

Anthony held her tightly in place. She couldn't fight his adrenaline-heightened strength. She was drained, entirely, and stopped pushing feebly against him.

Simon connected the ends of two wires to the tube and took another shot, this time springing open the green metal cabinet. He turned back one last time and waved, managing a weak smile. Anthony raised his hand and nodded. Behind them he could hear voices. He looked back to see some of the townsfolk coming down the path towards them.

Simon picked the tube up in one hand and gathered the two wires in the other. *Here goes nothing...*

~~~

By the time Pete and Mack had rowed out to the lifeboat, the giant wave overhead had receded. It stood there menacingly, watching and waiting. The people on the boat had managed to regain some measure of sanity, but their clouded single-mindedness had given way to their personalities returning to what they had been before the first timer had ticked down. Far enough away from the music to escape its effects, they were back in control – to a degree. They didn't even notice the second timer ticking down to zero or that the music had stopped.

Mike was in shock. He'd tried to persuade his new friends on the boat that Pete and Mack were bad news – that they shouldn't be let on. As disingenuous as he felt saying this, his guilt was strong. And he knew Pete would take his drugs. At that point in time, he was sure he had nothing else. Then the large man with the bald head had sidled up to him, taking his arm stiffly and whispering in his ear.

Everything will be all right. Give me the drugs. I'll make sure to return them later. You can trust me.

Then the voice came inside Mike's head, amid vivid images of the destruction he'd narrowly avoided: *We told you we like you. You're one of our friends. This will all need rebuilding. We need people like you.* Mike nodded. *We'll give you whatever you want. Whatever you need.*

Then it happened. The bald man shot back, his neck snapping violently up as he fell back against the side of the boat and collapsed. The drugs he'd just taken from Mike fell out of his hand, spilling onto the deck.

'Oh my God! What's happened to him?' A heavy-set lady wearing a bright orange lifejacket barged past Mike, then looked back at him with accusatory eyes.

Mike stuttered. 'Oh… he just… he just fell. Out of nowhere. I didn't…' He hadn't done anything at all.

Pete appeared at his side and for a few seconds they watched the lady attending to the fallen man. She muttered something about being a retired nurse. Pete looked Mike in the eye and nodded. He understood as much as he needed to. Mike was trying to wash his hands of those drugs. Some kind of epiphany perhaps. It didn't matter anymore.

Mike nodded back and shrugged. 'I didn't do this. We were just talking and…'

Mack appeared next and threw her arms around Mike. Pete joined in. Behind them, back on the shore a fizzing shockwave tore through the oil, vaporising it on the spot.

~~~

Stanley's final moment came at the same time his compadre took a gentler hit out on the lifeboat. The bald man had been lucky to survive, out of the blast range, but Stanley's little welcome home party, thrown by and for himself, was cut short. The poisonous, lethal electricity let loose two hundred miles away took him completely by surprise.

It came in an instant, fizzing through the cables and air and into his harem before it continued through to Steve's and beyond. Once it had shot through him, his tentacles simply fell out of the girls and seemed to burn away. The intricate web he'd constructed in the room, joining himself to all the girls at once, vanished without a trace as his very essence did the same.

Minutes passed until the silence of the room was broken as one of the figures moved. It lolloped forward and fell onto the floor, knocking the chair sideways onto another. The girl on that chair stirred too. The one on the floor feebly moaned as she reached up and tugged at her hood. It slipped off easily. As her eyes adjusted to the darkness in the room, she began to see the other girls. The one behind her stayed on her chair, having removed her hood too. She stood up and fell down to her knees, her legs too weak to take her.

Another of the girls leaned forward, her head swinging from side to side as she tried to speak. All that came was a soft, soulless cry. She reached up to her mouth and put her fingers inside, feeling for the tongue that wasn't there. Thoughts began to circle in her head. It had been two years since she'd had a thought of her own, or one she could recognise as such. She could see Stanley's face – his gentle, soft features belying his true horror. But she couldn't feel him there anymore, as if some cloud had cleared. A hand closed gently around her shoulder and she gasped, splitting the silence. She looked over to see the girl next to her, a pretty face unable to emote but offering some kind of comfort just by being there.

When Sarah had been abducted and brought to Stanley, she'd been fourteen. A happy student and a loving daughter to loving parents, stolen from her friends and boyfriend and a family who mourned as any would. Stanley had called her Beth. He always told her she was beautiful and cherished. She wondered, now that he was gone, if she was still beautiful and cherished.

~~~

George Lazarou didn't know what to do next. He'd whisked them away, his returned daughter and his spiteful bitch of an ex-trophy-wife, onto his yacht just a couple of hours before the oil came. Persuading them had been frustratingly difficult. It hadn't been the nicest of days for seafaring but sitting around at home waiting for the deathly spread wasn't an option for him. He'd worked so hard. Those friends he'd made in low places had kept their promise. Those disgusting things he'd done in their name had been recognised and rewarded. He'd turned on the charm offensive to get them to the marina. Once they were there, safely out to sea with him, he could return to his normal self.

George was a businessman. He knew how it worked. You shook on a deal and that was that. If you were lucky. And although he'd gone back on many such deals in the past, he knew he didn't have a choice in the matter when it came to these people. Except they weren't *people*. He didn't know what they were. One of the golden rules in business was to take the upper hand, and another to know your enemy. That he had been powerless to follow either rule in this case was frustrating but none of that mattered anymore. He had no idea what they were going back to, but he supposed it wasn't important. He was one of the founders of the new age, just as he'd been promised.

Lara and her mother had kept themselves entertained, too far from the shore to see what was happening. George had made sure of that. He didn't want to see it either. Muriel had tried to contact her friend Suzy but she couldn't get any phone reception and the wireless internet wasn't connecting either. George explained, quite harshly, that he wasn't an electrician and neither was she so bollocks to all of it.

~~~

Jez, Maria and the other survivors stood outside the supermarket, watching as the mass of boats and dinghies came back towards the shore. Bodies were slumped all around them, their possessions spilling out of pockets and bags. They were safe now. They'd passed another vote, to shut Benson in the freezer 'until further notice', and now back out on the street they could see both ways up the promenade. The oil was gone, leaving only its trail of death as proof it was ever there.

As they watched, Maria recognised the detectives coming up the stony beach, wet and cold and illuminated by the orangey-pink sunset behind them. She felt like the smallest molecule, a tiny piece of the giant puzzle of life, watching an incomprehensible and gigantic story playing out, her insignificance a mere subplot in it all.

Jez squeezed his arms around her. His world had ended too; a world in which he and his friends would get stoned in the park by day and watch amusing or dirty videos in the evenings – a world devoid of responsibility. At that point he felt enormous, overwhelming responsibility. Everything was gone but Maria. As he looked around he pondered the horror of it all and how inside that freezer, where they had expected shelter they'd created their own horror and condemned a man to death. *Benson*'s last sight was a rock-hard lump of meat smashing into his skull. They'd all killed him. *Survival of the fittest,* he thought. *Or survival of the shittest.*

Maria swivelled in Jez's embrace and kissed him. It was over.

Epilogue

Joe knelt down in the grass, cradling Louise's head on his lap. Tom lay next to her, face down, barely breathing. Louise had taken her last breath moments before, leaving Joe bereft. For so long she had been all he'd lived for. Now there just seemed no point. While the world outside had been turned upside down, his had been levelled.

It happened in a flash. Tom had vanished under the mass and that other man, their saviour, had sacrificed himself, thrusting himself into Louise's captor and tearing it apart. The room, growing and pulsating chaotically, had just exploded, or imploded, or *something*. The world had turned pure white as the mass screeched its final screech, and then to black as Joe was knocked out by the overload.

He had opened his eyes to a blue sky in a clearing, surrounded by tall and leafy trees with the sun baking down onto his face. Tom had been there too, thirty or so feet away, and Louise, further still. He had raced over to her, picking her up in his arms and stumbling over to Tom where he laid her down.

'I'm so sorry,' he sobbed. 'I couldn't... I couldn't save you.' He stroked her hair in both hands. 'Please. Forgive me. I'm so sorry.'

Joe's head slumped forward and he closed his eyes, still stroking Louise's hair. The only sound was distant birdsong, but he didn't notice it or Tom's shallow breathing next to him.

Please, God. If there is anything left in this world, bring her back to me. I promise... I promise I'll take care of her next time. I promise. She's... she's all I have. Please, God. If you can hear me, please. I beg you. I beg you. Please...

'It's okay, Joe.'

His head jerked up.

Louise looked up at him, her head upside down. Joe shuffled backwards as she swivelled to face him properly on her knees.

'Oh thank you! Thank you!' Joe looked up to the blue sky, his hands raised symbolically. He shuffled forwards and embraced Louise, careful not to caress her too tightly. *Thank you thank you thank you thank you...*

'How did you...'

'It's okay, Joe. It's over. You don't have to fight anymore.' She leaned back from his embrace and smiled at him, then stroked his cheek with the back of her hand. 'It's all finished.'

Louise stood up. Joe did too.

'I'm so... I can't believe we got you out.'

'You shouldn't have come back for me.' Her smile was gone, replaced by a flat expression.

'Why not? You came back for me.' He moved towards her.

'It didn't make any difference,' Louise said. 'What's done is done. None of it matters.'

'What do you mean? Of course it matters!'

'Not really.' Louise took a step back. 'That was just one. Just one of the Houses. There are three others. And we'll just build it back up.'

Joe's face darkened. 'We'll build what back up?'

Louise's face began to change – black tendrils breaking apart the flesh. Joe went instantly cold, his chest tightening and his stomach turning.

'Lou? What's...'

The tendrils shot forward and wrapped around his neck. Her mouth remained formed on her face while the rest seemed to writhe around it. 'We can really be together now.'

The oil snaked up and into Joe's face and back into his skull, caressing the geography of his brain. 'This is the only way, honey.'

Joe's eyes filled with Louise's new essence.

'I've learned so much.'

She drew Joe towards her, melding into him completely.

We love you.

House of Pigs Christopher Ritchie
FINALIST
2013 IndieFab Book Awards Horror
Surrey Life: *"Ritchie takes the reader on a frightening, disturbing journey that tests the imagination, pushing it beyond the limits of 'normal'.*

Slave Skin Derek E Pearson
Release July 2017

GODS' Enemy Derek E Pearson
FINALIST
2016 Indies Book Awards Fantasy
Read2Write: *"Texas 1883, a terrifying story that fuses sci-fi with history and theology. Pearson is in electrifying form"*

Soul's Asylum **trilogy** Derek E Pearson
FINALIST
2016 Indies Book Awards Science Fiction
The Sun ☆☆☆☆:
"a weird, vivid and creepy book, not for the faint hearted. But its originality and top writing make for a great read."

Body Holiday **trilogy** Derek E Pearson
Surrey Life:
"Pearson's galactic-sized imagination delivers, with veiled gallows humour, a compelling image of a chic, high-tech society infused with a toxic strain that feeds on extreme violence."